I0564592

From Grandeville – A Tale

Book 1 (revised)

PORTAL

A Fairy Tale.

Of Some Sort.

In Three Parts.

Of Varying Sizes.

George R. Mead

E-Cat Worlds Press

Comments and questions? –> gmead01@gmail.com

Portal (revised)

Copyright, 2015 by George R. Mead

LCCN 2015900069

Mead, George R.
  Portal /George R. Mead.
  p. cm.

  ISBN-13 978-0-9890927-8-4
  1. Portal (revised). Series. From Grandeville – A Tale.

E-Cat Worlds established its publishing program as a reaction to the large commercial publishing houses currently dominating the book industry and the smaller intellectual clones. It is interested in publishing works of fiction and non-fiction that are often deemed insufficiently profitable or commercial or that are not necessarily reflective of current literary trends and fads.

E-Cat Worlds, 57744 Foothill Road, La Grande OR 97850
www.ecatworldspress.com
SAN 255-6383
In the middle of nowhere - Creativity

Revised

Printed in the United States of America

Nonfiction

A History of Union County
The Ethnobotany of the California Indians, 2nd Edition
A History of The Chinese in The West: 1848-1880
Yachats. The Town Called "Dark Water at the Foot of the Mountains."

Fiction

From Grandeville – A Tale.
Portal (revised)
Lair
Search
Not Again
And Again.
Magiwitch
Rebirth
Offspring
Holiday
Treasure
E'Nilt
Braidna
Chyndra and Seemna

A Tale of The Feyra
Jonathon and Dee
Dee Of The Fontala
Dee and The People
Dee and The Golden Cartouche

The Seven Lands
(With Zakke L. Zacog)
Seventeen Siblings

Stream
Special Investigator

Why make a revision?

Portal was the first book written, those many years ago. Hence, as the first one, it had certain internal matters that I felt now needed to be addressed, i.e, revised.

So, that is why.

And this is that revision.

Three voices speaking.

Echoes from the past.

Of small numbers, but their valor quick for war.
Vergil, *Aeneid*, 19 B.C.

As good luck would have it.
Shakespeare, *Wives of Winsor*, 1601.

Adventures are to the adventurous.
Disraeli, *Ixion In Heaven*, 1844.

Three voices speaking.

To the future.

Who, of course, isn't listening.

OF THE THREE PARTS, THE FIRST.

KNOWN AS

THE TALE OF LUCK IS IN SMALL
NUMBERS.

Walk a Crooked Path to Paradise

A soft quiet voice whispered only to him.

It was a gift. Unasked for.
    The voice cat-caressed his mind.
And worked at its task.

    And sang a strange little song.

    Blackformlessness . . .
        Bottomless pit . . .
    Hidden,
        By cling-drifting cobweb fog . . .

The voice made subtle changes as it sang its song.

    And hummed.
        To both of them.

Stillshadow among the shadows . . .
    Something . . .
        Nothing . . .
          Behind you . . .

The voice paused.
    And smiled.
        And then . . .
          It stopped.

Deep, inner silence.

"Huh?"

They had been walking for the greater part of the day. The road they had been following had been all shadow gray, dark, dreary. The landscape had maintained an even, unwelcoming dampness. The road had run from here to there, and back again. Straight lines seemed to have been something that the road's designer had feared.

Now they were walking through a deep cut where the road deep sliced through a gently sloping ridge. It was still, here on this road, fog quiet, even more dim and damp than earlier.

The three figures, each at least twice the size of the one shorter than they were, walked along, side by side.

The trio were feeling hungry, uncomfortable, and more than a little irritable. Especially John Tinker. Who was more than a little irritable, he was deep down unhappy. And mumbling and grumbling to himself.

Of course, grumbling and mumbling, was, for him, not a very good indicator of his emotional state. He had grumbled and mumbled to himself from a very early age. It was, at times, a rather strange way of thinking through problems.

Then he said, mostly to himself, "This is some adolescent's idea of Dungeons and Dragons. And that, and this, is pure crap." Tinker glared at the road before them. It paid no attention to that glare, being just a rather damp road after all. "And if I ever get to meet up with the dingbat responsible for this, I think that I will rip his arm off. Maybe both arms." He frowned darkly at the road. "Starting at the ankles."

His mind cast back into the past. It was a long forgotten past, or perhaps, just not an event one would not like to reminisce about.

Hone and Lugar, Attorneys At Law.

Samuel Hone, a tall, elegant man and a very successful attorney, with the carefully controlled manner of one who had spent thirty years in court, tried not to show his displeasure at the presence of this person now sitting in his office, on the opposite side of his bare, clean desk, with one exception, a manila folder.

This person was moderately tall, about six feet, give or take a little, and dirty. His hair was long and tangled. He had shaved, but not recently. His clothes, as far as Hone could tell, appeared to be army fatigues in some sort of camouflage pattern. But the pattern was mostly hidden by the dirt and the stains.

He had been waiting in the outer office for some time wondering why this attorney had him tracked down and brought here.

His mind floated free and he thought of his earlier days.

Both parents had successful careers in unrelated fields. Very successful careers by very driven to rise higher and higher in their chosen endeavors. From a young age he had become accustomed to not seeing them except at dinner or later in the evening when they finally returned home.

Both parents had recognized that from an early age that their son had a quiet intelligent and as well, as all the coaches of all the sports had stated frequently during those parent-teacher conferences that his parents managed to attend, that their son was "a natural athlete," that is, he always knew, without thinking, where everyone else was, in a wide swath of space around him. They further added that any sport he happened to play, or at, he always looked as if it was just a normal and casual effort to do it.

So he grew up in a more or less personal existence with parents to intended to do well by him but where mostly involved in the careers. He knew, by the time he graduated from high school, that what they did for a living was not something that he was going to do. The basic problem was that he didn't know what he wanted to do.

His parents had died in an automobile accident just as he was signing up for a tour with the army. His grandparents were handed the entire inheritance to manage with the stipulation that this would end only when Tinker was no longer an active member of any of the armed forces.

Hone cleared his throat, bringing his client's attention back to himself, "Ahem. You are Mr. John Tinker?"

"Yep." He slumped into a more comfortable slouch.

"Did you bring some identification?"

Tinker fumbled a battered wallet from a chest pocket and fished out several items and shoved them across the desk top.

Using two fingers, Hone picked up the somewhat crumpled and dirty things and glanced from the photos to the face he saw watching him from across his desk.

He cleared his throat again, "Ahem, ummmmmmm, yes." And slid them back.

"Satisfied?"

"Yes."

"So, why am I here?"

Hone picked up the only the folder on the desk top, opened it, glanced at the top page, and nodded to himself.

"Mr. Tinker, you were a hard man to find but here you are. And my job," he winced, "is almost finished."

He left the folder open, spun it around, and pushed it across the desk top toward Tinker using one finger tip.

"Just sign there!" He reached out and touched, gently, a line at the bottom of the top page.

Tinker leaned forward, frowned, rapidly scanned the document, and looked up through his eye brows at the attorney.

"This is a joke?" he grumbled. "Right?"

"No, Mr. Tinker, it is not. When you sign that paper, under the dutiful eyes of my secretary, who will also notarize it, I shall hand over the passbook."

He slipped it from an inside pocket of his neatly tailored jacket and gently pushed it across the desk top.

"And you shall become a moderately wealthy young man." It almost sounded like a curse as he said it.

The door opened and the secretary slipped into the room, having heard some signal from Hone.

Tinker signed the document and it was duly notarized.

Hone handed over the passbook.

Tinker took it, shoved it into a chest pocket, and stood.

"I'm done?"

"Indeed."

Hone stood, but didn't offer his hand.

"We are done, Mr. Tinker. But I do not believe that your Grandparents had any idea of what they were doing."

Tinker shrugged, turned, and walked from the ever so neat offices of Hone and Lugar. He headed for the bank whose logo glittered golden on the corner of the passbook.

And then, somewhat later, he invited a group of "friends" to his place and began to acquire more of the aimless state that he had begun to develop after the army, after college, after losing himself in no-direction.

The party, if it could be called that, ran on and on, for months and months.

Until one cold and rainy day.

Tinker struggled to awareness.

It was cold.

He was wet.

He was shivering.

He was a mess.

He was huddled between a cold, wet brick wall and a cold wet metal trash bin that stood on short legs that ended in round iron wheels. He blinked and stared at his surroundings.

It wasn't any place that he recognized. It was just him and the trash bin, rain and more rain, and one wet angry cat lurking under the trash bin and glaring yellow eyes at him.

He had no idea of where he was, what day it was, what year it was, or how he gotten to this place.

He tried to stand and failed. He tried again. This

time he faded away from his wet world.

He woke in a storeroom of some kind. The air was filled with the wonderful smells of some kind of, for him, exotic cooking.

Later he considered it as the first day of his life.

Then his introspection was interrupted.

His short companion gently patted his elbow. "John Tinker," said the small voice. The elfin small hand patted Tinker's elbow again as he whispered, "We are being followed. Look, back there."

"Huh?" Tinker stopped walking. And looked down at him. His thoughts of a past event, long forgotten, now remembered for some reason, pushed back into the dim reaches of memory where they lived.

Sorrowful pointed as they both stopped and turned around, to stare into the moisture-dripping mist grayness that swirled around them.

Mountain turned with them, moved sideways, and grumbled loudly, "HUMPF! I told you that there was something watching us, did I not? Back there, when we first started out, that is what I said, I said, we are being followed. And now, see." He waved one great arm and pointed dramatically. "There it is. Right there. Right behind us, DOUBLE-DUMPF it all! Way back there. Behind us." The great man frowned a stony glare down at Tinker.

Tinker stared behind them, then he stared in front of them. Then he turned and stared at it, it now being in front of them, having been behind them, before they had all turned around. So, he stared at it, this object of their conversation. He nodded his head. There did seem to be some sort of vague, shapeless, black lumpish formshape on the road. It was a long way back down the road, a long way behind them. If that vague smudge was anything at all? It wasn't moving. Tinker squinted at it. It was just there, in the fogmist, a lump of something. Finally he decided. Yep, he thought, there was something there, all right. So he nodded his head, one more time, in agreement. "Yep."

Then his shoulders slumped as he sighed heavily. He wondered why this hoax just had to go on and on. And on and on. Now this thing appeared to be getting just that much more complex. And it really made no sense at all. At least it didn't make any sense to him. In spite of having had much time to ponder his predicament, he still hadn't a clue why anyone would want to kidnap him and play these not-very-funny games in this ever strange, getting stranger charade. He frowned, and thought, well, hoax, charade, bad joke, or whatever it is, he was definitely going to escape from his pair of keepers. And the sooner he did it, the better it would be. For him.

So who ever it was that was back there, sitting in the dim mistfog, that vague shadow blackness, it must be another part of this gang. Just sitting there, cutting off any plan he might have had of running in that direction. Obviously if he didn't act soon, he was going to be even more trapped than they thought that he already was.

It was time to think, time to rethink, time to rerun his private list of questions, created for just the situation he found himself in.

WHY?

That had been explained to him early this

morning. No good. There was no way he was going to accept a fairy tale explanation like that. So far everything that he had seen or had heard or had been told had merely reinforced his feeling that he was in the hands of a group of certifiable lunatics. Terribly clever ones, but still bug-nuts, one and all.

WHAT?

Another piece of bizarre logic. Tinker shook his head from side to side. Chosen One, indeed!

HOW?

Straight forward kidnaping, snatched right from inside his own home, right from his own living room. He didn't think that his kidnaping logically followed from the first two points, but, for now, he'd let that go.

WANT?

Definitely a set of bad assumptions all around. These escapees from a funny-farm, or circus, or whatever that they came from, had certainly missed the mark on this point. Just because they wanted something didn't mean that he was going to want it, regardless of where they held him, regardless of what manner of elaborate, and very goofy, game they had decided to play.

Tinker waggled his head and smiled to himself. Surprise, surprise. Escape is all that he wanted and nothing else. SOON! He must find the right time. And the right place. Now that they were finished staring into the fog at whatever it was, it was time to make that decision. He flicked his eyes from one of his companions to the other. One punch, if that would be necessary, should take care of the little one. Fast feet and some heavy duty dodging and hiding should help him elude the big one. And as far as anyone else that might pop up, why they would have a problem, a very bloody problem. This was certainly not a time or place for kindness or ethical considerations.

He set his feet and checked the others' positions.

Mountain caught his slight movement and fingered the handle of his cudgel. "There! There it is."

Tinker smiled and nodded at him. "Yep. There it is."

Mountain tapped himself on the chest with a finger. It made a dull thumping sound. "Just as I said, right from the very beginning. Right from the very start. Right when we left that DUMPFING-DAMP castle, BY RUMPF!"

Tinker nodded. "You're right. I do believe that you did mention something like that."

"Indeed I did. SO, by RAR-RUMPFING, I was correct." Mountain nodded vigorously.

Tinker snapped him another smile, "So what?"

"SO WHAT?" Eyes bugging out, Mountain stared down at him. "DOUBLE-DUMPFING rocks and stones, can you not understand? We . . . are . . . being . . . FOLLOWED! By that thing back there." He jabbed a finger toward the dark shadow in the dark shadows. It was another very dramatic gesture. It was just like the last one.

Tinker shrugged, thought that this guy was getting excessively theatrical, and sighed, mostly to himself. This is just what he needed, a gigantic thespian. "Oh we are, are we?"

"John Tinker?" Sorrowful tugged gently at his

sleeve, interrupting them, his voice a controlled soothing tone. "Perhaps it would be best if I hide in some small place and let it pass. That way we may find out what it is that follows us."

Now it was Tinker's turn to glower at someone. "And why would we want to do that?"

"To find out, of course. If I hide and wait for it to pass, then we will be able to find out whether it be friend or foe. It may be that which we were warned against."

Tinker yanked his arm away. "Come on Sorrowful, will you just knock off the nonsense."

The small man stared at him, eyes wide, puzzled by such behavior.

Tinker sighed. He crossed his arms over his chest. "O.K., I will agree, just for the sake of argument, that there is someone sitting on the road back there. All right? And that he is dogging our steps. All right?" Then he shot a fast glance up at Mountain who had mumbled something under his breath. "But we really don't have any idea who is back there, do we? Well, do we?"

Sorrowful shook his head. "No. We do not. Nor do we know if it is a he, or a she, or an it."

"DUMPING correct!" The great man nodded his agreement.

Tinker sighed. "Right. Let's just walk faster, shall we?"

Sorrowful shook his head again. "No, John Tinker."

"Why not?"

Sorrowful smiled up at him. Think, John Tinker, is it better for us to take action? Or wait . . . until action takes us?" He paused. "I suggest that we take action?" And dusted something from one sleeve. Tinker couldn't see anything there.

"BY DUMPF, Sorrowful is correct. COME, let us go stomp on it!" Mountain lurched forward, beckoning for Sorrowful to follow, unlimbering his great club.

"HOLD IT, RIGHT THERE, YOU TWO!"

They whirled around to face a glowering Tinker. Whatever it was that they were planning now, he didn't like it. One moment, they wouldn't leave his side. Now they were all ready to go running down the road, into the foggy mists. It was time to take control. After all, he was supposed to be their leader. At least that is what he was being told from time to time, part of the fairy tale he was supposed to accept. Might as well make use of it.

They stared at him. Waiting. Tinker demanded, "Am I not The Leader of this jolly little band?"

They both nodded. Mountain grumbled to himself.

"Then, I decide what we do. Or don't do. Correct!"

Tinker took a heroic stance. If it was dramatics they wanted, then he was going to give them some. It was time to lull them into carelessness.

"I make the decisions!" His arm jabbed toward the sky, one forefinger pointing sharply at the mists overhead. Sort of like Columbus finding the new world. Or something like that. He decided it was the best heroic stance he could think off.

They both nodded again.

Tinker dropped his arm. "Sorrowful, you still want to play peek-a-boo with that guy back there?"

Sorrowful nodded. He had no idea what 'peek-a-boo' was.

Tinker smiled at him. "O.K., then we'll do it."

Sorrowful smiled back. It was a small acknowledgment. "I will stay well hidden. And let it pass me. Then we shall see what it is that comes by, what it is that trails so carefully behind us."

"Fine." Tinker waved an arm, he didn't really care who it was wandering along behind them. "Come on Mountain, let's go."

They walked off while Sorrowful searched for a place to hide, Tinker congratulating himself on letting them separate themselves, one from the other. Now he only had one keeper.

Sorrowful threw his hood over his head and slid behind a bush and into a narrow crevice behind it. He vanished. The dark velvet of his clothes made him a shadow indistinguishable from the other shadows.

Tinker strode rapidly up the road trying to gain as much distance between them as he could possibly get before Sorrowful realized what was going on. Just a little farther away and he'd make a break for it. He got ready to run. He was sure that he could outrun that great lumbering hulk walking next to him. He didn't get far in that plan.

" T I N K E R R R R R R !
HEEEELLLLLLLLLPPPPPPP!"

Tinker spun on his heels and stared. "Now what's going on?" There was nothing back there, just swirling fogmist. But someone had screamed in real terror. He charged back down the road toward the spot where Sorrowful had chosen to hide. He couldn't help himself. It hadn't sounded like play acting to him unless Sorrowful was a better actor than he appeared to be. Mountain thundered behind him, his feet thudding loudly on the road surface. In a moment, they could see a small crumpled form lying on the road.

They thudded to a halt and stared at the small man, sprawled loosely on the road. No blood on the road, no signs of violence on Sorrowful. Tinker bent over and touched him with a tenuous fingertip. Sorrowful mumbled something indistinct. Mountain bent and peered over Tinker's head. Tinker reached down and straightened up, lifting Sorrowful to his feet. Mountain jumped back.

Sorrowful's eyes popped open, pupils dilated, black openings in a pale white face. Whatever he was seeing, it wasn't either of them. He clenched Tinker's arm in a painful grip.

"Darkness," he hissed.

"What?"

Sorrowful's eyes focused on Tinker's face. "Darkness, John Tinker, darkness!" Then he shuddered and wiped his hair back with a nervous gesture, his eyes darting from side to side. Clearing his throat, he whispered harshly, "Darkness." Clearing his throat, again, loudly, Sorrowful released Tinker's arm.

"I stepped out from my hiding place to take a closer look after it had passed. I made not a sound, yet it heard me. It spun and ran right over me, knocking me down. And disappeared." Tinker had to lean forward to hear the ever softening words. "Straight up."

Tinker shook his head and grumbled mostly to himself. "Stepping out like that wasn't any too bright.

You were supposed to stay hidden." He knew that what would come next he wouldn't believe, but he had to ask. "So, little guy, what did you really see?"

The small man rolled his head from side to side. "I do not know what it was that I saw. Certainly nothing in my experience, which is considerable if I must say so, has ever prepared me for this. As for that. It certainly was not shaped like us. Of that I am positive, absolutely positive. And I swear to you, by all the tales told and yet to tell, that it had great, yellow-gold, orange, eyes that seemed to glow. They stared right into my face, into my very being, then it vanished. Upward."

Tinker slowly shook his head, he knew it, more fairy tale nonsense. These guys just piled it on, deeper and deeper. Why they thought he would accept all that was beyond his understanding.

Sorrowful began to brush specks of dirt and debris from his clothes, quick dainty strokes, checking for damage.

"And yet, here I stand, uninjured. So what could it have been? Certainly not a demon."

Extracting a small, neatly folded cloth from a back pocket he polished some smudge from the tip of his left boot. A few quick strokes, satisfied it was properly clean again, he straightened up, refolded the cloth and settled it back in the correct rear pocket.

Now it was Tinker's turn to roll his head from side to side.

"Well I am sure that I don't know. Monsters and demons are really out of my line." More hum-buggery. But why did they keep it up? Sorrowful obviously hadn't been expecting something like this to happen.

And he had been more than a little shocked by the event. So who had been following behind them? And why this addition to an already not very funny game? Tricks upon tricks upon tricks. But why would anyone play tricks on his keepers?

Tinker looked over at the other one. "What about you, Mountain, any guesses?"

"NO! Only that we should proceed from this place as quickly as possible. Who knows what kind of creatures prefer to lurk in such cold and dampness as this? Besides, I am hungry." His stomach made a loud rumble as if in agreement. "We carry no food and have no way to make shelter. Before nightfall it would be nice if we could somehow acquire some of each."

Tinker turned back, back toward the direction that they had been headed. "Well you are certainly right about that." He waved one arm and started walking. "Come on, let's go." He figured that he would just have to find some other place to ditch this pair.

Much later in the day, mid-afternoon, getting on toward late afternoon, having left the fog belt far behind them, they found themselves trudging up a steep grade in bright sunshine.

Mountain was telling them that this was a much better region than the one that they had left behind. This area was warm and sunny and dry, all very positive attributes as far as he was concerned. He almost smiled.

Tinker carefully studied their surroundings, and agreed with him, but for different reasons. It certainly wasn't as gloomy. But it wasn't as open either. Much more brush. More hiding cover. Clumps of trees. All in all, he felt that this was as good a place as any to make a break for it. He began watching for the right place. It was time to go, time to part company from his watch-dogs, such as they were.

"BY DUMPF, food and shelter."

Tinker snapped his attention from his survey and stared around them. "Where?"

"Just ahead. Why?"

"I don't see anything."

"Can you not see the rooftops just beyond the ridge in front of us?"

"Nope."

"HUMPF!"

"You have a distinct height advantage, big guy."

Mountain smiled, a very shy smile. "Well, John Tinker, I *am* large, even for the quarter from where I was taken. But I am no giant." He made that term sound like a curse.

Sorrowful tapped Tinker lightly upon his elbow. "Yet, John Tinker, to one of my dimensions, you are extremely large, while he is almost beyond comprehension. It appears that being a giant is rather a relative term, does it not?"

Tinker had to smile. They were an engaging pair in spite of being his captors. And he rather liked them. Of course, that didn't lessen his desire to escape, it just made them more, well, human, in a manner of speaking.

"Seems so, Sorrowful, seems so. Ah . . . one question, if I may?"

"Yes, John Tinker."

"Seeing as we are taking about relative size." He laughed.

"Yes, John Tinker."

"I take two steps, at least, for every one of Mountain's. And you take at least two steps for every one of mine."

"Yes, John Tinker."

"Soooooo, how come you don't seem to be getting tired? What's your secret?"

Sorrowful beamed at him. "No secret. It is like this, John Tinker. The world from which I was so rudely taken is one where the preferred mode of transportation is the one that we are currently using." He pointed down at his feet, "We walk. It is considered a casual trip to walk all day and all night just to visit a friend or neighbor."

"Neighbor?"

Sorrowful nodded. "We prefer to live widely separated, we do. Now as to how we travel so easily over these distances and durations, it is quite simple."

He paused. And held their attention.

"We tell tales. As we travel, we tell tales to each other. As we travel, often in small groups, such as this one, we utilize the time for good conversation with merry companions, telling entertaining tales."

He shrugged his shoulders, looked sad. "But, so far, this trip has been noteworthy for its lack of either aspect."

Sorrowful waggled one cautionary finger into the air. "But, as I am, ahem, ahem, rather well known for my tale telling abilities, perhaps it would be best if I went first. That way you two might see, and hear, how it is done. Learn a little something."

He smiled at each of them in turn.

Tinker smiled back. Mountain frowned. Tinker was beginning to realize that frowning was Mountain's normal expression, not an indication of his mood. Most of the time. At least as far as he could tell.

"This is *The Tale Of Surprise and Discovery*."

Sorrowful took a deep breath. And started.

"SO! In a time and at a time, it seems that there was once a certain one-legged traveling salesman named Brim'tr'imble. Now Brim'tr'imble was a man who traveled far and wide throughout the Six Lands, selling his wares.

"And, as chance would have it, one stormy night, in the Land of In-And-Up, he knocked upon the door of an isolated greenstead. It was his good fortune, for it was known high and low, that in his land, the land of In-And-Up, it was the custom that weary travelers were always made *most* welcome. Brim'tr'imble felt that he should be well fed and well housed, or at least given a warm and dry place to sleep." He paused.

"Imagine his surprise, then, when the door was answered by . . . "

Sorrowful hesitated. Mountain and Tinker looked at him, both wondering why.

"Ah, perhaps I should finish this tale some other time for it does appears that we are about to be joined by another traveler."

"WHAT?" Tinker's head snapped around. Not another one.

Sorrowful pointed ahead of them at a cluster of trees and shrubs. "Yon individual, there, seems to be waiting for us, does he not?"

Tinker sighed. Heavily. And muttered to himself, "Damn, damn, damn." He should have made a break for it, not walked along listening to strange stories.

Sorrowful waved and called, "Hail Fellow, travel with us?"

The figure flowed from beneath the deep shadows of the tall trees, his blue robes surging about him. He waited for them to get to where he stood. A soft, weary, impatient voice whispered from the depths of his hood.

"Greetings, Chosen One. Greetings to the Seven Who Are One. I am The Blue. I have been waiting a long time. It is my duty to see that you are given shelter, directions, and food."

At the mention of food, Mountain's stomach gave a loud, rumbling gurgle. The newcomer jerked his head around, causing his hood to fall back from his face. He stared at Mountain's mid-section.

"After dawning next, I will escort you as close as I may to the evil that you *must* face. Come!" One arm waggled slowly through the air. "Through the village to the inn on the far side."

Suddenly The Blue jumped back, his eyes jerking wildly. "SEVEN!" he screamed. "There ARE supposed to be SEVEN. Where is the other?"

Tinker shrugged his shoulders and looked around. There were only the three of them and The Blue. He wondered what kind of mathematics this guy had learned.

"Beats me, G.I. But what you see is what you get. We are it. Let's go." He was still planning on escape and was getting anxious to find a good spot. Especially now. Whoever it was that was responsible for his predicament, kept adding people. First some mystery guest, now this guy.

The Blue snapped his hood over his head and stalked off. Tinker nodded and followed him, thinking to himself that now he had three keepers, telling himself that he had better make his move pretty soon before any more of them turned up, especially this mysterious seventh person. And the other missing three.

The small group strolled up over the ridge and down into the village nestled on the back side. As they strolled down the road through the twisted main street, Tinker stared intently at the houses, seeking clues as to his whereabouts. It wasn't terribly productive.

Most of the structures were low, single-story things with thatched roofs. Here and there were tile-covered structures, walls and roofs, the roofs in shades of red, yellow or blue. A few of these were quite tall, thrusting hard towers into the sky. It had been the tips of these that Mountain had seen from the other side of the ridge.

Tinker stopped and stared around. He knew he had never seen such a place before, not even in the pages of the *National Geographic*. So where on earth was he? This region had to be one big special stage set. But why? Who could afford to pay for it?

Tinker turned to his newest keeper. "Where are all the inhabitants?"

The Blue, as he called himself, pointed back toward the way they had come. "All fled. They have all fled the danger that you *must* face, Chosen One."

Tinker ran across the street and through one of the doorways. He slammed it shut behind himself and began a hasty search. A table was still set as if for dinner. The cupboard doors still hung open, its shelves bearing quantities of food, apparently left behind.

Tinker laughed out loud. It was perfect. This was it, then. Tonight he would just give these guys the slip, come back here, load up with provisions, and be on his way. To freedom.

The door behind him popped open, The Blue walked in, grabbed Tinker's sleeve and tugged him gently out of the building. Tinker allowed himself to be led. Why not? Tonight this nonsense would be over and done with.

Back out on the street, The Blue bustled about, urging them to hurry, looking very agitated at their unwillingness to do as they were directed. He kept glancing up at Mountain's frowning face. And the great club that hung at his waist.

"Come, come! Please? We must leave this place and get to the inn. We really do not have time to dawdle."

They started walking down the slope, out of the village, into the woods. The Blue hurried them along, down the ever twisting road. Soon, they approached a cluster of sprawling, interconnected buildings of varying sizes and shapes that nestled together forming an untidy three-sided courtyard. A large and very ornately carved wooden sign was mounted over what looked to be the main entryway. They stepped over and peered up at it.

It informed all who might care to look up and read:

REST AND LODGINGS
THE BEST OF FOODS

Suddenly the front door slammed open, thumping heavily into the wall, sending thick clouds of dust spiraling across the courtyard, coating them in a gray film of grit. A short, thickset man shot from the inner dimness toward them. He grabbed one arm of The Blue and gabbled at them, his words spilling out rapidly, anxiously. "Inside, inside. Quickly, quickly. Before that, which cannot be named, becomes aware of yur presence."

Yanking the blue-robed figure headfirst through the doorway. The door slammed shut as the last of them quickly scurried inside. Dust from this last blow shifted down upon them from the ceiling, adding another layer to their first coating.

They stood and squinted in the faint light of the hallway. The inn-keeper shoved them from the hall and into a large, open room framed with rough-cut and oddly shaped timbers. Waving one burly arm, he bade them seat themselves at the solitary wooden table in the room. The table gleamed softly in the faint light, its top polished smooth from years of service. Mountain thumped down into the twice-sized chair. Sorrowful hopped up into the half-sized one. Tinker and The Blue sat in the other two, both Tinker-normal in size, both shaped identical to the other two.

Tinker looked around the room. Other than themselves it was empty. Well, he thought, judging from the chairs, it must have all been planned well in advance.

The inn-keeper bustled away and quickly returned, his arms laden with dishes and serving platters. Rapidly these things were plunked down in front of them and portions were ladled out: stew, biscuits, gravy. And in a minute, bottles of wine.

Noticing that none of the others hesitated to eat, Tinker joined in. The food was quite good. And he was hungry. Their burly host, who he assumed must be the Trunk of the sign, hovered in the background.

The instant that it appeared that they had finished with their meal, he pounced, urging them from the room with the same vehemence that he had expressed when dragging them into the building. He waved The Blue to remain seated at the table.

"This way, this way. Yur room is just down this hall, this way." His arms windmilled them in the direction that he wished them to go, "They, The Blue, will stay behind to guard yur backs. But yur *must* be out of sight. Quickly, quickly."

The inn-keeper rushed them along the hall and into a large room with three beds. He yanked the door shut behind them. A resounding thump. More dust sifted down.

"HUMPF, John Tinker, what do you think about all this?"

Tinker looked around their room and then at the big man.

"Well, Mountain, to tell you the truth, I think that this rigmarole has gone on for just about long enough. Even for a hoax, it is getting awfully elaborate."

"HOAX? John Tinker, you can not be serious." Sorrowful bounced in front of him, glaring up at him, both hands bunched on his hips. "You will get us killed for sure if you keep thinking like that."

Mountain snarled his agreement "BY DOUBLE-DUMPF, you are right in that, Sorrowful!" And crossed massive arms over an equally massive chest. His frown was dark and real this time.

Tinker glared back at both of them. "And what's that supposed to mean?" Then he smiled, relaxing. "All right, all right, come on you two, a joke's a joke and all that, but I think that green wine was putting it on just a bit thick."

Sorrowful stared at him, surprise written on his face, not believing what he was hearing. "Humly, nothing wrong with green wine."

Then he carefully, very patiently, very slowly, began to explain, patting Tinker's hand gently as he did so.

"John Tinker, this is neither hoax nor joke nor game of any sort. Mountain and I were here long before you arrived. And we know. And what exactly is wrong with green wine?"

Tinker threw both his arms out, spun around, and walked over to the single window and examined it. It was fixed, it couldn't be opened. The shutters were on the inside. He slammed them shut, no escape there. He turned and faced his two room-mates.

"What do you know?" He waggled a cautionary finger at them. "Ah, ah, let me go first, if you will. I'll tell you what I know. I know that I have been kidnaped. I know that I have been plunked down in Wonder Wonderland. And I know I am here in this room with you two. I know that I'm supposed to believe all sorts of cock-a-mamey nonsense, like being followed by things with glowing orange eyes that disappear straight up and leave no trace of themselves behind. Correct?"

Sorrowful nodded. "Yes, John Tinker, that also?"

"WHAT? ALSO?"

Mountain glared down at Tinker, his frown even deeper. "And we didn't ask to be here either, BY DUMPF! And it is not Wonder Wonderland, never heard of such an elseplace. And it is because of *you* and The Thought that we are here. This is not our world, DAMP-DUMPFING, RAR-RUMPFING place that it is!"

"Oh really now?" Tinker glowered back. And laughed. "My fault?"

"Yes, really now, John Tinker," said Sorrowful soothingly. He gestured around the room. "You must see that this is all too real. And not to be dismissed lightly. And it is."

"HUMPF! Sorrowful is right by DOUBLE-DUMPF! How could this not be real?"

He gave the wall a flat-handed slap. Dust trickled down from the high ceiling. He glared at Tinker as it drifted past their noses. "YOU are supposed to get US home from here, John Tinker. YOU!" He stomped across the room and gave another wall a heavy slap. The ceiling creaked ominously. A piece of plaster clattered to the floor.

"Some joke, I'd say," he rumbled. "Trapped in this place with an unbelieving dwarf and a yammering flyspeck. Hoax. HUMPF! Deathtrap more likely." The top of his head just brushed against the very high ceiling. "DUMPING small room."

Tinker stared at them and decided to try a slightly different tack. "Well, Mountain, Sorrowful, I will tell you what we ought to do."

They stared at him, waiting.

"We will just wait until morning arrives, get a good night's rest and a good morning's breakfast, and then, why then . . . "

Tinker smiled at them and threw his arms wide. "Why then we will just see how we go about escaping from all this reality of yours' with our lives and limbs intact. O.K.?" He gave them his best salesman smile. At least what he thought was a salesman smile.

Mountain frowned, at least it seemed to Tinker that he did. "Well, BY DUMPF, John Tinker, I do not see that we have much choice in the matter, not that *we* ever had. You are The Leader after all." He picked up his bed and placed it across the doorway, blocking it completely. Then he crashed down upon it, grumbling deeply. "There. No one may attempt to enter without first waking me."

Tinker nodded. And thought to himself, and no one could slip out late at night either. Damn, damn, damn, DAMN.

"Good night, John Tinker. Good night to you also, tiny man." Mountain rolled up in his blankets, clothes and all, and promptly fell asleep.

Tinker laughed softly. "Well, surly to bed and surly to rise. Pinch out the candle will you, Sorrowful?"

In the dark, Tinker squirmed about, seeking a soft spot in his bed, pondering this very strange, and getting ever stranger, situation. As he relaxed and headed into sleep, his mind began to drift back over the past day, reviewing all that had happened, searching for clues, seeking some way out. And asking himself, "Why me?"

In the night dark silence, a large shadow flowed up the roof, over an eave, and merged sable soft under one of the many large odd-shaped projections that ornamented the roof. It observed the surrounding area. It studied their shuttered window with yellow-gold, orange eyes that seemed to glow with their own inner light.

And waited.

Humming quietly to itself.

To Sleep, Perchance to Dream. Or Something Like That

The body could have been that of a dead man, lying so still. It looked like a dead man sprawled loose-limbed in a sparsely made bed in a cold, hard room. But. Such was not the case. A very careful observer might have noticed the imperceptible rise and fall of the chest. Perhaps.

He was alive. And awake. He just wasn't ready to let anyone know that, yet. One was always served best by large amounts of caution when waking in strange places. It was always best to be careful.

Deja vu (all over again).

He almost laughed, but instead decided that it was time to ask himself that old, familiar question. The one he had asked himself so many times before, in the past. Of course, this time it was different. He didn't have a hangover. His mind was clear. His body was fit and ready.

The question was old and disused. It had been gathering rust for just over ten years since he had last asked it. Now, in this place, in these circumstances, it came back. Unbidden. Unasked for. It came.

Now what's going on?

Once asked, it had to be responded to.

So he did.

Nothing, that's what. My life has been quiet and

orderly. For ten years. So there was nothing going on. There is no reason for this. Not now. Not any more. Not at all.

In spite of his answer, he lay still and listened intently to the silence. A very quiet place, was this. He breathed gentle, soft feather breathing. Even with his eyes closed, he knew. He knew he was not where he should be, where he ought to be. The bed felt strange. It wasn't his. Nor was it any other bed of recent memory.

So? Where was he?

A very good question, John Tinker, he said to himself. It went with the other good question. Too bad he couldn't produce a really good answer, to either question. This was beginning to feel like the bad, old days again. And that wasn't good. Not even a little bit.

He wasn't ready, or willing, for that kind of life again. Not ever. Never again. That was the past, a not very nice past. The past was over and done with. Kaput! He was quite happy with his calm, somewhat regulated lifestyle.

He was alive.

He was living.

He was comfortable.

He somewhat, moderately, well-off: mentally, physically, economically. He had a few good friends, who really were *good* friends. He lived quietly. He had lived happily. For ten good years, plus or minus a little. Good years, filled with study, exercise, contemplation, writing.

So? Now what was going on?

He readied himself. His eyes popped open as he sat up and quickly looked at his room. Nope, this silent place was certainly not a familiar place at all. Flopping back, he crossed his hands on his chest, closed his eyes and thought. What on earth had he been doing before this?

"Well, let's see," he grumbled into the silence of the room. It was an old habit. One that broke out every now and again. He decided that it didn't really matter whether anyone knew that he was awake or not.

"Just go back a bit, just back to last night. Evening is always a good place to start."

He knew what he had been doing last night. It was what he had been doing regularly for many evenings for the past ten years. He had been in the dojo, training, working through several kata, the formalized sets of martial arts movements, with Master Chen, Adam Liu Chen, his friend and teacher. Then, afterwards, over tea in the living room, they had discussed the evening's workout, analyzing subtle details, small points of form.

And then?

Then Chen had left and Tinker had sat at his desk and worked on the notes for his newest book. And ate popcorn. And then he had gone to bed. Alone.

And then . . . what?

And then . . .

What? . . .

And then it was morning. He had woken up and crawled from his bed, just as he always did. Then he did the next thing, always the same next thing: he had sat, in his favorite chair, in the living room, and watched the world outside through the large window.

Out there the world was covered with the blue-gray twilight of that moment that precedes just-before-sunrise. He sat and watched as the golden band of coming dawn marked a border along the dark silhouette of the mountain ridges that defined the far side of the valley. His hands had been curled around a large mug of coffee filled with his favorite blend. He sat, sipped, and listened to the fire crackling inside the wood stove. Its radiant heat welcomed him to a new day. It was a friendly beast, that wood stove. It muttered to itself whenever the wind blew hard against the house. It was doing that now. The stove muttered, the house creaked. They were two old friends holding a conversation in the early morning light.

Today was his birthday. Actually, now he supposed it was yesterday. He had turned thirty-eight years old going on twenty-six. He had always liked that age, twenty-six. No special reason, he just did. He thought that maybe he could convince Chen to bake a large chocolate cake. He could invite a few friends over. J.C., Hard, Doc. Maybe one or two others. J.C. could bring his ex-fiancé and still best friend, Shannon, and her spouse. It would be fun, quiet fun. Very relaxing fun.

They could sit, talk, take it easy. And eat. And drink, a little.

He remembered staring out the large window, watching early light come a'creeping over the nearby snow-dusted foothills. He remembered wondering about the morning star. He didn't remember that it had ever sparkled so brightly before. The thing just hung there, right over, so it seemed, Frank's Flat. It was a bright point of crystal ornamenting dawn's sky.

And then what?

He remembered . . . NOTHING!

So that was it. It was that star. That was the last thing that he could remember until now. Just a bright point of light that had flashed deep into his mind.

And now?

And now . . . he was here.

"O.K., Tinker, where is here? Now?"

He laughed, loudly.

"Well," he grumbled to the room. "It certainly isn't good old Grandeville, Oregon, the garden spot of the Universe."

Smiling broadly, he looked at the ceiling. "Time to get up, time to find out where we are, John Tinker."

He stretched to his full length, slightly under six feet, his arms bumping against the wall, his feet popping out from under the covers. He sat up and wiggled his toes. "Hi guys, how's everything down there." Then he slowly examined the room.

The ceiling was high. The room was narrow. The walls and floor and ceiling were all made from large pieces of rough-carved, grey stone. One corner of his mouth puckered, definitely not a place that he had been in before. Nope. Not at all.

"So then, where are we?" He continued his careful inspection of the room. It was sparsely furnished: one bed, one chair, one small table with a large wash basin sitting upon it. Clothes hung on a row of wall pegs. Dark clothes, shadows of softness. Below them, on the floor, sat a pair of boots, same color, same vague blackness.

He rolled from under the covers and stepped over to investigate. "Must be mine, it seems." He was shivering in the cold air, goosebumps marching up and down his bare skin. But where did his other clothes go?

The clothes fit. The boots fit. The boots were soft yet sturdy. The trousers had large pockets and elastic cuffs. The cuffs snapped over the boot tops. The shirt-jacket was cut on the large roomy style with an attached hood. There were elastic cuffs on the sleeves also. He looked down. He was a walking shadow. Everything he wore seemed not to reflect the light but to absorb it.

He ran his hand over his loosely-cropped, sandy-brown hair, scratched behind one ear, and looked for a mirror to check his appearance. No mirror. The wash-basin held water. Cold water. He splashed some on his face, rubbed his eyes, and wiped his hand across his hair, then finished the job with the towel. He was ready for the day, assuming that it was day. The room didn't have a window, either.

He sat in the chair and waited. He was very good at waiting. It was a skill that he had developed early in those ten years that he counted. Someone would have to come by sooner or later to check on him, he supposed He was ready. He slipped into soft inner quiet and smiled to himself. He always adapted to new situations rather quickly, now. Always in the past ten years. Before that didn't count.

Long, many moments later, heavy blows rattled his door, snapping Tinker from his deep, contemplative mode. He rose and silently set the chair to one side, out of the way, creating an open, uncluttered space in front of himself, between where he stood and the door.

The blows repeated. The door shook.

Then it slammed open, crashing back against the

wall and swung closed again.

Tinker waited, slightly turned to the right.

The door swung slowly open again and the creature peered into the room. It appeared to be the bad results of a genetic mismatch of a frog and an alligator. It grimaced in his general direction, showing rows of shark teeth and gurgled at him.

"You are John Tinker," it said, all liquid wet tones. "You are The Chosen One. They are waiting. Come."

Whatever, whoever it was spun around and scurried down the outside corridor with a scuttling hop, its flat feet plopping loudly against the bare stone floor.

His curiosity aroused by such an apparition, Tinker hurried to follow this thing, wondering to himself why anyone would bother to dress in such a bizarre costume. What kind of bug-house was he in, anyway?

The corridor they were in was long and narrow, with many twists and turns. It was a lightening stroke of a passageway. The floor, ceiling and walls were all constructed of the same material and in the same manner as his room. Same high ceiling.

As he hurried after whoever, he realized that neither his boots nor his clothes were making a sound, not even when he jumped up and down and waved his arms vigorously. Impressed and engrossed in this discovery he failed to notice that his guide had stopped in front of a large wooden door. Tinker walked into his back. The guide ignored him.

After a few moments of silent waiting, Tinker having stepped back a few paces, just to watch, the door opened silently inward. The whatever hopped through,

Tinker right on his heels, still deeply intrigued by the overall Halloween atmosphere of his present situation, each of them dressed in their own costume, such as they were.

The high ceiling of the chamber that they had entered was lost in the darkness of drifting haze. The haze came from a number of swirling clouds of smoke that drifted upward and waved lazily in the faint air currents astir in the great room. These smoke columns rose from a scatter of stone figurines standing in a ragged line around the chamber. They held, with cupped hands, open bowls that sputtered and spewed small flames and much smoke. The statues stared outward with round, myopic eyes.

Tinker stared back. Neither side blinked. Off to one side he heard a faint noise. His head snapped in that direction followed by his body. He faced a raised platform upon which sat three ornately carved thrones. In them sat three silent figures carefully studying him. Between each of the thrones and marking the end of the line were more of the figurines holding bowls, spewing more smoke, adding to the general air pollution.

Tinker ambled carefully into the middle of the vast space, expanding his awareness, and stopped to face these three people. Just as he opened his mouth to speak, they did.

(Left) "You are The Chosen One."

(Right)   "We have sent for you."

(Center)   "We have a mission which you must do for us."

(Unison)   "WE ARE THEY -- YOU ARE THE CHOSEN ONE."

"You . . . "

"Must . . . "

"Obey . . . "

Tinker stood quietly and waited for more conversation, his face a blank mask, considering this situation, and what he had just been told. They watched him carefully. This was worse that he had thought could be possible. He must be somewhere in Southern California. He'd been nabbed by some really strange religious freaks. It was time to work actively on getting out of here. The three of them just sat there looking at him, apparently satisfied that they had accomplished what they wanted.

He looked up. He smiled at them, and took a quick glance over at the door, it was still open. And cleared his throat. The hall outside beckoned escape.

"Forget it, troops. I am not interested in being drafted into your, ah, peculiar group."

He waved his arms at his surroundings, letting his anger show, but controlling it, starting the adrenaline flow.

"I don't like your theatrics, your play-acting, your B-grade movie setting, or your costuming." He turned away mumbling to himself, "This has got to be the weirdest thing that I have ever been in. This is really and truly a bad dream." Looking over one shoulder he waved goodbye to the raised platform and its inhabitants. "Sayonarra, mothers." It wasn't nice. It wasn't polite. But then he wasn't feeling terribly nice or polite at the moment.

He walked toward the door. Once he was outside in the hall, he fully intended to run for his life.

"STOP!"

"You are The Chosen One."

"We have sent for you."

"This is not a dream."

"To make you understand . . . "

"We send you . . . "

"Pain . . . "

Three creatures, costumed thugs he assumed, launched themselves at Tinker from where they had been standing along the far wall. They gurgled and grunted as they rushed toward him, teeth bared. They were green. They were ugly. They looked just like the one that had guided him to this chamber. One of them was.

Startled, and more than a little surprised, Tinker gasped, "What's this, more costume freaks?" Then he saw that two of them were carrying weapons.

He took a deep breath. Relaxing, exhaling softly. *Zanshin.* He watched their approach, judging their positions and rate of speed. Then he ran and jumped.

One foot caught the nearest one on the chest, the other foot struck it on the forehead. It went sprawling. Tinker dropped to the floor, rolled to one side, and kicked across the kneecap of the next closest one. Howling in pain, it crashed to the floor, a sword clattering to one side. Tinker continued his roll. A wooden pole bounced off the floor next to his head. Bounding to his feet, he grabbed, twisted, and spun, pulling and kicking. The staff was his. A quick jab with it sent the third attacker backward, clenching at its throat.

The first, recovered, was stumbling toward him. Twirling the stave, Tinker belted it alongside the head, dropping it to its knees. It toppled to its side and lay there. Tinker leaped sideways at number two, who was hobbling toward him, still snarling. A hard jab in the stomach stopped the noise. A second jab stopped its motion.

Tinker danced into an open space, looked, took two hopping side-steps, and launched his javelin at the central figure seated in the thrones.

That being leaped to his feet, snapping both arms upward, palms out, commanding, "STOP."

A bright red, crackling wall of flame roared from floor to ceiling. With a sharp *crack* the wooden pole exploded. Tinker raced through the smoking splinters raining down, hurtling toward the door and freedom.

The door vanished. It became solid wall.

"What the . . . ?" Tinker ran up the wall, tumbled backward, twisted, and landed on his feet, facing the room, ready for the next bunch.

"You are The Chosen One."

"You *must* help us."

"We *need* you."

'THE THOUGHT WILL GUIDE YOUR WAY."

"We are . . . "

"At your . . . "

"Mercy . . . "

Without a sound they faded, disappeared. The thrones sat empty. The flames went out. The rising smoke thinned and disappeared.

Tinker straightened up and looked around the room. Well, he thought, that is pretty impressive. Very nice special effects, indeed. These guys must work in some of the movie studios. He slowly scanned the room, looking for someone else, something else. The room was empty. Silent.

He carefully walked around the edge searching for some sign of the exit, any exit. Nothing. There didn't appear to any way to get out. He rapped on the walls, here and there. They always sounded solid to him. Shrugging his shoulders, he walked over and clambered up and began to check the surface of the platform for signs of trapdoors. Nothing up here either.

He walked over and sat in the middle throne. It looked like a comfortable place to sit and wait. It was. Slouching into a slightly more comfortable position, he waited. And watched the smoke disappearing up near the high ceiling. Must be some sort of venting system up there, he thought. But out of reach.

Long, many moments later, a sad, hollow voice broke into Tinker's silent, inner world. His eyes refocused and took in the chamber. The smoke had long ago disappeared. He felt something. Someone. Standing quietly, standing deep inside the shadow hidden far end. Just the hint of movement.

"John Tinker, I am The Thought. If you would come with me. Please. I will explain why you were brought here, where here is, what it is that has happened to you, and to us, and why we need your help. Please. Come with me."

Tinker rose to his feet and stepped off the platform, asking himself, "Now what's going on?"

A tall figure, dressed is a deep green almost black colored robe emerged from the blackness. The hood was swept back by one arm, revealing a face all too human, deeply carved with furrows and wrinkles. Wearing an air of great fatigue. He beckoned gently, and waited for Tinker to come to him. "Come, John Tinker. I am now harmless and old and tired, so very tired. I am the *only one* who can tell you how you may regain your own elseplace, ah, your own home. But, of course, only after you have finished your, um, shall we say, um, assigned duties."

Tinker shrugged his shoulders and walked down the long chamber and stopped, five paces away, "O.K., MacDuff, lead on." For just a moment, Tinker thought he saw the faintest flicker of a smile, then nothing.

The Thought turned and led him through a doorway hidden behind heavy, flat black, wall hangings. It hadn't been here earlier. From there they traveled but a short distance, into another room. Tinker stopped, keeping a wary eye on his new surroundings and this newest actor in this play he had yet to figure out.

This room was also large, but not as large as the chamber they had just left. Massive half-columns edged into the room along the walls. Between them impenetrable shadow painted the walls. In the center of the room sat a long, rectangular table. Lying upon it were three weapons: a long, black, two-handed sword that reflected no light; a massive, wooden cudgel, longer than the sword; and, a short, brightly shining dagger whose edge glittered in the light. Next to the weapons lay a belt and for the smaller edged weapon, the dagger, a scabbard.

The Thought walked around the table and sat in the only chair. He gestured for Tinker to stand opposite him, just by the sword.

Tinker did, carefully checking his surroundings one more time, searching for an exit. He couldn't see one. Where the door they had entered had been, there now seemed to be nothing but solid wall. He nodded to himself. The special affects in this place were amazing. He stood easy, relaxed, and watched the seated figure.

For a brief instance it had appeared as if the ornate carving on the chair's back was visible, shining through the man seated there, watching him. Tinker quickly glanced around, searching for the projector. Nothing visible.

The Thought cleared his throat, just to get Tinker's attention. It worked. "I am sorry, but you will have to stand while I explain all this. It is part of the ritual. And ritual can not be changed." He flashed a quick smile at Tinker and resumed his explanation.

"It is all part of the process and will not take long. I am called, as I just stated a moment ago, The Thought. I am the most skilled of my kind. I am also, for now, the last one of my kind. Until the Young Ones awaken there will be no others to serve. We serve those three individuals you visited earlier. The three are a kind of collective unit, which we call They. They rule and The Thought guides. Between us, we maintain, or used to maintain, the harmony of this our world, this elseplace. Once, not all that long ago, all here lived and worked in peace and, if not in happiness, at least in contentment."

Tinker frowned and leaned forward to rap the table top with one knuckle. It made a loud, sharp sound. "Hey there, hold on, just wait right there."

"What is it?"

"I have a question. Actually I have a lot of questions, but we can start with just this one. And you can turn off the lies and soft sell, all right?"

"Lies? What lies, John Tinker, called The Chosen One? Soft . . . sell?"

Tinker straightened up and relaxed. He had begun to lean across the table, his right hand tightening into a fist. "Right the first time. I am finding it hard to believe in bug-uglies and B.S."

"Why is that? Whatever bug-uglies are?"

Tinker sighed. "Elementary, my dear Watson. Just now you said how peaceful and harmonious and content this place is, or was, right?"

"Correct."

"Weeeellllll, it seems to me, it does, that any

place that holds such claims, peaceful, harmonious, etc., etc., doesn't go around setting their dogs, or as you probably are aware, three lunatic costume freaks pretending to be fanged monstrosities, on their guests. Now do they?"

Tinker answered his own question. "Of course they don't. But that is what happened, didn't it." He stepped a half-step back from the table edge, his voice settling into a low menacing, flat tone. "So, despite what you think, or They thought, I am not interested in having any part of this funny farm or its inhabitants. Not now. Not never. I am not joining up. Not with you. Not with them." He jerked his thumb back over one shoulder, then stepped backward to gain a little more free space, knees flexing, his weight dropping low, ready to go in any direction. He watched The Thought and both sides. "And," he growled. "I do not enjoy being yanked from my home to Spookland just to play nutzy games with costume-ball ding-dongs."

The Thought sat and watched him, calm, thoughtful. He smiled gently. And nodded.

"You do have a point, John Tinker. Of a sort. But please understand this simple fact. Desperate people do desperate things. In some ways it was my fault. I told them that you were The Chosen One of Legend. Which fact just happens to be true, whether you wish to believe it or not. I told them that without your help we were finished, every last man, woman, and child. And that is also true, whether you chose to believe it or not. Of course, when the bodies begin to pile up you probably will, but then it will be somewhat late for those of us already dead. So, John Tinker, Chosen One, when you told them you were not interested in what they were saying, they panicked, that is all that was, just panic. Please accept my explanation. And my apology."

He steepled his fingers and rested his chin just above them. "And as for anything else, everything else, that has happened, I suppose I could sit here, and you could stand there, and we could debate the merits of the process, but we do not have that time to waste. Besides, it is all an academic point anyway. For after all, here you are." The Thought gestured at their surroundings. Then he gestured, not too gently, for Tinker to remain quiet. And he continued his story.

He told Tinker, the others had already been told, of how this world, this elseplace, was threatened by a member of The Thought's own order gone astray. This person had chosen evil over good, an age-old problem. This individual was now trying to infect all the times and places of the universe. The legends of this world, this elseplace, had predicted that such an event would occur. They also told what would have to be done in order to solve this problem once it arose. It was told that The Chosen One, from a different elseplace, would come and lead his companions on the dangerous quest that would finally rid the universes of this plague. But only after much danger, some minor, some major.

The Thought and all the members of his order had merged their minds and had called for help. Then, first from this elseplace, and then from that one, certain individuals were selected. They were to be The Chosen One's companions. The bright star that he had seen was the focus of their calling minds. He was called last, The Chosen One of Legend. Now here he was. The Thought straightened up and waggled one cautionary finger at Tinker. "Ah, ah, for now, no more questions or argument. We must save that for . . . later. For the moment just pretend that you accept what I have said. You are here, as was foretold. You have been here a long time, in a deep sleep. This gave us time and opportunity to prepare you, your clothes and your tools. As we prepared the others who will help you. Companions, would you please step forward?"

From the darkness, on either side of Tinker, two individuals stepped out. They both were clothed in the same type of clothes as he was but there the similarity ended. One was very small. The other was very large, larger than anyone Tinker had ever encountered or heard about. By several times. Short, tiny folk he could understand. But huge colossal he wasn't so sure about.

The Thought spoke loudly, bringing Tinker's attention back to him. "These two are your companions. There is one other, who you will meet soon." He pointed at the small figure. "This one is called, in his elseplace, Sorrowful Mistidings, and is, by profession, a teller of tales." The finger shifted. "That one is known as The-Mountain-That-Walks, a person who is most knowledgeable of rock and stone."

Then he pointed at Tinker. "You are the center that completes the group. These two understand, as does the other, that they must follow you, and obey all your commands, if they wish to ever return to their own respective elseplaces."

The Thought sat and gazed from one to the other for long, silent minutes. Then he beckoned them to step up against the edge of the table. "John Tinker, stand in front of the great sword named Slayer. The-Mountain-That-Walks in front of the cudgel called Crusher. Sorrowful Mistidings, you stand just there, in front of your sparkling dagger, Cutthroat by name." He smiled at them. "The names are fanciful." He shrugged, then reached out and lightly touched each weapon in turn. "These are special tools, created just for you, which I may touch now, but never again. From now on, only you may do that, or those that you trust completely. The jewels set in their hilts are called Golden Eyes. These beings are unique, no others exist. We have spent the treasure of this world, and the energy of this world, to make them. And to bring you and them together, in this time, in this place." His hand pulled back and dropped into his lap.

"Hold out your hands, weaponkin, your right hands, palms up please, we must finish the binding before time has fled. Do it!"

The three of them glanced at each other and then did as directed. With a quick flick of his hand, The Thought sliced across each outstretched palm. A thin line oozed blood. He pointed at the weapon.

"Grasp them. Do not let go. It will take but a moment or two."

Tinker reached out and grabbed the sword hilt, wondering now what? Some more of the hocus-pokus it seemed. The others followed suit.

The Thought's hands flowed in intricate patterns as he said something, slowly, carefully, mumbled words, phrases, patterns, words of command.

Tinker felt his palm begin to tingle. He stared at his hand as he felt thin electrical tickle crawl from his fingers, up his forearm, then up to his shoulder. The sword quivered and jerked. Then it began to dance, a rapid clattering on the table surface, an extension of his rigidly extended arm.

Sudden flaming pain lanced from sword tip to shoulder, rocking him back upon his heels. He lurched forward, sudden sweat pouring from his face, dripping puddles on the table and floor. The sword flailed wildly as Tinker fought to contain it. It was like a wild thing, trying to escape its captor. Then he was cold, shivering cold. But relaxing. He slumped forward, knees quivering, using his left hand, flat on the table top, to hold himself up. The sword lay quiescent. His arm, fingers, and shoulder felt fine. He glanced up and then from side to side.

His companions didn't look all that well. The giant was breathing in deep, rumbling rasps. The other was lying upon the table top.

Tinker straightened up and pried his fingers loose. The Thought smiled and handed each of them a small, brown wafer. "Eat these and recover, Weaponkin. You are now more than you have been, but less than you will become. No questions, yet, please. My time draws short and I have much to impart to you."

Sorrowful Mistidings shook his head and slipped from the table, wobbling from side to side, but carefully watching everything none-the-less.

The Thought nodded at each of them. "These are now you and your's. The six have become three and almost one. There is yet one more to complete the shape, the shape of seven. Then the one. Smoke will be a guide. Smoke will complete . . . the design.

The Thought's voice drifted in and out as he slumped back. "My time has run through. Follow the path . . . always. It will lead you to the evil one that you are to eliminate. And back to your homes."

The Thought now was transparent, casting no shadow. He gestured feebly behind his chair. "Follow the path. It begins just . . . outside the door. Smoke . . . is . . . outside. To aid . . . you. To . . . become . . . of . . . the . . . one. Goodbye, Brave Ones, my time has run throughhhhhh."

The chair sat empty.

The three of them looked at each other then Mountain and Sorrowful looked at Tinker. He stared around the room and shrugged his shoulders. "Well then, shall we start?"

"Wait," said Sorrowful, hastily grabbing his dagger, sheath, and belt, and putting everything together and on. He patted the dagger. It was a gesture of unfamiliarity. Mountain swung his thick belt around an equally thick mid-section and hung the cudgel in place. And nodded.

Tinker headed for the only door he could see. The door hadn't been there just a moment ago. He stopped, sighed, and spun around. Mountain and Sorrowful jolted to a halt, surprise on their faces. And jumped back, away from the swinging sword. "Do either of you have any idea, any guess at all, of what he was talking about?"

They shook their heads.

"Figures," he mumbled as he turned back to the door and, without thinking, swung his right arm around and up over his left shoulder, swinging the great sword over and around. It flapped against his back and clung there, the hilt sticking up, within easy reach. He hadn't remembered picking it up. He stopped, his eyes sliding sideways at the great bat-like thing, disbelief on his face, and mumbled, "Now how did I know that? And how does it do that? This is getting curiouser and curiouser, as Alice said."

Sorrowful looked up at Mountain. Mountain shrugged. There were times what Tinker was saying didn't make any sense, to them.

Tinker pushed at the door and stepped through as it swung open. The light outside was faint and dismal. After a short pause to check the immediate area, he walked into the gray, dreary scene. A narrow, somewhat overgrown, path started just outside the door and ran twisting away into the thick fogmist swirling around them. As he walked up the path, Tinker frowned and mumbled to himself, "This certainly doesn't look like sunny, southern California to me."

Things Are Where Things Are

Tinker's eyes popped open. He was awake. Waking much faster than his usual approach to a new day. He had decided. What to do about all this, this stuff he was involved in, with, whatever. Go with the flow, gain their confidence, make'em relax. Then bug-out. He laughed to himself. Today was as good a day as any.

He eased from his bed and slipped silently across the room and threw open the shutters covering the window. Sunlight, bright golden sunlight streamed into the room, cutting yellow bands across the floor and over the other two beds and the occupants therein. He smiled as he gazed out and up at the blue sky. Well, maybe he was in Southern California after all. It looked sunny enough. Behind him he heard a loud creak, the sound of a bed on the verge of collapse.

Mountain sat up and stretched, great arms seemed to span the room. Then he gave a heave and thumped upright, both feet thunking on the floor. He was still wearing his boots. He stood, turned, and picked up the bed and gently set it back in its original spot, grumbling in low bass tones about someone's idea of how to start a day.

Tinker grinned at him. "Awake, awake, big guy. It is truly a bright and sunny day that beckons." He saw Sorrowful tossing bedclothes and waggling his arms.

"Breakfast awaits large, and small, appetites.

Hark, hark, adventure calls to one and all." Tinker cupped his hand around one ear. Then sat and finished dressing. Sorrowful stared at him And his strange behavior.

A heavy hand pounded upon their door. The landlord called to them, "Time ta eat, time ta eat. Time ta be on yur way."

Tinker laughed. "See, I told you." He headed for the door. Sorrowful beat him to it and through it. A very quick mover. And fast riser.

They hurried down the short hall and into the dining room. There they found their blue-robed guide, already seated at the table, and already well into his breakfast. The Blue shoved another large mound into his mouth and peered out at them from deep inside his hood. Swallowing noisily, he spoke through half a mouthful, "John Tinker, The-Mountain-That-Walks, Sorrowful Mistidings, we have little time left before us." Another heaping forkful disappeared. The empty fork gestured at the table, beckoning them to seat themselves. "Eat. Prepare yourselves."

The Blue leaned forward and wiped his platter clean with a large slab of bread and popped it into his mouth. "Doom lives on the horizon," he said as he chewed. Then he sat back, eyed the platters just being set before the others by the landlord, shrugged to himself, and sipped from his cup.

Tinker took his seat and frowned across the table at The Blue, who pretended not to notice. Then Tinker pointed. "The only thing that I could see on the horizon this bright, ever so sunny morning, was a small storm boiling up. Nothing else."

The Blue banged his cup down upon the table,

"Chosen One, that storm is Doom. An evil presence that turns away the very sunlight itself. THAT is your destination. THAT is the very goal for which you four have been brought from your elseplaces to face, to face here. WAIT!" His head jerked around as he scanned the room's interior. He hissed, "There are supposed to be four of you." One arm snapped his hood back. "Where is the fourth?" he demanded. One fist thumped on the table top.

Tinker shrugged his shoulder and began to eat. "Beats me, G.I. Where is the fourth?" He wondered how many more times they would have this kind of discussion and how come The Blue now said fourth instead of seventh. He must be a rather confused person.

The Blue sank into his chair, slumping deeper and deeper, total despair written on his face. He was almost crying, struggling not to. "There are supposed to be four. Four," he mumbled. "Without the fourth, we are finished. We are all dead."

He jerked himself upright and cautiously checked the room's interior again and whispered to them, "The fourth must join you soon. You must have four to eliminate Doom."

"On the horizon?" suggested Tinker, taking another helping of food, being helpful. Sorta.

The Blue nodded. And slid one of the platters over and began to eat. This hero, he thought, speaks a very cryptic language.

Tinker smiled at him. It seemed to him as if escape lay right out there, on the horizon. Nothing like a small storm for running and hiding. He loaded his fork. "Well then, I suggest that we eat our breakfast so we can be on our way as soon as possible. I imagine that the fourth member of our little troop will join this jolly gang out there somewhere."

At his side Tinker heard Mountain mumble not all that quietly. "BY DUMPF, if this blue bottomless pit before us hasn't eaten everything already." The Blue was helping himself to just a little more breakfast. Again.

The Blue relaxed. The Chosen One had indicated that the fourth awaited them far ahead.

The innkeeper returned and set down more food and drink, bustling around them. The Blue sat straighter and helped himself to yet another serving, or two. And nodded to himself. The Chosen One was very sly, just hinting that the fourth was outside, waiting for them. Not saying it exactly. It was the way of the clever and devious. All good qualities in a hero.

They sat and ate and waited for Mountain to finish. It was taking large quantities to fill the huge man. Finally, he was done. The inn keeper had stopped bringing food.

Tinker rose and started for the outside, beckoning for the rest of them to come along. It was time to lead, seeing as he was supposed to be The Leader and all that sort of thing. Time to find a place to run. Tinker waved one arm to hurry them along.

"O.K., let's go, it is time to hit the road, to head for yon dark and dreary horizon. And you, our Blue Guide, can tell us all about whatever it is that you think it is that we must hear. We can just walk along and chat." He banged The Blue on the shoulder. It was a comradely thing to do.

Outside, as they started up the road, Tinker

pointed. "It doesn't appear to be all that far away."

The Blue nodded, and rubbed his shoulder. "It is far enough, Chosen One. And close enough. But, I may not go as far as you. Beyond a certain point, you must proceed by your selves. Only those who have been properly prepared may enter that fell realm ahead. You hold the fate of all of us in your hands. Our lives and our elseplace depend upon your success. If you should fail, we are finished. All of us."

Tinker sighed.

The Blue pointed dramatically at each of them with one sharp fingernail. "And your's. And your's. And your world as well, Chosen One. And the missing one's as well, the fourth." Then he increased the length of his stride. "Come, we must hurry."

Tinker stayed by his side as Mountain and Sorrowful trailed behind them. But not too far behind.

After a few minutes of silence, Tinker addressed the group at large. "O.K., everybody, all of you, I want no comments, or interjections, or any of that other nonsense for awhile. I need time to think. It is time for me to find the root to this particular problem, whether you-all like it or not. It is truly time to take a look behind the facade and find out why all the special effects and this cast of characters. And then come to some conclusion as to what this is really all about. So be quiet!"

He waved both his hands, cutting off any comments that they might have wished to make. He was beginning to get an uneasy feeling just there, deep in the pit of his stomach. Intuition was trying to tell him something. Right now he didn't want to hear what it had to say.

"Now, let's see . . ," he sighed. "They could have put something into my coffee, unbeknownst to me, I suppose." He glanced over at The Blue. No reaction.

"An induction coil under the table, or some such thing, might very well account for the tricks with the weapons. Other than that, it is just lots and lots of special effects. But why and to what affect? In this post-Disneyland era all that stuff is practically old hat, just so much flim-flammery. Tis naught but games within games, me'thinks." He jerked one thumb up over his shoulder. The Blue gave a start and jumped hastily one step sideways.

"And where they found this pair is anyone's guess. Some circus, I suppose. But how come? Aye, there's the rub. Who in their right mind would want to go through all this trouble? Snatch me, especially me, build elaborate sets, spend all that money, go through all this effort? Of course, they might not be in their right mind. Now there's a spooky thought. Weeelllll, as the King said to Anna, it's a puzzlement."

Behind his back, Mountain and Sorrowful cast puzzled glances at each other. They weren't really following much of Tinker's rambling monologue. Sorrowful shrugged and held his hands out, palms up. Mountain frowned and rumbled deep in his chest.

The Blue paid no attention to the one-sided conversation. But he kept a wary eye on Tinker's behavior, and watched the ever darkening horizon. That, he was worrying about. This person, walking at his side, speaking about peculiar things, was The Chosen One of Legend. The Blue knew that creatures of myth and legend behaved in wonderous ways, ways that were usually obscure to mere mortal minds like his.

However, nothing he had ever studied had described behavior like this. He had expected someone more, much more . . . heroic!

Around them the light was failing. Each step took them further into darkness, wan sickly, pale light. The grass on either side of their path was no longer green. It looked gray, dying. The few shrubs were stunted and sere. Black shadows lurked beneath the sparse trees and watched their progress up the hill with glittering eyes.

Suddenly Tinker gave a start, jolted to a halt, and stared around them. He had just noticed their surroundings. "Guide, what's going on? We've only been walking a few minutes. Do all your storms move this fast?" Dig for information, he told himself.

The Blue shook his head. "No, Chosen One, they do not. That is not a storm." He waved one hand vaguely at the dark in front of them. "It is we who have traveled so fast, not the other way around. In this region, time and distance do not follow the old rules. LOOK." He pointed back the way they had come.

They all turned and stared. The stood near the top of a high ridge. On the far horizon they could see the village, outlined in bright sunshine. Down the slope they could see the dot that was the inn where they had stayed. They had traveled miles in minutes.

Tinker felt his knees tingle, a chill coursed through his body. "Just a minute." He turned slowly around and carefully looked at everything. His shoulders sagged, he took a step up the slope, and sat down, legs tucked under, in the middle of the road, with a heavy thump. Dust eddied around him.

"OH NO," he sighed, a long drawn out loud

sigh. "It can't be true. Say it isn't so."

The Blue stepped to his side and leaned over, brows furrowing in concern. "Of course, Chosen One. It isn't so."

Tinker looked up at the serious face staring down at him and rolled his eyes. He could feel the blood draining from his face as the realization finally hit. It couldn't be true. It shouldn't be true. He was having the thoughts of the demented. Intuition was babbling over rationality. "It is true, isn't it?" His voice came out all harsh whisper and rasp. Intuition had won.

The Blue nodded at him. "Of course, it is true. Reality is reality, after all." He sounded quite puzzled.

Tinker's voice cracked, "Reality? Some reality this is. I am really trapped, aren't I? Deep inside a fairy tale?" His eyes darted back over the warped landscape. "This is reality?" Now he wondered, which was it: bad dream, nightmare, or insanity?

The Blue dropped one hand gently upon Tinker's shoulder and knelt by his side, pointing up into the gloom, speaking softly but firmly, "Chosen One, here I must leave you and your companions. There is your destination." He was beginning to wonder whether someone hadn't made a dreadful mistake. But it was too late to change things. Now.

Looming in the fastness ahead stood a monstrous shape, clouds swirled around it, fog seeping soft tendrils downward. Bent figures could just be seen crabbing their way across the tops of crooked walls and shattered pinnacles. Dark growth, twisted and bent, clung to precarious soil around the structure that seemed to pulsate gently. It was half hill, half castle. It looked to be no more than a mile or so ahead of them.

It was a dark mound, blotting out the sun, oozing darkness. Tinker shuddered and closed his eyes.

The Blue straightened up and stepped away. "Inside lives the evil self-named Doom. You will succeed." He certainly hoped so. "Farewell." He turned and swiftly ran down the path they had climbed, dwindled to a dot, and disappeared.

Tinker sat straighter and began to regulate his breathing. Then he stood up, swaying from side to side, pushing away the shock, pushing away everything. He took another deep breath, and slowly exhaled. He eyes refocused, he faced the thing ahead.

"Sludge."

"Sludge, John Tinker?" Sorrowful had stepped to his side. That was a rather strange curse to make.

"Right. Sludge, sewage sludge. A large mound of solidified sewage sludge. Big. Black. And ugly."

Well, now he knew, really knew, what he, they had to do. Go through there. Escape was somewhere through there. This was one adventure he could really have gone forever without having. He didn't need it. Not . . . at . . . all. Not now, not never.

Tinker turned and looked up at Mountain, then down at Sorrowful. He gave them a weak smile. It helped. Just a little.

"Well gang, it seems we have to go through there. This fairy tale has to be faced. Shall we start?" He tried another smile. This one worked better. Then he laughed and shrugged his shoulders.

"Nothing to worry about," he told them. "We are the heroes. Homes are on the far side, apologies to Gary." The more he thought about it, the more he decided there wasn't all that much to really worry about. As he had said, they were the heros. And he reminded himself once again of that fact. In all the fairy tales he was acquainted with, the heroes always won, the villains always lost. And they were the heroes. So, the quicker in, the quicker out. That was a comforting thought. Time to go in there and win. Then home. Can't be too hard.

Mountain and Sorrowful stood, waiting. Mountain crossed his arms on his chest and frowned, into the darkness. Sorrowful cast an expectant glance at Tinker.

Tinker nodded at them. "O.K. so far. Let's see if we can find a way in. I think we will just give a creep through those woods. Shall we start?" He looked from one to the other. They weren't being very helpful. Or very responsive.

"Look gang, it seems we have to try and find our way into that place, and then go out the other side, unless one of you was given better instructions than I was. Well?"

Both of them shook their heads.

He nodded. "Right! Then let's go. Chop, chop!"

Mountain's voice rumbled from deep in his chest, "John Tinker, those woods are low-limbed. You and our tiny companion can slip through them with ease. As for me, I shall have to run along the edge of the road and trust to the shadows."

Tinker looked up at the frowning face and nodded. "But let's move as quickly as we can. I don't like the idea of being out in the open. Sooner or later something up there will see us."

He turned and trotted up the path, then into the forest, Sorrowful right at his heels. Mountain jogged along the road edge merging with the shadows, watching the other two shadows flitting from dark patch to dark patch.

As he ran, Tinker could feel his body recovering, his energy level rising. From the little exercise he was getting he was beginning to feel better and better. He had set disbelief aside. For the moment.

Darkness.
Sudden and swift.
No twilight.
Just night.
With a hint of light filtering down through the foliage overhead.

A heavy thump followed by a muffled oath rumbled through the midnight ink enveloping them. Then, two more thuds followed by soft, very creative swearing.

"By DOUBLE-DUMPF it all, John Tinker," the low bass sotto-voice of Mountain carried through the black forest. "I seem to have run headlong into this castle mound. It rises straight up before me much like a cliff. What have you found?"

Tinker responded in a hiss, "Much the same thing. In much the same way. What can you see over there?"

"DIM-DUMPFING little. From what I can feel, this structure is constructed of large cut-stone blocks with sizable cracks between the courses. Very shoddy workmanship. One of us could probably climb up and find a way to let the others in."

"Not a bad idea," spoke a low voice at

Mountain's elbow. It was Tinker. In the darkness, he and Sorrowful had slipped up upon Mountain, unseen and unheard. "You know, if you hadn't been speaking to us, we couldn't have found you at all. These clothes hide us in this darkness."

Tinker ran an exploratory hand over the rough stones in front of them, slipping his fingers in and out of the deep cracks. "You're right. One of us ought to be able to climb this wall fairly easily. Sorrowful is the smallest and would be the least visible once he gets to the top. How about it, Sorrowful, want to give it a try?"

The small voice whispered to them both, "Yes. But I would like to make a small observation."

"What?"

"It seems to me, it does, that for all the alleged large amount of preparation we were told has gone into this activity that we are upon that we are singularly unprepared for the first obstacle we should meet."

"DUMPFING correct in that," softly grumbled Mountain, well, as softly as he could.

"Well, we can't just stand here holding a debate about that," stated Tinker firmly, impatient to end it, to be on his way. And back home.

Sorrowful reached out, carefully felt his way, and crept up two layers of the large stone block layers and whispered into their faces, "True, true."

He slipped higher, then stopped to whisper down at them in a very pedantic tone. "This reminds me of *The Tale Of The Sid'ler That Dangled*. Which I shall have to relate to you upon my return. So, and so. Make yourselves comfortable, I shall see what can be found up there." He slipped a bit higher and stopped to whisper back down at them. "On my way up I think that I shall compose a new tale that I shall call, in honor of this occasion, *The Tale Of The Solidified Sewage Sludge*. That title has a certain flow to it, don't you think?"

Tinker hissed at him, "CLIMB! We can hold academic discussions of story telling later. After we're done here and on our way home. GO!"

Overhead the slight scrambling sounds faded and disappeared.

Then silence.

No night sounds.

Deep deadly silence.

Broken only by the faint sounds of Mountain and Tinker breathing.

Then.

Something else.

Sorrowful's harsh whisper drifted down to them, "Do you hear something?"

Mountain and Tinker held their breath.

A deep vibration came up through the soles of their boots. They could feel it in the vibrations in the castle wall. It was a deep, heart beating sound. Surrounding them.

It grew louder.

And louder.

It spoke to them.

doom . . . doom . . . doom . . .

It came from . . . everywhere. It surrounded them. The ground, the castle's walls shuddered with menace.

Something came down the wall toward them.

doom ... doom ... doom ...

Sorrowful dropped to the ground with a soft thud.

"OOF! John Tinker, I am glad that you changed your mind about all this. If you had not, I fear that you would have gotten all of us killed. And I, for one, do want to return home."

Tinker sighed, loudly he sighed. "Sorrowful, no-one is going to get home unless you climb back up there and find a way for us to get inside. Now, will you get back up there?"

"Most certainly, John Tinker. But it seems to me, it does, that whatever it is that is responsible for that thumping noise must be aware of our presence, does it not?"

Sorrowful started climbing up the wall again.

There is no need for that, John Tinker.

"What did you say, Mountain?"

"Not a RAR-RUMPFING thing. It is you and Sorrowful that are making all the noise."

"You didn't?"

"That is what I just said. I said, I am not making a RAR-RUMPFING sound. What I said, I said!"

"Well, I thought that I heard you say something. Hurry up, Sorrowful, we don't have time to waste."

There is no need for that, John Tinker. I am here.

"Hold it up for a minute, Sorrowful. I did hear, I do hear, something, someone talking to me."

"As you wish, John Tinker," called Sorrowful.

doom ... doom ... doom ...

"All I hear, John Tinker," snarled Mountain, "is that DUMPFING sound. Although I did, just for an instant, see a movement off to our right side."

Tinker reached for his weapon.

There is no need for that, John Tinker.

"WHAT? WHO ARE YOU? WHAT ARE YOU? WHY CAN'T THE OTHERS HEAR YOU?"

"John Tinker, who are you yelling at?" Sorrowful had climbed back down the wall and was clinging just above their heads.

"SHHHHHHHHH," cautioned Tinker, "there is something out there, over to our right. What are you doing back down here?"

doom . . . doom . . . doom . . .

Sorrowful sidled across the wall and peered into Mountain's face. Mountain shook his head slowly from side to side.

doom . . . doom . . . doom . . .

It is because I am inside, John Tinker.

"Inside what? My mind?"

"SHHHHHHHHHH, yourself, John Tinker," cautioned Sorrowful in his turn. "You will be heard up there. At the top."

Yes, John Tinker, the top is the way in. Up there are watchers and the entrance.

Something barely seen shot up the wall. It made no sound. Then from high overhead they heard it, a soft crunching.

Tasty.

Something thudded into the forest duff nearby. Sorrowful scrambled down the wall and ran over to see what it was. It was a body, a strange figure dressed all in dark leather. With no head. Dark fluids oozed into the forest floor.

Two more bodies thumped down, barely missing them.

Tasty.

Sorrowful tugged at Tinker's sleeve. "I do not like this, John Tinker. What was that which we could barely see? Who were you talking to, that we could not hear? What is happening in this place?"

Tinker pursed his lips and whistled soundlessly. Then he sighed.

"Sorrowful, I think that the answer to all your questions is that we have been joined by the fourth member of our little troop just as The Thought said would happen. The one that The Blue was so agitated about. Well, now, I guess we now are four. But I don't know what number four is. And I don't know why only I can hear it. And, I don't know what it is, either."

Tasty.

"Why do you call it, it?" Sorrowful frowned at him.

doom . . . doom . . . doom . . .

"Because I don't think that it is human. Because it is up there eating the guards, or part of them. Because I think that The Thought has played a rather grisly joke upon us."

Far to one side several more things crashed down through the trees.

I am not a joke, John Tinker. That is not a nice thing to say. Climb up, the way is clear.

A coil of rope whipped past them and landed in a tangle next to Sorrowful, who leaped sideways crashing into Mountain's legs.

"BY DUMPF, watch what you are doing, fly speck."

"Mik! Mik, mik, mik!" Sorrowful kicked Mountain on the side of his boot and grabbed the rope, swiftly making a neat coil of it, slipped it over one shoulder, and started back up the wall. "Wait here, please. I will anchor this firmly at the top." He disappeared into the darkness. Into the silence.

Moments later, the uncoiling rope hissed past them. Tinker grabbed it and swarmed up the wall. When Mountain clambered up and over the parapet, he found his two companions facing in either direction, weapons in hand. Tinker gestured and started along the walkway. They followed him.

doom . . . . doom . . . . doom . . . .

Inside.

Tinker pointed at the dark rectangle of an opening and started forward. Sorrowful darted past him and through it before he could say anything. After a short pause, a small hand popped out and beckoned them forward.

Tinker and Mountain stepped into the castle.

"Don't go running off like that," hissed Tinker. "The last time you were by yourself something ran over you, remember?"

They walked carefully along the dim corridor,

Mountain mumbling and grumbling to himself as he wobbled his head from side to side dodging the ceiling beams.

doom . . . . doom . . . . doom . . . .

The beat was louder now that they were inside. The further they progressed, the louder it became.

In the faint light Sorrowful's eyes gleamed happily. "It would seem that we are headed in the correct direction, John Tinker."

The small morsel is correct.

"Seems that we are, Sorrowful."

Ahead they could see more light, pulsating softly. It was shining into the corridor from one side. Sorrowful pointed at it. "Wait here." He ran toward the light.

"WAIT . . . damn it, I wish he would stop running off like that."

Far ahead, near the light source, Sorrowful stopped and peered cautiously around something. Then he waved jauntily at them and disappeared.

doom . . . . doom . . . . doom . . . .

They stood and waited, Mountain shifting back and forth, from foot to foot. "By DOUBLE-DUMPF, John Tinker, we shall have to move soon as I cannot stand bent over like this forever. This hallway was not built for one such as I."

"Patience, patience. Where I come from the giants were always noted for their patience. At least, that's what all the tales say."

"HELP! JOHN TINKER! HELP!"

It was Sorrowful, his voice echoing down the stone corridor.

Tinker shook his head. "Oh no, not again. Well, come on, let's go see what happened to him this time."

They ran toward the corridor into which Sorrowful had disappeared. Two silent shadows.

"Low RUMPFING CEILINGS. OUCH!"

"HELP, HEEELLLLPPPPPPP. HELP, HELP. HELP."

doom .... doom .... doom ....

"Oooof. OUCH. DOUBLING, DUMPFING, RAR-RUMPFING CEILINGS!"

"Will you be quiet, they will hear us coming."

doom .... doom .... doom ....

"HUMPF! From the noise that Sorrowful is making, we will be expected anyway."

They charged around a slight bend in the corridor and into a shaft of bright light streaming from a large doorway set in the hall side. The heavy door slammed shut. Pushing, shoving, and kicking wouldn't budge it.

doom .... doom .... doom ....

Mountain unhooked his great club and waggled it gently in one hand, motioning for Tinker to step back.

Then arching his back, he wedged himself into position and swung the cudgel back and up. It fell, whistled through the air, grazed the floor, and crashed into the lower central panel of the door. The explosion blew Tinker backwards, pieces of door spattering down around him and into the room.

The flash had blinded Mountain momentarily. Then, blinking his eyes, he stumbled forward and lurched out into a vast, open space.

doom .... doom .... DOOM ....

The sound was originating from this room. An evil pulsating heart.

Mountain straightened up and looked around.

He was standing in a large hall, a large hall flooded with light. The ceiling was high, the walls far apart. He kicked the remnants of the door away, clearing a space around his feet.

"WHOA, what have we here?"

Tinker hurtled into the room, his sword in hand. He stopped, spun around, and faced one end.

Something was seated there. Something was seated there in a golden throne set high up, set upon a raised dais. Around the throne and its occupant hung a dense, black fog that oozed in soft swirls into the air. They drifted along lazy air currents to bump against the ceiling and to finally drift away to somewhere.

"Ooops," said Tinker, "another smog maker."

DOOM .... DOOM .... DOOM ....

A voice spoke to them from the eddying

darkness. Softly it spoke. Kindly it spoke. Gently it spoke.

"Welcome John Tinker, called Chosen One, to my home. I have been waiting for you to arrive. Have you and your's come to offer me your obeisance? It would really be best if you did so. Otherwise you may find yourself sharing the fate of your minuscule associate who hangs just there writing his farewell." A languid arm raised, one long finger pointing lazily, one long talon, tracing the path of a tendril of ink curling and roiling over their heads, and finally to the far wall.

Spider wrapped in a dark cocoon, Sorrowful hung upside down. His right arm was pinned to his side, his dagger still firmly clenched in his hand.

DOOM … DOOM …. DOOM ….

The ebony pendulum swung with the sound, casually thumping its burden against the wall.

DOOM …. DOOM …. DOOM ….

Sorrowful was managing to twist and to ward off the wall with his free hand and arm. He smiled a bright and upside down smile at Tinker.

"Well, John Tinker … OOF … do not just stand there gawking at me … OOF … get me down from here …. OOF …. before I wear out … OOF. It is quite dirty … OOF … up here."

DOOM …. DOOM …. DOOM ….

The soft voice spoke again, demanding Tinker's

attention. He turned back to face the throne and occupant.

"Well, John Tinker, do you wish to save your friend? If you do, then throw down your weapons and swear your faith to me. You will not even have to mean it. Just say the words, that is all. It is such an easy thing to do. Just SAY THEM!"

Doom waved one arm. The fog swirled in the agitated air. "This elseplace is mine. Just say the words. Save yourselves. If you do . . . . then you may leave. Unharmed. Intact. Through the portal. There."

The hand pointed to one side, past where Sorrowful was hanging, thumping back and forth. Something shimmered and materialized. A doorway appeared, its surface swirled and shimmered with heat waves. Fire-snakes roiled and hissed around the edges, bathing in the heat. On the other side, quivering in the heat distortions, Tinker could see green fields and bright sunshine, a pastoral scene.

Doom curled his fingers into a tight fist, one talon pointing arrow-straight at the portal.

"Through there lies Paradise. When I have finished with you, I mean to have it. It is next. Paradise will be mine. However, first things first, as we are always being told. Do you and your's, John Tinker, join with me? Or, do you chose to die?"

He must stand and leave his throne.

DOOM ... DOOM .... DOOM ....

"Enough of your nonsense." Tinker waved both arms wildly.

Mountain jumped sideways as Slayer flashed

dangerously close. "DUMPF!"

"Who are you to dictate to us? Come out from behind that black smog and show yourself, Oh Mighty Afraid One." Sweepings his arms straight out from the shoulder, he took a deep, mocking bow.

Mountain jumped sideways as the sword tip flashed past. "Careful!"

Doom leaped to his feet, face twisting with rage, and stalked forward, still wearing his mantle of blackness.

DOOM.... DOOM.... DOOM.... DOOM.... DOOM.... DOOM....

"WHAT? You pitiful fools would dare to mock me? I am Doom. And doomed is what you are. HERE! Here is a small gift for your small companion."

One gnarled finger jabbed toward Sorrowful. A bright ball dripped glowing fire oozed from the tip and floated lightly across the room. It delicately touched Sorrowful on the side. Purple light flared and died. Sorrowful's face contorted as he stifled his cry of pain.

Doom pointed again. Another ball formed. It shot straight for Tinker's face. Slayer twisted and sliced, the ball flashed into non-existence. Doom jabbed again and again. The blade flashed as missile after missle sought to strike the dancing figure inside the protective shield woven by his weaponkin. The air was crackling, filling the chamber with the sharp smell of ozone.

"Mountain . . . that way. OUT!" shouted Tinker, "That way."

His sword danced, seemingly by itself. Think about it later he told himself.

Mountain lumbered for the wall, his great club singing through the air as he hurtled forward. Dust erupted from the wall under the initial impact. Stone shards flew outward and rattled over the floor.

DOOM....DOOM....DOOM....DOOM...
DOOM...DOOM....

"STOP! I so command you. STOP!" Doom was shouting, screaming at them. "STOP!"

Mountain struck the wall again. It visibly shook as a long crack snapped upward following the edges of the stone blocks. Rubble and stone fragments showered down. The massive club thudded to the rhythm of the insane beat of doom.

DOOM...DOOM....DOOM....DOOM....
DOOM....DOOM....

In front of Mountain, carved blocks of stone tumbled outward as a section of the wall collapsed. A deep concavity was rapidly taking shape. A stone toppled from the side of the doorway. It stood unaffected. The fire-snakes hissed at the monstrous being flailing wildly at the wall. Mountain kicked his feet and grumbled at the fire snakes snapping and hissing at him. His feet were buried past his ankles by rock fragments and plaster dust.

"STOP!" Doom leaped forward. "You would see what you face, would you?"

He stalked to the edge of the dais, arms held stiffly at his side, fingers clenching and unclenching.

The black fog drifted away.

He glared and snarled at them, "Then look at your DEATH."

Two black tentacles snapped forward, out and down, groping for Tinker and Mountain.

Tinker's sword snapped up and around, slicing through them. They exploded with an electrical crackle. Doom staggered back a step.

DOOM....DOOM....DOOM....DOOM...
DOOM....

The chamber quivered under the rhythmic energy twisting the very castle-mountain itself.

Doom rocked back on his heels and pointed at them. Insane laughter stabbed through the din.

Over their heads the black mists began to coalesce and take on form and substance. Light arced and pulsated over the forming surface repeating the jagged pattern on Doom's robe. A great, dark sphere floated overhead, lightening flashed from it, striking walls and floor.

DOOM....DOOM....DOOM....DOOM....
DOOM....

Doom smiled at Tinker and pointed.

The globe drifted toward its victim, lightening strikes etching a pattern along the floor. Molten rock seeped from the steaming gap.

Suddenly Doom screamed, loud, piercing terror. He twisted violently from side to side.

Something had grabbed him from behind. Two large, black, fur-covered paws gripped his forearms, pinning them to his sides as the ebony claws slipped from hidden sheaths and sank into the folds of his sleeves.

Doom's cries echoed from the walls. Crimson stains crept down his sleeves, blood began to drip from jerking fingertips.

The black sphere, undirected, hung motionless. Lightning continued to pump downward. The stone floor glowed red, then white, then it began to sag, ever so slowly.

DOOM . . DOOM . . DOOM . . DOOM . . DOOM . . DOOM . . DOOM . .

A large head reared up from behind the still struggling figure. Large, round, yellow-gold, orange, eyes peered at them over one shoulder. Vertical pupils, now mere slits, closed against the bright light, stared at Tinker. A great muzzle yawned wide, ivory teeth glistened as lips pulled back in a horrid snarl, great saber canines glittering. The thing struck, fangs plunging to the gum-line. The head snapped back. The paws released. Doom crumbled forward, eyes wide, staring, vacant. A red jet gushed from the ragged hole where neck once joined shoulder.

"Oh, oh!" hissed Tinker.

The large thing sat on its haunches behind the twitching body, jaws dripping gore. A smile seemed to play across its face as its long tongue licked away facial stains. It rose in one fluid motion and flowed off the dais toward Tinker.

"Oh, merde."

Tinker stepped back, snapped a quick glance

around the room, and waggled his sword in front of himself, warning it away. This fairy tale had just turned into a nightmare of the worse kind.

The horror slipped closer and closer, the great paws silently touching down, the claws now retracted. The eyes totally focused upon his face, all attention focused upon him. A predator's stare.

Mountain began pounding upon the wall again.

DOOM . DOOM . DOOM . DOOM . DOOM . DOOM . DOOM . DOOM . DOOM .

The heavy beat had returned, its force now released, out of control. The castle shook and trembled. The globe continued to arc crackling bolts at the floor. The fog dissolved, fading away rapidly.

Mountain caught Sorrowful and held him cradled in his left arm as he swung with his right, intent upon reducing the wall to rubble.

DOOM . DOOM . DOOM . DOOM . DOOM . DOOM . DOOM . DOOM . DOOM .

The floor heaved and split, dust poured from the ceiling.

The thing stopped just beyond Tinker's reach and peered into his eyes.

Through the portal, John Tinker. It is our only hope for survival.

"What? What are you?"

I am Smoke. In one bound it twisted, leaped, and sailed through the portal.

DOOMDOOMDOOMDOOMDOOMDO
OMDOOMDOOMDOOMDOOMDOOM
DOOMDOOMDOOM.

You have no choice. Leap!

Tinker turned and waved frantically.

"Mountain, that way. Through the portal."

The floor ripped open, belching flame. The far end settled heavily, cracks snaking in all directions. The walls bowed outward. The ceiling sagged and groaned.

Mountain lunged for the portal with Tinker charging after him almost stepping on his heels.

They hit the ground and tumbled rolling across the cool, lush grass. Behind them, the portal disappeared in a brilliant flash of electric green.

Tinker sat up and looked around at their new surroundings.

It was a nice, pleasantly warm, sunny day. They were sprawled high up a gently sloping plain that stretched into the distance. All around them was a dirty gray smudge. Where the portal had been, the gray ended in a razor sharp edge.

He looked at his companions. Sorrowful was rousing as he lay cradled in Mountain's lap. The black thing sat next to them cleaning its face with its paws.

Tinker stood up and scanned the immediate vicinity. Well, he thought, now which way is home?

Over there is a path.

Tinker stood, turned his head, and saw it. "Now what?"

He walked over. It was a wide path, winding its way through the grass and down a back slope. It seemed to be made of metal. It was about six feet wide.

Tinker bent over and touched one of the paving bricks with a finger tip. They were smooth. They were gold. This path was made from gold bricks.

"Crazy." He straightened up and saw the sign off to one side. It hadn't been there a moment ago.

It was a small, wooden sign mounted on a short, stout post. There was something carved on its face.

Shrugging one shoulder, he walked over, stopped in front of it, and read:

WELCOME TO PARADISE.

We're off to See the Wizard

Tinker stood by the path. It didn't make any sense, not given all the things that they had been told. He looked at his surroundings. Other than the strange path, everything in the environment here looked like home. Everything looked just like the mountainous area just west of his place, his rural home ten miles outside of Grandeville except he didn't believe that was where he was. He scanned his surroundings again. Then he looked at the sign again. Then over at his companions. He wondered about them. He wondered how he could be inside a fairy tale.

So, he asked himself, what are they? One big guy. One small guy. One . . . something?

He walked over to take a better look at the it, the something. Whatever it was, out here in the sunshine it looked a little less nightmare and much more like some large, mutated feline kind of a thing. Tinker laughed silently to himself. Yep, he decided, in some strange way that didn't really make any sense to him, he was definitely trapped inside a fairy tale of some sort with a rather standard fairy tale cast of characters. An elf(?), a giant(?), and a, ummmm, something.

Then he laughed out loud, his basic optimism surging to the surface. A carefully developed optimism from the past ten years. "When in Rome do as the Romans do, or some such thing," he mumbled. And reminded himself, once again, of the basic fact of this fairy tale: we are the heroes and the heros always win.

Now what's going on?

It was that old familiar question, long unasked. It echoed in his mind. It wasn't him asking. He glared over at the cat-thing and snarled at it, "All right, you, stop that."

Long rabbit ears lifted as the head turned to look at him. Then it arched its back and stretched. He could see each muscle rippling smoothly under the thick fur. The monster stalked slowly over and past him, to sniff and prowl along the edge of the golden pathway.

Tinker turned slowly, always keeping it in sight, and watched what she was doing. He took another look. HER! Suddenly, he knew. It, that something, was a female. Something. A big, female something and she certainly was big. She was tall, almost five feet to the top of her back. Her muzzle protruded, more dog-like than cat-like. Great canines, saber teeth, stabbing downward from upper jaws, glittering bright white. The long rabbit ears ended in fuzzy tufts of hair. The ears twitched and danced as she listened to faint and far distant sounds. Her tail, an amazingly long, long tail, floated and drifted here and there, jerking and swaying with a rhythm of its own. She was a shadow. Her fur seemed to absorb the light. Just like their clothes. He smiled and thought, four of a kind. And laughed.

Tinker smiled, Smoke was a good name for her. He took a careful step closer and asked, "Well, Smoke, what do you think?"

This path smells of powerful magic. Mind-made magic.

He rolled his eyes at her and kicked gently at one

of the bricks. "Magic?"

Yes.

"Like you."

No. Different. I am not magic!

"I suppose." He shrugged.

Look at me, John Tinker.

He did.

He was staring at the most beautiful, flower-covered bush he had ever seen. Soft perfumes seeped out and caressed him. The odors were strange, yet overpowering. Enticing. Irresistible. He had to walk a little closer. He didn't want to. But he did.

The bush vanished. Smoke's nose was just touching his. Her great eyes stared into his. That long tail was draped over his left shoulder, across his back, and curled around his neck. It was a snug, velvet noose. The tip lightly brushed one cheek. She yawned widely. All he could see was the inside of her throat and rows of white, gleaming teeth. Her upper canines touched the top of his forehead, the lowers nudged under his chin.

Do you understand?

He managed to gasp out a ragged "Yes" as she snapped her jaws shut with a loud pop, just in front of his face. Her tail slowly uncoiled and slithered away, allowing him to take a faltering step backward. He inhaled deeply, taking several calming breaths. Then he spoke, "Oh yes." Tinker looked down at the path. "So this was created by someone's mind, right?"

She looked at him.

"But why gold bricks?"

Smoke sat down.

"I don't suppose we might be lucky enough to be

back home, my home, that is?"

One ear twitched at him.

"Right. But why a yellow brick road?"

Her tail flicked from side to side.

He laughed. "O.K., O.K." He looked over at Mountain and Sorrowful.

They were sitting side by side watching them. Waiting. Wondering what he was doing. Wondering why he was doing whatever it was that he was doing. And wondering why he was talking with that large creature.

"It look's like everyone is sufficiently recovered to carry on. We might as well get going." He waved at them. "So, let's get going. We have to find our way home."

They stood and walked over. Sorrowful had a slight limp. He patted at his scorched clothing. "Not as bad as it appears, John Tinker." And smoothed out his shirt.

Tinker pointed. "We might as well follow this thing, this, ummmmmm, path. It starts just here and runs over that way. Soooooooo, if it is all right with you guys, ah, you two and her, let's hit the bricks, so to speak."

"Her?" asked Sorrowful.

"Right," said Tinker. "Her."

"Oh." Sorrowful bowed to Smoke. "Madame."

"HUMPF!" snorted Mountain.

Tinker started, walking down the middle of the pathway, singing, not exactly on key, "We're off to see The Wizard, the wonderful Wizard of Oz . . . " It seemed appropriate to him. He wondered whether they were going to meet green witches and flying monkeys.

It was a fairy tale after all.

The others stood and stared at him. Mountain and Sorrowful looked puzzled. Smoke just looked. He stopped, turned, and beckoned violently at them.

"Come on, come on. This is the pathway to adventure, to excitement, to HOME." He laughed, and mumbled to himself, "I hope." Then he called to Mountain, "And, if we are lucky, maybe even something to eat." He started down the yellow brick road again.

They hurried after him. He was walking slowly so they could easily catch up. He had decided to give this fairy tale he was trapped in his very best effort. And reminded himself of what he felt was the basic fact, this above all. WE are the heros! WE always win!

Sorrowful gave a tug at Tinker's sleeve, just above the elbow.

So Tinker stopped walking. They all stopped walking.

"John Tinker, what is this wizard of which you are singing? Is this some kind of a tale?"

Yes. What sort of wizard being are you leading us to see?

Mountain rumbled something deep inside his chest.

Tinker looked from face to face. "Well, gang, it is a long story." He patted Sorrowful on the shoulder. "But I will tell you anyway. It is one of my favorites."

Then he held up one finger, a cautionary finger. "But I shall have to assign each of you a role to play. It is the only way to truly understand this tale."

"A very strange way for a tale to be told," stated Sorrowful, firmly, frowning.

"MUMPF," agreed Mountain.

Tinker looked from one to the other, then at Smoke. "Ah, ah, ah, it is my tale to tell. You will just have to take it as is."

He stroked his chin and looked very serious. "Now let us see, which one is which one? Ummmmmmmmmm? O.K., I shall be Dorothy."

Tinker snapped a fast glance from Mountain to Sorrowful to Smoke. "And no smart remarks about that? Mountain can be the Tin Woodsman. Sorrowful will be the Scarecrow, and Smoke will be Toto. Ready?"

Sorrowful and Mountain nodded, slowly, two very puzzled individuals. Smoke sat and stared at him. They hadn't traveled very far down the yellow brick road.

Suddenly Sorrowful beamed, clapped his hands together and bounced up and down on his toe-tips. "Ah, ha, John Tinker, ah, HA! You are more civilized than I had thought. Or you had previously indicated. We shall play the parts. Say on, say on." His eyes twinkled with anticipation.

"Gee, thanks, Sorrowful. O.K., gang, here we go." He started down the pathway again, waving both arms. "The Scarecrow walks on this side on me, the Tin Woodsman on the other side. Right. Toto just sorta scampers about, running from here to there."

Smoke lopped lazily back and forth across the pathway in front of them. It felt good to get some exercise. Whatever a Toto was, it felt good to run about like one. She stretched her legs and bounded in elastic arcs.

Tinker laughed loudly. "RIGHT, by George I think you've got it, you've really got it." He checked his right and left sides.

"Now you two have a little dance to learn. It goes like this. Try it." Tinker danced just to show them how. For this bit he was following the movie version. Sorrowful followed his example, then Mountain. They were both fast learners. More or less. Tinker sighed. "Well, that will have to do. It will get better as we move along." He took a deep breath. Then he started the tale.

"Once upon a time, in a land called Kansas, there lived a little girl named Dorothy, that is me, and she had a little dog named Toto, that is Smoke. Now Dorothy lived on a farm with her Aunt Em and her Uncle Henry and . . . "

They danced, and gamboled, their way down the yellow brick road. Behind them the yellow bricks faded away. The back edge was keeping pace with them. And as the bricks faded they left no trace of their existence. None at all.

The four travelers didn't notice, engrossed as they were in Tinker's tale.

". . . and so Dorothy clicked the heels of her red shoes together, that is in the movie, in the book they were silver, and made her wish. Then there she was, back in Kansas."

Tinker looked down and smiled, a broad smile. "Well, Sorrowful M., was that enough of a tale for you?"

Sorrowful beamed up at him, nodding his head enthusiastically. "Oh, yes, truly, John Tinker, that was a traveling tale to be told. Now I must make a confession." He blushed. And brushed some small speck from his shirt front. "I am most impressed.

Earlier, in that other place," he glanced quickly back over his shoulder, "it did not seem as if you would be the type of person who would know such tales or would even be interested in them. I shall treasure this one mightily. I look forward to the time when I may tell, retell, it to my own folk."

His face saddened "That is, assuming that we should somehow find a way to finish this trip, ah, alive. And, oh me, to find a way for me, ahhhh, us, to return home again, that is . . . "

Tinker nodded, his own smile fading away. He felt the gloom resettling around them. "Yes," he sighed, "that is the problem, isn't it?"

Tinker glanced down at Sorrowful, then up at Mountain, and then out at Smoke, who still trotting about, and spoke softly. "You know, I was sure that this wasn't real, that is, not real in the manner The Thought was speaking about. It was hard, it still is hard, for someone from my home to believe such things are true, especially when you are asked to live them." He waved his arms at their surroundings. "But here we are, where ever this is. It looks like home to me, but it can't be. I doubt that I will wake up and find out that everything so far has been a dream." He laughed. "Welcome to reality, of some sort or another. What can we do about it?"

He answered his own question. "Live it, that's what. We make the best of it and push on. Right? Right." Tinker looked up."So what do you think, Mountain?"

The bass voice grumbled down at him. "By all the ROCKS AND STONES, John Tinker, I think that if we do not find something to eat soon that I shall shrink right down into a small, insignificant fly speck like our tiny friend here, BY DUMPF!"

One large hand swung down across Tinker's chest and plucked Sorrowful off his feet, casually swinging him high into the air. Sorrowful smiled, a rather weak smile, down at Tinker as he sat on Mountain's shoulder. One hand clenched a handful of the gigantic man's hair.

Mountain pointed ahead, his stomach rumbling gently, his stride lengthening. "COME! Perhaps if we stretch out our legs some small amount we might find food and shelter all that much quicker. Perhaps these woods we are approaching harbor some edible berries or leafy vegetables. COME, let us hurry."

Tinker danced around and ahead of him and poked Mountain sharply in the stomach. Like hitting a stone wall. It grumbled back at him. "HEY THERE, slow down, slow down." Mountain did. Otherwise he would have walked right over Tinker. "Toto . . . er, Smoke, why don't you just scamper ahead and see what might be lying in wait for us in the woods. Just to make sure that we don't get some new surprise. Or something."

Smoke bounded ahead and disappeared. Tinker blinked his eyes. One moment she was there, the next she was gone. He couldn't see her anywhere. Not a trace. He walked slower. Behind him Mountain, stepped carefully.

Tinker waved one arm. "Come on, come on, don't be chicken."

Mountain took one step and walked by his side, "A strange thing to say, John Tinker. Chick un."

"Ummmmm, I suppose it is." Tinker looked up

at Sorrowful, who grinned back. "Well, up there," asked Tinker, "what do you think? That looks to be a very well-manicured forest. Not very wild."

Sorrowful waggled his eyebrows and shrugged one shoulder.

They entered the forest. It had all the appearance of a formal garden, a gigantic organized plot of trees and shrubs and flowers. Vast open spaces, the grass neatly trimmed, flowering shrubs and flowers poking up everywhere.

Then they saw it. Up ahead of them.

Another sign, right by the edge of the pathway. It faced the yellow brick road partially hidden by some low bushes.

Tinker looked around and called, "SMOKE. HEY THERE, SMOKE!" He carefully scanned their surroundings, frowning deeply. "O.K., now where did she get to?" And slowly began to turn around, taking another, more careful look. "Now what? SMOKE. HEY, ARE YOU THERE?"

Yes, I am here.

"Well then, talk to me. What's on that sign? What does it say?"

It would be better if you read it.

Tinker's frown deepened. "What? I assume that from that, that the coast is clear?"

I got lost in thats.

"Is there anything around here waiting to pounce upon us?"

Only me.

Tinker sighed. "Just what I need, a fur-coated comedianne." He stomped forward, headed for the sign. Smoke didn't bother to tell him that she had no idea what kind of a thing a coast was that was supposed to be clear. He stopped in front of the wooden sign, bent over and read it.

The sign was very similar in style and construction to the first one that they had seen. It could have been its twin. This one said:

100 AKER WOOD

Beware the Jabberwock, my son.

Mountain gently sat Sorrowful down so he could bend over and read the sign. He looked at Sorrowful for some explanation as to what this strange message could mean. Sorrowful shrugged his shoulders. They both looked at Tinker.

Tinker looked from one to the other. Then back at the sign.

The frustration with his predicament roared back, full strength. He kicked the sign squarely in the center. The post shifted a small amount. "Fairy tale or not, this is just too much. It is just too damned, double-be-damned, tooooo much."

He kicked it again. It tilted back the other way, leaning even further over.

"Just tooo much, toooo much." He wrenched sign and post from the ground and slammed them down. Then he jumped on his victim, dancing, kicking, STOMPING. The sign cracked, crumbled, began to splinter.

"Too much, too much, just too much. Damn, damn, damn, damn, DAMN!" He kicked splinters of wood far and wide, then heaved the post into a large clump of brush. Finally he stopped, panting heavily.

From a safe distance, Mountain and Sorrowful stood and watched, expressions of fear and wonder crossing their faces. Satisfied that Tinker had stopped his violent activity, Mountain cleared his throat and spoke to him in a very gentle voice, gentle for him.

"John Tinker? What is too much?" He took one cautionary step forward. "You are beginning to worry me, BY DUMPF. You are The Chosen One, the one who is supposed to get us home. Yet, instead of finding a way to do that, you are here, on the edge of this forest, screaming and kicking, crying out loud and strange incantations, jumping up and down on a small wooden sign. Were you making kindling?"

Mountain pushed at some of the wood splinters with the toe of one boot. "Surely that is not what you were doing, getting ready to make a small fire? Were you? If you were, then by DOUBLE-DUMPF, I could have broken it up with a lot less effort." Swiveling his head from side to side, Mountain slyly searched their surroundings. "Is there something to eat here that I haven't noticed?"

A smile tugged at one corner of Tinker's mouth. "Not that I know of, Mountain, not that I know of. Smoke?"

Perhaps. I do detect some faint traces of life.

Tinker swung back to the pathway, giving a farewell kick to parts of the sign, and headed deep into the forest. He waved at them to follow. "O.K., gang, that is the last demonstration of frustration. From now on, it is Straight Arrow plunging headlong into the stuff of fairy tales and magic. No more doubts. No more backward glances. No more wondering how come.

Let's find a way home."

He stopped, turned around, and hissed at them, "Well, just don't stand there gawking at me. Let's go. We have to find our way home. Isn't that what you-all want? Isn't that what we are supposed to be doing? So, move it!" He glanced up into Mountain's ever-present frown. "And maybe we will find something to eat."

Sorrowful looked up, Mountain looked down. Neither of them had ever heard of a thing called a straight arrow. Then they both walked up to Tinker. He turned and started off. They walked at his sides. Smoke drifted from shadow to shadow, her sensenet stretched far, watching in three dimensions, listening to Tinker.

Tinker waved one arm. "O.K., let me explain, if I can, why that sign now lies back there in splinters. It is this way. We are walking down the yellow brick road, just like Dorothy and all the rest, right? Right!" He preceded to tell them all about what the words on the sign referred to, about the children's tales mentioned. Winnie The Poo. Alice's Adventures In Wonderland. His arms waved wildly as he explained. Sorrowful and Mountain carefully kept their distance.

"So," concluded Tinker, "if any of that makes sense to either of you, you too, Smoke, then you just let me know. Cause right now, at this very moment, right here, stompin' down this ever-lovin' yellow brick road, I am a pretty confused duck, believe you me." His pace increased as he hurried them deeper and deeper into the forest. Sorrowful and Mountain wondered what a duck was. And why one would be confused. Smoke peeked inside his mind and saw it. It looked tasty. She licked her lips.

The sun filtered down through the foliage of the towering trees, soft, misty subdued pillars of light, yellow through green. Butterflies flitted from flower to flower, darting back and forth, flashing bright colors as they flew in, out, and around the golden columns. Everywhere there was the grass. Emerald green, closely cropped, thick, luxurious, beautiful.

The place reminded Tinker of a Disney movie. Maybe it was, he mused, turning his head from side to side, just in case he might spot Bambi running toward them. He wouldn't be surprised if that should happen. Not any more. Nothing would surprise him any more. He smiled to himself, imagining the Seven Dwarfs hiking along, whistling their happy tune. Then he grinned, it might be very interesting to meet Snow White. Maybe he could convince her that he was Prince Charming.

The yellow brick road took a sharp turn to the right around a dense clump of shrubs and trees.

They found another sign.

"Triplets," grumbled Tinker. He walked over and read it, out loud.

NUTCRACK
(Straight ahead)

☞ Food & Lodging

Propr. Big Red

Next to Tinker something made a loud gurgling

sigh. Mountain delicately rubbed his stomach. It rumbled softly. He nudged the sign post carefully with one boot tip. The sign wobbled and leaned.

"NOW that is what I call very good news, John Tinker, good news, BY DUMPF. Whatever kind of place Nutcrack may be, it has food, lodgings. So there must be an inn there. Forward, forward. It is time for some haste."

Mountain peered theatrically around them, staring at the woods with one hand cupped around his eyes. He searched the very peaceful scene that they had been walking through for some hours now. "We have walked a long time and have yet to find a single threatening thing." His eyes rolled as he looked at Tinker. "With the exception of a certain sign that was properly demolished and put out of its misery."

"Sorrowful, what say you?" Mountain bent over and gently patted him on the top of the shoulder. Sorrowful's knees buckled. "Race you to Nutcrack."

Twirling around, Mountain straightened up and lumbered away, the ground booming under the heavy thudding of his feet. Sorrowful hurtled along at his side, his legs a blur.

STOP! Go back, go back. FLEE!

A black shape flashed past them in the opposite direction.

In one elastic bound, Smoke disappeared up the tree next to Tinker. Before he could react, a great paw snapped down, hooked gleaming claws into the hood of his jacket and yanked him high into the tree. And then let go.

Tinker gasped, yanked his jacket into place, and rubbed his throat. Then he looked around. Far below he could see the ground. They were sitting on a thick limb. "Wha . . . what's going on? Now what?"

A giant, John Tinker. Just ahead, a giant."

"Well, so what? He reached over and gently ruffled the fur on her back. And smiled. "We have one of our own, of a sort, for a traveling companion. He can take care of the problem. One giant ought to be able to talk to another giant, don't you think?"

Her tail jerked back and forth as she leaned forward, eyes staring into his. *Hold tight to this limb and do not let go, I will give it to you.*

He quickly grabbed a handy limb. Then he was on the ground.

He was moving silently and unseen, drifting from shadow to shadow. He could hear much more than normal. The colors were brighter, the shadows less dense. Even the air had a different sparkle to it, a different odor. Up ahead he could feel the presence of something that dodged his ability to detect.

He was Smoke.

Hold tight.

Then he listened to the discussion around the sign. He flowed into a shadow next to a large, brownish mound, the top of which had a most peculiar formation. This thing had a very strange smell to it. From the top, another formation rose straight up and disappeared into the dense foliage above. Then he heard Mountain and Sorrowful start their race.

PEEK-A-BOO, I see you. A voice whispered in his mind. A pair of monstrous hands reached down and parted the treetops, allowing a vast face to see her. This mound was a boot with a leg rising up and up. She twisted and fled, back toward the others, at full speed away from DANGER.

He was sitting on a tree limb. Tinker eased his fingers from the branch he had been clenching and pointed toward the ground.

"We have to get down from here and try and stop those two before they run into that thing." He started to slip one leg over the edge and stopped.

A loud voice spoke to them. "It is too late." The leaves rustled from the volume. "But take your time, John Tinker, and Smoke, take your time. I have your friends with me. They are . . . perfectly safe. We will meet you at the bottom of your tree. Here kitty, kitty, kitty. Oh, ho, ho, ho, ho, ho."

Tinker looked at Smoke. "Now what?"

She stared down at the ground.

Come on, let's see what we find at the bottom of our tree." Tinker started down. "Whatever it is, it certainly has a weird sense of humor. Here kitty, kitty, kitty, indeed." On the way down Smoke slipped past him.

At the bottom, after landing with a soft thump, Tinker turned around and looked from Mountain to Sorrowful and then at the thick-set man who stood between them.

He was dressed in red. Every article of clothing was some shade of red. Red jacket over pale red shirt tucked into soft chamois-cloth pants of a dark red hue tucked into leather boots of a deep burnished scarlet. His hair, and full, neatly trimmed beard, were a rusty red color. His skin the rosy hue of an outdoorsman. Sparkling blue eyes twinkled at Tinker. Over one eye waggled a red feather that jutted out from the bright red alpine cap perched on his head. He was taller than

Tinker by half a head, more burly and heavy set.

Tinker took a step toward him. "All right, sport, who are you?"

He laughed. "Me? Why John Tinker, I am Big Red." He thumped his chest. "As you can see." He pointed at the forest around them, "And this is my world. You are most welcome here. I am, and shall be," he swept his cap off and made a deep bow, the feather sweeping the ground in front of him, "your most humble host."

Big Red straightened up, reset his cap at the proper jaunty angle, and looked at Tinker again. Then he pointed in the direction that they had been walking and smiled at them.

"Come with me, John Tinker, come, The-Mountain-That-Walks, come, Sorrowful Mistidings, come, Smoke of The Velvetmist. Come with me. Let us away to my most humble of abodes to eat, drink, and relax. If you wish, over the groaning board, we can discuss your adventure, or adventures."

"Well?" He watched Tinker closely.

Tinker hesitated.

"Come, John Tinker, why do you hesitate. Are you uneasy? Afraid?" Big Red grinned and laughed heartily. "Don't be, for we share the same cultural background, the same elseplace, although our creations were rather different. Come, let's away go."

Tinker looked from one of his companions to the next.

Mountain and Sorrowful nodded their heads.

"Smoke?"

Yes.

Tinker looked back to Big Red. "O.K., let's go.

You lead the way."

"DONE!" Big Red clapped his hands together. They made a loud *POP!*

The air shimmered around them.

"And done."

Tinker stared around them. The forest was gone. In one blink, it was gone. They were now standing in the middle of a large courtyard facing a large, rambling two-story building that had a very Tudor architectural influence in its design.

Big Red pointed at it. "Well, what do you think of it? It ain't much, but I call it home." He thumped Tinker on the back. "It was nothing, John, really nothing at all." He laughed, a loud, happy laugh. "After all, if we had walked it would have taken several hours to get here. I could see that you all were rather hungry. So I just thought I would save you some time. And effort." Big Red started for the front entryway. "Well, come inside. I'll see what we can rustle up for dinner."

The door swung silently open. Big Red stopped and beamed. "Ahhhhhh, here comes my wife now."

Tinker looked toward the door and felt his jaw drop open. He knew it was dumb, but it couldn't be helped. A beauty like that couldn't be real. Jet black hair, smoky gray eyes, a glowing golden tan.

Big Red swirled around, sweeping one arm around her waist as she stepped quietly up beside him. He gushed, "My dear, may I present our house guests, three very hardy, and hungry gentlemen. John Tinker, who is their leader. His two companions are, The-Mountain-That-Walks and Sorrowful Mistidings. This young and very beautiful lady is Smoke of The

Velvetmist." Big Red smiled at each of them as did his wife. "And this is my wife, Dancing-All-The-Day."

She gestured toward the house. "Won't you please step inside and make yourselves comfortable. Supper will soon be on the table." Her voice was soft and resonant. She nudged her husband in the ribs with her elbow. "And don't pay too much attention to him. He tends to carry on and on and on."

Big Red frowned, a mock frown. Then he smiled. His wife turned and led them into the house. Then down the hall to a large dining hall.

In the middle of the room stood a long, wooden table set with five chairs and six place settings. Steaming bowls and platters with lids covered the top. There was an appropriate sized chair for each of them, an empty space for Smoke. Big Red's chair was upholstered in a heavy red corduroy. The rest of the chairs were finished in shades of green and brown.

Smoke slipped into the empty space and eyed the food heaped platters in front of her place.

Big Red flopped into his chair and boomed, "Well, don't just sit there and wait for an invitation. We don't behave with much formality here. DIG IN. We appreciate hearty appetites. Good company with mountainous appetites, ho, ho, ho, ho, ho." He winked and began to heap his dish with quantities from the nearest serving dish.

Mountain opened the bowl in front of himself, peeked inside, and beamed in surprise. Sorrowful did the same thing. He had the same reaction.

Puzzled by this, Tinker reached out and dragged the closest dish over for inspection. He wondered what was so surprising about a good Hunter's Stew. Then he realized that it was one of his favorite dishes.

Each has their own favorite dish, made from ingredients native to their own homeland.

"Quite right, Smoke, quite right," chortled Big Red. "And I do hope you will all enjoy your dinner." He raised one hand as they all turned toward him. "But no questions until we have finished eating and drinking. Please." Hoisting a large goblet set by his plate, he took a deep draught, smacked his lips, banged it down on the table top, and smiled at Tinker. "Some red wine, John?"

Tinker smiled and held out his cup. Dancing-All-The-Day reached out and filled it from one of the carafes. It was a deep, red, full-bodied burgundy.

So they ate . . .

And drank . . .

And then . . .

Big Red pushed back his chair, stood up, and scanned the table. It was now some time since they had first began eating and everyone was sitting back looking pleasantly stuffed and relaxed. He waved one arm. "Shall we retire to the living room and stretch out in more comfortable settings? We can talk, discuss what it is that has been happening to you, and any other thing that might cross your minds. My wife will join us shortly with a little after dinner libation."

He turned and walked out through a large rough-hewn wooden door that swung open as he approached. So far, everything, every opening and door, was large enough for Mountain to pass through without ducking.

The room they trooped into was a vast cavern of

beams and stone. At one end an oversized fireplace filled a goodly portion of the wall. Inside it a fire burned and crackled merrily. Facing the fireplace, at just the proper distance, was a U-shaped setting of chairs, each sized appropriately for the varying body shapes and sizes.

Big Red waved them forward and waited until all were seated. Then he looked at Tinker. "So, John, what do you want to know?"

Tinker stared at him, then smiled. "O.K., . . . who are you? Where are we?"

"Ah, ha." Big Red beamed at him. "Very good, very, very good. Straight to the point. No messing about. The Thought chose well, he did, yes he did." Big Red smiled broadly, crossed his hands over his belt buckle, and plopped backward, slumping deeply into his chair.

"Ohhhhhhh Kayyyyy, as you would say, John, O.K. My name is, as you already know, Big Red. This is my world, my elseplace, as others would say." His brow wrinkled. "What else is there to tell? You have met my wife, so I need not mention her. OH. This is my house and you are free to wander where ever you wish, when ever you wish, at your leisure, as, and if, you wish."

He sighed, and pushed himself up, just a little.

"Well, that about does that. Oh yes, one other small item that almost slipped my mind." He winked at Tinker. "I do enjoy a joke. Some small pun. Might as well enjoy life." He beamed happily at his company.

Dancing-All-The-Day quietly entered the room carrying a large serving tray and handled each of them a glass, except for Smoke, of course, serving Big Red last. Setting the tray on the floor next to his chair she sat on one wide, heavily padded arm of the chair and laid one hand on his shoulder.

Tinker straightened up and leaned toward them, shaking his head. "Not good enough. That explanation didn't explain anything. What you told us, we already knew, more or less. How about explaining the yellow brick road, the 100 Acker Wood, and that stuff? Ah, if you would?"

"Ah yes, John Tinker, ah yes." Big Red sounded exactly like the recording of W.C. Fields that Tinker had heard as he pushed up from the soft confines of his chair. "You see, it is really quite simple, it has to do with how I came to be." He paused dramatically and looked from face to face. A master story teller.

"I was created in the imagination of a young girl with a most unusual, but very pretty name. She was six or seven at the time she did this. I was her imaginary playmate, a gigantic Rhode Island Red chicken whom she named Big Red, who lived in this place called Nutcrack." Big Red looked over at Tinker. "She is a neighbor of your's, John. Lives just over aways, at, the next place, down the road to the left, name of CatAshleigh."

He paused, smiled to himself, then continued.

"Well, anyway, she had this imaginary friend as many children do. But then, one day, through some process that even I do not understand, suddenly, all of a sudden, there . . . I . . . was. Just sitting there. Perched right in the middle of nowhere. Just sitting there, feet firmly placed upon nothing. Just floating there right in the middle of time and space, admiring the darkness all around me and the stars and stuff like that there.

However, I was now human, no longer an oversized chicken." He sat up and plopped his hands on both knees.

"Weellll, luckily for me, she made me a magical imaginary companion, and that trait stuck. So I created Paradise." Frowning deeply, Big Red sat back.

"After all, it is rather dull just hanging about in the emptiness of space with nothing in particular under your feet. Now the really interesting part of all this is that this young lady had also, in her imagination, created my wife, who, by the by, is not magic. As soon as I created Paradise, puff, there she was, standing there, smiling at me. For this I am most grateful. Just think how dull life would have been otherwise." Big Red waved one hand and answered their unspoken question.

"Of course I could have created my own companion. But then there would have been no mystery to them at all. All predictable. No mystery, none. Not a bit. Also rather dull." He smiled, and waggled his fingers at Tinker. "So there you are, John. Welcome to Paradise."

He laughed. "And that explains all the allusions to the various tales and stuff. As you ought to realize by now, we have the very same cultural background, you and I, John."

Tinker nodded and leaned back in his chair. "O.K., that explains that. Some of that. What do you mean, you are magic?"

"Quite simple. I am magic. I don't do magic. I am. Magic. You see?" He squinted his eyes and peered around the room at the several kinds of blank stares.

"Hummmmm, I see, you do not. See. Maybe this

explanatrion is better. I am magic personified. I am that quantity often referred to as magic. I am not merely a being such as you-all are. I am a stuff, a particular kind of stuff. Magic. That makes me unique. Nowhere, no how, no time, not here, there or elsewhere, not in any other place or elseplace or universe, in all the universes of universaes, is there another. Not even my wife."

He sighed deeply. "It is my fate, as it were. In some way, it has to do with how I was created. How I came into being, not as an oversized chicken, but as a human being. However . . . I can, if I wish . . . lay eggs. See."

Big Red held out his hands, cupped together, palms up. In this nest a large goose egg slowly materialized. It was large. It turned a golden color. He opened his hands. The egg hit the floor with a solid thump.

"I could be that goose, too."

Tinker smiled at him. "One final question. For now. How come the name, Paradise?"

"Ho, ho, ho, quite simple. Simple, simple simple. I stole it. Actually I borrowed it." Big Red jumped to his feet and gestured dramatically. "I took it from Omar the Tentmaker. I am sure you are familiar with him, John. You know how the verse goes, those most famous of lines . . . ahem, ahem."

He clenched the edge of his jacket and declaimed.

> "A loaf of bread, a jug of wine,
>> And thou singing beside me in the
>> wilderness.
> And wilderness would be **Paradise**, enow."

Sweeping one arm widely, he caught his wife and pulled her against his side. "And when I saw that I would have my wife with me, singing in the wilderness, so to speak, that verse leaped into my mind. And there it was, Paradise. So I named it. So it is. Don't you think?" His eyes scanned the room.

Sorrowful shrugged his shoulders. "Is it truly so innocent? Are there no pests in the seams of Paradise?"

Big Red laughed. "Now that is a loverly image. But no, there are no pests in Paradise. In this place, there is nothing to fear, nothing at all. Not allowed. Not since that first visit."

"What first visit?" asked Tinker.

Big Red sank back into his chair, his wife resettled herself on the chair's arm. "Oh that." He shrugged. "It was just The Evil One. Popped in, unannounced. Just paying a visit. Quite some time ago. Tried to interest me in his little scheme. I wouldn't have any part of it. Or of him, either, for that matter." He vigorously shook his head.

"Showed him the door, in a manner of speaking, actually it was the Portal, the one you came through. I told him to leave. But that bastard . . . OH, your pardon ladies, ummmm, that villain stole it when he left. That is part of the reason, ahhh, why you are here, you know. Not here here, but here doing the job you were given, the quest you are upon. That's the thing, you see." He looked from face to face.

Four faces looked back. Two quite puzzled expressions, one blank. Smoke twitched an ear.

Big Red nodded. "Oh, I see. You don't. See. That is. Well, it is this way. The doorway, the Portal, the one you came through to get here, that is mine, I built it. He shrugged his shoulder, depreciating this effort.

"I was just noodling around one day, out there in the courtyard, just trying this and that, and came up with this idea of how people could have an instant passage from one elseplace to another. Just a tiny hole, a spot, a portal. All one would have to do is just take a single step. In here, and out there. I figured that it would be very useful for those who didn't have, ummm, certain rare qualities." He smiled.

"Well, anyway, there I was working on that thing when up walked this stranger."

"Hi stranger."

"Hello Big Red. My name is Dram, often called The Evil One. I need your help. Between us we could rule all the elseplaces of all the universes that are and will be. I have already starting collecting them under my rule. I have most of Murk Wildweald, but The Thought is keeping me from my rightful place."

"And what place might that be?"

"Why, ruler of the elseplaces, of course."

"OH. Of course. And how may I aid you, Evil One, you don't mind me calling Evil One, do you?"

"Oh no, it is quite all right. I have a straight forward proposition to make. If we work together, we would only have to say *let it be done* and it would be done. Without your help it is going to take me quite a bit longer. I would rather finish sooner than later. With your help I can do that. But either way, the end result will be the same. So you might as well help me."

"Ummmmm, I see. Sorry. No sale. Begone."

"Not yet, Big Red, NOT YET."

"Yes. Yet. BE . . . . GONE!"

"Noooooooooooooo ...."
"Bye, bye."

Big Red watched his audience, then smiled. "And with that, I just blew him back to where he came from. Woooooosh, and back he went. He didn't want to go, but he really had no choice. But, the sneaky evil had put a loop of magic around the portal and yanked it after him. After that he moved rapidly, leaving no trail, no trace. So, I figured that I had overdone it and just blown him and the portal into non-existence." He paused.

Tinker shook his head. "Nope, he was alive and kicking, at least for awhile. We finished his business for him, castle and all."

Big Red gave his head a faint shake. "That wasn't him, John. That was only Doom, one of his lower echlon staff. Fraid to tell you this, but your quest isn't over, it is barely started."

Tinker sprang to his feet. "WHAT?"

Big Red waved him back to his seat and waited until Tinker was resettled. Then he sighed and continued his explanation.

"All of you, one, two, three, four, have to rid the universes of The Evil One. He is in for a surprise. He figures you are stuck here in Paradise because he has the portal. But he is wrong. Evil is always wrong in the long run of things. Always. In the long run." Big Red thumped his chest. "I will send you on your way. Now that the portal touched here, I can find it. That was his first mistake. He will make others. For now, you will need some R and R, rest and relaxation. And maybe some little additional assistance. When you're ready, I will see you on your way. Then . . . "

"WHAT?" snapped Tinker, glaring at their host.

"Why then, John, you will kick The Evil One's butt into non-existence where he belongs. How's that?"

Big Red rose to his feet, took a deep drink from his flagon, stretched and yawned. "Ahhhhhhh, yaaaaaaa, it is time for bed, time to hit the sack and catch some Z's. You may give me your reply in the morning. See you then. Just follow the guide lights to your room. Nighty-night."

He and Dancing-All-The-Day vanished.

They sat and looked at each other. Smoke had been lounging against Tinker's legs. He pushed at her until she released his feet. "To bed?"

"Fair thought," replied Sorrowful as he headed for the door, faint lights winking on ahead of him, dancing in the air, leading them to their room.

Tinker followed, Smoke padding silently behind him, her head peering over his shoulder.

Mountain stood, stretched and followed them. As the door swung shut behind them, the fire faded and blew itself out.

The small lights drifted ahead, leading them down a hall, and up a staircase, until they were inside their room.

It was a large room, well furnished, beds and chairs suited to their tastes and comfort zones.

Sprawling back on his bed, Tinker asked, "Well, what do you think? Is Big Red all he says he is, or what? Any opinions?"

Sorrowful sat on the edge of his bed and bounced gently up and down. "I think he could, if he so chose to do so, with just a snap of his fingers, he could turn you into a Shin'dle, that is what I think." With a sharp

'POP' of his fingers, he demonstrated. "POOF, you are a Shin'dle."

"Nice thought," grumbled Tinker. "What's a shin'dle?"

Sorrowful bounced up and down. "John Tinker, a Shin'dle is a small thing that wizards can turn you into with a snap of their fingers when they have a mind to do things like that. It is a small, furry thing that lives under the leaves of the Shin Bush in the Land of Round-About. They are the creatures from a series of children's tales. In one such, a wizard changes a traveler into a Shin'dle and this traveler, so altered, has a series of adventures until he can get himself transformed back again. This tale is called *The Shin'dle-Tin'dle Tale.* Remind me to tell it to you one of these days."

"MUMPF-DUMPF," rumbled Mountain. "It seems our small friend is full of tales, a veritable ball of yarn. The point to be taken by us, BY DOUBLE-DUMPF, is that Big Red is what he says, and that there is little that we can do about anything that he might chose to do. SO, we might as well get some sleep and see what next day has to offer." With a heavy crash, Mountain fell backwards, rolled up in his blankets, and dropped fast asleep.

Tinker sat up, looked over at the large mound, and laughed softly. "Well there he goes again. We might as follow his example. Night all."

"Fair evening, John Tinker, fair evening."

The lights faded away into darkness.

Soft sleep.

OF THE THREE, THE SECOND.

KNOWN AS

THE TALE OF SCATTERED LIKE LEAVES
BEFORE THE STORM

Aphorisms really aren't a whole lot of help.

Live dangerously and you live right.

Goethe, *Faust*, 1806.

Some roads lead further than others.

Pindar, *Olympian Odes*, 468 B.C.

Accident. An inevitable occurrence due to the action of immutable laws.

Pierce, *The Devil's Dictionary*, 1906

That is what John Tinker always said.

One Day in Paradise

The sun rose perfectly.
    As it always did.
  It was another morning in Paradise.

After breakfast, Tinker, his companions, and Big Red, strolled outside and walked up a slight rise near the house to sit relaxed under a brightly colored, red-striped, awning stretched between some trees. It was a fine place to sit and admire the early morning hours.

The grass was cool, the air slightly warm.

Each of them was sipping from a mug or cup, except, of course, Smoke. Tinker's cup held coffee. He had wondered what each of the others had, but quickly decided not to ask after noticing that Mountain's looked like one of the mud pots he had seen on his last trip to Yellowstone National Park.

Smoke sat by Tinker's side, her eyes slitted to thin lines, a deep rumbling coming from her chest and throat. She sounded very cat-like. She looked very cat-like. Completely relaxed. But she wasn't. Her attention was firmly fixed upon Big Red who sat on the grass against one tree. He was smoking a thick, very aromatic cigar, and staring out over the vast, green velvet of the rolling plain that stretched to the far horizon.

"Ahhhhhhhh," sighed Big Red, blowing a great cloud of smoke skyward, "it certainly is pleasant out here, isn't it?"

Tinker nodded by way of answer. Then he spoke, "Yep. Certainly is."

Big Red turned and looked at him. "So ask your questions, John. I know you have a few."

Tinker smiled. "Right. I think we all have some more questions. This is all rather perplexing, to say the least. Magical creatures, and being here, are all the stuff of fairy tales. Not reality. But here I am, inside one, like it or not. Takes some getting used to. So tell me, tell us, what's really going on?"

"What's really going on, indeed." Big Red's cigar rolled from one corner of his mouth to the other. "It's fairly complicated, the explanation. So, you will just have to be a bit patient while I explain." The tip of the cigar glowed brightly.

"Let's start with you-all. You are all related to each other. It is a relationship of time, distance through time and space, hence the term I used yesterday, elseplace. Your homes, your elseplaces, are all interconnected."

He jabbed at them with his cigar. Ashes tumbled onto the grass. The grass wiggled and shook them off.

"Sorry," said Big Red. He continued his explanation. "Sorrowful and Mountain are direct manifestations of the different cultures, different elseplaces, different worlds, different futures, of your own people, John. Smoke is something else." He laughed. "No pun intended. She is a divergent evolutionary line caused by some small split in an elseplace, so to speak."

A smoke ring drifted gently from Big Red's mouth. It sank to the ground, sat on one edge, then rolled down the slope, bouncing lightly over the grass. He watched it disappear, then resumed his explanation, first sighing heavily.

"The Thought is/was also part of your distant future. A future that stretches link by link by link through the great chain of elseplaces from Tinker to Sorrowful to Mountain and out along various side-branches even to such ones as Smoke and her kin. The Evil One, Dram of whom I spoke, was next to The Thought in ability, but his baser side took over. He left Murk Wildweald before he could be contained."

Then Big Red told how The Evil One's influence had spread out into many of the elseplaces. The Thought had attempted to do something about this, but found that there was a law of being that prohibited such forces from colliding. The Thought then isolated himself in his quarters and worked upon his problem seeking an answer. And through searching ancient records, and vast introspection, he had finally arrived at an answer. The answer turned out to be Tinker and present company. The Thought's solution was to gather those few beings whose relationships were removed and yet connected. They could be set upon the quest, the quest of removing The Evil One from the elseplaces.

So, he had gathered them up, designed and manufactured their clothing and their tools, and had made certain modifications to their very persons. Now they could communicate with each other, and others. And eat the foodstuffs of all the elseplaces they might ever visit. However, The Thought had run out of time before he could complete his task. He and his entire order had perished in their efforts to make everything ready.

Tinker leaned slightly forward. "Why didn't you do all that? As magic, or whatever you claim to be, you should have done all that. Easily. Right?"

"WRONG. But I tried." Big Red slumped against his tree, puffing violently on his cigar. "I could see how things were going on Murk Wildweald. I found that there are rules, there are always rules. Even for magic. And, as I found out, these rules cannot be violated. Not even by me. Rather bothersome, that. Everywhere, in all the elseplaces the universe of universes, certain *laws* can't be touched, no matter what."

He frowned at nothing in particular and heaved another great sigh. "The Portal is a result. I was trying to find a way around things. Around the end of The Thought. But things proceeded in their own good time, at their own good pace."

Big Red stood and said quietly, "If the three of you would excuse me and Tinker for awhile, we have some talking to do of a private nature?"

As soon as Sorrowful and Mountain had strolled off to walk through some nearby hills and Smoke had slipped into a large clump of trees and disappeared, Big Red gestured Tinker to follow him. They walked far out onto a point of land and stood looking down into the vast greenness of Paradise.

"Well, John, here we are. Two beings from the same elseplace. But not exactly the same type of being, eh?"

"I am still puzzled by that. And other things."

"Oh? Like what?"

"Like. Why me?"

"Is that all?" Big Red laughed. He thought it was very funny.

Tinker frowned. "No. So what's really going on?"

"Really, John, I've already explained all that. What is going on is what is going on, exactly as I told you." Big Red thumped Tinker's chest with the tip of one finger.

"I didn't have anything to do with it. It was all The Thought's doings. And choosing." At the continuing disbelief still displayed upon Tinker's face, Big Red tried a different explanation. "Well then, look at it this way. You were in the military at one time, were you not?"

Tinker nodded, slowly. He was not one to overly glamorize being in the military unlike those who never had been.

Big Red reached out and gently patted his shoulder. "Then you will understand. You have just been volunteered. All four of you. Surely, none of you would have come if merely asked? Would you? Of course not, who would. It is, as you've said, the stuff of fairy tales." He began to giggle.

"And who would want to jump right into the middle of a fairy tale? Certainly not John Tinker, product of the 20th century, Grandeville, Ory-gun, U.S. of A. But here you are, like it or not. Might as well get used to it, you're in for the duration. It is just like a recruiting spiel. You will get to travel, visit exotic places, meet exotic folk, like Smoke, for instance." The magician stared toward the trees.

Tinker followed his gaze. "Well, she certainly is exotic, and interesting. And you know what?"

"What?"

"I am getting used to her."

"Just like magic, John, just like magic. One gets used to it. After awhile."

"Speaking of magic, why didn't you just zap Dram when you had a chance?"

"Like I said before. I couldn't. Well, at least not directly. Not yet. Such a clash would rip the fabric of the universes. Then we'd all be in trouble. I can make things like The Portal. Of course, that was partially prompted by boredom. I was really bored with lots and lots of just plain, old-fashioned boredom. BORED!"

The last word roared out over the plains and forests causing small dust devils to swirl into the air. Branches and leaves blew from the trees.

"Bored, bored, BORED!"

Tinker jumped away, quickly checking his surroundings, searching for an escape route. He asked softly, "Why so bored? I would think that you would never be bored at all."

"HO, HA! Ho, ho, ho, ho, ho, ho . . . . " Big Red rocked back on his heels, tears streaming down his cheeks. He finally stopped and wiped the tears away. "So you think being magic isn't boring, huh? Then think upon this, John. I AM magic. I don't do magic. So, it has a tendency to get boring."

"Why?"

"Well, suppose that anything you thought about would just be. Any thing. Then add this to the equation. Nothing can harm you, nothing. Threats are just wished away. Want or need something? Think about it. Poof, there it is. Food? Any kind. Trees? Flowers? Shrubs? Buildings? Anything your little heart desires."

All around them the air crackled and flowed, objects appearing and disappearing in dizzying quantities.

It was a demented slide show. Snow fell, rain slashed the ground, lightening crackling across the sky. Silence. Sunshine. All was returned to the condition that it had been.

"See what I mean. If I can have anything, where are the surprises? Where are the adventures? Surprise makes life interesting, adventure tingles the blood. But for me, everything is as I wish it to be. And thus it is. And thus it will be. FOREVER. So take it from me, that is boring." Big Red stepped away and walked further out on the brow of the ridgeline, Tinker trailing along by his side. Big Red mumbled, "Only one saving grace in the whole thing, my wife. I didn't create her. She is my mystery, my wonder. I never know what she will do or say." He waved one arm widely. "Somehow that little girl, CatAshleigh, and her imagination, triggered the forces of the universes, blowing me into existence. And my wife. And you know what?"

Tinker didn't reply.

"It is these same forces that make it necessary for you and the others to do the hard work of cleaning house, so to speak. You may, and probably will, receive aid from many places. But it is on your backs that the burden lies. Only the intermediaries may meet, never the absolute forces, not directly, not unless things are just so. Of course," he smiled broadly, "you may attack that force of darkness. You are our force. You will meet his. Doom was only one. There are others, much worse. Enough of this, here, a small gift."

A large table materialized. Big Red stepped over

and shoved a small wooden box from the table center toward Tinker. "It doesn't look like much, but it is all your's."

Tinker reached out and pulled it over. Then he unhooked the lid and dumped out the contents. He smiled and poked at the things with one finger.

Small toys. A white, plastic wind-up goose with orange feet and bill. A wind-up toucan. Two wind-up robots, one red, one blue. There was a small yellow chicken made of fuzzy material straight from some child's Easter basket. Jumbled around were an even dozen wooden soldiers painted to look similar to British Grenadier Guards. The last toy seemed out of character. It was a large rubber stegosaurus colored an outlandish purple-red. On it's belly was impressed *Made in Taiwan.*

Big Red walked around the table and began to put the toys back into the box. "This is part of the aid that I just mentioned. Do keep this box with you at all times. Don't lose it."

Tinker latched the box top as Big Red spun away.

"Let's stroll back to the house, John. It is almost time for dinner."

Tinker grabbed the box with one hand and followed him, amazed that the day had managed to somehow pass by so quickly. He wondered how anyone would, or could, use a box of children's toys.

Dinner flashed by in a blaze of sumptuous enjoyment. Big Red had constructed a feast that had everything that any one of them could have wished for, and probably had at some time or another. Even Smoke's tastes had been accounted for. All around them there was entertainment.

Much later, as they all sat back, or lounged, or sprawled, contentedly, their host explained.

"It is just magic, you know. Nothing to it. My pleasure to be able to do something for someone other than myself and my wife. You are all splendid company. Besides, like all magicians, I just love to have an audience." Beaming broadly he raised his wrist, checked a non-existent watch, and began to fade away. In moment all that was left was a ruddy glow at one end of the great table, pulsating gently in the ever dimming light of the dining hall.

"Good night. Sleep tight. Don't let the bedbugs bite."

The glow vanished.

Tinker smiled to himself and leaned back in his chair, wondering when they would be on their way out of here. He couldn't wait. He wanted to get out of this fairy tale as soon as possible. Back to Grandeville. Back to Oregon in the good old late 20th century. Home. Back home.

Two days, John Tinker.

"Huh?"

We will be leaving here in two days.

"How do you know that?"

I peeked, of course. She smiled in his mind. *Tonight I will sleep outside. I do not like caves unless they are necessary.* Smoke rose, stretched, and padded silently away. The door opened for her. Tinker pushed back his chair and headed for their room.

Mountain and Sorrowful remained at the table, each lost in their own thoughts, staring into the flames of the great fireplace. The flames flickered and danced for as long as their visitors wished, far into the night.

So Where Do We Go from Here?

Dawn came up like thunder.

In Paradise.

The bolt of sound snarled past their bedroom window. The walls, floor and ceiling shuddered violently. Plaster cracked, the door banged open. The three sleepers snapped awake and stared wildly about.

"What the hell was that?"

"BY DUMPF!"

"Oh, dear."

Big Red stood at the foot of Tinker's bed and smiled a wan apology at him. "Ah, um, sorry about that, John. Goes for you also, Mountain and Sorrowful. It was just a bit of a joke on a rather old cliche, you know."

Tinker stared at him blank-faced. Mountain and Sorrowful shook their heads.

"Didn't register, did it?" Big Red stepped back and giggled. "Dawn just came up like thunder, you see. But I fear that I used a bit too much thunder. Now I will have to fix the ceiling." He rolled his eyes dramatically as dust flittered down past the end of his nose.

Tinker looked up just in time to see the ceiling cracks filling themselves.

Big Red made a dusting motion with his hands. "There, all neat and tidy. Have to practice that a few more times. Perhaps I will put a big bay out there for the dawn to come up over. Maybe like San Francisco. We can discuss this over breakfast." He glanced around the room, smiling happily. "Well, now that everyone is awake, breakfast calls. Adventure calls. To horse, to horse." He disappeared. Far away in the distance, they could hear the clear clarion call of military trumpets.

They crawled from their beds, dressed and headed down the hall for breakfast. Tinker was really beginning to worry about their host's behavior.

Dancing-All-The-Day met them at the foot of the stairs and directed them outside. Once outside, they headed for the large table under the multi-striped awning. Big Red and Smoke were already there, staring into the opposing face. He was sitting. She was lying, feet tucked underneath, head erect, ears up. Sorrowful and Mountain made for the food, Tinker walked over to Big Red and Smoke. He wanted to see what they were doing. As he came close, he could see that the air between them was filled with objects flashing in and out of existence. Sensing his presence, they stopped.

Big Red beamed at him, "Morning, John."

Early day, John Tinker.

Big Red ruffled his fingers through the fur on top of her head, "We were just enjoying a small game, Smoke and I. She is a most talented young lady. You ought to be glad to have her with you."

Yes.

Big Red hastily yanked his hand back as Smoke's tail whipped around and flashed through the space where his wrist had been.

"The Thought chose well. This holds true for the rest of your company as well. Each of them is quite remarkable in their own way. Ah, ah, ah." Big Red held up a restraining hand, "Don't ask, you I shan't tell. Finding out is part of your quest, part of the challenge. Each one will have to find within their own beings that inner uniqueness that will carry them forward and through this adventure to completion."

He stood up, looking over at Mountain and Sorrowful, "Let's to breakfast go." He headed for the table.

Pulling out chairs, they sat down.

"How do you like your eggs, John?"

"Over easy."

"Done." A dish appeared in front of Tinker. Then Big Red took orders from the rest.

As they ate, Big Red began to ask them about the thunder, what kind or type he ought to use, and how much of each should sound as dawn came up. He held out for the snarling, crackling variety.

Tinker suggested a long, low rumbling type that build up to a thumping finish.

Sorrowful suggested that what they really needed was one more sun, of a different hue and not so bright, please.

Mountain grumbled that the basic problem was that it was too DUMPFING cool.

Smoke just twitched her ears.

Each suggestion was tried. The sky flickered as the sun appeared and disappeared, as clouds scurried back and forth and around and around. The air sizzled around them from the lightening bolts and trembled as changes in the intensity of thunder roared and tore from horizon to horizon. Finally, Dancing-All-The-Day gently dropped one hand on her husband's arm and quietly suggested that perhaps it would be best if they first ate their breakfast and maybe later worked on this problem.

The heavens stabilized, the birds sang. Breakfast reassembled itself. They all turned back to eating.

Big Red beamed at his wife and addressed the gathered group, "After we're finished, let's take a walk down by the lake and sit and relax on the sand. I will tell you what I may of your quest. Down there. All right?"

They all nodded and watched as a nearby grassy slope sank and became a wide valley. Water began to fill the hollow.

A clear blue lake sparkled in the sunshine. Trout leaped at flies while an eagle soared high overhead eyeing the fish below.

Soon they strolled down a long, wandering path, down to the lake's edge, down to the broad, sandy shoreline.

Big Red waved one arm at the scene before them, "I think I will just leave it as it is. There is something restful about sitting down next to a lake on a warm, sunny day like today. Don't you think so, John?"

"Sure. Maybe after this is over you could just sorta slip on onto my property? Not too far from the house?"

Big Red shook his head sadly. "Fraid not. NOT that I couldn't, you know. Not that at all. It is how you would explain such a sudden appearance. In some other time, some other place, the folk would agree that it was truly a miracle and just let it go at that. But not in your elseplace, I'm afraid. Your place would be crawling with curiosity seekers, scientific or otherwise.

No fairy tales for them, no miracles. Maybe Mountain or Sorrowful or Smoke would like one?" He beamed happily at that thought and peered over at them.

Sorrowful smiled, a soft faint smile. "A most kindly offer, but I do not really need one. We already have a great quantity of shoreline. I rather prefer things just as they are." He shrugged one shoulder by way of emphasis. And flicked some small speck from a sleeve.

Mountain looked down his nose and glowered, "Lakes and water BE DUMPFED. Much too cold, much too damp. What I would prefer, here and now, is more heat and less humidity. If you please?"

Big Red laughed softly. "Ahhhhh yes, I forgot. Your elseplace is much more hot and much more dry than here, all rocks and desert. Breaks of the game, I'm afraid, here it is green and golden. Have some more coffee, or whatever pleases you. We ought to get down to business, ah, such as it is." He stood and walked away, down the sloping sand, to another table, this one covered with a white cloth. Various shaped pots and mugs covered the top, artfully scattered in random patterns. Each of them made a choice, walked down to where the magician waited, seated on the sand, and resettled themselves around him.

Smoke flowed down to the water's edge, took a drink, then flopped down next to Tinker, flat on her side, basking in the warmth.

Big Red cleared his throat and started talking to them.

"Let's see, I told you that you now may eat, drink and be merry in any elseplace in the universes of universes as your stomachs are now capable of eating, and digesting, almost anything."

He glanced slyly over at Mountain. "This is, no doubt, good news."

Big Red shrugged. "However, the rest of the preparation must come from deep inside each of you. It will be a matter of your spirit and your determination that will carry the day." His eyes widened. "OH, and always follow the portal. Just one step, in and out, all it takes. Now remember this single important fact. The mythic reality guided The Thought in all his endeavors. And the mythic reality called each of you forth. So I rather suspect that you will prevail in the long run."

Tinker hissed at him, "You get rid of The Evil One. Just send us home."

"Can't do that, John."

"Why not?"

"I told you yesterday. Besides, he has to be bound. FIRST."

"Bound?"

Big Red cleared his throat, "This song sings this way:

> Evil reigns in a hollow bowl;
>> Casting spells through time, unbound.
> No spell, no magic, can touch;
>> Only golden eyes, one, two, three, unbound.

> The Chosen One, The Four are One, The Company bold;
>> Gold and gray, red and green, binding.
>> Evil ends on greed stricken;
>>> Jewels and jewels and jewels and

jewels.
BOUND!"

"HUMPF!" grumbled Mountain. "Doesn't say much."

Sorrowful leaped to his feet, hands on his hips.

"It seems to me that there is much to be learned there. It mentioned John Tinker, The Chosen One. And us, The Four." He smiled at Mountain.

"I would suggest, most gently, that the rest of it tells us all we need to know. It is just at this moment we do not know what to do, or how to read this song properly."

He spun on his heels. "Is that not so, Big Red?"

Big Red nodded. "Just so. You will have a real adventure finding out. A search, a journey, an expedition."

"Wonderful," mumbled Tinker.

Big Red ignored him and smiled at Sorrowful, and said to him, "You should enjoy this quest as it will supply you with great quantities of material for tales to be told." Then he looked from one to the other.

"But what the rest of you will gain, that I cannot see or guess. Perhaps merely some small insight. Perhaps some personal vision. Maybe something else. Maybe even death. There are no guarantees, you understand." He stopped and left them to their individual thoughts, pondering what their immediate future might bring, what their fate might turn out to be.

Tinker stared out at the lake with blank, staring eyes and wondered about everything that had happened. It was beginning to make a strange kind of sense. He was beginning to realize that it was as Big

Red had said, a quest. For him it had begun just over ten years ago.

Master Chen had jolted him into realizing that what he had been doing was in and of itself a steep path leading to its own evil conclusion. Sudden wealth, sudden friends, sudden everything. No reason for it, just do it. No thought, no reason. Just do it. Then wake up in strange places not knowing how or when you got there. Unrestrained. Chaos.

Chen had dragged the limp, sodden body from the backdoor of his restaurant and deposited it in his storeroom. And there, for reasons never explained, he had bludgeoned his find onto a new path, a different path. As Tinker's understanding grew, and his body had rebuilt itself, he had begun to understand what had been happening to him. From his deep internal self awareness, the oriental world of the self-healing of the martial arts, he had become someone else, ten years ago going on eleven.

Now here he was, an unwilling participant in all this stuff, none of which he really was interested in at all, not even a little bit. But now he also realized that, somehow, his personal search for meaning, his personal rejection of the evil he had seen, had coupled him with this strange fairy tale quest.

He turned his head and stared at his three companions. They must have been chosen for similar reasons. If they were parts of his future, then whatever evil they had rejected must have been similar to that which had ensnared him. Hard to imagine.

He looked at Smoke. What kind of evil had she faced. What kind of evil could exist in a land of telepathic carnivores? What kind of horror loomed in minds that could reconstruct reality around them?

A soft tendril of thought reached out and lightly touched his mind. Then he saw it. Black, ravaging horror that ripped asunder the very fabric of the mind. Foul visions. TERROR!

Tinker leapt to his feet, sweat pouring from his face, trying to shake the sudden chill that the sun seemed incapable of dispelling.

It is called soulrive, the terror of the mind. From the very deepest recesses it comes. My mindmate and it became one. Because of the linkage between us, it was my duty to become The Scourge.

Tinker peered out into a dim space, a clearing under vast trees whose limbs nearly closed off all light from above. A battle raged between two beings, all razor sharp claws, slashing teeth, and mental projections. It was Smoke and the Soulrive.

A silent battle, roiling quiet. All around, hidden in shadow spaces he felt the others, watching.

A sudden liquid ripping, a scarlet gushing. An eruption splashing the opening with the remains of the Soulrive.

Slipping from the darkness they came, The Velvetmist, her clan members, encircling Smoke with their minds, easing the pain, easing away her sorrow, easing away the loss of the death of her mindmate, so newly found, now lost.

Much, much later, she was healed, made whole again. With one exception.

Deep within her a small point of fire growled angrily. It hunted an evil thing that laughed in delight at the creation of things vile.

And so. . .

She was selected.

He stood dazed as she released him from her reality.

Then she began to feed him the events that had brought Sorrowful Mistidings to this quest.

"NOOOOooooo!" Tinker twisted away from her. "STOP IT, STOP IT! No one needs to knows things like that, no one."

He ran. Away from their agony. Away from their hurtful past. Down the sloping shoreline and out and around the lake, he ran, his mind blanked out, focused only on the physical act of running itself.

Big Red watched the small dot running, running, circling the lake, legs pumping. "Smoke, I don't know whether that was wise or not."

She sat and watched this man, running, far on the other side of the water. Her head turned slowly as he came around the lake, tracking him, focusing upon him. She felt a Velvetmist tingle.

Big Red nudged her with his toe. "Ahem, he is the key to the quest, the very focal point of it all. If you lose him, well . . . you know."

Yes. Her tail jerked. Then curled around and across her feet.

Tinker jolted to a halt, his face flushed, weaving slightly from side to side as his breathing slowly came down. Then he sprawled forward, face down, letting the heat from the warm sun above and from the warm sand below sink into his body, feeling his muscles loosening. No thought.

John Tinker?

"I am all right," he mumbled. "Don't worry

about it."

Big Red stood next to him. "I can see that. You are remarkable in your resilience."

Tinker rolled over to look up at him. "Just one of life's many lessons. Now what?" He wiped the sand from his face.

"NOW WHAT?" Big Red gestured wildly. And dramatically.

"Now what? Why now, we relax. And rest. And enjoy the rest of the day. For today we shall eat, drink, and be merry. For tomorrow we may diet. Eh?"

No one laughed. He shrugged his shoulders.

"Well, I thought that it was funny. Let's have a little snack." He pointed up the slope.

Up there, just at the edge between sand and grass stood the table, groaning with dishes, hot and cold.

"Ohhhhhhhh," sighed the table. "Ahhhhhhh," moaned the table. "These dishes are sooo heavy. I think that I am going to collapse under their horrid weight."

Big Red shouted at it, "Be quiet. It is not all that heavy."

The table stopped making noise.

Tinker sat up, giggling until tears ran down his cheeks.

Sorrowful laughed quietly.

"HUMPF!" Mountain stood up and headed for the table. Food was not something to lightly make jokes about.

Smoke drifted in the same direction, the tip of her tail stroked Big Red under the chin as she passed by.

He smiled. "Yes. Enough of this nonsense, shall we eat, drink, etc., etc.?"

They did. Periodically Tinker burst into a fit of

giggling.

For the rest of the day, and into the evening, they made idle conversation, sitting or strolling aimlessly around the lake. Everyone was pushing away the tension they felt about what tomorrow would bring.

Then relaxed and ready, they headed back to the house. And soon fell asleep.

"HALLELUJAH!"

The rousing chorus shook them awake and from their beds.

Tinker stumbled over to the window, threw it wide and leaned out, searching for the sudden noise. Stretching before him was a vast bay surrounded by low hills. A thick fog bank was creeping cotton gray feelers over the steel blue water. Just protruding from the heavy blanket were bridge towers. They were painted a rust red color. It was the San Francisco Bay and the Golden Gate Bridge.

"HALLELUJAH!"

He looked upward.

Hanging in iridescent clouds of light and motion, beings swirled and sang, flashing color.

"HALLELUJAH: for the Lord God Omnipotent reigneth."

"Pretty impressive, what?" Big Red nudged Tinker's shoulder with one of his own. He was smiling proudly.

The chorus overhead hit its full stride, ". . . and He shall reign for ever and ever."

Tinker grinned at him and nodded. "Right. Pretty impressive all right. But don't you think that the Hallelujah Chorus from Handel's Messiah is a bit too much?"

"Welllll, the thought did pass by my mind. I thought we had enough thunder after yesterday. Besides, you guys are on your way today, so it seemed appropriate. Ah, in a manner of speaking, that is. Never mind, let's to breakfast go. Then ready ourselves for the job at hand." He disappeared, leaving behind only his smile which hung in the air. Then it vanished.

Mountain stomped out the door, grumbling about someone's idea of how to start a day. Sorrowful was right on his heels.

As Tinker followed them into the hall, Smoke poked her head over his shoulder and licked one of his ears.

Tinker jerked sideways, ducking his head, "Yeeeetch!"

Ready?

"As I will ever be."

Dancing-All-The-Day greeted them as they settled themselves around the breakfast table. "Big Red will be right in. He said he would fetch the portal and then join you. So start. He will catch up."

They did.

Just as they were finishing, Big Red clomped into the room, a heavy scowl on his face.

"That bastard. He didn't want to release it. OH . . . your pardon ladies." He flushed.

Dancing-All-The-Day patted his arm. "That's all right, dear. I understand."

Yes, dear, I understand.

"WATCH IT, SMOKE, you will get me in trouble." He gazed around the table. "As I was saying, that bast . . ., ahhh, The Evil One, didn't want to give back the portal. I had to yank it away from him. He is getting stronger. That's what took so long. It is really time for you to start. Shall we go?" He turned and led them outside.

They trooped after him. He waved them over to stand near his device, the portal.

It stood there, the surface shimmering from the heat waves, distorting the view on the other side. Fire-snakes roiled and hissed around the edges.

Big Red grinned broadly. He was very proud of his device.

"Magnificent, isn't it? I really think that this is one of my finer creations." He spun and thrust a small box at Tinker. "Here, John, you wouldn't want to leave home without it." Tinker grabbed it and held the box in one hand.

Stepping to one side, the magician made shooing motions with his hands.

"Well, off you go. Step through, step through. And bon voyage. Good luck. Have a pleasant trip, write when you have time."

Sorrowful walked up to the door and stepped through and disappeared. Smoke bounded after him.

Mountain clasped one gigantic hand on Big Red's shoulder, then turned and stepped through, ducking as he went.

Tinker hesitated and turned to one side.

"One last question, if I may? Why me? Why am I the leader of this mob?"

Big Red chuckled softly. "It is really quite simple, quite simple. You, John Tinker, are the past, their past. The past always leads the future, does it not? Off you go." He reached over and shook Tinker's hand. "Have a good time."

Tinker turned and peered through the portal. He didn't see anything over there. He started to turn to ask another question.

Big Red was chanting.

A realm awaits that without you cannot come

into being.
Think of life, find a new meaning.
Deep within.

"What?"

Big Red said, "Oh, just a misquote."

Then he gave Tinker a hard shove in the middle of the back and sent him stumbling through the portal.

"Bye, John."

He turned to his wife, who had walked over to watch the party depart. He threw one arm over her shoulders.

"Do you think that I should have told them that the portal was flickering just a wee bit. Some slight effect of being in The Evil One's possession, I suppose. He probably messed with it, or tried to. Well, it shouldn't take long to fix. First, let's have a nice quiet cup of coffee. Just you and me, my dear."

He took her arm. They strolled back to the house, arm in arm.

Behind them, the portal quietly flickered.
From color
to color
to color . . .

OF THE THREE, THE THIRD.

KNOWN AS

THE TALE OF MANY PATHS,
ONE DESTINATION

Small words of wisdom.

Spoken quietly.

> *It is a kingly action, believe me,*
> *to help the fallen.*

Ovid, *Ex Ponto*, A.D. 13

> *All life is a stage and a play, so*
> *learn to play your part.*

Palladas, *Epigram*, A.D. 425

> *Enough is enough.*

John Heywood, *Proverbs*, 1546.

If anyone cares to listen.

Darkness Itself Does Appear to be a Thing of Comfort

Sorrowful stepped from the portal and found his feet sinking deep into the dank, spongy ground. Water seeped up over the top of his boot tips. He stepped quickly to one side to make room for Smoke. He had seen her following him just as he stepped forward.

She dropped lightly to the ground and padded over to sit next to him, eyes fastened upon the portal.

It disappeared.

Suddenly.

It was gone.

Sorrowful spun on his heels, his eyes darting from place to place, searching for it. He assumed that it had relocated itself.

Smoke sat. And watched him. Her head turned, tracking him as he scampered here and there.

He stopped. And spun around. Once. Twice. Then he stopped to stare back at her.

"Oh dear, oh dear, oh dear. It appears we have been abandoned . . . marooned . . . cut off . . . severed and . . . separated."

He carefully looked around the small opening, squinting into the green dimness.

"As John Tinker was, is, so fond of saying, now what?"

He walked back to where she sat and looked into her face.

"Well, what do you think? Is this some part of what Big Red could not tell us? Is this a surprise? Of some sort? But why?"

He turned around. Rank odors assailed his nostrils. He shook his head and looked at his feet, slowly sinking into the ground.

"Not a very appealing sort of a place, is it? Not the least to my tastes. Not at all. What about you?"

He turned and looked up at her.

Smoke sat and looked down at him, her ears cocked forward. Then she carefully examined their new location.

They were standing in a small clearing surrounded by dense, towering witch-tangled vegetation. Overhead, green things grew together, forming a dense canopy. What little light made it to the ground was faintglow. This was a world of soft, green-tinged twilight. Dense shadows in coarse growth. She could see narrow trails piercing the verdant walls. Tunnel paths.

Smoke's eyes dilated, the yellow-gold pushed to a narrow, outer ring. For her, there was enough light. These plants were strange, differently formed in shape and behavior. The temperature was slightly higher, the humidity noticeable higher. All in all, it reminded her of home.

She cast out her sensenet. Nothing. Then, but for a fleeting moment, out at the extreme edge, something flickered past. Too fast to see. Or taste. But not looking for them.

Sorrowful?

No response. She was isolated from him. And they were isolated from Mountain and Tinker. Her tail jerked back and forth. She was slightly agitated. But not worried.

She checked the trails leading from this clearing, seeking some small clue as to which direction they ought to follow.

Nothing.

So.

She sat.

And waited.

For Sorrowful to decide.

Patience was a highly developed skill in a carnivore.

Sorrowful walked over to her, having just completed his second trip around the edge of the clearing, stood on his tip toes and looked into her face.

"Well, Smoke, have you found anything? Is one of these paths better than any of the others?"

He paused and watched her expression. Big round eyes stared down the long snout into his. He smiled.

And bobbled his head.

"Nod your head. You could nod your head. That way I could at least get a yes answer or no answer from you. We are going to have to work out some form of communication."

He stopped talking to her, frowned, and then asked in a very soft voice.

"You can at least understand what I am saying, can you not?"

Smoke's head rose and fell.

He sighed heavily. Then he smiled. "Good. That is good." He turned away and stared at their clearing. He was now thinking of it as *their* clearing.

"If we can find some way to get more out of you than a simple yes or no, perhaps we will be ready for, ah, . . . OH, for what? I do not know. I do not think either of us really knows for what."

Sorrowful turned away and waved one arm at their surroundings.

"Pick a trail, I will just follow along."

Smoke sat and stared at the back of his head.

He stood and waited.

So did Smoke.

Whirling around, he bunched his fists on his hips.

"Why do you just sit there?" Then he briskly walked away and peered into one of the narrow passageways.

'Oh dear, I suppose I must do it."

He looked back at Smoke.

"This one looks as good as any other."

She stood up.

"This one? Yes, I suppose so. Well then, shall we go?"

He turned from her and walked into the growth.

Smoke flowed silently behind him. It didn't really matter to her which of these paths they followed.

Six paces down the trail, Sorrowful twisted his head to look back over his shoulder at Smoke's head swaying slightly from side to side as she padded along behind him. In the soft soil neither of them made a sound.

She is so big, he thought, and walks so silently. Sorrowful hadn't noticed the fact of his silent passage, yet.

Well, he said to himself, at least she does not look

worried. But how should I know how she looks when she is worried? Who can read an expression on a face covered with fur? I wonder what she is thinking about? I wonder what we will find at the end of the trail? I wonder where the rest of our company is? I wonder how will we ever get back together again?

He shook his head violently, and answered himself. I think that I had better stop wondering so much and start paying attention to where we are going. And to what, if anything, there is ahead of us before I wonder myself, ourselves, into trouble.

Smoke twitched one ear, amused by his thoughts, and wondered how long this was going to go on. Simultaneously she was seeking far ahead of them and far to all sides. As she walked she was the central point of a large dome of sense-space. Within this bubble she saw everything.

And nothing.

There was nothing around them but rank vegetation and a few, fairly small, nothing to be worried about, animals. Her tongue idly licked her lips. Some small snack, perhaps. But no danger.

Subtle changes in the light told her that night was rapidly approaching. They must have arrived late in the day of this elseplace. She probed for a sleeping lair. Just ahead of them, she saw a good space. It was a deep concavity nestled under and within the intertwined undergrowth. It was a perfect place.

Stretching out her neck, she bumped Sorrowful on the back of his neck with her nose.

He twitched, hopped forward, and spun around.

Smoke was just merging with the brush. The tip of her tail hung in the open space of the trail and waggled at him, beckoning. Very cautiously, he walked back and peered into the growth. Then he stepped through the slowly closing opening she had made.

Within the gray-green enclosure, Smoke lay sprawled comfortably, her head nestled on her forepaws, preparing to sleep.

Sorrowful hunkered down against one of the tree trunks and fished around in one of his pockets for some of the provisions that he had prudently stashed there. He nibbled on a small piece of dried biscuit, then offered a chunk to Smoke.

One of her eyes popped open, stared at it, and dropped shut. One ear twitched slightly.

"Humly, I suppose that it is not much to offer, not to one such as you. But, it is all that I have to offer. Perhaps on the morrow we shall be able to find something better to eat. From what I could see of this place there certainly does not appear to be all that much to chose from, does there?"

He reexamined their small space again.

"So, this is where we spend the night, yes? Well . . . fair evening, then."

Sorrowful fussed and wiggled about, trying to find some comfortable position, some comfortable spot, to curl up and sleep. He stood up, and stumbled over her feet.

"Sorry. Rather damp place we have here."

Smoke's tail snapped up and around, coiled around his waist, yanking him backward.

"WHA . . . . . . OOOOOOOOF!"

He fell into a deep, soft, fur-covered nest. It was Smoke.

She had pulled him into the curve of her belly

and chest. She humped and squirmed, stretching her legs out on either side of Sorrowful, and resettled herself. Then, uncoiling her tail, she slipped it free. It drifted softly across and over his legs and over her nose and back across her neck. The tip idly ticked back and forth to some special, inner rhythm.

Sorrowful felt nice and warm. And comfortable. And very safe. He fell asleep, her deep breathy rumble sang a lullaby in his ears.

But . . .

Part of Smoke remained alert.

As always.

Watching.

Dawn.

Smoke's eyes popped open. She had seen something. Small figures had moved along a trail just at the far reaches of her sensenet. She carefully marked the place and flickered the end of Sorrowful's nose with the tip of her tail.

He wiggled, shifted about. And woke up.

"Do you know that it tickles, doing that? Yes, I suppose you do, else why did you do it? Time to go? Yes, yes, I suppose so." He stood up.

"You pick the direction this time." He nodded at her.

Smoke slipped away through the vegetation.

He crashed out onto the path after her, stretching and yawning. Then he gave two leaps into the air and hopped madly back and forth, first on one foot, then the other, waving his arms wildly.

"Aaaaaaahhhhhhhhhhh. There. That does it."

He looked at Smoke. "Which way?"

She bumped him heavily with her head. There was only one way to go, the way that they had been traveling.

Sorrowful started down the trail.

Smoke trailed behind him, her head swaying over his, humming a silent melody to herself. It was The Dawnchant, the Song of The Sensenet sung by the Memser of the Velvetmist, The One Who Guided The Body as they prowled throughout their domain.

As she sang, Smoke thought of her sister, Soft Tendril, and imagined her doing the same thing as the Velvetmist aroused themselves from their sleep. It was her right -- the elder to follow the younger. It was her right -- as a female. The males usually did not have the strength to project as far or as solidly. Besides, their primary duty was to be consort. Some, a very select few, even became mindmates.

Her thoughts drifted to John Tinker, the one chosen from that strange elseplace. She could visualize him as a mindmate. It was a strange thought. He did have certain characteristics, a certain focus to his mind, something deep within. Her tail coiled and danced.

Here was a unique situation. She was far from her homeborn. She was far from the focus of her new group. For now there was little she could about it. She set one part of her mind to thinking on these things and focused the rest on the here and now.

The here and now was not all that tasty. All she had for company was this small mouthful with the dead mind. Her fur rippled in agitation. This was a challenge, an unknown without precedent.

Since she had been taken, she had only seen these strange, sapient, two-legged folk with the dead minds.

It had been a surprise, finding such unusual beings as these. Nowhere in her memories was such mentioned. And it had been most uncomfortable to not have another mind, joining, sharing, being.

She huffed a soft breath through her mouth. She was The Memser, The Focus of The Center. She could, she would, take care of this small parcel of meat until they rejoined John Tinker and Mountain. Her tail stopped its violent lashing and drifted in a soft rhythm. She clacked her teeth together. A single sharp sound.

Sorrowful's head jerked around. He looked back and up at her face. He was not sure that he approved of what he thought he could see in her eyes. She appeared to be staring right through him. It was a hungry look. At least, that was the way it appeared to him.

Hastily he turned his attention back to the path and shuddered. And thought a comforting thought, she was one of The Four, part of The Quest. Yet, it had been a most unnerving gleam that he had seen in her eyes. He felt just like a tiny fin'dle caught in the six clawed grasp of a zhregan'dle. UGH, UGH, UGH, that was a most discomforting thought to be thinking.

Then a most strange image popped into his mind. He almost laughed out loud. They were such a strange looking pair. Both dressed in black. Both treading silently along some strange trail in some strange region of some strange elseplace.

But she was so big.

He had been feeling his diminutive stature ever since he had been first taken by The Thought. Were all the elseplaces filled with folk as large as those he had met so far? Was only his elseplace peopled with the small?

He took another quick glance behind. Why he could almost walk beneath her belly without the top of his head tickling the thick fur. Smoke's protruding canines gleamed in the faint light. He stared down the path and lightly touched his dagger. Not much comfort there. Her weapons were as long and sharp as his. And she had two of them. But there was something safe in the feeling from the slight tingling he felt from his weaponkin.

The incongruity of his situation cheered him up. His pace quickened and became more lively. This was the stuff of great tales, a great Walking-Tale. He would have much to tell and retell. This might become one of the grandest, a renown tale. It would require a special name, a carefully chosen name.

What to name it? *The Quest of The Four?* Too dull, sounds wrong. He would just have to think about it.

In his excitement, Sorrowful almost hugged himself as he danced down the pathway. It was a grand idea, a great tale for telling. He began to chuckle, it would be such a fine tale to tell, a series of small episodes. He could see the children's eyes sparkling as they heard of the various and unusual characters.

He laughed out loud. And snapped his fingers. He would probably receive the red bar to wear down his left sleeve. One and all would know him as *Sorrowful Mistidings, Master Teller.*

He felt much better. This was, after all, just another journey, although this time it was with exotic companions in exotic lands. Then he remembered his obligations as a traveling companion.

He was being remiss. It was his duty to tell tales to his traveling companions to lighten their steps and to shorten their journeys. He would have to tell a tale to Smoke. He quickly began to sort through his vast storehouse of tales, searching for the one that would be most appropriate for this setting. And to his traveling companion, strange as she was. She would probably not appreciate the subtle humor and the droll happenings. But how would he know? She doesn't appear to smile. She certainly can't laugh? Get on with it, he commanded himself, a difficult audience has never fazed you before.

Sorrowful stopped, twisted his head around, and peered back and up at her, attracting her attention. Looking back at the trail, he spoke loudly so she could hear him.

"Ahem, my dear Smoke, it is the custom of my folk to tell tales as we walk along on various hikes and journeys. We do this to lighten our journeys and to shorten the distances traveled. Therefore, here and now, I propose to tell you one of my very favorite tales. It is called *The Tale of The Two Lost Wanderers in The Land of Through-And-Back*. It is one of the renowned tales told for shortening journeys. If you are ready, I shall begin."

He looked back up at her.

Her ears canted forward.

"Humly. Yes." He decided that meant she was ready. He took a deep breath. And began.

"SO! In a time and at a time, it seems there were two lost travelers, wanders really, who, one day, found themselves in The Land of Through-And-Back. How they managed to get themselves in this land is a different tale, to be told at some other time. Suffice it to say, there they were, somewhat lost, in The Land of Through-And-Back. The names of these two travelers were *News* and *Views*. The first because he delighted in telling all that he had ever been told. The other spoke in pronouncements utilizing a kind of editorial prose. They were a complementary pair for between them they covered the full spectrum of everything that ever had to be said." He paused for two beats, and sucked in a deep, silent breath.

"Now they had been walking for a goodly portion of one day, telling each other variations on the minor walking tale, *The Thing That Hobble-Bobbled*, and trying each new invention upon the other, and thus passing the time in pleasant company. And being most concerned with what they were doing they did not notice exactly where they were going or exactly what kind of path they were treading. They walked right up to a Min'dle-Min'dle, a fearsome creature that only exists in The Land of Through-And-Back. It stood there, in the center of the path, blocking their passage, and it spoke to them. It said to them, it said . . . "

As he walked along, deep inside the telling of his tale, Sorrowful began to caress the hilt of his dagger, his thumb sliding back and forth over the cold smoothness of the jewel set in the hilt.

I see you, Sorrowful.

In mid-sentence, in mid-stride, he stopped and sprung high into the air.

"What? WHAT?"

Landing in a crouch, Sorrowful spun around and stared at Smoke. Then he straightened up. "Did you say something?"

His face flushed. "BIN'DLE! Did I just say that? Of course you did not"

Smoke's tail coiled over her back in loops of

frustration as she stared into his eyes.

He turned away and starting walking again, mumbling to himself. "So and so, it has to have been my imagination. Too wrapped up in the tale." He frowned, "Now where was I? Oh, yes . . . "

"And then the Min'dle-Min'dle said to them, 'Tell me something that I haven't heard before and you shall know my secret.' So they told it of the Princess Windfall and the Commoner Mud. But it snarled before they were yet finished, 'Even a pup Min'dle-Min'dle knows that.' Then it bared its terrible teeth and inched closer. And it said . . ."

Don't take your finger off the Golden Eye this time.

"WHAT? WHAT?"

Sorrowful soared high and spun around before returning to the ground.

"THAT IS not what it said!" He goggled at Smoke and quickly scanned their surroundings.

"Oh dear, oh dearie dear me. Smoke, I do seem to be losing my mind. There must be some strange and powerful substance in the atmosphere of this elseplace." He reached out and lightly touched the thick fur on her chest.

"Smoke, my traveling companion, will you try and see that my empty hull is somehow returned to my elseplacc? Friends and relatives would be pleased? And sad, of course."

Smoke's ear snapped back against her neck. Her tail coiled up as she lowered her head. Sorrowful took a step back. Her claws slipped free, digging into the soft soil. He saw her muscles rippling as she prepared to spring. He began to back up, trying to gain some distance, running backwards, his hand snatching for his dagger.

"WHAT? WHAT? What? Oh no, no, no, no, nooooooooooooo . . . "

She pounced.

One huge paw batted his chest as she slammed him backward, throwing him onto the pathway. The rest of the air gushed from his lungs as he landed flat on his back. Her great weight held him firmly in place. He could smell the sharp earthy odors of the humid turf. He could feel the dampness pushing up against the back of his head. His legs wouldn't move. She had them trapped. So he took a deep breath. It was all he could do. He lay very, very still. Only his eyes moved.

So, he thought to himself, this is how it ends. I am to be a light snack for this gigantic beast in this most foreign of elseplaces. Not even at home. He had always wanted to die in bed, his bed, at home.

By craning his neck he could peer down his body and see the tips of those ebony claws just peeking from the downy softness of one immense paw covering his entire chest. The other held his right arm firmly in place, his weaponkin tightly clasped in his fist. He couldn't even wiggle that hand.

Her head dropped down, great golden eyes stared into his. The tips of her canines just touched him.

Sorrowful decided that struggling was a waste of time. It would be best to just have it over quickly. One bite and goodbye.

He smiled weakly and stared back at her. Then he realized where he had seen those eyes before. It was in that dismal fog enshrouded road on Mirk Wildweald. It had been her. He cleared his throat and moistened his lips.

"Humly, my dear Smoke, it does seem that you are forever knocking me about."

A bold front was the best way to end a career all too soon terminated.

"Is there, my dear, something that you want from me?"

He knew that he was about to become a before dinner snack, but in his position, he had to smile at the pun, there did not seem to be much he could about that. Except to be polite.

Smoke sat back and released him. He sat up, rubbing his arm and stared at her.

She stared back.

"What? What?"

She watched him, carefully.

Sorrowful began to inch, very slowly, very carefully, his weaponkin back toward its sheath. Her prehensile tail snapped forward and coiled tightly around his wrist. Sorrowful went rigid and stared in fright as her paw reached forward and lightly touched his hand.

He waited for her to tear his arm off. He could visualize the blood and gore shooting everywhere. He twitched.

One ebony claw had nudged his wrist. With the delicacy of a surgeon dissecting a mouse, she gently slipped his thumb from its position around the dagger hilt and up to the Golden Eye. Through his terror, he could feel the smooth coolness of the polished surface.

Now keep your finger there. Do you understand?

"WHAT? WHAT?"

He tried to leap to his feet.

She casually batted him back and lightly laid one

front paw upon his chest, pinning him in place. And once again manipulated his hand, still held tightly by her tail curled around his wrist, with a razor sharp claw.

Keep your finger on that Golden Eye!

Sorrowful looked down at his hand, then up into her face. He smiled.

"Why Smoke, you can talk?"

She backed away and sat, releasing him, lowering her head to peer into his face.

Sorrowful sat up, his smile growing larger and larger.

"That is, now you can talk to me. I, of course, could always talk to you. Tale stuff, I am like John Tinker. Amazing."

Not the same. You require the Golden Eye.

His smile lost five degrees of radiance.

"OH, I see. I think. With me, it takes the intercession of this jewel to work properly. Is that correct?"

To work at all. As long as you touch it, I may impart.

"Ahhhhhhh, ha. How far can you impart? Is there a limit?"

Now I cannot espy John Tinker. When he was within the sensenet, always. With the Golden Eye contact, I do not know.

"Well, well. Well, well, welllllll, WELL!" Sorrowful bubbled with joy. He almost kissed her on the nose, restraining himself at the last moment. He gushed.

"You just do not realize what a great pleasure it gives me to be able to converse with you. I had thought myself to be doomed to an eternity of silence, an era of nods signifying *yes* or *no*. Horrible, HORRIBLE! We folk of The Six Lands live for good conversation, the play of words, the gambol of dialogue, the telling of tales. To be locked in a situation where one could not communicate, or barely, in this case, is horrid indeed! Yaaaaaaaaagh, it makes my skin fairly crawl and itch just to speak of such an existence."

The Six Lands?

"My home." He frowned at her. "Perhaps if I might be permitted to rise, I could explain?"

Smoke sat further back, lifting her paws from his legs.

Sorrowful stood up, daintily smoothing out the wrinkles in his clothes (there really weren't any, but he thought there were), and quickly patted the fragments of decaying vegetation off.

She stared at the top of his head.

He whirled around, finally satisfied that he was neat and orderly again, and announced, "THERE!"

Taking a few steps backward, he grinned up at her. And pressed his thumb firmly in place.

"SO! The Six Lands is the given name of my elseplace, humly, as I've mentioned, I do believe. There, in my home, are, as you suspect, from the name, six lands, each one separated from the other by varying widths of open sea. Outside, surrounding all the land is emptiness, The Clear Water. The six lands are named, in this very order: In-And-Up; Through-And-Back; Over-And-Up; then there is Around-And-Return; Cross-And-Recross; and the most beautiful of them all, Middle-And-More."

Sorrowful lightly tapped his chest.

"I am from Middle-And-More. It is, as you might suspect, the land in the middle. The others, the other five, are across The Inner Arm which enfolds my home in blue embrace. Across this azure delight some of the others are close, some are far." He paused.

She stared. *Finish.* It was a focused predator stare.

"Yes. Among those who study such things, there is a tale, a peculiar tale. This tale tells that in a time, and at a time, the six lands were but one. Vast currents, unseen and unfelt by the folk, broke the one into the six. Now, as the tale tells, we are all adrift, sailing off in all directions." Sorrowful drew himself up into a very vertical stance. "I, for one, do not know about this, but that is what *they* say, those who study such matters. That is The Six Lands."

Smoke stood up. *Yes. Ahead there is a branching on the trail. Go to the right. We have company.*

"Company?" Sorrowful whirled around and stared into the dim greenness.

I see life forms. Small pieces of meat, like you.

He spun back to face her. "Small pieces of meat?"

I shouldn't have said that. She dropped her head and licked the top of his head.

Sorrowful jumped back and hastily wiped his hair back in place. "Quite all right, quite all right, my dear."

I apologize.

"For what? I am rather petite, at least compared to you, I am. And I am, one might say, a small piece of meat." He looked decidedly uncomfortable at the sudden image of being someone's raw, dripping ingredient for a meal.

A derogatory term among my kind. Ahead is a tunnel. Enter it. And don't act surprised. Or frightened.

Or startled. They radiate kindly.

During all this conversation they had been walking and now found themselves at a branching in the trail. They turned to the right.

"They?" Sorrowful strode confidently into the tunnel. Inside the vegetation seemed to be pressing closer. The air was heavy, a stillness more still than before. The light fainter.

As they passed deeper into this structure, Smoke could feel the ceiling just brush along her back as she followed Sorrowful.

All around them, inside the green tangle, faint lights blinked on and off.

My, thought Sorrowful, this is certainly an unusual elseplace. No sounds. No small animals. Nothing. A verdant desert. What manner of creatures could inhabit such a place? What king of small small pieces of meat?

He stepped carefully ahead, his left hand tightly clenching his dagger, thumb firmly pressed against the jewel.

Just ahead. Around this curve. There is a large opening.

"Just ahead?"

Yes. They are gathered there. Many.

"Many?"

Yes, many.

"How many is many? Is that a large crowd?"

Yes. One! Some! Many!

Sorrowful straightened his back. He assumed the air of Someone Important. He became The One Who Knows What He Is About. He knew where he was going. He strode unhesitatingly around the curve, through an opening, and stepped into . . .

darkness.

And stopped.

Smoke gently nudged him forward with her head.

Sorrowful carefully stepped further into the darkness. When she stopped pushing, he stopped walking, and stood still, very still.

They waited.

Suddenly, all around them appeared a row of bright lights. They were at the same height as Sorrowful's eyes. They didn't move. They blinked. One here, one there.

The interior of the dome began to glow, softglow, and slowly, ever so slowly, details could be seen. All around, lining the edge of the dome stood figures, staring at them. They were all Sorrowful's height.

One set of bright lights detached itself from the still row and approached Sorrowful. He squinted into the dimness at the shape approaching. It stopped.

Then it moved.

Then it stopped.

He could see that it was vaguely . . . what?

It stepped closer.

And stopped.

Now Sorrowful could make out the fine pattern of scales that covered its skin. Hands and feet were delicate in structure, both had obvious webbing between the digits. The creature was thin and linear, shoulders as narrow as hips.

It stared at him over a distinct muzzle. With great black eyes, it stared at him, from gray bone encircled eye sockets. Its eyes were four times the size of Sorrowful's. Deep in their centers Sorrowful could see a glowing speck of light. The being seemed to be able to regulate the strength of the glow.

It stepped closer and scratched its finger tips on its chest, rasping the scales. From the silent staring row came an answering echo. It spoke to him, a dry hissing voice.

"We are The Gryerd, swimmers of Growing Deep. What are you? What do you do here? . . . You may speak." It scratched its chest again.

Sorrowful gave the creature a halting bow. Then he drew himself up to his full height, just slightly taller than his inquisitor, straightened up, he had been leaning forward, and started.

"My name is Sorrowful Mistidings and my companion's name is Smoke of The Velvetmist. As to why we are here, I am not sure, not at all. It appears to have been an accident. Although, perhaps, it was by design. But that is yet to be seen."

"I am Greengrim. I am the Heart of the Gryerd, Band of Greenglow. This is our intersect. The place of gathering. The place for decision making, for good or ill. We will speak on it."

Greengrim paused and appeared to be speaking/listening with the still figures evenly spaced around the open floor of the domed structure.

"You are not of Growing Deep. Never have there been such as you, here. There are weak ones far beyond the spot. But they are not the same, not the same. Never, there has never been such as that which now stands behind you. Is it mute?"

Sorrowful shook his head. "Humly, not exactly. We can . . . communicate with each other. But she does not speak otherwise."

Greengrim leaned sideways to peer around Sorrowful. "It cannot speak with us?"

"Yes. But I can tell you what she wishes to say."

Greengrim straightened up, his eyes glowing brightly. "Then you may speak to us, so we may feel the decision to be made in this place of decisions. The place of gathering. The place for decisions for good or ill."

"Yes. Ahem, it is a rather lengthly tale so you will have to be patient."

Greengrim waited. Staring. Immobile.

Sorrowful sucked in a deep breath. And began.

"SO! In a time, and at a time, it seems that I was summoned to an elseplace than my own by an individual who was named The Thought. And in this elseplace I was summoned to . . ."

Sorrowful related the entire adventure as he saw it and experienced it. He told the Gryerd how they had rid Murk Wildweald of Doom, the ensuing collapse of the warped castle, and their flight through the portal. Then he told them of their stay with Big Red and of the things they did there, in Paradise. Finally, he explained how he and Smoke had stepped through the portal and into this elseplace and of their hike to this meeting spot.

He stopped and waited.

The Gryerd stood silently around them, staring.

Moments passed into minutes.

Silence.

Sorrowful clasped his dagger hilt, thumb rubbing the jewel.

They are ready to make a decision. Stand patiently.

Greengrim scratched the fingers of both hands on his chest. The circle answered. The sound bounced from the walls.

"I am Greengrim. I am the Heart of the Gryerd, Band of Greenglow. This is our intersect. The place of gathering. The place for decision for good or ill. We will speak of it."

Greengrim looked at them, his eyes flared brightly.

"We have heard all that which you did say. It has been decided. You are Gryerd-tied." The fingers rasped loudly.

The circle began to move sideways, feet stamping, a short jerking, pounding. The tempo increased rapidly until the thrumming footsteps blurred into a single sustained note.

And ended.

Sudden silence.

Greengrim stepped forward and touched Sorrowful lightly on the chest. Then he stepped around him and reached up, touching Smoke. His head swiveled around as his fingers sank into the thick fur.

"This one has a strange covering upon it. Even stranger than yourself.   '

He stepped back and returned to his place, facing Sorrowful.

"Would you like to have something to eat? Sit here, in the center, the spot of honor."

The Gryerd rushed toward them, hands reaching out to touch and press, each one satisfying a curiosity as to what these most unusual creatures were that had come into their midst. Finally, after all had satisfied their curiosity, Sorrowful and Smoke sat, surrounded by shadowy beings with glowing eyes, and ate the banquet of assorted food stuffs that the Gryerd had gathered from their surroundings.

Once every member of the throng had finished its inspection, they took some article of food and sat down to eat. Finally when all had eaten their fill, Greengrim scratched lightly upon his chest scales, silencing the softly murmuring crowd.

"We have heard all that which you had to tell. Your exit from our land may lie in a place we rarely visit, The Blasted Spot."

He curled both hands around his eyes and ducked his head. All the Gryerd made the same gesture. Then he looked up and continued.

"This place, whose name we do not like to utter, is a place that the Gryerd do not swim. The Screaming Terror, whose rage is transmuted into the beauty and light we enjoy so, touches the surface there. A terrible place, many intersects wide, many intersects from here. It is empty. Few live near. None dare enter."

The Gryerd murmured assent.

"But some do. As a foolish youth, I did. Once did I creep, come creeping, into that place. It was the time when the eyes may see. Into the center did I creep, into the honored spot itself. There I found strangeness, tangled tall. The ancient voices do speak of a thing from above coming there, being there, causing there. Thing is for thing."

The Gryerd murmured awareness.

"That strangeness may aid your strangeness, your exit, this stuff called quest. We will guide, the Gryerd, Band of Greenglow. Thus you swim, swimming. But not in. Magra, magra."

Sorrowful looked puzzled, was puzzled. "Magra?"

"The stone undo them, it."

Sorrowful looked back at Smoke. "What do you think?"

"You are . . ."

I think we should visit . . .

". . . talking to it?"

. . . The Blasted Spot . . .

Sorrowful nodded. "Yes, I am."

. . . and see what magra is.

Sorrowful smiled at their host. "Greengrim, we wish to thank you for your hospitality. We would like to visit this spot."

Greengrim's eyes flickered.

"We will guide you, guiding, to the next intersect, the next band, the Gryerd, Band of Shadowflick. We will ask them to swim with us as we guide you, guiding, to that spot whose name we do not like to mention. Come." He rose to his feet, gesturing Sorrowful to stand.

Sorrowful leaped to his feet and threw out his arms. "WAIT! Wait. We feel that it would be better if you did not come along with us."

Yes.

"We both feel that it would be dangerous to you and unnecessary. We feel that this is a thing that we must do alone. We feel this to be true."

You have the matter by the throat.

Sorrowful slowly turned and addressed the watching circle of Gryerd. "Facing that place is our purpose and our function. Please do not come with us."

The watching band shuffled their feet.

Greengrim spoke, "In this spot truth twines free. We feel you speak pure. It is your growth to do so. We, the Gryerd, we, the Band of Greenglow, give you these."

With long fingers, Greengrim opened a pouch in his chest and extracted seven stones. They were round and green. He carefully placed them into Sorrowful's outstretched hands. They were heavier that their size suggested.

Greengrim stepped back. "From the past, our hearts heard the following call."

He began to chant.

> "To a'demon black, large and small,
>> With daggers gleaming three.
>
> Give the stones, the stones,
>> Give the stones of the tree.
>
> The stones do demons slay,
>> But only A'Demon knows the way."

Stepping one pace back from them, he continued, speaking in a low, solemn tone, "It is a voice from the past. Use the stones well."

Greengrim continued to retreat until he was one with the circle. The Gryerd feet beat a rapid tattoo.

"Farewell. For some distance we will watch as we swim, swimming."

They closed their eyes. The thrumming stopped.

Sorrowful peered into the dim space around them. He and Smoke stood alone.

"Well, Smoke, which of the many paths should we take?"

There is only one.

Sorrowful circled the doom, checking the wall.

"Why, you are correct. All the openings are gone, save this one. Not much choice. It seems that the Gryerd are guiding us as they said they would."

Sorrowful strode into the tunnel, Smoke close behind him. The tunnel curved to their right. Then they stepped out onto a normal pathway, into the normal light.

Sorrowful laughed. "Do you know, I feel much less constricted out here. Interesting, is it not? Before we entered the dome, these pathways seemed so closed and dark. Now, why now, they feel positively open and light."

I hadn't noticed.

"Oh."

He increased his pace. Then he began to carefully distribute the stones into various pockets, trying to even the placement of the weight. Several stones were moved from here to there and back again. Once he was satisfied with their disposition, Sorrowful began to hum a walking-tune to himself. It was a very nasal sound interspersed with whining, very high-pitched notes. Every high note he warbled caused one of Smoke's ears to twitch violently.

Sorrowful?

He finished a stanza. "What?"

Stop. Your song is painful to my ears. It is like backing into a grantz plant.

"A grantz plant? What is that? I do not believe that I have ever heard of such a plant before. Nor do I remember you ever speaking of such a thing."

A grantz plant is of my elseplace. A tall plant with

but a single leaf waving at the top of the stem. The stem appears soft. But if it is touched tiny, tiny spines jab forth and make very painful, very itchy wounds. Lasts for days. One does not like to touch a grantz plant.

Sorrowful nodded his head. "Yes, I would rather think so."

Then he shook his head. "In Middle-And-More, I am known far and wide for my sparkling clear singing voice. I am almost as well known for my voice as I am for my tale-telling ability."

In Middle-And-More, that may be true. Here, in the Land of the Gryerd, to one of my hearing, you are a singing grantz plant.

"Singing grantz plant."

Yes.

He jolted to a halt and whirled around, waggling a finger at her. "Some traveling companion you are! FIRST!" one finger pointed straight up. "I am called a small piece of meat. SECOND!" another finger pointed straight up. "I am knocked about on this damp terrain. AND NOW!" a third finger waggled next to the first two. "I am called a singing grantz plant."

He leaned toward her.

"I am beginning to think, Smoke, that," his voice rose, her ears folded back against her neck, "that your folk are not a very pleasant people at all. Not at all!"

Of course we are a pleasant people. Have I not formed an appreciative audience for your outlandish tales. Did I not provide a most pleasant nest for sleeping?

Her tail drifted out and around. She lightly poked the tip into his ear.

Sorrowful danced away.

"He, he, he, he. Stop that, it tickles."

She lightly danced forward after him.

I know that. His ear was attacked again.

"Ho, ha, ha, ha, ha, ha, he, he, he, heeeeee. STOP!"

Sorrowful whirled around, dodging back and forth, batting away the offending tail, and turned and raced away down the trail, legs pumping hard.

Smoke lopped along behind him, enjoying the sudden burst of light exercise.

Far down the trail, he suddenly jolted to a halt, his chest heaving.

She skidded heavily in the soft turf, claws digging furrows in the paths surface, barely avoiding running him down. She had just been beginning to enjoy the running rhythm that could carry her for miles and miles.

Sorrowful, may I make a suggestion?

"What?" he gasped, taking deep breathes from his bent over posture.

If you will not take it as an insult of some kind?

"What? What?"

I realize that your folk have a certain strong feeling about walking.

"Yes? Yes?"

How about you ride?

He straightened up and stared at her. Sorrowful's shoulders hunched up around his ears as he glared up at her.

"DO ... WHAT?"

Ride.

He glared right through her. "RIDE?"

On my back.

Flapping imaginary dirt from his clothes, he

regained his composure, and announced in stern tones, "In the Six Lands only the lame and infirm . . . ride!"

You've been insulted. Again.

Smoke sat down and cocked her ears forward.

Sorrowful vigorously shook his head back and forth.

"NO! No, no, no, no no, no! It is not that at all. Not at all. It is just . . . it is just, well, not done."

He frowned heavily at her. "NEVER!"

We could move faster. You are quite small.

"Small?"

Compared to me. Not compared to the Gryerd.

"I am not riding."

It would be quite a tale to tell.

He thought about what she said for some time. Then he nodded at her.

"So and so, it would be that, would it not?"

Quite different than most tales.

Sorrowful was losing his stern look. He stepped closer and looked at her back. She stood up. He reached up. There was no way to clamber aboard.

Well?

"I suppose it might be acceptable, ahem, given the particular circumstances we find ourselves in."

Yes. Especially given the circumstances.

"In that case, we might try it. BUT!" he waggled a very stern finger under her nose and demanded, "you will have to promise to tell me if I become too heavy for you, too much of a burden. Do you agree?"

Yes.

She crouched down and waited while he crawled up on her back. Then gently she stood up.

Now, if you would just wiggle a little further toward

the front. Right there is fine. Hold on to my fur. Can you stay on with only one hand?

"I think so."

Smoke started down the trail, using an easy walking stride, enjoying the freedom to finally give her muscles a stretch.

I can walk much faster this way. We should cover much more ground in a day.

"Well," said Sorrowful. "Well, well," he said, looking right, then left, then over the edge, smiling to himself.

"I must say that this is very interesting, being way up here. Very novel. Quite pleasant, in fact. Do you know, your fur is very thick and ge'pin'dle soft?"

I have been told something like that on one or two previous occasions.

For a brief moment, Sorrowful felt just a lightening undertone in her comment, some flashing past erotic tingle. Then he wasn't so sure about what he had felt. It just faded away.

Smoke padded along feeling completely relaxed, stretching her legs, hardly noticing her burden, such as it was.

Her passenger had become very, very quiet, totally immersed in his new experience, the act of riding.

All Things Are Gay That Is Green

The blow Big Red had delivered carried him into, through, and beyond the portal.

Multiple colors flashed around him. He wondered if that was normal for this device.

As John Tinker stumbled forward through the portal, he glanced down at where his feet ought to be.

His left foot hit the ground hard. He staggered, felt his right foot tangling in something, and spun sideways. The other foot shot forward, some small stone rolling out from under him.

He saw it, from the corner of his eye. A tree. He was spinning into a tree. Throwing up one arm to protect his face, he blocked the tree with the other. And just as he smashed into the rough bark, he realized two things.

His toy box was sailing high into the air, flung there as he fought a losing battle with the local vegetation. The other thing was what a dull *thunk* his head made hitting the trunk.

Then he crashed into a deep, soft, darkness.

He straightened up and looked around. He was sitting in his favorite chair in front of the wood stove, listening to the wind blow and admiring the view through the big picture window. The coffee was hot. He took a sip. It was his favorite blend. It tasted wonderful. He looked out and watched the first dawn light oozing up and over the nearby hills. A bright star caught his eyes and he wondered about that one burning so brightly over Frank's Flat. Then he took another sip of coffee and laughed. What a strange dream he had been having.

Then dimly, over the sound of the wind, he heard a voice. It seemed to be addressing him. It was low and unintelligible. But it grew louder and louder, more and more insistent. It was an unfamiliar voice. It repeated the question.

"Lord Tinker, be you awake?"

He turned his head, searching the dimness of the living room. How could anyone have gotten into his house without him knowing it?

"Lord Tinker, you must awaken. Toucan, see if thee canst do something, he must bestir himself."

Tinker's eyes popped open. He couldn't see anything, all was just a blur, an out-of-focus mess. He was lying flat on his back. Large somethings knelt next to him. They seemed to peering at him. Tinker squinted his eyes. At the things.

The things demisted and came into focus. A rather handsome male face looked into his. The man stood up. He was on the thin side, an athletic stranger dressed in black, wearing a white shirt.

Someone walked up to stand by his side, placing one hand on the man's shoulder. She leaned forward to stare down at Tinker and looked very worried at what she saw. She was dressed entirely in glowing yellow attire.

Tinker decided that they must be related to each other as their faces seemed so much the same: same sandy-brown hair, same bright blue eyes, same somewhat long, somewhat narrow faces.

The man spoke to the woman, "Princess, I know not what we may do but wait til fair sense do return in own sweet time. Goose did check ugly head wound. 'Pears to be most minor, though foul blow do strike most strongly, but a'glancing."

The woman noticed that Tinker's eyes seemed focused upon them. "Toucan, it do 'pear a'me that Our Lord Tinker has returned to this, the land of the living."

The man leaned over and helped Tinker to his feet, hastily brushing away the few leaves and twigs sticking to his clothes. He stepped away and gestured apologetically. "My Lord, we do but find you lying so. Nowhere do we find sign of foul assailant who do strike you down. Be you recovering, Highness?"

Tinker nodded carefully and gently rubbed the lump on the side of his head.

"I think I am, yes." He pointed.

"The assailant is right there."

Two swords whipped from scabbards as the man and woman spun to face in the direction he had pointed.

"Easy, gang! It was only that tree. I, somehow, managed to get my feet tangled up as I stepped through, twisted around, and rammed my head into that tree. It struck the first, and only, blow."

Swords slipped back into sheaths as they turned back to face him. Both looked relieved.

"Who are you?" asked Tinker.

The man made a low, courtly bow with many

hand flourishes.

The woman made a courtesy, somewhat less ornately done than her companion.

The man spoke, "My Lord, I do be The Prince Toucan, and this do be mine own sweet sister, the most Noble Princess Chicken. We do be your most obedient and most humble of servants." He smiled warmly and gestured with his right arm.

"As do be all of The Company."

Tinker turned his head and stared in the direction indicated.

In a small clearing stood two ranks of very large men, twelve in all. They were all dressed in the same costume. Red tunics over blue trousers loosely tucked into high black boots. Down the side of the trousers ran a broad red stripe. Each head wore a black beret perched at a rakish angle. Each face wore a large, handlebar mustache, the ends fiercely curled. From every belt hung a huge two-handed broadsword.

Directly in front of them stood another, dressed all in white. He appeared to be the twin of Toucan. Catching Tinker's eyes, he smiled, and barked a command, "TROOP!"

Twelve pairs of heels popped together as one while the figure in white swept his sword from its scabbard and up in front of his face in the classic military salute.

Toucan walked over to Tinker's side and announced proudly, "My Lord, may I present my brother, The Noble Prince Goose. And The Guard."

Then he suggested, "You may inspect the troop, if you do so wish, Highness. In the rearmost rank you will find Two-Byte. Yonder is Tai."

Tinker looked where Toucan indicated and saw two short things moving around behind the two ranks of soldiers. They looked like mobile garbage cans. One was colored a bright red, the other a bright blue. Then he looked off to one side, following Toucan's outstretched arm. A large, a very large animal was shuffling in the deep shadows munching grass. It was a reddish purple color. It stepped into an open, sunny patch.

It was a stegosaurus.

Tinker shook his head, once, and took another look. Then he carefully looked at each and every one of the others standing, watching him. He gasped, turned and ran back toward the tree that had abused him.

Then past it, searching in the tall grass. And found it. The shattered remains of the toy box. That was the last thing he had seen, other than the tree, the toy box flying high into the sky, flung upwards during his frantic attempt to stop the oncoming collision. He bent and picked up the fragments. Then he turned and stared at the folk standing behind him.

Prince Toucan and the Princess Chicken waited a respectful three paces away, deep concern upon their faces. He held up the shattered container.

"Highness?" asked Toucan.

"My Lord?" queried his sister. "Has some most fine treasure been lost?"

"Toys!"

They both looked puzzled.

Toucan frowned. "You did lose some child's things?"

"You are the toys. From the box." He held out the bits and pieces. "The one that Big Red gave me."

Toucan gasped and with Chicken dropped to one knee. Tinker looked over and saw that Goose had done the same thing. All three bowed their heads as Toucan spoke.

"Highness, Mighty Lord, we do be at your service and at your pleasure as of this very moment. Speak and t'will be done."

Hastily Tinker spoke to them the only thing he could think to say, "Rise. Rise."

They did, all turning to face him. And waited.

Tinker looked from one to the next and then the next, "Ahhh, how about everybody relax?"

They all did. And waited.

He sighed and walked over to Toucan and Chicken.

"This is going to take some getting used to, gang. First, I find out that I am in a fairy tale. Then, we are entertained by a chicken of a magician. Now, it's this. All this." He waved both arms. "What's next?"

Toucan and Chicken cast questioning glances at each other. She spoke, "Only but what you should command, My Lord?"

Tinker looked from Toucan to Chicken.

"If I tell you to change back, can you do it?"

Toucan's eye darted to Chicken, then shook his head.

"Nay, Highness. Of that we are not capable. Tis most beyond our control, not of our volition for it as you did be'speak, we were naught but toys, of neither volition nor thought. Of that we do have nary a memory nor control."

"Ummmm, I see. I think?"

"Highness?" Toucan hesitated. "If I may but

ask?"

"Sure. What?"

"Do be you alone?"

"WHAT?" He spun around and rapidly scanned his surroundings. He had completely forgotten about the rest of the group. So where were they?

Right now everyone was standing in a small clearing on the edge of a dense forest. From here Tinker could see a vast plain rolling in gentle waves out to the far horizon. It was covered in knee-high ferns. A velvet green sea gently surging back and forth under a soft summer breeze.

Tinker hurried from place to place, searching what open ground there was. He didn't find what he was looking for. Not one sign of a large or small footprint, not one paw print either.

He snapped around, hissing angrily to himself, surprising the waiting royalty who had followed him on his search.

"I knew it, I knew it. I should have suspected that something like this would happen. This whole thing has been a botch-up from square one. Damn The Thought to hell and back again."

The Prince and the Princess watched him, carefully maintaining expressionless faces.

"Where did they get to? Where did I get to? Either of you know?"

Toucan took one pace forward. "Highness?"

"Where are we?"

"'Tis but most great a mystery for us as but a moment past, a temporal wink backwards, we all do be naught but childly pleasures inst small, wooden chest as you do so tell us. What do be your wish, Highness?"

Tinker shrugged his shoulders and smiled at him.

"Now that's really a very good question, Toucan. May I call you Toucan?"

"As you would wish, Highness."

"Ummmmm, yes." Tinker took a new, a more careful look at his new companions, then at his new surroundings.

"O.K., who of you is the best, militarily speaking, that is?"

Toucan turned his head and called, "GOOSE! Hither!" The figure in white ran over as Toucan explained, "He do head The Guard, you see."

Tinker smiled at Goose and waved his arm in a wide sweeping gesture, indicating their present position.

"We can't just stand around here and wait for someone to come and find us. We have to go, somewhere. Which way do you think we ought to go?"

Goose ducked his head and then pointed out over the fern sea, directing their attention to some spot on the horizon.

"SIRE. From here I do see neither trail nor path through verdant expanse before us, yet on yonder horizon, or beyond, there do be some small wisp of gray smoke arisin'. Somethin' ought be the responsible agent. Should it please you, Sire, we might travel thence and see, with some subtle caution, what manner of bein's do reside in such a place as this."

"O.K., Goose, sounds like a plan."

Tinker strode out into the greenery headed to the far horizon.

"SIRE! WAIT!"

He stopped and swung around. "What?"

Goose ran up to him, frowning deeply.

"Sire, I do believe t'would be best The Guard should go before all. Followed by your Royal Self, accompanied by the Nobles, Prince Toucan and Princess Chicken. Behind shall prowl Tai and Two-Byte. Thus, in such a manner and in such a way, we do best be able to protect such nobility as do stand now here before us."

"Protect?"

"Just so, Sire. Tis our mission. Of that we do know most firmly."

"Your mission? OH, now I see." Tinker smiled at the puzzled Goose.

"This must be what Big Red meant by aid." He slapped Goose gently on the side of the shoulder with an open palm.

"Very well, Goose, deploy your troops. And myself, as you wish."

"At once, Sire. SERGEANT, TO ME!"

Goose spun smartly on his heel and strode briskly toward the waiting Guard as one member stepped toward, stopped and saluted he his leader.

"Yes, SAH!"

"Sergeant, do deploy a broad skirmish line, back curvin' arc. Head for yonder curl of smoke. Just there." Goose pointed.

"Yes, SAH!"

"Move out, man."

Goose turned back to Tinker, snapped into a rigid stance, his sword now held at his side, and waited until Tinker approached.

"My Lord Tinker, shall we then proceed?"

Tinker laughed. "Sure, let's do it."

Goose giggled, turned and ran off, becoming the center point of the line formed by The Guard. They surged out into the ferns. Tinker, accompanied by Toucan and Chicken, walked after them followed by Tai and Two-Byte.

"Ahhh, Toucan?"

"Highness?"

"Tell me about those two things, Two-Byte. Why do they go by only one name?"

"They do be Siamese twins."

"They don't look like Siamese twins."

"They do be linked by electronic band, Highness. In dim light tis plain to see. Individually they do be called Red-Byte and Blue-Byte, collectively Two-Byte. Ummm, which they do prefer."

"I see. What kind of things are they?"

"Electronic beings, Highness, with powers far beyond the likes of you or me. They, as are we all, do be charged with seeing to your safety. As do great lumbering beast."

"And its name is Tai?"

"*Her* name, Highness."

"Ah. Her name."

"Just so, Highness."

They walked easily through the ferns, up and down the slight undulations of the low rolling hills. When they were on top, they could see that the forest behind them stretched in a dark edge from horizon to horizon. In the ferns it was like walking on a frozen sea. From the top of a swell, they could see forever, well, far and wide. At the bottom, in a trough, only the surrounding, waving greenness. The breeze was comfortable warm. It as just right for a long walk on a sunny day. Behind them, they could hear the faint electronic crackling that was the robotic twins' communication with each other. Tinker wondered whether they could talk to anyone else. Deep counterpoint to the static sound played the soft, snuffling, grunting sounds of the giant lizard as she ambled along behind them, snatching mouthfuls of plant growth in passing, munching contentedly. Toucan walked on Tinker's right, Chicken on his left.

"Highness, tis a most interesting blade that you do wear most strangely."

"It certainly is that, Toucan. But don't ask me how it does that, it's all a mystery to me."

"Tis most strange a'witchcraft, having no scabbard, that it do stick most leachlike to your back. Truly a magical mystery."

"Just one of many on this quest."

"Quest, Highness? Praps you wouldst speak to us of this quest so we do be most properly prepared for to aid you?"

"Oh yes, My Lord, pray do." Chicken laid one hand lightly upon Tinker's arm as Goose drifted back to them, having waited for them to catch up.

He smiled broadly. "Quite right, Sire. One can't command The Guard to correct action if one knows naught what comin' action do be about, y'know. Of course, what do come along wilt in all ways be handled with most great dispatch."

"Whoa there, gang, simmer down. No rush, we have all day." He waved his right arm wildly.

"Let's just enjoy it. I will tell you everything I know as we stroll along."

The three nobles carefully restrained their impatience, Goose taking a position on the other side of Princess Chicken.

Tinker cleared this throat, twice.

"Ummmmm, let's see, you remember that you are, were, the toys, from the box, right?"

Each one nodded and replied.

"Yes, Highness."

"Yes, My Lord."

"Quite right, Sire."

"And nothing more?"

"Just our duty to you, Highness."

"Righto, Sire."

"Nothing more, My Lord."

Tinker looked from face to face and felt their concern. And realized that he felt very relaxed with his new company. With them, he didn't feel alone. They were familiar in their archaic ways, not so alien, not so strange. He realized he was feeling better and better. He smiled.

"O.K., gang, here we go, the story of how I, we, got here. It all started this way. One morning, as I was waking up, just sitting in my chair, admiring the early morning light coming on, enjoying my first cup of coffee, I saw this bright star. The next thing I knew, there I was . . . "

They walked slowly through the ferns, following The Guard, as Tinker told his new companions all that had happened to him and his adventures, from Doom to Big Red to here, where ever here might be.

" . . . and so there you are. And here we are. And maybe we will find out where here is, shortly. Doesn't it look to you that the smoke is just a few rises away?"

"Aye, Highness," replied Toucan, placing a gently restraining hand on Tinker's arm.

"If I might suggest, it do appear a'me best we do wait whilst Goose and The Guard proceed before and investigate said yonder smoke."

"Umm, O.K., as you wish. Go get 'em, Goose."

"Righto, Sire. SERGEANT!"

"Yes, SAH!"

"Two lines, well spaced."

Goose charged down the slight slope and up to the slight ridge before them, waving his sword. "TALLY-HO, LADS!"

He disappeared down the back side followed by half of The Guard.

"Tally-ho?"

Chicken smiled and gently nudged Tinker with her elbow.

"My Lord, the Noble, but oft quirky Goose, do tend toward silly, betimes."

"Oh."

They stood and waited. And watched while the rest of The Guard ran after the group that had gone before. They stood and waited some more. Time passed very slowly.

Tinker scuffed at the turf and stepped from side to side. The others might as well have been statues for all the movement they made. By the time he had made a rather large, brown scar where he stood, Goose reappeared, walking casually back over the hill.

He called to them, "Do come ahead, Sire. There be no one down there alive."

Puzzling over this most cryptic message, they hurried up to join Goose and follow him back down the back side through the ferns.

At the base of the hill was a large blackened area, obviously the result of fire. Charred debris littered the area. Standing in the center of the scorched spot were the remains of two structures. Smoke still drifted lazily upward from smoldering embers. This was the source of the air-borne smudge that they had seen.

A narrow, well-beaten path wandered along the base of the fern slope, through the destroyed area, past the structures, and then up into a small canyon in the adjacent hills. Behind these hills they could see distant mountains. They were standing at the edge of the fern sea, at the beginning of the foothills stretching back and upward to the distant peaks.

The Guard were evenly spaced around the burned splotch, facing outward, swords in hand, watching everything carefully. Goose guided Tinker into the mess, pointing out what had been the house, and what had been the barn. And the remains of the inhabitants.

"It do appear, Sire, that these most unfortunate ones have been hacked and slashed, not burned to death. Most strange apparel they wear. See here." Goose poked with the tip of his sword.

"Bells. They do all be a'wearin' most small bells. These cuts 'pear more like claw than blade. What think thee, Toucan?"

"Me'thinks thee do be most correct, Brother Goose. All look unarmed and do lay as if slain whilst a'running from what got'em."

Goose looked at Tinker.

"Sire, hast thoughts pon this matter?"

"Fraid so, guys. This is probably the handiwork

of The Evil One or one of his henchmen." Tinker waved an arm at their surroundings.

"It seems that I, we, are on the quest after all. Your coming alive was a timely event, for me. I think that I am going to need all your help." He looked up the narrow track leading into the small canyon.

"Which way? Into the hills? Along the edge of this plain?"

"Toward most fair hills, Sire."

"How come?"

"There be more dead that way. All did seem to run that way 'fore death. Thus, it follows that yon way lies safety. And thus, if what killed them be your enemy, then yonder must live allies."

"Sound all right to me. How about you, Princess, into the hills?"

"As mine Brother Goose thinks, so do I. Let us away to the hills go."

"Right, let's do it, Goose."

Goose ran off to gather up The Guard, calling for the Sergeant. Tinker, Chicken and Toucan joined him just as he finished issuing instructions. Goose turned to Tinker.

"Sire, I do feel we ought proceed thusly as afore. The Guard and me, first. Then you three. Then Tai and Two-Byte."

"As you wish."

Goose spun on his heels "SERGEANT!"

"Yes, SAH!"

"Start 'em off."

"Yes, SAH! ALL RIGHT YOU BLOKES, OFF YOU GO! Hustle, HUSTLE!"

The first section of The Guard hurried up the

trail, each man separated from his mate by a twenty foot gap. Tinker leaned against a convenient boulder and waited. Time passed slowly. Again.

"SERGEANT, let's away."

"Yes, SAH!"

Goose started up the trail, followed by the rest of The Guard.

Tinker traced small patterns in the dusty soil with his boot. Time oozed by.

"Highness, tis time."

Tinker's head snapped up.

"What? Oh, must have been dozing. Right, let's go." He started up the trail flanked by his two escorts, his two new companions. He looked from one to the other and smiled at the incongruity of it all, him being accompanied by Nobility of some sort, right here in this fairy tale, of some sort.

"Well, Princess, it seems we have a nice day for a stroll. Or rather, our continued stroll."

"Indeed, My Lord, the weather in this abode do appear to favor us with its charms."

"What's the frown for, Toucan?"

"Highness, the narrowness of this dusty track do give us not maneuver room should such a need arise."

"Does seem rather close now that you mention it. However, with The Guard ahead of us, I feel rather safe. Don't you?"

"Tis not our safety with which we do be concerned, tis thine. For without you, all t'will end."

Tinker shrugged his shoulders and didn't reply. What was there to say? Besides, that last comment took away all the sense of well-being he had just had. He took another look at his two fellow travelers. They were pleasant enough company. Bright, very well spoken. Toucan sounded well-educated. The Princess was certainly a very attractive person, although a bit on the quiet side. He puzzled over them and whatever it had been that might have been in Big Red's mind when he gave him that box. Behind them, Tinker could hear the buzzing/crackling noise and soft huffing of their rear guard. What a combination that was. He made a mental note to try and check on Tai's belly later, just to see whether it still read *Made in Taiwan*. He smiled.

Chicken's arm dropped lightly on his arm. He turned his head and looked straight into clear blue, sparkling eyes. For a moment, he found it hard to remember that just a moment ago, just a short portion of a day away, she and the others had been just a strange collection of toys in a box. He smiled happily at her and thought, oh well, what did it matter. In fairy tales all manner of things like this happened, didn't they?

"You do 'pear most pleasured pon some fair thought, My Lord." She smiled back.

"I was just thinking about one of my other traveling companions and what he would think about all this."

"All this? Another member who should have accompanied you here?"

"I don't know about that." He shook his head.

"That is, I don't know where we really are, or whether where we are is where we ought to be. Things like that there. Maybe they are where they ought to be and I've gotten off the track, somehow."

"Tis a conundrum, My Lord." She frowned.

"Yep, it is that all right. But I suppose it is just all

part of the quest, such as it seems to be."

"Oft times quests do be'magic'd things. Pray tell us of your lost companions. Be they gifts? Also?"

Tinker looked up the trail and laughed at that thought.

"No, Princess, they were certainly not gifts. They all came from different worlds. I mentioned that, didn't I?"

"Indeed, My Lord."

"Did I describe them well enough?"

"Nay, My Lord. It do be hard a'seeing these beings in mine imagination." Her hand continued to ride ever so lightly on his arm. Tinker pretended not to notice. It was the royal thing to do. Besides, it was rather enjoyable having such a beautiful young woman walking at his side, touching him lightly, even if she wore a rather large sword.

"I was thinking about Sorrowful, the little guy. Mountain's the big one. Then there is Smoke, of course, Smoke of the Velvetmist. Now there is an amazing young lady. And you know what is really strange?"

Chicken shook her head, slightly.

"She is rather attractive. And that is really amazing, really amazing and rather strange when you think about it."

Chicken bristled, her fingers gripping his arm tighter.

"My Lord, We do find that neither strange nor amazing. For, if we may be permitted to venture such an opinion, you do have most passing fair mien. We wouldst imagine most goodly number of hand-maidens and Ladies of your Court do be most heavily stricken and a'jostling for your favors."

"What court? My court?"

"Why the Court in your own Land, My Lord."

"I see. My court? And the Ladies therein?"

"Quite so." She nodded.

"Ah, well you see, it is not quite that way."

Chicken waited, beginning to frown, just a little.

"In my country I have no court. None at all. No ladies, or hand-maidens, waiting either."

Her eyes rounded, she gasped, and quickly recovered.

"OH, My Lord." He jerked his head back.

"You have banished been. Tis why this quest do be set upon you."

Tinker quickly shook his head and worked hard to restrain his laughter. Her expression was far too serious for levity.

"Nope. Not banished, just snatched. No court. No castle either. Just a small farm and me." He decided this was no time to speak of friends and neighbors.

"Passing strange, My Lord."

"Not for my time, Princess. Not for my time." He thought about late 20th century Grandeville, Oregon, and knew that it was certainly not ready or willing to accept knights constructed from toys, and deformed castles, or demons and wizards. Or royalty, or gigantic, telepathic carnivores either.

Chicken broke into his chain of thought.

"Well. . . when this quest do be over and done with and we do be but returned to your right and proper lands, then t'will be most fit and proper that we wouldst do something about that. My Lord." Her expression was very grim, her step more firm and determined. Her grip on his arm remained. But tighter.

"SISTER! I do be'think me thee do forget thy proper place."

Chicken jerked her arm away. Toucan was glaring at her.

"Yes, Brother Mine. Your pardon, My Lord." She bowed her head.

"We meant not to presuppose, nor for to make bold attempt . . ."

"WAIT! HOLD IT! STOP!" Tinker looked from one to the other. Chicken frowned. Toucan looked puzzled.

"I don't, didn't, mind the questions. In fact, I find it rather relaxing to have familiar company. But, you will have to ease off on all that royalty stuff, that I am not used to."

Now Chicken looked puzzled as well.

"And besides, I don't really know where any of this, umm, quest, is going to end. That is, how it is going to finish and whether any of you will actually be going home with me. Hell's Bells, look what happened to Sorrowful and Mountain and Smoke. They are all someplace else." He grabbed each of them by the arm.

"So, the same thing could happen to you. But, for the time being, you guys are all the court I have, all the court that I am ever going to have, I suspect." He smiled at them.

"And a grander court no lord could ever ask for. O.K.?"

Toucan nodded and spoke, slowly, "Highness, the points you make do be most well spoke. I, for one, do be most content to serve as I may, when I may, where I may. Sister mine?"

Chicken bowed her head again and murmured,

"Brother mine, as always, thee do be most correct." She looked up, clear blue eyes fastened upon Tinker's.

"My Lord, We do Ourselve share Mine Own Brother's thoughts." The faintest of smiles tugged at the corners of her mouth.

"But, may We you make some small query?"

"Sure."

Her expression shifted subtly, her eyes flicked to Toucan and back again.

"Do your Good Lady Smoke have some place in your heart?"

"SISTER!"

Her expression stated exactly what she thought of Toucan's admonition.

Tinker started to laugh and then quickly stopped when he saw her hurt look. Quickly he explained.

"It wasn't your question, Princess, it was the thought of Smoke being called the good Lady Smoke." Then he couldn't help it, he started to giggle. Toucan was still frowning deeply. Tinker stopped, giggling and walking.

"Uncloud your face, Toucan, I will try to explain." Toucan's eyes darted from Tinker to Chicken and back. Then he nodded.

Tinker smiled broadly and stepped back so he could look at both of them and held one hand even with the top of his shoulder.

"Try to visualize her this way. Smoke is a bit taller than I am, ummm, more or less." He bobbled his hand up and down.

"Her shoulders stand just about even with the top of my shoulders."

"Her shoulders, My Lord." Chicken had a very

puzzled expression of her face. She was only a few inches shorter than Tinker.

"Yep."

"She is . . . tall, then?"

"In a manner of speaking. But long would be more like it."

"Long?" Her brows furrowed, then she smiled. It was some sort of fey royal joke.

"Right. I would say she is about nine feet long, more or less."

"More or less," echoed Toucan, frowning at him, very puzzled.

"That would be my best guess. Somewhere about there. Of course, her tail is a lot longer than that."

Chicken's eyes popped open, wide.

"A demon? For Noble Consort you hast mistress demon?" She took a careful step backward. Tinker noticed that Toucan was also trying to slyly place more space between them.

"Whoa there, Smoke is no demon, not at all. She is rather like a cat. Well, not exactly like a cat, but sorta, in general shape that is. Covered with thick black fur, big ears, protruding canines. She is the fourth and last member to join the group, or was until you-all showed up." He smiled at them, especially at Chicken.

"But I don't really know whether one would call her a Lady or not. Not after what she did to Doom. I did tell you about that, didn't I?"

Chicken nodded.

"Indeed, My Lord, you did. But in most sketchy a'manner. T'was The Smoke?"

"Right."

She glanced over at Toucan.

"Brother Mine, it do appear a'me that Our Lord Tinker hast far greater powers than we assumed judging by such fearsome companions as he do have and command."

Toucan nodded.

"INDEED. It do most certainly seem thus. All the more reason for thee to mind thy station."

Tinker laughed, quickly interrupting them before they could start that argument again.

"Well, I wouldn't worry all that much about any special powers that I might have. As far as I can tell, I don't have any, not at all."

Toucan walked closer, shoulder almost touching shoulder, a question on his face.

"Yes, Toucan?"

"Highness, we do be ennobled a'being your court, in the here and now. If I may but offer some small words of caution?"

"Caution? Ah, sure."

Chicken edged closer as she strode along by his side, matching him, stride for stride. Toucan's eyes glanced slyly sideways.

"My Noble Sister, The Princess Chicken, who do hath curiosity in great boundless measure, wouldst verily talk your very ears from head but given half a chance, therefore . . . "

Chicken started to interrupt, Toucan suddenly pointed.

"Something do be afoot. There do stand Prince Goose."

They all looked up the trail. Goose was standing next to a gigantic gray stone outcropping, his sword dangling from one hand. He was obviously waiting for them. They hiked up to him, their conversation set aside.

"What's up, Goose?"

"Sire, I know not. One of the Advance Party, a'smellin' smoke, do run ahead. He do report yet another smoky column. I do set some small detachment a'runnin' up trail and do here now a'wait. Fore leavin' with The Guard me'thinks t'would do be best if you do wait here until beckoned on. Sire?"

"Right. We will wait here until you call."

"As you command, Sire." Goose saluted with his sword and ran up the trail followed by The Guard.

"But we will just walk slowly so they don't get too far ahead."

They did. Slowly the hills rose higher and higher around them as the trail wound back and forth and upward. All around them was a landscape of brown. Sere brown, stunted grass, a few scattered clumps of brush where water seeped to the surface. The trail followed the narrow water course, frequently switching from side to side as the side slopes made passage difficult. As they stepped around a boulder they entered a small junction of the trail with another. In this wide spot waited two of The Guard, great swords in hand.

One spoke. "Princess, My Lords. The Prince Goose do command us thus: Wait here and speak of trouble on trail ahead and bid them to await till proper signal do come for to call them forward."

Tinker glanced from Toucan to Chicken and answered, "Gentlemen, we'll do as you say. We will wait right here until Goose calls."

They both saluted with their swords, speaking in

unison, "At your service, Lords and Lady." They spun away and walked a short distance up the narrow trail, blocking it totally.

Toucan walked up to them and asked, "Know you what trouble yonder lies?"

"Nay, Lord, only that tis yet another thin smokey column rising up and that Prince Goose do say he was afeared that t'would be a repeat of that which we do not so long ago visit."

"Ummmm, I see." He turned around and walked back down to Tinker and Chicken.

Tinker had found a proper sized boulder to sit on. He gestured for them to do likewise.

"We might as well relax while we wait."

Toucan and Chicken shook their heads and wandered around the small space, glancing here and there, checking the slopes above, never still, always watching.

A rattling, clattering noise brought Tinker's attention back to the present, he had been dozing lightly. One of The Guard trotted in.

"Lord Tinker and Nobles, The Prince Goose do request your presence up yonder." He pointed with his sword.

"Tis yet another blasted place, totally destroyed." Tinker nodded.

"O.K., tell Goose we are on our way."

The three Guard ran up the trail followed, at a slower pace by Tinker, Chicken and Toucan. Behind them came Two-Byte, then Tai. As they hiked, Tinker asked, "Toucan, what do you think of this path of destruction we seem to be following. Have you seen any signs along the trail of whatever it is that we are following?"

"Nay, Highness, I have not. Merely footprints of our Company in soft dust. What manner of thing we do be following do leave nary a trace of foul passage. Hardly comforting a'thought, that." He shrugged.

Tinker nodded.

Chicken shot a fast and worried glance at Toucan. He gave her a slight twitch of his head by way of answer.

They walked steadily uphill, the trail still twisting deeper into the hills. Looking back, every once in awhile, they could see, now far below, the fern sea, before the turn closed off the view completely. Then they stepped into a wide open, mostly flat meadow. At one time it must have held a small cluster of buildings, some sort of settlement. Now rubble lay scattered far and wide. Black stains splashed up the hill slopes. All the structures had been destroyed, trampled and thrown into heaps. Fires still smoldered in piles of shattered timber. The ground was gouged and ripped, deep furrows crisscrossing the opening. Bodies lay where they had fallen. The odor of burned wood and other things filled the air.

Goose was wandering through the rubble, poking at things with the tip of his sword. The Guard were, once again, evenly spaced around the perimeter, carefully watching the surrounding hills and the trail. Goose glanced up as they entered, stepped carefully toward them, disgust written upon his face.

"Sire, tis as was before. Inhabitants slaughtered as they tried to flee." He pointed up the trail.

"More of them yonder. None barin' weapons. This be the killin' of the innocent. A most terrible thing.

We do seem to follow what be causin' this. Praps, if we do but hurry, we just may catch these most fell of agents and swift reward as do befit them. What say you, Sire?"

Tinker had been slowly scanning the meadow and its grisly contents. He nodded his head.

"Loose your dogs of war, Goose. We will follow. I think with Tai and Two-Byte we will be safe enough. GO!"

Goose spun and ran. "SERGEANT!"

"Yes, SAH!"

"On the run, Sergeant, on the run!"

"Yes, SAH!"

Goose jolted to a halt just as he entered the trail, spun and bowed deeply to Tinker, a grim smile on his face, a bright gleam in his eyes.

"By your leave, Sire." He turned and ran up the trail, The Guard closing ranks behind him.

As they disappeared around the first bend, a hand lightly touched Tinker's elbow.

"My Lord, t'was that wise?"

"I hope so, Princess, I certainly hope so. Whatever is doing all this, it either isn't aware we are behind it, or it doesn't seem to care. Let's hope that Goose and The Guard can distract it from any more of that." He pointed into the meadow. Then he started toward the narrow trail.

"Come on, we will have to get a move on if we expect to catch up with Goose and gang before night fall. Somehow," he stared at the destroyed settlement, "I think we all ought to be together before then." He hurried up the trail, Toucan and Chicken right on his heels. Tai and Two-Byte followed.

As twilight faded into gloomdusk, the three

began to jog along the trail-ledge they were on. Then, in the dimlight, they could see that the deep floor of the canyon was rapidly rising until it reached the level of the trail. They clattered out into a meadow, another black spot of destruction. The whiteness of Goose drifted ghost spectral though the ruins. The Guard, as was their wont, stood facing outward, watching carefully. Goose walked over, shaking his head from side to side.

"Carnage, destruction, murder, Sire. Tis a most evil and foul thing we do follow."

"Fraid you are right, Goose. But, we will have to camp around here somewhere. It is almost dark and I do not think we should be running up that trail in the dark with whatever it is ahead of us."

"Quite correct, Sire. If you wouldst follow, I will show quarters, such as they be, to you. A small shelter, easily defended, somehow not destroyed."

Goose beckoned and they followed, past a high pile of shattered rock, around and through a small grove of trees clustering green against a gray cliff. Pushing through the dense vegetation, Goose stepped into a small stone structure overgrown with vines.

"Here tis, Sire. Not exactly palace, but intact and secure. A shallow cave with dry masonry front. I do lay small fire which even now awaits some small ignition. The Guard, and I, stand guard and watch round about. Till fair morn." He stepped backward with a great sweeping flourish of his sword and disappeared into the dense growth. They could hear shouted commands as he reassembled The Guard.

The interior of the room, it was only one room, was visible in the faint, yellow light spreading soft glow almost to the walls. Tinker looked up, the roof appeared complete and tight. He knelt and stuck a cigarette lighter into the kindling in the fireplace. Toucan and Chicken watched over his shoulders, marveling to each over his magical device.

Tinker spun around, still on one knee and announced, "Well gang, it ain't the Castle Hilton, but it will do for one night. I would much rather sleep outside, but I doubt that Goose would think kindly of me. I suspect he would insist on my staying in here."

Chicken nodded. "Most true, My Lord." Then she hastily added, "But Brother Goose has nought but your safety in mind."

Tinker smiled at her serious tone.

"I realize that Princess, but Brother Goose will have to understand that one is not protected by being wrapped inside a ball of cotton."

"We do suppose so, My Lord. If you wish it otherwise, t'will shall be so!"

"That is not what I meant. I wasn't trying to be ungrateful. I was just trying to say that I am not used to being fussed over all the time. Also, I am tired. See you in the morning." He stood, yanked several straw pallets from a pile in the corner, shoved them into what he hoped would be a comfortable mattress, and lay down. After a few experimental wiggles and squirms, he fell asleep.

Toucan and Chicken sat, in opposite corners, so they could watch the door and the sleeping figure. Each of them held their drawn swords across their laps. From outside came the faint buzzing/crackling of the twins and the soft thud of heavy feet.

Morning.

Overhead blue sky. The sun, having sailed high enough to clear the surrounding ridge lines, shot a brilliant shaft of light into the shelter and struck Tinker full in the face.

His eyes popped open in surprise. Toucan stepped through the doorway. Behind him stood Chicken.

Toucan spoke. "Fair morn, Highness. Didst sleep well?"

Tinker rolled from his bed, stood and stretched. "Yes, I did. Time to go?"

"In but some few moments more. Goose did send some portion of The Guard forward some time past. Even now, he do leave with the rest. We follow as yesterday. Pears to be yet another day of fair weather."

"Well then, I suppose it is time to go." Tinker stepped through the doorway.

"My Lord?"

"Princess?"

"We carry supplies none."

"Yes." Tinker rubbed his stomach.

"A little matter we will have to figure out pretty soon." He pushed through the sheltering trees and into the clearing. Spinning around, Tinker stared back at them and wondered how sunshine managed to penetrate and hit him in the face. Off to one side, Tai and Two-Byte were standing and waiting.

"Looks like it is time to go. Shall we?" He started across the meadow and up the trail. Chicken and Toucan stepped up to either side, matching his gait, their swords making soft popping sounds as they were slid back into their sheaths.

In a short while, the trail became, once again, a narrow, twisting gash, twisting and turning, rising higher and higher.

Every flat place, where once stood some structure, some settlement, was destroyed. Black destruction preceded them.

It was a silent party that walked along. Their shadows shrunk as the sun rose higher and higher. Finally, around noon, Tinker figured, judging by his lack of a shadow, they walked into a very long, very narrow, arrow straight canyon. In the distance they could see a white flash and small objects turning what looked to be a corner.

When they finally arrived at this point, Tinker could see that the long ago dead river had cut a sweeping turn around some hard rock outcropping now forming a steep cliff. They strode around it.

And found Goose and The Guard blocking the way.

"What's up, Goose?"

"Sire, yonder, just by black talus slope next to yonder great gray rock, we do see some small movement. Just there, a'hidin' betwixt and between boulders grand. Now watch. THERE!"

"Right, looks like quite a few of them."

"Aye, Sire, just so. No maneuver room there. T'will be straight ahead and over the top."

"Head on? Do you think that is wise? Whatever, whoever, we have been following isn't exactly a nice bunch, you know."

Goose pointed with his sword tip, waggling it.

"Sire, those lurkers do be not the agents we do

seek. Me'thinks those foul creatures t'would hesitate not in their attack."

Tinker squinted up the trail and noted the furtive way the figures moved from place to place.

"Ummmmm, looks like your right. O.K., Goose, go ahead. Let's see what happens."

"Righto, Sire." Goose spun on his heels.

"SERGEANT!"

"Yes, SAH!"

"Advance, Sergeant, advance."

"Yes, SAH!"

The Sergeant bellowed his commands, The Guard started their advance up the trail, a double column of determined men, swords in hand. As they approached the rock piles, they charged. A yowling mass of figures bolted from the cracks and crevices and pelted away, up the trail, running as hard as they could, The Guard at their backs.

Goose stopped, twisted, and called for Tinker and the rest to follow. He spun and ran after his rapidly disappearing troop.

Tinker jogged up the trail, followed by Chicken and Toucan, both with sword in hand. Far ahead came sounds of cries echoing off the near vertical rock walls. It certainly didn't sound like the sounds of medieval combat to Tinker.

The trail changed into a set of steps, winding up and around, leaving the gorge, taking them up to something else.

At the top, they stepped off onto a floor, a vast, open space. They stared into a dead-end canyon paved with red-brown slabs of stone. Almost at the far wall, they could see two groups of racing figures. The second group was Goose and The Guard. They appeared to be losing the race. The gap between them and their quarry was widening.

"They're trapped."

"Nay, Highness, tis structure not cliff."

Tinker squinted in the direction Toucan pointed.

It was a structure, set into the cliff face, part of the cliff face. The first group was veering toward it.

"Looks like they are heading for the front gate." Tinker stared to run.

Winded and panting heavily, they charged up to Goose and The Guard. They were all standing and staring at an immense wooden gate set in an outer wall. The gate hung open. The Guard were trying to watch every direction. Goose was leaning slightly forward, peering into the darkness within.

"Bloody fast on their feet, that mob. Chased 'em in there. Thought it best not to follow. They do give us no fight. Nought but a'howlin' and a'yowlin'."

He stared harder.

"Think you we dare enter?"

"Your guess is as good as mine." Tinker stared into the dark interior but couldn't see anything in there.

"I don't see anything at all. Looks awfully empty. Ominously quiet. Anything happen since you got here?"

Goose slammed his sword into its scabbard and shook his head.

"Nay Sire, nary a sound, nary a movement. When first they do enter, footsteps gave most hollow and tomblike sound, most like some great hall, praps great cavern."

"Could be. Certainly looks like it." Tinker leaned

forward, cupping both hands around his mouth.

"HALLOOOOOOOOOOOOOOOO, ANYONE HOME?" His voice echoed back from the dark interior space. The gate creaked and slammed shut.

Everyone jumped back a step. Some of The Guard ran up. Tinker laughed.

"I'd say that they are not feeling any too friendly right now. Goose, any idea of where we are?"

"Nay, Sire, only the obvious. Tis but one way in, one way out. To leave, we must get ourselves back the way we do come. Away back yonder I do note some branches in trail. Mayhap one do lead up and out of these mountains. Brother, Sister, what say thee?"

Toucan shrugged one shoulder.

"I do leave such matters as these to thee. To mine own eyes it do but seem these rising walls naught be scaled by mortal men. For the nounce, tis here we camp for dark night come a'creeping. In fair morn retrace our steps we may, then find ourselves some small twisting way out. Sister?"

"For Ourself, We do say, do as you wish, Brothers. If Our Lord do but agree. Fair light do even grow faint enow. T'will be hard a'camping pon bare and stony floor. My Lord?"

Tinker looked from one to the other.

"Right. We camp here and see what the morning brings. Goose, set The Guard. We will stay here, more or less in the middle of this space. But I certainly agree with the Princess, it will be hard camping all right. No pun intended."

A low crackling/buzzing swept up behind them. Two voices, in unison, addressed them.

"John Tinker, we have made the necessary

computations which indicate to us that we can open that door. A black force is approaching with evil intent and just now is entering this canyon. We have figured the odds. It would be best to open the gate and retire inside before these things arrive."

Tinker whirled around and stared at them.

"Well, I'll be . . ." He stopped and stared at the robots.

"They can talk, ahhhh, you can talk. Ahhhhhh, fellows? Can you open the gate, really?"

"Indeed we can, John Tinker."

"Do it, please."

Motors humming loudly, the robots slipped around the small group and stopped before the gate. They began to chant loudly, their voices weaving in and out of the rhythm of their song. Tinker looked at Toucan.

"What are they doing?"

"Weaving a spell, Highness. To tell great gate for to swing wide."

"A spell? Two mobile computers are weaving a spell? Of all the . . . "

The wood creaked and groaned. The gate swung open. Tinker turned around and peered down the canyon. Far away, he could see a thick, oleaginous fog oozing toward them.

"From the looks of that stuff, I say we had better get inside." He waved both arms.

"Let's go. Everybody inside. That means everybody, Two-Byte and Tai included. GO!"

Goose bellowed, "SERGEANT!"

"Yes, SAH!"

"On the double man, on the double."

"Yes, SAH!"

Goose and The Guard ran inside followed by the robotic twins and Tai. Tinker, Toucan and Chicken ran after them.

"Everyone here?"

"Indeed, Sire."

"Close the gate, Two-Byte."

Their voices rose again, filling the emptiness, the spell echoing, returning, demanding attention. The gate quivered. And slowly swung shut. The thump reverberated from the hollow space ahead of them.

They were standing in a small courtyard. Set in the cliff face was yet another gate. It stood open. Tinker walked over and peered inside.

"Only way to go. So, let's see where it takes us." He started down the wide tunnel, the rest warily following behind him. The floor slanted downward. The air was cool, slightly damp promise of cavern and cave, the light paledim.

The second gate slammed shut, just missing the tip of Tai's tail. Two-Byte sang out, "Not us, John Tinker, not us."

Tinker stopped and faced his small crew.

"Well gang, it looks like we're committed now. Someone knows we are here and doesn't seem to want us to leave. Shall we play the game?"

"What game, Highness?"

"D 'n D." Tinker turned and started inward.

"What ever, Sire."

Blades slid from scabbards, hissing sibilant song.

"We know not such a'game," whispered Chicken to Toucan.

It was a silent place. Their footsteps echoed

softly. The only other noise came from Two-Byte and Tai.

Deeper and deeper. The light remaining all around them. Just enough to see by, not enough to see well by, to see how the tunnel was constructed.

"Whish, My Lord." Chicken had slipped up to his side. Ahead could be seen a faint, light. They were approaching an opening.

Tinker laughed softly.

"As certain politicians would say, I see the light at the end of the tunnel.""

"You jest?"

"Not really, Princess." He stopped.

"Goose, you ready?"

"Into the fray, Sire."

"Let's go."

They stepped from the opening.

Into open space.

Large, open space.

And stopped.

They were looking into a great square. Overhead, soft haze obscured the ceiling. Narrow shafts of light slanted down into cathedral space. Dust mote dancing beams touched the tops of the people's heads. Rank after rank after rank. Their backs to the tunnel opening. A sea of bodies. Standing silently. Waiting.

For something.

Chicken clenched Tinker's arm and gasped, "My

Lord!"

"Right, Princess. It seems we have found the population of this place."

Doubting Castle, Giant Despair

He dropped heavily to the ground.

"DOUBLE DUMPF!"

He leaned backward, arms wind-milling wildly to catch his balance. Looking down, past the tips of his boots, down the face of a near-vertical cliff, he watched small stones, dislodged by his arrival, listened to them ping as they bounced toward the bottom.

Mountain whirled around, his arms wide spread to catch and keep the others from tumbling after the stones.

Then he stared.

At nothing.

His jaw dropped open. Sputtering, he spit out some small flying thing that had investigated a potential home.

Slowly he scanned his surroundings. The portal wasn't there. None of his new companions were there. All he could see was the flat, open, rocky ground stretching into the distance. Frowning deeply, Mountain turned around, took one step forward and stared downward.

Just along the base, just at the edge of the talus slope, he could make out the thin line that was a path of some kind. It followed the edge of the cliff, wandering from somewhere to somewhere.

He leaned forward. Where those crumpled bodies lying on the rocks? He leaned further over the edge and booted a small rock over. It sailed outward and finally smacked into the path, a puff of dust marking its point of impact. The dust drifted through the bodies. They were only shadows.

"HUMPFING strange. Where is everyone?"

He turned around and began to carefully scan his new surroundings. Not a tree. Not a shrub. As far as he could see, and his visual acuity was better than most, there wasn't anything up here at all.

"RAR-RUMPF it to there and back again, those clumsy midgets must have fallen over the edge and splattered themselves amongst the boulders. Three dead bodies down there. Now I have to find them, just in case one might still be alive. But, by DOUBLE-DUMPF, they're most likely ugly lumps now. Who gets to carry on alone? Might have known it. HUMPF!"

Grumbling and mumbling, occasionally kicking a stone over the edge, Mountain moved along the cliff edge, making a slow and meticulous search for the way down. Eventually he found it.

It was a narrow crevice, just wide enough to admit his bulk, just wide enough for his purposes.

Lying flat he peered down the jagged crack in the cliff face. Finally satisfied by his careful inspection, he turned around and gently lowered his legs until both feet had found firm purchase. Carefully, slowly, moving one foot or hand at a time, he began to descend.

The sun glared warmly on his back and from the surrounding stone. Small fragments rattled and banged downward as he dislodged loose materials.

Mountain almost smiled. This place reminded him of home. Of course, he knew he wasn't home. The colors weren't quite the right shades. It was just a touch on the cool side of being just right. Still, it was a much better place than that dank and wet Murk Wildweald or that place of ever changing landscapes, Paradise.

"BY RUBBLE-RUMPF, give me the solidity of rock under my feet any where. Horizontal or vertical."

He began to hum one of the old songs. And to study the rock face just inches from his nose. He noted the weakness in the rock matrix that had allowed this crevice to form. Then he stopped and turned around, both arms firmly bracing his position. He looked outward, admiring the view.

Down below, the land lay flat and unbroken, most similar to the cliff top. Far, far out, he could see something, some faint smudge of horizon fixed grayness. Mountains? He shrugged, sending a few more rock fragments to the bottom. It was too far to tell. This was a strange land. Straight down was a desolate, sun-baked expanse. Far over there, sand dunes. Ranks of them. Multicolored ones.

The sides of his mouth crinkled. Just a bit. This was a lovely land. Just a bit strange. He had never seen multicolored sand dunes like that.

"Now that is truly strange. Not just a bit strange, but truly strange. The truly strange ought to be investigated, BY DUMPF! So Mountain, it seems that some little trip is needed just to see what goes on out there. Later. After you take care of whatever remains of our past companions remains. Ho, ho. The seven who became one. HUMPF! It is ONE now. This so-called quest has gone to ruin. Mudstone in a flood." He ripped a piece of rock loose and hurtled it far out and watched it sail and tumble and clatter noisily, down there.

"SAND AND GRAVEL, Mountain, you know full well there is no use grumbling over tumbled stone. Just find their bits and pieces, scoop it into a small crack, cover them with rock, and speed them into Next World with a sending-song. Then, off you go to see this place. HUMPF, HUMPF, HUMPF!"

He turned around, readjusted hands and feet, and started down again. At the bottom he headed in the direction he expected to find the bodies, walking along the narrow trail.

Standing at the correct spot, he knew it was the correct spot, Mountain looked around, kicked a few stones, and mumbled loudly to himself, to the cliff and to anything else in the vicinity. There was nothing here but rocks and stone. There were no battered remains splashed over the jagged cliff debris. There was no sign that something, in this case several somethings, had fallen from above.

"DOUBLE-DUMPF it, Mountain, this is most strange. Nobody above. No bodies below. You have been abandoned, that is what. Abandoned, a pebble booted from the path. You should have known. Portal. Demons. Nonsense, the entire passage, all nonsense."

He looked to his left, he stared to his right.

"Well, which way? No virtue standing and mumbling, RUMPF-A-DUMPF, which way?"

Shrugging his right shoulder, Mountain turned that way.

"Why not? Might find a cave. Might find

something to eat." His stomach rumbled a deep bass note.

"Never know, it might be days. HUMPF, that is an unpleasant thought." He drew in a tremendous breath of air and exhaled slowly through his nose.

"At least this is a fairly pleasant land."

Mountain stomped along the trail, his right shoulder almost brushing the cliff face. The talus slope plunged steeply to the plain far below just beyond the edge of his left boot. Far ahead, he could see a place where the cliff bent to the right, hiding what came beyond.

Much later Mountain hiked steadily around the curve. Behind him, unseen, a stone came up the path and nestled against another sitting there. At contact they made a sharp *click*.

Mountain eased up on his hiking pace, slowing down just a little. He had decided to enjoy the scenery. There was something about this place. It was very pleasant and relaxing in the beauty of the stark visage opening before him. Truly, this was the first time since he had been taken from STUMPF that he had felt so comfortable and so at ease.

The last time it had been a day much like this one.

He had just been taking a short tromp, ambling casually across The Rocky Flats, deep in thought, pondering all the varieties of forms on the flat, and upon the terror that some travelers felt when crossing this region. Suddenly he had stopped, looked around, thinking that he had heard someone calling his name. Perhaps this is what created the terror.

The next thing he knew, there he was, deep in the

dark and enclosing quarters of The Thought.

He gasped, "Mountain, you really have been Demon-taken, BY DUMPF!"

His first reaction was to make a hole through the walls. They were only stone. Their strain lines clearly showing. A few well placed blows and that portion next to the door would collapse nicely. Then what?

He would be free. But free to do what? He hadn't any idea of where he was or what was on the other side of these walls. It would be better to wait and see. Then take action.

From the feel of the place, damp and cold, it couldn't be Stumpf. His folk didn't travel from their world. Traveling from their world wasn't a thing to do. They couldn't. His mind hurt at the thought. This must be demon-wild. This was worse than first thought. A soft voice spoke to him from deep in the gloom.

"You are in an elseplace called Murk Wildweald. My name is The Thought and I have brought you here. Soon there will be others, three others. There is something that I must ask you, all of you, to do for me, for us. Then you will be returned home. Follow me, please. We will get you something to eat, show you your quarters, and explain what this is all about."

So he had followed along, eaten great quantities, and listened to the explanation mostly not believing it. Then Sorrowful had arrived.

He was hard to believe. Never had Mountain seen such a small person, fully grown that is. The top of his head barely reached to Mountain's kneecap. And he talked. People on Stumpf kept their thoughts to themselves unless asked otherwise. This little one never stopped talking. He talked and talked and talked and talked.

After a while, much to Mountain's surprise, he found that he enjoyed listening to these never-ending tales being spun and respun. It was a long wait. Then John Tinker had arrived and they were on their way. Supposedly home.

Now, BY DUMPF, that did not appear all that likely. Here he was, stranded on yet another place. This time without companions of any sort, big or little.

click

A soft sound. The sound on one rock touching another.

click

There. Again. Mountain gazed up and down the slopes, carefully searching for signs of slippage, signs of imminent collapse, ready to run for it. Nothing, this place was stable. Must have been a few stones coming down one of the many cracks in the cliff face. It was lined with them.

He kept walking, scanning his surroundings. Then he suddenly stopped. Now wait a pause, he said to himself, just wait one, black revolving stone of a pause. Rocks and boulders do not mumble to themselves. Something around here was mumbling to itself. It wasn't just him and an echo.

Slowly he turned, his eyes examining every crack and crevice. He stared at each stone. He checked his path. His footprints were clearly visible. There was not a sign of anything else. Then he carefully scanned outward. Far to the horizon. In all directions. Nothing there. Nothing moving out there. Nothing moving right here. Nothing moving anywhere.

CRUMPF, HUMPF AND DOUBLE-DUMPF! Whatever it was, it was hiding. And it was well hidden.

> *Rock and boulder,*
> > *Gravel and sand;*
> *Whoever you are,*
> > *Leave me alone.*

The Travelers Prayer came to his mind, the one used for crossing The Sand Barren. Probably would not do much good in this place. Different spirits.

Well, roll on, mighty rock, as my twice parent would say, there is no sense just standing in one place and wondering and waiting for something to leap upon your back.

Mountain started down the trail again. The trail was now twisting and turning around sharp cliff edges of the many-toothed edge. It seemed to him that every time he stepped around a bend that he could hear it. Behind him. A sharp *click*. Now this sound was changing. It was developing an echo. *Click . . . click.* The first sound was behind him. The other was starting to come from in front of him. He didn't like it. But he hadn't decided what he could do about it either.

So he stepped around the next turn. And stopped.

The ground ahead rose sharply. The trail did not. It was cut level, disappearing into a narrow trench.

"HUMPF!"

Mountain stomped into it. His shoulders brushed

either side. Small stones littered the floor. They were getting thicker as he preceded. He was having trouble stepping around them.

He stared upward. They must be falling from somewhere up there. He couldn't see where they were coming from. He hurried, worrying about one falling and hitting him on top of the head. He stopped and stared at what he had found, just around the next bend.

The trail was blocked. A waist-high wall of these same small stones was neatly stacked up, forming a wall. It was a dry wall, not a sign of mortar in a crack.

"DOUBLE-DUMPF, just have to climb over." He stared over the wall. The trail now pitched sharply downward.

Placing both hands of top of the wall, he leaned heavily. It held. So he swung up. The wall was very wide. He stood on top and stared downhill thinking that there ought to be water somewhere down there, at the base, always a good place to find water. That was a good thought. Mountain sat and dangled his legs over the edge. The trail down hill was bare of small stones. At least he would not slip on one of those walking downhill.

The wall collapsed.

Mountain fell on his back and began to slide. Downhill. Feet first. All those small stones, those round small stones, underneath, between him and the trail. He was out of control, gaining speed.

Mountain flailed his arms grabbing for something, anything to slow his descent. Nothing. The trail steepened. Way down there, he could see the trail bend, framed by the gunsight of his boots, he could see it bend. Beyond it, nothing but blue sky. Any moment now and he would be flying, like a great stone. It would be a short flight.

He could hear someone yelling, cursing all the gods and their stony silence. The trail curved. He careened up the wall, shot the curve and hurtled onward. Mountain sucked in a great breath of air. The yelling stopped.

Then he dropped, his stomach banging against the back of his throat. The trail had pitched down, even steeper. He felt like he was standing up but he knew better than that. The bottom was speeding toward him. He was speeding toward it. Down there was a wide clearing. On the opposite side he could make out the shadow darkness of an opening. Some large cave.

Squinting his eyes, Mountain judged the angles and his speed. If he was lucky he would shoot the clearing and hurtle into the cave. He hoped for a large cave. Empty, free of debris. Well, BY DUMPF, here he came.

The trail curved gently, depositing Mountain and the remains of the stone wall as both hurtled into the clearing. Rocking from side to side, he tried to change his trajectory. He skidded to a halt, dust billowing up around him. Dazed, he looked up through the gray and watched as it slowly drifted away on the slight breeze. He drank in the blue of the sky, blinking his eyes. Well, by all the rocks and stones, he was alive and, as far as he could tell, well. Somehow he had stopped.

He sat up. He tried to sit up. He couldn't. He was stuck, flat on his back. All those stones were stuck to his clothing. Can't be all that heavy. He tried again, muscles straining. He felt a seam in his shirt begin to tear. Relaxing he decided to lay here and think about it.

No sense ripping his clothes off. Then what would he do.

Rolling his head back and forth, he checked the clearing. He couldn't see anything. Nothing to explain this strange predicament. He was stuck. Like a rock in a mud flat.

Mumbling choice and better to be unmentioned curses, he thought about this strange place. Then he heard something. A strange sound. From the cave, from deep within the cave, something was coming. It made a heavy, stone crunching sound and a basso click that echoed from the reaches within. It sounded very large, very heavy, and headed his way.

"Better unclothed than mashed, BY DUMPF!" Mountain strained upward. All around him things were making higher pitched replies to the thing in the cave.

Too late.

A large shape slid from the cave. It stopped in the glare of sunshine just past the overhang. It was a gigantic, rough-hewn boulder of sandstone.

Mountain blinked his eyes and stared at it.

Two cracks opened up. Two pairs of eyes stared back at him. A grinding, rumbling earthslide voice spoke.

"Who are you to come to The Land of The Gett and to disturb them so? Rise, strange creature, and explain."

A series of soft popping sounds and Mountain sat up. Lurching to his feet, he wobbled from side to side, and faced the thing. Small rock-beings scurried away, whispering among themselves. He stood in a small, open space.

Mountain cleared his throat. "HUMPF! My thanks to you, Great One, for releasing me from my bonds. How I came here and why is a lengthy story. I am called by my people The-Mountain-That-Walks and I come from a land called Stumpf. It is on Stumpf where this strange tale begins." He began to tell the tale.

"One day as I was taking a short hike across The Stoney Flats, I thought that I heard someone calling my name. I stopped to look around and . . . "

Mountain described all the events of his recent past, the places and things he had seen, and walking down the trail.

" . . . and so there I was climbing over what appeared to me to be a wall laid up of small stones. The next thing I knew, there I was, flat on my back, BY DUMPF, and careening downhill." He waved one arm at his surroundings.

"So here I am and there you are. I am the only member of the group left. I suspect that my being here has something to do with the quest but I do not know the why or when of it. I just feel that it must be so."

The creature spoke. "An interesting story, strange creature. Perhaps we have an answer. It will wait until day returns. The Bringer of Heat settles, it is time for us to settle. Do not leave. We will continue after First Heat."

It dropped to the surface with a heavy thump. All around him came answering thuds. All the rock-creatures were settling down, hooking their lower edges to the bare rock. Silence reigned in the space before the cave.

Mountain looked around, strode over to one, and gently rapped it with his knuckle. It didn't stir.

Mountain could feel night approaching in the cooling breeze drifting down the canyon here at the base of the cliff. From somewhere close he could hear the music of water tinkling over something.

"HUMPF, it seems these things have dropped off to sleep like a rock. Ha. Ha." He headed down the path seeking the water, hoping that there would something to eat as well.

A hundred yards down the trail, he found it. A small glen with water flowing into a quiet pool and gurgling melodic song over a low barrier. Mountain dropped to his knees and plunged his face into wet coolness. The water level dropped noticeably before he straightened up. He had replenished his body's water balance. Now he could go for days without drinking. Or eating. It wasn't something that he enjoyed doing.

Slowly his gaze wandered over the local vegetation until he spotted what looked like fruit hanging from limbs inside a thicket of brush. He thrashed his way inside and tasted one for palatability. His stomach rumbled and gurgled satisfaction. He began to eat his way through the supply. Finally, coming out the other side of the brush, he searched for a comfortable spot, and finding it, dropped down and fell asleep.

The first bright rays of dawn ricocheting from the cliff face woke him. He took a small sip of water and headed back up the trail to see what these rock-things had to say. If he didn't feel they had anything useful to tell him, Mountain planned to head out into the flat spaces.

Stomping into the clearing, he looked around.

They were still sleeping.

"BY DUMPF, it seems I will have to sit and wait for them. Sluggards." He judged that from the temperature of the air that it would be at least two pauses and a nod before they roused themselves. Searching the place carefully, Mountain selected a rock, he was sure it was just a rock, to sit upon. And to wait.

"Strange things, these Gett. Certainly fooled me. Thought the whole scatter were nothing but pebbles and stones."

He sat, conversed with himself, and felt the heat of the day slowly increasing.

Faint crackling noises drew him from his dialogue. The smaller Gett were stirring. As they woke, they lifted up slightly, making a faint crackling sound. Watching carefully, Mountain could see several clawed feet underneath.

Soon he sat encircled by a vast number of them. More were arriving all the time. Many came straight down the cliff face. A few walked over the lip of the cave, across the roof, and then down a wall and outside again.

"BY DUMPF, they are at home any side up."

Some of them had popped open a segment of their shell and were wandering about picking at things in the dust with various of their short arms, arms that ended in sharp pinchers.

The boulder-sized Gett woke.

CRACK!

"Warm Greetings, strange creature. I am The Gett'tda. I am the oldest and the greatest of The Gett.

During the dark I have pondered the question. I have thought on all that you said. We have decided, we have, that you may become Gettish. It is a great gift. It will last until this quest is finished. Then our gift will fade away."

"In exchange for this great gift, we ask that you do a thing for us. A monster calling itself Darkness has taken a treasure from the Gett, the Gett'ta'gaz, a string of jewels with much power. The Gett'ta'gaz has been long among us, as long as there have been Gett. And we are a long-lived people. Our memory stretches back to the time when this place was green and golden." One long arm waved at their surroundings.

"The Gett'ta'gaz cries to us to return home. When evil has been banished, it will find its way back to us. Darkness belongs to The Evil One. We have mulled our history. A Gettphrase murmurs back:

> It is known that the Gett'ta'gaz,
>> when in the power of Evil,
>> and looked upon by Golden Eyes, Three.
> Three are Six,
>> Six are One,
>> Four will destroy Evil itself,
>> all the power of Evil.
> The Gett'ta'gaz will return,
>> The Gett will rejoice,
>> The Gett will rejoice."

The Gett'tda crunched toward Mountain and stopped very close to him.

"You, strange creature among us, called The-Mountain-That-Walks, are our agent. We see, we do, that you are to take the Gett'ta'gaz from Darkness and carry it to The Evil One. You must do this. There is no other way."

Mountain tried to step back. The smaller Gett blocked his way, heaping up behind him. The Gett'tda paused and then continued speaking. It explained that Darkness had separated from The Evil One and now wished to rule The Land of The Gett alone. This action had unbalanced the primal forces and that Mountain had to redress this imbalance.

"DOUBLE-DUMPF!"

"You will do this by taking the Grett'ta'gaz from Darkness and by delivering it to The Evil One. We will aid you in this endeavor by giving you The Gift of The Gett. Take this." A large claw reached out and handed Mountain a small device.

"Place it on the end of your weapon."

Mountain took the thing and looked at it carefully. It was a lens with four fasteners. They gripped the end of the cudgel shaft, projections slipping into four grooves. The lens nestled into the shallow depression. It clicked. He tugged at it. The thing wouldn't come off.

Mountain looked at the Gett'tda, started to say something and changed his mind, pursing his lips instead. He dipped his head, just a bit.

"I thank you for this fine gift, Greatest of The Gett. What do I do with it?"

The Gett'tda rumbled, "That is not The Gift of The Gett. That is a small thing of legend. It fitted itself to your weapon, thus you must be a thing of legend as well. It is how we see it, we do. And how we see it that you will aid us in clearing The Land of The Gett of foul

Darkness."

"BY DUMPF, what do I do with this thing?"

"That will come in its own time and place. The legend does say to us, it does not. The legend will answer by itself, in its own time and place. NOW, you must wait by the pool. It is time to prepare The Gift of The Gett."

All around him the Gett began to mumble. A narrow path was opened up for Mountain to walk through the assembled mass. He carefully tread across the clearing and down the trail puzzling over what they were doing. Halfway to the pool, he spun around.

Waves of Gett were pouring into the clearing. Thousands rattled and clicked against each other filling the available space, piling themselves up into peaked mounds. Streams were pouring down the cliff face, rocky torrents streaming downward. Others were spilling up over the edge of the trail, joining the mounds. From the central spot, half buried, the Gett'tda boomed at him, "WAIT AT THE POOL!"

Mountain whirled around and stomped downward.

"HUMPF, HUMPF, HUMPF! Who will believe me when I speak of this motherland. Little rocks that run about on tiny feet in any direction. STONE-DUST and GRAVEL-ASH, so I am supposed to get rid of something or someone called Darkness. And with what, BY DUMPF! A little sparkling thing that clings to the end of my cudgel and their mysterious Gift of The Gett. HUMPF, CRUMPF, AND DOUBLE-DUMPF!" He booted a real rock into the shrubbery.

"Well, as one rock said to another, it is all part of the same outcrop. HA. HA."

He thudded into a sitting position on some soft grassy stuff, stretched and yawned.

"This sitting and talking for two days is not the stuff for me." His fingers swished the water in the pool back and forth. Sounds drifted down to him. Crackling, grinding sounds. Accompanied by a dull, rhythmic thump. It went on and on and on.

Slowly the sun crept across the sky.

Mountain leaned back against a large boulder, not caring whether it was truly a boulder or not, and fell asleep. The boulder didn't mind. It was just a boulder after all.

Long shadows stretched from rock to shrub when the sounds finally stopped. A small creature whose shell reflected bright red flashes of light gently crawled up Mountain's boot and began to tug at one lace

"YOP, what is this?" A brilliant flash shot into a nearby crevice.

"Well, BY DUMPF, something lives around here besides The Gett. Some little red creeper. Some little red, hungry creeper. HUMPF, I don't hear them up there. I will probably have to wait another day."

Heavy crunching, ponderous and loud, moved down the trail toward him. Mountain looked up. The Gett'tda came toward him, hordes of Gett streaming behind. It carried a large, stone vessel tightly clenched by four pinchers.

"Rise Mountain and drink. DRINK! It is The Gift of The Gett."

Mountain stood up and peered over the rim of the cup at the contents. Something vaguely liquid, definitely blackish, roiled thickly about.

"Drink?"

The Gett'tda shoved the cup at him.

"It is The Gift of The Gett."

"MUMPF!" Mountain raised the vessel to his lips and took a small, precautionary sip. It didn't taste bad, UMMMM, NOT TOO BAD. It wasn't all that good either. Barely drinkable. He squinted at the stuff.

"DRINK!"

Mountain did. He set the empty container at his feet.

"Now what?"

"We are done."

"Done? That is it?"

"Of course, strange creature. You now are as The Gett. Your path crosses the Field of Rock to Rock Meets Sky. There dwells Darkness. The legends murmurs to us, they do murmur:

A Golden Eye,
> gleaming bright.

Slays Darkness,
> in its might."

"Farewell."

The Gett'tda heaved itself around and creaked up the trail toward the cave. The Gett streamed after. In moments, he was alone. Mountain looked around the glade. Twilight was swiftly arriving. Water tinkled softly at him. He walked over, found his previous sleeping place, sat, and then lay back. And fell asleep.

His eyes popped open. It was morning. Two pair

of crystal eyes peered at him.

It was a Gett, sitting on his chest. It scampered off.

Rolling to a sitting position, Mountain took another look. This one was as large as his head. It had a light brown streak running across its shell.

Mountain grunted at it. "Morning to you."

"Warm Greetings, strange creature. I am Quartzeye, your guide. I will lead you across the Field of Rock to Rock Meets Sky. It is a good name to aid you on your journey. The Gett'tda so speaks, they do."

"They do, do they? HUMPF! Can one so small keep up with one so large?""

"If you would remember your journey down the trail, it would seem so. The way leads this way."

Quartzeye scurried down a well worn trail that soon curved away from the cliff and out into the open space.

Mountain jumped to his feet and hurried after the rapidly moving Gett. The stream trickled alongside the trail for some distance and then disappeared into a narrow crack. The vegetation disappeared. They were on a rock plain. Mountain could see the far horizon, a flat, horizontal line.

As they traveled through the openness they passed single boulders standing in massive isolation. Sunglare reflected from the hard surfaces changing browns and grays into glowing yellow and white.

The Gett scurried along just in front of Mountain easily adjusting its pace to match Mountain's stride. A slight plume of dust kicked up behind the Gett, rock motorboat in a dusty sea. Great clouds puffed up around Mountain. The heavy material dropped quickly behind them covering their tracks.

Overhead, the sun made a leisurely track across the blueness overhead while behind them the cliff shrunk and faded from view. By the time the sun had settled toward the horizon, the unbroken flatness of the terrain had shifted into rugged, stone littered, undulating country. The trail they were following wove back and forth through a mazeland of tumbled and broken rockmass, flat, dull surface all reds and greens.

Then, as Mountain's shadow stretched far ahead of them, they entered a cleared space bulging to one side of the trail. Two large slabs of stone leaned against each other, providing a small cave shelter.

Quartzeye scrambled into the den.

"This is the first Standstill. Here we will settle." With a slight plop, it settled to the smooth rock surface, retracted arms and legs and snapped shut both eye covers.

Mountain stared down at the Gett.

"Well, BY DUMPF, that was short notice. This is the first Standstill, is it? Well, for this strange creature, there is still some day left and some things to look at, some things to see."

He strode away, wandered around the clearing, peeking and poking into and under other small openings. Mountain knew he wouldn't get lost, his mind was automatically recording the landmarks and his position. It was second nature to a native of Stumpf. Then he straightened up and snorted.

"HUMPF! Not much here to sing about. No food. No water."

His stomach grumbled loudly.

"Just rock. Rock, rock, and more rock. This place

is almost as blighty as The Rocky Flats."

He clambered to the top of the largest rock mass in the immediate vicinity and slowly searched the horizon, turning slowly, until he faced the direction they were headed. Ahead he could see the multicolored sand dunes he had noticed from the cliff top. They appeared to cut across the trail he and the Gett were following. The soft breeze plucked at the crests, feathers of sand eddied out and down.

"Well, BY DUMPF, crossing there will be unpleasant. Nothing quite as unenjoyable as wading through sand and sand-dunes and sand-storms." He stretched.

"Ho, hum. Sleep time."

As he carefully worked his way down from the top of this rock pile, he thought he could hear faint voices calling. The sound drifting faintly in his direction from the dune field. They were calling his name.

Mountain stopped and tilted his head. The sound was gone.

"HUMPF!" He jumped, landed with a thump, and hurried back to the shelter. Stretching out next to Quartzeye, he sank into a troubled sleep. He dreamed of sand-dunes that sang and called his name.

When he woke the next morning, Quartzeye told him that it would take all day just to cross the Dune Field. The Gett hurried away, Mountain following. The deeper they entered the Dune Field, the sandier it got.

"HUMPF, just what I expected. Sand, sand, and more sand."

At first it was just small eddies twisting around small collections of loose rock. Then, they walked around long streamers that trailed across open, bare patches. Then they entered the realm of the sand dunes.

Mountain craned his neck. They looked much as he had anticipated. Although each of the dunes had a separate color.

"Tell me, Quartzeye, how do these dunes keep from getting their colors mixed?"

"Sand-Trells."

"Sand-Trells?"

"Yes, strange creature, Sand-Trells. Each dune is the home of a Sand-Trell. They keep their sand to themselves. Each one is careful of the others. They will not allow their sand to mix with another dune."

"What do they look like, these Sand-Trells?"

"That is hard for me to say. They rarely come out during the day. Mostly at night, so it is told. I have never seen one. I have only heard the tales. But the tales are vague. It is told in these tales that the voices of the Sand-Trells are beautiful when they sing."

"Sing?"

"Yes, strange creature, they sing."

"HUMPF! Perhaps, then, I am ahead of you in this. Last evening, after you had settled, I thought that I heard someone calling my name ever so faintly. This calling seemed to come from this direction. Could what I heard have been these Sand-Trells?"

"It may have been. What did these voices say to you?"

"Nothing, BY DUMPF! They just called my name. I did have a strange dream though."

As they talked, they trudged deeper and deeper into the Dune-Field. The trail wandered back and forth, at times almost looping back upon itself. It was clear and smooth, this trail they were following.

"Quartzeye, how does this path remain so clear of sand? Why does it not disappear under these sand heaps?"

"The trail frequently does. The Sand-Trells always make another. This Way is never the same, yet it is always the same, always here. Somewhere. There is always a passage through the Dune-Set. Long in the past, The Gett and the Sand-Trells made a covenant. One part of this pact resulted in the Way always remaining clear."

The dunes towered above them The light, here on the trail, was diffused and multicolored from the reflections of the sand around them. The blue sky capped a small world of rainbow violence. A bright green dune stood next to a pale glowing orange mound. They passed a shocking pink dune that seemed to lean against one of yellow so bright that Mountain had to squint his eyes to protect them from the glare.

All around came the sound of the breeze caressing the edges of the dunes which sent sand soft slithering song down a steep leading edge of a dune, slowly moving forward.

There were no other sounds. Somehow, on this hard, clear trail, their footsteps were muffled, soft. They stepped in front of blue mound and past the edge of a soft brown one edged in gray.

"Quartzeye, didn't you say that the Sand-Trells would not allow their sand to mix?"

"True."

"Then, BY DUMPF, what about those two?"

Mountain pointed at the pink and yellow mounds behind them.

"This brown that we pass, its Sand-Trell has died. The yellow and pink are in conjugation. Soon, a new Sand-Trell will take a color and move with The Set."

"UMPF!"

They walked around the brown, twisted in and out of the tail of a metallic bronze, and stepped out into an open space that stretched into the distance. Their shadows stretched long, the sun was touching the horizon. Not far ahead stood the next Standstill. Quartzeye hurtled down the trail, anxious to settle. Here in the open, the temperature was noticeably cooler away from the heat-retaining dunes.

They were now on a rolling plain covered with water-worn stones of varying sizes and shapes. The litter stretched to the far horizon.

Squinting and straining, it seemed to Mountain that he made out the dim forms of mountains, ever so faintly the peaks of craggy mountains. BY DUMPF, two more days, two more days to go. Well, he reminded himself, it is not the longest that you have gone without food and water. But, it wasn't something to look forward to.

"HUMPF!"

Mountain stomped into the Standstill. It was nothing but a larger clearing in the midst of open spaces set in the middle of a sea of gray stone. The Way entered one side and exited from the other. He looked around and almost missed seeing the Gett. Then he spotted his companion. Quartzeye was the only round-backed stone in a jumble of flat-backed ones. His shell had taken on the coloration of his surroundings.

Mountain shoved a few stones out of his way and sprawled on the hard surface.

"BY DUMPF," he grumbled, "this is not much of a bed. So far, this has not been much of a comfortable place either. Just some like home, DOUBLE-DUMPF it. It is a pleasant night, lots of sky-twinkles. And the air is warm. And we are no longer surrounded by sand."

He crossed his arms over his chest, took a deep breath and fell asleep.

"Mountain .... Mountain, Mountain."
"We see you."
"Come play with us .... come sing and dance..."
"Mountain...................... Mountain, Mountain."
The soft voices caressed his dreams and woke him.

In his dream, he rose and walked back into the Dune-Set.

Tall, beautiful creatures stood on the sides of the dunes, waiting for him. They sparkled with the color of their dune. They floated upon the sand surface and beckoned to him, laughing joyously.

"Come, Mountain .... Mountain, Mountain. Come sing and dance with us."

"Join our celebration for a new Sand-Trell is to be born."

"We have waited a long time. We have sat immobile for a long time."

"But this night we can move again ....
Come."

Laughter rang from all sides, whispering silky music tinkled down the dune faces. The sand rippled with the sound. The Sand-Trells linked hands and began to dance lightly over the dunes. The soft moon light refracted from the fairy beings coating everything with pin-pricks of color. Sand-Trells streamed from all sides.

Mountain was whirled away in a swirling iris of color. He felt his feet lighten, he felt his body lighten. Then he was spun up and away to join the laughing and dancing and singing crowd.

Light as the soft breeze of day, they flew over and around the Dune-Set. On and on and on they spun.

Laughing.

Dancing.

Singing.

In the moonlight. Then, as the moon touched one horizon, and as dawn's first hint seeped from the other, they gathered in a hushed throng at the base of the dark brown dune.

The pink and yellow dunes had parted. Between them stood a tall, slim figure stretching and yawning. She sparkled and twinkled in the fading light. She was colored a majestic, royal purple. The Sand-Trells oohed and ahhed among themselves.

"She is beautiful."

"A wonderful color."

"When is the last time we had such color?"

Then someone said, "To nest .... to nest."

And voices answered, "It is time to call the wind."

"It is time to mooooooooooove."

"Goodbye, Mountain .... Mountain, Mountain."

"Come play with us again."

"Goodbye, Mountain ....Mountain, Mountain."

"Goodbye …………"

Light as a feather he was floated back to the Standstill and settled back to the ground. He fell from his dream into a deep sleep.

"Arise, strange creature, warmth is well upon us and it is time to follow the Way."

Mountain's eyes popped open. He looked up at the sky. He wasn't lying inside the shelter, he was outside on the open ground. It was a clear blue sky day. He lay still.

"Quartzeye, I have had the most unusual of most unusual dreams. Last night I dreamt that I sang and danced and frolicked with the Sand-Trells. They had a celebration for the birth of a new one. She was colored a magnificent dark, royal purple. It was so dark and so luxurious that you felt you could fall right into that color and fall forever."

He sat up and stretched and yawned. Then he stared around at the littered ground.

"BY DUMPF!"

The space around Mountain was sparkling with streamers of multi-colored sand. Particles winked back sunlight from his clothes. He brushed his hair and more sparkles fell to the ground.

Standing up, he stared out over open space to the Dune-Set. A strong wind was blowing across their peaks and ridgelines. Sand was cascading down the windward sides. The Dune-Set was on the move. Just beyond the metallic bronze dune, almost hidden inside the swirling sand, he could see flashes of deep purple.

"Well I will be DOUBLE-DUMPFED! It was not a dream."

"You must be truly legend, strange creature. Few have ever played with the Sand-Trells. They are powerful friends, but terrible enemies. Perhaps they will aid you on your quest. But we must hurry from here. The Way of the Dune-Set will soon cross this place and few creatures can withstand their abrasive caress."

The first sand particles were already swirling into the clearing.

Quartzeye scurried down the trail.

Mountain had to trot to catch up with him. From behind, he could hear, ever so faintly, a distant singing.

"We see you Mountain .... Mountain, Mountain."

"We see you."

They both ran as the wind increased its force.

Much later, as they hurried along, Mountain gestured at the gray rock landscape that stretched all around them.

"What is this called?"

Now in the far distance could be seen a towering mountain range. Sharp, jagged peaks tore upward into banks of clouds. Lightening flashed in their depths.

"This place is called the Dismal Blight. It is well known that some folk, after leaving the Dune-Set, are so depressed by this unending grayness that they go fastly mad. How do you feel?"

Mountain thumped his chest.

"Me? BY DUMPF, I feel just fine. Although, and this I will confess, I am just a bit tired after last night's revel. Are these craggy ranges I see ahead our destination? Or should I say, the destination that I was told to seek?"

"Yes. That is Where Rock Meets Sky. Far above

Darkness dwells."

"HUMPF, far above is correct. These mountains rear straight up. They look to be a dark and dreary place."

"Once The Gett roamed happy and contented there. Then came strange happenings and the arrival of Darkness. So we crossed the Field of Rock to Cliff Land where you met us and we met you. When you have been successful it will be good to return home."

"Why didn't you do so long ago."

"We Gett could not withstand the power of the Gett'ta'gaz in the hands of Darkness. But once you have taken it from him, we will return. Home."

Mountain sighed, heavily.

"Home. Yes. Soon you will be able to go home. When will I be able to do that? HUMPF!"

They hurried through Dismal Blight. Through the grayness. The rock was gray. The Way was gray. Their shadows were gray. Even Quartzeye had retained a gray shading in its shell. The dust that coated both of them was gray.

Looking upward, it seemed to Mountain that even the sky had taken on a gray look. Mumbling to himself, he understood why people walking for a few days through all this gray perplexity might get depressed. Without realizing it, he found that he was jogging to try and keep up with the faster moving Gett.

"Quartzeye .. what is . . . the . . . hurry?"

"We must get to Standstill Overlook before this day ends."

With an additional spurt of speed, Quartzeye ran faster. The gray dust rooster-tailed higher behind him. As they ran, Mountain could see a small dot forming on the horizon. Soon it took on the shape and form of a tall tower.

When they got closer, he could see that it was made of gray stone, a beacon that called to them to hurry . . . to hurry.

"Faster, faster, strange creature. The shadows are lengthening. We must be inside by dark start."

The Gett spurted ahead. The dust shooting as high as Mountain's waist as the Gett rocketed along. Mountain had to really stretch his legs to keep up. The gray tower reared just before them.

As the faint sliver of the sun disappeared below the horizon behind them, Quartzeye shot into the tower door and up the central column of the winding stair and disappeared.

Mountain charged inside, whirled around and barred the door shut. When he lurched out onto the very top level of the tower, panting heavily, he found the Gett nestled in a corner, fast asleep.

Mountain leaned on the parapet, breathing deeply, and admired the view. It was magnificent. In one direction the gray stretched back toward the way they had come, all the way to the horizon. The other direction was something all together unexpected.

The tower was built on the edge of the cliff. The cliff ran arrow straight to his left and right. Far ahead another cliff. And beyond that . . . mountains.

Great mountains.

Gigantic mountains.

An entire mountain range.

Mountains soaring and roaring upward, jagged masses of black and gray slashed by narrow canyons. Here and there long waterfalls plunged from heights to blow fogvapor away before reaching the valley floors.

And there were clouds, banks and banks of them, hiding the peaks, flashing with lightening, thunder echoing and reechoing, bouncing from face to face to face.

"BY DUMPF!" He almost smiled at the sight. Between himself and all this magnificence was a dry arroyo filled with sand. Flowing down this river of sand, neatly dissecting it, was a meandering line of mist. The mist eddied, billows surging back and forth, a blue fog river in a yellow sand sea. This fog line was coming from somewhere and going somewhere. But craning his head right and left didn't answer that question.

Mountain looked back at all that wonder ahead. From behind him, the low setting sun shot spears of light into the rock range. Verdant valleys flashed green.

Now he did smile to himself. A slight movement by the side of his mouth. Tomorrow. Tomorrow, BY DUMPF, he would be there. Out of all this wasteland and back into a place to climb, a place to enjoy, a place to find something to eat and drink. His stomach grumbled loudly in anticipation.

He turned his back on the sight, slipped down the wall and dropped into a pleasant dream, legs sticking straight out. He dreamed of the Sand-Trells, singing and dancing.

He didn't hear the snuffling, growling sounds as things prowled across the sandy reaches below the cliff.

Mountain stood with his elbows propped upon the top of the flat stones capping the wall and admired the morning. The clouds had parted, the sun touched the sand sea. It glowed yellow then turned a deep gold.

This golden river seemed to flow between two flat gray walls. Down its center the blue-green mist roiled, its edges tinged reflected bronze.

"A beautiful sight, strange creature."

Quartzeye sat next to Mountain's elbow.

"But that beauty below hides much that is ugly."

"Ugly?"

"That sandy reach was once a mighty river, The Blue Bent. It flowed swift and true, filled bank to bank. That was long ago when the world was green. That mist swirled and sang upon its surface. And creatures sang in the depths while others drank from the shores. Now you see but a trace, forever shrouded in mist, the river Murk-Mist. The way crosses at but one spot where a small span leaps from side to side. It is a poor image of the mighty span that once arched high over The Blue Bent.

"COME! It is time to start. I will take you only to the start of the sand way. You must cross alone for I am to return back. Beware of the warped things that burrow in the sand."

The Gett scurried down the wall and out of the tower. Mountain lumbered down the stairs to catch up. Quartzeye led him to a mound of broken stone.

"This is all that remains of the mighty span. From here the way leads down the cliff face and over the sand to the Silver Span. You can see it shining in the sun, even from here."

Mountain peered and saw it, a sparkling over the mist.

"I leave you now. Farewell, strange creature. May your way be clear."

Quartzeye shot away and turned onto the way

leading back into the Dismal Blight. Mountain watched until The Gett could no longer be seen. Then, for a few moments longer, he watched the high dust plume, until it also disappeared.

"Farewell Quartzeye. May your way be clear."

Mountain turned back toward the wide expanse of sand below and stared at the narrow way pointed arrow straight across the undulating sand. Carefully he worked his way down the jagged pieces of the broken stair. The closer he got to the bottom the stronger his sense of something wrong grew. Somewhere out there, somewhere around here, there was something making him feel very uneasy. He stopped and carefully scanned the sand below, the cliff face on either side.

"HUMPF! Nothing much to see around here. Nothing stirring down there." Yet he felt uneasy. He knew some thing was watching him. Of that, he was certain, whether he could see anything or not.

"Well, DOUBLE-DUMPF, do not stand there quaking in your dusty-dust. Time to cross this waste."

At the base of the cliff, he gingerly stepped from the wreckage of the stair and started down the way, across the sand. Mountain started to trot. He had decided this was no time for viewing the sights, such as they are.

As he ran he scanned his surroundings, near and far, ears straining to catch the faintest of sounds. Nothing moved, nothing was heard, just his feet thudding on the way.

Then, from the top of one of the many sand swells he saw it, just a short distance ahead, the silver span crossing Murk-Mist. There were three more humps of sand to cross. Then he would be halfway. He started running harder, counting.

"One . . . "

"Two . . . "

"Three . . . "

"BY DUMPF!"

The sand in front of him heaved and swirled. Mountain skidded to a halt and jumped back from the boiling mass. All around him the sand began to move.

"Trapped, BY DOUBLE-DUMPF, trapped."

The sand in front of him humped and twisted upward. Torrents poured off the thing from underneath. It rocked back and forth upon clawed feet. Two long arms dragged furrows as it took a step toward him. From the oversize head a rasping voice growled at him.

"Who are you that dares to cross our river of sand, Sand Bent?"

"Yes, yes . . . "

"Yes . . . yes . . . "

"Yes, yes, yes, yes."

"Yes . . . '

"Yes."

The ragged chorus echoed agreement from all sides.

Slowly Mountain turned to see what was speaking. Numbers of the creatures hunkered on the sand, staring at him. They were all versions of the thing that had spoken to him. Some were larger, some were smaller, a few had more arms and legs. One of them had two heads, each with but a single eye that glinted darkly at him.

They stood and shuffled their feet and twitched their claws, leaning toward him, anxious to rend and tear.

Mountain shrugged and turned back to what he supposed was the leader of this mob, his fingers caressing the hilt of his club.

"Begone, noisome creature." Mountain waved one arm at the thing.

"I have no business to discuss with you. Clear the way."

It leaned forward and roared, "CLEAR THE WAY? The way IS CLEAR. Or it soooooon will be. After, huk, huk, we have had our fill. TWO-BEAK."

One clawed fist jabbed two thumbs to one side.

Mountain whirled. The two-headed one pounced. Mountain forearms shot up. Both sets of fangs clamped down, ripping into the sleeve of one arm. Shards of crystal struck Mountain in the face and chest.

"OWWWWWWWWWWWWWWW!"

Two-Beak leaped to one side, hands swiping at mouths.

"MY FANGS, I broke my fangs."

Mountain stepped sideways and smashed another thing in the face with a fist as a third attempted to bite his lower leg. The leg biter rolled away as a massive foot thumped down.

"STONE!" cried one.

"STONE!" yelled another, wrenching from Mountain's grasp. "Our meal is made of stone."

The sand demons charged at him from all sides, raging, eager to tear this unknown beast to bits. Battle fury surged through Mountain as he spun, stomped, pounded, and clubbed everything in sight. Gouts of sand and pieces of sand demons flew and fell on all sides. The sand continued to heave and spew forth ever increasing numbers. They would soon overwhelm him by weight of numbers.

Mountain headed for the silver span, staggering under the weight of three monsters that were attempting to rip his head from his shoulders. Tromping heavily upon the one grabbing his ankles, he lurched forward, and spun. Around and around and around, faster and faster and faster.

As his tormentors flew off to thud to the sand, the great cudgel smashed them back into sand rubble. Freed, he charged for the span, just ahead of his pursuers.

Behind him they came, lopping, scampering, chittering, eyes squinted tight as they faced the sun. The closely packed herd knew they were about to have their prey at last.

Mountain jolted to a halt and stood to one side of the silver span, just on the edge of the bank, spun and faced his tormentors.

Howling, snarling with rage, they thundered down the slope at him.

He leapt upward, grabbed the edge of the silver span and twisted out of their path. The leaders of the pack tried to change direction. The pressure of those behind thrust them forward as they screamed, "TURN, TURN, TURN . . . "

The pack disappeared into Murk-Mist, the trailing edge never looking up to see their prey smiling down at them as they tore past.

Mountain leaned on the railing and peered down into the swirling blue-green. Roars of fear followed by violent splashing. Then silence. Nothing but silence. He turned and walked up the slope of the silver span. And paused at the top.

He stood and looked back toward the tower, then turned and thumped the railing with one hand.

"BY DUMPF, that was something. Or some things. Heh, heh. As ugly a bunch as ever was. Just as Quartzeye said."

Holding up one arm, Mountain peered at his hand. Then he bent over and yanked up one pant leg.

"UMPF, not a scratch, not a mark. Now that is strange, very strange."

Straightening up, he yanked a crystal fang still stuck in his sleeve loose and pulled the sharp tip across the back of his hand.

"Tickles." He peered at his hand. There was no mark. Wincing in anticipation, he jabbed down, hard. The fang shattered.

"By DOUBLE-DUMPF, DUMPF, DUMPF! What have The Gett done to me?" He leaned heavily on the rail and thought back to what the Gett'tda had said after he had drank that strange stuff.

". . . you are now as The Gett. You have the protection of the very cliffs themselves . . . no enemy may harm you, no blow will disturb you . . ."

He rapped one knuckle sharply against the metal rail. It rang, the rail rang, a soft bell-tone.

"RUMBLE-RUMPF, rock and stone, they have done something to my skin."

"You are Gettish."

The Gett'tda's words echoed through his mind.

The Gett were rock-like creatures. That stuff had made him like them. Mountain probed his arm with one finger. It seemed as soft and pliable to him as it usually did. Yet, he was stone hard. He rapped the railing again. It chimed back at him.

"Dust and gravel!"

Mountain leaned and pondered this new puzzle and stared at the mist below as it eddied and swirled in the sunlight. The heat seemed to be drawing it upward. On Stumpf, that curseword named planet, as words ending in -pf were, he had often stood and watched the fogs lift as the sunwarmed air moved them from here to there and back again.

"DUMPF!"

The blue-green softness had surrounded him. It tickled featherfeel across the tips of his boots and rose high all around.

Soft voices whispered to him, "Friend of The Gett, friend of the Sand-Trells, enemy of the Sand Demons, we greet you."

"WHAT? Who are you? Where are you?'

"We are here. We are the dwellers of Murk-Mist. Be not afraid. We will aid you if we can. How may we help you?"

"Well, BY DUMPF, I do not know. HUMPF, maybe I do. Can you tell me where Darkness lives? I seek this place but do not know which way to go."

"We know this. Darkness is Evil, a vile thing. Why do you seek it?"

"To end it. It is my quest."

"To end, to end it."

The voices whispered among themselves. The mist swirled higher. Mountain stood in a small open space surrounded by climbing . . . something.

"We have heard that The Gett have sent a legend to rid us of Darkness. Are you that legend?"

"The Gett think so. I do not know about that. All I know is that I drank their potion and have become Gettish."

"It is so. We saw. Help you we will. Trust us. All of us. Step from the silver span. Step into Murk-Mist."

Mountain stared at the dense fog, tendrils eddied over his feet and caressed his legs.

"Step, step into Murk-Mist."

"Twice-parents, you raised a child of some daring," mumbled Mountain to himself as he swung his legs over the railing and stepped out. And dropped.

He sank up to his chest and stopped, bobbing gently. He could feel a soft dampness enveloping him, but nothing else. Then he began to float away from the silver span, drifting upstream, pulled by a current he couldn't see and barely could feel.

"Darkness is far ahead," the fogsoft voices mistwhispered to him.

"We will carry you there, to the place of beginning. Sleep and rest, friend. We will wake you when we arrive. Have no fear, nothing can harm you while you journey with us. Friend, rest and sleep."

Mountain didn't feel sleepy, not in the least. He watched the surrounding land sweep by. Soon the cliffs closed in. They swirled up a narrow canyon. The canyon gently curved one way then the other. And then up against the base of a darkening mountain range.

Soon, soon, his head began to nod, his eyes fluttering up and down, relaxed by the gentle rhythm whose soft motion lulled him into a deep sleep.

The blue-green of Murk-Mist swirled and eddied and covered him over. And buried him deep from prying eyes.

Hands off Is Fair Play

Tinker stared into the vast space.

"Sire," hissed Goose from behind him. These do be the chaps that we do so merrily chase. Me'thinks we do be trapped. Not even The Guard can withstand such a multitude as there now stands before us."

A solitary figure, standing in the middle of a high podium set front enter, stretched out an arm and beckoned to them. It was a command. A command to step forward.

Tinker turned his head and spoke softly, "O.K., gang, this is it. Let's get formed up. Princess, take my arm. Toucan and Goose walk behind us. The Guard will follow them, in a column of twos. Finally Tai and Two-Byte."

They quickly rearranged themselves. After a quick scan of their ranks, Tinker nodded.

"Well, then, here we go. Slowly. Regally."

Tinker started down the open path, walking at a very measured pace. Princess Chicken lightly held his left arm, her hand riding on his forearm as he held it over his hip. Behind them the rest followed with The Guard putting as much space between their ranks as they could without being too obvious, making their ranks look as large as possible.

As the little group approached the last rank of the throng, a path opened before them. Heads swivelled to watch them pass. They walked into the densely packed mass.

Checking the crowd with quick eye movements, Tinker realized that there were several times more people in one rank than his entire company. And they were a long way from the front row.

Each rank parted as they approached, melting together as they passed. Their slow pace gave Tinker and group time to inspect the crowd.

Everyone was dressed in clothing that utilized the same color combination, all red and white. Not one appeared to be wearing exactly the same garment. It was an unending variation on one theme. All wore small bells fastened to their clothing. As they shifted, gentle music played softly, delicate, bell whispering crowd murmur before the opening curtain to some arcane play.

Tinker looked at Chicken and spoke in normal, conversational tones, "Princess, these are not the people who were responsible for the carnage that we saw. These are the victims."

"Indeed, My Lord, I do believe you are most correct."

After what felt like a very long time, Tinker and Company arrived at the front. They stopped, facing the podium. All around, throughout the vast chamber, not a sound was made as the throng watched them intently. The figure waiting for them jumped lightly down, landing in front of Tinker.

He was, as were the rest of the population, about three feet tall and almost as wide. What they lacked in height they made up in thickness. Yet, in spite of the massive build, the man walked lightly upon his feet. Not one bell on his garment made a sound as he flowed, dance smooth, toward them. Smiling at Tinker, he swept his hands out in a welcoming gesture.

"Welcome. Welcome to Lord Tinker. Welcome to His Company. We were told by Eye-In-The-Sky that you were coming. And here you are. We were told to aid you in all ways that we can. And we will do so. We were told you would aid us, rid us of Dread, which even now rides toward us upon Edondeath. Help, us Lord Tinker. Help us."

He stepped back and waited, face a carefully controlled blank.

Tinker cleared his throat. "Well. It seems we have come to the right place at the right time after all. Certainly we will help you."

The throng rang wave after wave of thanks. The man chimed silence. All sound stopped.

Tinker smiled at him, and nodded.

"We would like to wait until morning, ah, if that will work out. Is that possible?"

He wasn't ready to charge out into the darkness and face whatever Dread and Ebondeath were.

The figure before them nodded back.

"Of course, Lord Tinker, you may do so. The Gate will keep Dread and Ebondeath outside forever. Although we would consume all the food here long before that. Come, I will lead you to your chambers, your food, and your baths."

He turned and walked away. They hurried after him. Exiting the great hall through a small portal, they walked down a long hall, passing numbers of side corridors and chambers until, finally, they arrived at their assigned quarters.

Their guidehost waved them forward and took

them on a quick tour of their rooms. The rooms were large, well furnished. The beds appeared soft and comfortable, the baths were already filled with steaming water. Bowing, their host left the rooms.

Goose bustled about and settled The Guard in a large adjoining hall, which appeared most barrack-like, and quickly joined Tinker, Toucan and Chicken at the large table set for dinner. Even through the heavy door they could hear the raucous laughter of The Guard as they relaxed.

As they started to eat, their host's head popped back through the still open door.

"Your, emmmm, animals are well taken care of and are well quartered."

"Where are they?"

"The large beast and its strange companion remain in the main hall. We are bringing vast quantities of greengrowth for the great one. The others did not wish to eat."

"No, they wouldn't." Tinker smiled. "Thank you."

"Lord, till morning then."

He bowed, again, and shut the door quietly.

The four returned to their meal.

When they had finished, Tinker announced, "I am going to take a long soak and then hit the sack. See you in the morning." He rose and left the room.

Behind him, the others stood and wandered toward selected their rooms.

After wallowing for some considerable time in the hot water, Tinker crawled into his bed and dropped into a deep, untroubled sleep.

"Time to rise up, My Lord." Soft lips caressed his ear.

"Tis a bright and fair morn, so We do suspect. Time to rise and to shine."

"UMMMMMPPH? . . . Huh?"

"Tis the morn, My Fair Lord. Time for to be astir."

"WHAT?" Tinker's eyes popped open, staring straight up. He was lying on his back.

A pair of bright blue eyes peered down at him. They blinked at him. The face seemed familiar but was too close for focus. He rolled toward that side. There was someone in bed with him.

"PRINCESS! CHICKEN!" He jerked upright and stared at her.

"What are you doing in here? In my bed? Here? What?"

"T'was naught but a'sleeping, We was, My Lord." She smiled at him, covers held tucked up beneath her chin.

"Here?"

"Most true, Fair Prince, My Own." Her smile broadened.

"In the flesh as t'were." She lowered the covers.

He nodded, frowning.

"So it seems. BUT, what are you doing here. Or rather, when did you, ah . . . I don't remember you being here. Not when I fell asleep."

She shook her head, slowly, made a sad face, and sighed very dramatically.

"Most true, My Lord. You do be sleeping so soundly that it do seem all to the better that you should sleep on." She sighed again, a very dramatic sigh.

"I see, I suppose. Well, it is time to get up, as you said. So, pop out of here and get back to your room before . . . " He wasn't sure how to finish that sentence.

"Before what, My Lord?   "

Eyelashes fluttered at him as she smiled.

"Ah, ummmmm . . . before I, WE, ummmm ... BEFORE one or both of your brothers find you here."

"Not possible, My Lord." Her smile shifted to pure mischievous.

"No clothes."

"No clothes?"

He hissed at her, "What do you mean, no clothes?"

"Just so. Nary a'stitch."

Blue eyes fastened upon his.

"Our hosts do gather all saying they wouldst clean them and repair as do be needed. We will me'self here remain til fair clothes returned do be."

She lay back and slipped deeper under the covers, one hand reaching over and gently tickled his ribs.

Tinker jerked away.

"Stop that, I'm ticklish. QUIT IT!"

She laughed deep in her throat.

"Your every wish do be naught but Our most binding command. What do be your most royal wish?"

The blanket was now held just over her nose, eyes gazing steadily at him over the edge.

Tinker looked down at her.

"Look, I do not want to have to fight a duel with your brothers or be thrown to The Guard or whatever else they might feel is appropriate when they catch us in bed together." He jabbed one finger at the door.

"So, you will just have to leave. NOW! Take one of the blankets."

She draped one corner of the cover around her head.

"The Noble Princes Toucan and Goose will mind not, My Lord. For We do tell them whither We t'was bound err last We do see them."

"YOU DID WHAT?"

"Do tell them, My Beautiful Lord."

"You told them?"

He shot a quick glance at the door.

She nodded, and smiled at him.

"Indeed."

Tinker's shoulder sagged, he felt that somehow he was losing the sense of this discussion.

"And what did they say, these Noble Princes of your's?"

She frowned at him.

"Why nothing, of course. Oh, Goose do giggle. He do be rather silly be'times."

She lowered the blanket to the base of her neck.

One corner of his mouth twisted.

"I think you mentioned that once before."

She smiled.

"Most so. And Toucan . . . "

"And Toucan?"

"He do raise one eyebrow, thus."

She shot one eyebrow up, framing a round, sparkling, blue eye, looking sage.

"I see. So there's nothing to get excited about because one brother giggled and the other waggled his eyebrow?"

"Well bespoke, My Lord. For We ourself do be

Warrior Bold, as do they. Warriors choose for themselves where, and with whom, or not-whom, they do choose for to bed. Howsoever the case may be. So, you see . . . " She smiled warmly.

"Yes, I suppose I do. But, is that wise? I mean, the Lord consorting with his staff?"

"Oh aye, Me'Lord, most wise and prudent. Tis old court custom, the Lord consorting with staff merrily. T'was thy staff We do be a'thinking pon."

"I see."

"You do?" She sat up. And dropped the blanket.

"Ohhh, yes." He leaned toward her.

"You are a very beautiful princess, Princess." His fingers lightly touched her cheek.

"Lovely lips . . . lovely face . . and . . ."

"My Lord?" She smiled again. And leaned toward him.

Their lips brushed gently. His fingers brushed silk smooth softness.

"Oh, billy be'damned!" growled Chicken, jerking back, frowning deeply.

He snapped his hand away.

"What's the problem?"

"Fraid there be nay time, My Lord. Mine Elder Brother do just now approach."

"Your elder brother?"

Tinker gasped and lurched backward. He felt his heart take a sudden lurch.

"Aye, My Lord. We do hear nought but most heavy footsteps now a'clumping this'a way. It do be The Toucan."

The bedroom door flew open and Toucan stepped through.

"Good Morn, Highness, and Noble Sister Mine."
One eyebrow shot up.

"I do bring clothes, fresh clean."

Chicken stepped from the bed, one cover wrapped toga fashion over a shoulder and around herself, walked over to Toucan, gave him a kiss on the cheek, snatched her clothes from his arm, and stalked haughtily from the room glancing neither right nor left. The door slammed shut.

Tinker rolled from the bed and began to dress, Toucan acting as a valet. Tinker's pulse settled rapidly as he realized that Toucan was totally unperturbed by his sister's behavior.

The cleaning process has restored the deep, flat blackness of the material. He sat down to bend over and snap the pant cuffs over the tops of his boots.

Chicken popped back into the room, her yellow costume casting golden tones from the walls and floor.

"Many thanks for bringing us our very own clothes, Brother." She stuck out her tongue at Toucan.

Tinker, fussing with his belt, missed both her expression and her gesture.

"Yes, many thanks, Toucan. Our hosts certainly did a good job on cleaning and repairing our clothes."

Toucan made a quick nod with his head.

"Quite so, Highness. Breakfast do be most ready. And then . . . "

"And then, Toucan?"

"Then foul Dread do awaits pon us, Highness."

Tinker flashed him a bright smile.

"Right. Dread awaits. But, breakfast first. The way this quest is going you never know when you will get a decent meal."

Chicken flashed Toucan a dark look.

"Or most decent a'bed." She stalked out the door followed by Toucan and Tinker.

The table had been set for four. In the center sat a cluster of steaming dishes. Goose sat, waiting, gleaming white. He set down his cup, rose and grinned brightly at Tinker and his sister.

"Fair morn, Sire, Brother. Sister my own, I trust that you do . . . sleep well."

She banged his shoulder sharply with a fist and sat down.

"Indeed, Brother, we do sleep well." Uncovering the dishes, she looked up.

"May We serve you, My Lord?"

Tinker dropped into a chair.

"Huh? Oh sure, thanks, Princess. It certainly looks good."

They sat and addressed themselves to the food.

Periodically Goose giggled to himself.

Tinker glanced jumped from one to another. Goose seemed as unperturbed as Toucan although he seemed to be enjoying some inner joke all his own.

Tinker, relaxed, noted that these three made a handsome trio. Toucan, sober and somber. Goose, bright and beaming. And Chicken? Well, he thought, she was certainly something, all right. Although it seemed to him that there was a stubborn trace rubbing up through all that beauty.

He jerked his eyes back to his food. She had caught him staring.

Her brothers, sitting opposite each other, engrossed in their own conversation, appeared to be unaware of his glances or her returning smile. So, cradling his cup and leaning back in his chair, Tinker enjoyed their company. As he did so, he began to ponder what sort of reality he was living. Then, unbidden, that old question floated up into his conscious.

"All right, John Tinker, now what's going on?"

Every Parting Gives a Foretaste of Death.

Sorrowful rode along, half dozing, then jerked suddenly awake. Smoke's ear twitched at his sudden motion. He had been dreaming of home, drifting in a boat, enjoying the quiet company of friends and family. Quickly he composed himself. He leaned forward.

"You know, Smoke, I have been thinking. I have been thinking that I should compose a special tale about all this. And I think that a proper title would be *Riding On The Back Of A Cloud Of Smoke*. With a title such as that I could weave and re-weave without revealing what it was all about until I reached the very sudden and surprising ending. What do you think about that?"

Her ears waggled a bit. Then he realized that he was no longer touching the Golden Eye. He hastily grabbed the dagger's hilt with his left hand.

It would be all right, I suppose.

"It would be all right, you suppose?"

Sorrowful bounced up and down, forgetting where he was. Smoke paid no attention to his antics.

"That does not sound like a very enthusiastic response to me. Especially as you would be the very essence of the tale, its object, the heroine, in a manner of speaking."

I am not familiar with all this tale-telling. I have to leave such judgments to you.

"Oh . . . . I see, well."

He looked around. It was the same scenery a before.

"Are The Gryerd still with us? I do not see any signs of them."

Yes. They move very quickly through their surroundings. Another intersect lies just ahead. There is another of their bands.

Smoke stopped in front of another entrance tunnel and sat down causing Sorrowful to slide down her back.

"OOOF!"

Sorry.

He walked around her and into the tunnel. She followed.

As soon as they walked into the dome they were quickly surrounded by the gathered Gryerd. But they had left an open space. Into this space a figure stepped and scratched the fingers of both hands on its chest. From all around came the answering sound.

"I am Shadowbank. I am the Heart of the Gryerd, Band of Shadowflick. This is our intersect. We welcome you. Greengrim, Heart of the Gryerd, Band of Greenglow, spoke to us of you. We greet you. We give you the stones of the tree."

Shadowbank handed Sorrowful four stones, similar in size and weight to those given to him by Greengrim. Sorrowful thanked their new host and quickly distributed them into various of his pockets. As soon as he was finished, Shadowbank stepped back, feet stamping a rapid tattoo upon the turf. The Gryerd around them began to sway.

Shadowbank spoke, "Your way is clear, follow

the path."

The drumming stopped. The Gryerd slipped back into the dense undergrowth, passing out through the walls of the dome.

"My, they do that quickly." Sorrowful looked around the dome.

"It appears that once again we have only one choice, only one way to go." He strode to and through the opening.

"Then let us proceed."

As soon as they reached an open pathway, Smoke regained her passenger. Sorrowful had reconsidered his revulsion toward riding. Besides, this was not home, this was a strange place where strange behaviors were acceptable.

During the next three days they wandered the paths of the Gryerd, passing through numbers of intersects, always being guided toward their destination. They met the Bands of Treespear, Leafbright, Bushwiggle, Barkboil, Groundtrot, Moldmunch, and Springlimb. From each band they received more of the strange stones. Sorrowful's pockets bulged and sagged.

As he added seven more stones, just given to them by the Band of Springlimb, he grumbled loudly, "If we meet many more of these Gryerd I think my pockets will rip away and my trousers will be tugged down around my ankles. I must weight half again as much as I did when first we started. How is your back holding up?"

Even with the stones, you are no weight. Now we leave the Gryerd behind. In front there is only wrongness.

"Wrongness?"

Yes.

"What do you mean?"

Come.

Smoke crouched and waited for Sorrowful to reseat himself, then she started down the trail at a fast trot soon changing into a lope, then a full run, her ears laid back alongside her neck. Sorrowful leaned forward, his face pressed close to one ear. It was an awkward position, trying to speak to her and maintain his hold on the Golden Eye.

"How much further?"

Some.

She galloped around a sharp curve and charged out into a wide corridor of blasted and torn vegetation. Everything was torn and trampled. It was a path of destruction twenty feet wide. The far end disappeared into the gloom ahead.

"We are going that way?"

Yes.

Smoke slowed to a walk and picked her way down the center of the swath, walking easily upon the mashed and compacted plant growth. The trees along the sides hung with shredded bark.

Here, in the center, we walk upon the path we were following. All has been pushed outwards. Wrongness is ahead.

"Smoke, is it all right if we talk?"

Yes. Danger is some ahead.

"In that case, tell me of your land, your elseplace. Was it like this? You seem so at home here."

No. Not so hot, not so steamy, not so closed in. Not so dimlight. Would you like to see it?

Sorrowful bounced up and down.

"Oh yes. I am always interested in seeing new places. But how could I do that?"

We will stand for some. It will be safe. Ready?

"Yes."

Sorrowful was standing in a forest. It was a forest such as he had never seen before. The grass under his feet was thick and soft. In all directions there was open space. Gigantic, rough-barked tree trunks punctuated the space. In the far distance they faded into a soft blue haze. The bark was coarse deep fissured brown-grey. He looked up. The lowest branches were high above.

In some ways it reminded him of the park in the capital city of Center in the Land of Cross-And-Recross. However this park stretched forever. Here and there clumps of shrubs and bushes crowded together forming dense clusters. Small animals scampered from hiding place to hiding place and raced along the great limbs. He knew that up there were multiple pathways formed from the many interlocking branches, many multiple levels of pathways. The canopy was a riot of growth and color. Petals drifted softly down from unseen flowers. They littered the grass with colorspots. This was a world of light and color and shadow, dark and dense shadow.

He stared into the corridor of blasted vegetation.

Well?

"It is a beautiful place. You must miss it. You must miss it a great deal. I know I would."

I miss it. I miss many things.

For the briefest of instants Sorrowful had the impression of a face flickering through his mind. It appeared to be John Tinker. Then it was gone. Then he was not sure that he had seen anything.

Come. If we are ever to regain our homes we must move forward. Soon, not far ahead, I will leave you to move through this growth. I want to see this dreftizt ahead. It has an evil nature.

"Dreftizt? Evil nature? What is ahead? What do you see?"

Bad is what I see. Here, here we must part. Do be careful.

Smoke sat down. Sorrowful slid down and stepped back. She slipped away and disappeared, blending into the shadows.

He looked around and laughed, a very nervous laugh.

"Careful? Have I ever been otherwise?"

Staring forward, he began to redistribute the stones, trying to get his load properly adjusted.

Talking to himself, shuffling stones back and forth, from pocket to pocket, he walked slowly down the open corridor. He hadn't noticed it before but now he did. The vegetation was decaying rapidly. Under foot it was turning slick. The odor was close to overpowering. He fingered the smooth coolness of the last stone and peered at it. It was very pretty. He turned it this way and that way, admiring the play of colors, the subtle glow from the interior, not paying attention to his surroundings.

Something crashed ahead. He peered into the dimness. Something grunted ahead. Not far ahead, it seemed to him, the vegetation appeared untouched. He inched closer and closer. Several somethings were moving around just ahead, making grunting noises.

"Oh . . . dear."

Sorrowful quickly searched the vegetation for Smoke. Nothing there. He started to back away.

Something made a high-pitched whistle. Some shapeless thing turned and began to stalk toward him. It stumbled, lurched, and staggered, changing shape as it came. Tentacles oozed forward, stretching and wiggling. Feather soft they touched the mashed ooze, seeking prey, a meal.

The others turned and spread across the corridor and followed.

Sorrowful backed up, into something mushy.

"AH!"

It was a pile of refuse that he hadn't noticed.

That thing in front of him reached, its foul breath plugging his nose. It bared its fangs and crouched.

Sorrowful grabbed for his dagger. He was still holding that stone in his right hand.

It leaped. He snapped the stone at its face and threw himself to the ground.

The stone struck the creature's forehead. The demon disappeared in a roar of flame and noise. Fire gouted backward and sideways, igniting the others. The corridor echoed with the explosions blasting gaping holes in the corridor walls. Acrid fumes and smoke boiled outward and slowly seeped upward through the thick cover.

Silence.

A mash of plant limbs and unidentifiable parts sat up. Sorrowful stood and hastily began to brush the stuff from his clothes.

"UGH, UGH!"

He leaped sideways and snatched his dagger, whirling around. Something was behind him.

Smoke sat just beyond his reach, her ears standing straight up. It looked like she was laughing at him.

"OH! You certainly startled me. I thought that another of those things had turned up."

She watched him as he relaxed, then put his dagger away.

He waved his arm grandly.

"Did you see what happened to them? They exploded. PUFF! Just like that, PUFF!"

Sorrowful danced and gestured wildly.

"Flame and smoke, one after the other. BANG! BOOM! Crackle, crackle, PUFF!"

She sat and watched him.

"Well, was not that something? Ugly horrors coming from every whichway. Then . . . BANG! PUFF! BOOOOOOOOOM! Gone . . . Well, what do you say ?"

His face flushed red.

"Oh dear me, I forgot." He slid his left hand up the hilt of his dagger and caressed the Golden Eye.

It was the stone. The demons were created by that thing that the Gryerd call the Light-In-The-Dark. The stone released the energy from which they were constructed. Now the creature knows we are here. We must move quickly along this path. It leads to the Blasted Spot.

She walked over and settled next to him. Sorrowful scrambled back to his seat. She trotted off. All around them the plant growth was as silent as before. Now Sorrowful felt a dread seeping from the density pressing down around them. He didn't like it. He had to know.

"Smoke, how did you know that these things were created by this Light-In-The-Dark being?"

Easier to show you than explain. Grasp that jewel tightly and clench my fur strongly. And don't fall off.

He looked out and saw the land of the giant bluish trees around him as he glided silently through the open spaces. He was aware of all the space around him, all sides and above. He sensed the multiple layers of activity even the chirping song of the flyers in the clear sky. He was the center, the very hub of a large three-dimensional space. Inside this sensenet he knew where everything was and what it was doing.

The others were spread out, their thoughts flowing in and out, back and forth, conversations crossing and recrossing, point and counterpoint. With a start, he realized that he was Smoke and her clan, sliding through the open spaces, gliding from shadow to shadow.

HANG ON!

They were a single entity, a multiplicity of eyes, minds, bodies and limbs. At its hub, Smoke, controlling the body as it searched.

The Velvetmist were on the hunt. Ahead they sensed their prey, a large herbivore. The outer edges of the clan moved faster than the middle, the circling net swiftly inclosing the object of their attention. Then all motion stopped.

Smoke looked into the opening. An image formed. A plant grew and grew and became a great mound of shimmering leaves and flowers. The colors of the rainbow sparkled from the leaves and reflected from the glossy petals as a delicate odor drifted from the plant and floated through the grass. From the thick tree limbs above, large blossoms lowered on thick vines and swung gently, back and forth, waiting, waiting.

Soon, into the silence, rumbled a large, beige furred, many-legged grazer, fatally attracted to the plant. It paused outside the ring of hanging flowers. The perfume grew stronger, more enticing. The grazer trotted forward. The flowers fell and clung to its back. It paid no attention as it staggered toward the plant and collapsed.

The plant and flowers disappeared. More black forms dropped from the trees. Three of them stood on the back of their crumpled prey. The Velvetmist clustered around their meal leaving an open path for Smoke to approach and start the meal. She was the hub. It was her right.

Sorrowful stared into the dim light, one hand buried deep in the soft fur of Smoke's neck, clenching it tightly.

Do you understand?

"Yes. Yes . . . I think I do, understand. You create things. Just as you and Big Red were doing that day in Paradise. Mental things?"

Correct.

He carefully cleared his throat, "Ahem. How often do you do that sort of thing?"

What?

"Ummmm, what I saw?"

Not often. The Food do not reproduce very fast. We are adapted to it. We can go a very long time without eating. Although a little snack now and then is enjoyable. Don't you agree?

She twisted her head around and rolled one large, yellow eye at him, curling her lips back to expose gleaming white teeth.

"I DO! As a matter of fact, I do. But, ahhhhh,"

he hastily changed the subject, "who is taking care of your group while you're gone?"

My sister. It is her right. She is the eldest.

Eldest?"

Yes. The youngest female is The Hub, then the eldest. We have a limited reproductive span, mostly females, few males. When the child bearing is over, then the youngest is trained, accompanied by the eldest. Thus it is, and thus it will always be. I was trained by my mother and her mother and her mother's mother. My line tends to be more long lived than most. It gives us an advantage because of the training. Most can only learn from their mothers. We, the Velvetmist, of all The Kind, have the greatest range and the greatest imagery.

"I see."

He rode for sometime in silence feeling trapped in a narrow world of sight and hearing. He felt as if his world has shrunk somehow.

Then he shrugged his shoulders. Was he not Sorrowful Mistidings, teller of Walking-Tales, renowned through the Six Lands? He knew what to do. He would set this new insight into a new tale? This tale would be a new form, a base for others to copy. Rapidly he became lost in internal musings as he pondered the warp and weft of this tale yet to be woven.

Smoke padded silently on, watching everything. Ahead of them she could see the Blasted Spot.

On her shoulders, swaying from side to side, Sorrowful finally roused himself and stared out at the vegetation with new vision. Before it had been merely a dense tangle of dank vegetation. Now he saw dread, a terrible wrongness oozing from the undergrowth, seeping onto the path, closing behind them. He could feel it, sense it, taste it. Something with dead eyes was watching them. Waiting, waiting.

"Smoke?" His voice broke. He tried again. "Smoke?"

Yes?

"Is there something really out there? Or is it my imagination?"

It is there. I cannot exactly locate it, but it is there. Just ahead. In the Blasted Spot.

She began to lope. Sorrowful dug both hands into her fur. Not far ahead he could see bright patches of light sparkling through the tangle.

The path bent one way, then another. Suddenly, they were out in the open, standing on the edge of a sunlit clearing.

Squinting his eyes tight, he jumped down and plunged into the shoulder high grass, dazzling in its emerald brightness. Soaring up around the edges, the plant life of Growing Deep, a tightly woven wall of twisting, intertwined growth. The great treetops disappeared into a layer of white mist,

Above the Blasted Spot no clouds formed, no mist hovered. Unabated sunlight burned down. The green glare from the grass carpet cast a viridescens glow upon everything. Squintpeering toward the center, Sorrowful could see a towering mass of shrubs, vines, and unidentifiable things resembling a structure. He pushed through the grass toward it.

Smoke drifted off to one side, ears up, twisting this way and that, tail thrashing angrily, as she tried to locate the thing that dwelled here. They both could feel it, watching them, waiting for them. Waiting, waiting.

At the center, Sorrowful was disappointed at

what he found. It was just a tall mound of plant life crawling over, intertwined with, the wreckage of some ancient structure. As he poked about its ribs, he decided that it would be of no use at all. Pieces of the structure canted one way, pieces canted the other way. Whatever it had been, it had fallen into ruin long, long ago. It didn't look all that safe either. How was this pile supposed to help them escape from Growing Deep? This was one mystery he felt that they would never be able to answer.

"Smoke, what do you think? Do you see anything in this mess that will help us find a way out?"

No.

"Neither do I. Well, I suppose we might as well check the entire thing over before we leave and head for someplace else. When we get done we can decide what to do next."

Sorrowful crawled into the maze and began to work his way higher and higher. There was nothing to find. At the top there was an opening. Poking up and then standing free, he looked out and across the Blasted Spot. There wasn't anything to see.

"Smoke? Where are you?"

Here.

"I cannot hear you move."

Below. Some folk are not as noisy as other folk.

He looked down past his feet and squinted his eyes. He thought that he had just seen a shadow flow past and below him.

"Smoke?"

Over here. I am casting a net. What is bothering you?

He shuddered and stared out into the green opening below.

"I really do not know. But suddenly I feel most afraid. Like I am being watched by something horrid, something evil. It is the same dread that I felt as we approached this place, only stronger. Now I know why the Gryerd called this place the Blasted Spot. There is certainly something wrong here."

Correct. It is out there and it is coming this way. It would be better if you were down there at the base where you would have a greater freedom of movement.

"Yes, you are quite right."

He started down, scrambling through the tangle. Popping out at the bottom he peered across the clearing. It seemed to him that the light just at the edge of the clearing was getting noticeably softer. It was as if something was sucking it away. He stared at one spot where he had thought something had moved. Then he saw it.

A thin edge, a thin black edge was seeping into the grass. It thickened and flowed outward, covering the grass.

Sorrowful turned and jogged lightly around the base of the tower. On all sides he could see the black stuff oozing outward, slowing filling the clearing. Unbothered by the sunlight, it flowed, the front edge seeming to bubble. As it drew closer he could see that the front edge was writhing. From this edge came a high-pitched gibbering. It was the same sound that he had heard earlier, from those things in the corridor.

The writhing edge was a mass of things. A mewing horde, lurching, jumping, staggering toward them. Their eyes glowed red, bright coals even in the sunstream. All eyes turned toward him. He could feel their hunger. Sorrowful circled the tower again and again. There was no escape, no opening across the clearing. It was almost filled, edge to edge with the black stuff.

"SMOKE! What do you see?"

Blackness, all around. Monsters. Terror. Far out there is a spot of light, glowing in the mass of it. This must be the Light-In-The-Dark spoken of by the Gryerd. It belongs to The Evil One. Use the stones. They are the only weapon we have.

The first wave scrambled up the tower's base toward them.

Sorrowful's first stone struck a wolf-faced thing in the chest, just below a second pair of eyes. A crackling flame raced around the rapidly enclosing circle. The dark mass recoiled. The flame died, the mass surged forward, a new wave of horrors scrabbled toward them.

Frantically Sorrowful threw stone after stone. Demon hordes exploded, reformed, and charged again. The air in the clearing dimmed, clouded by oily vapors. Their nostrils ached from the stink of burning blackness. The thing didn't stop its slow, inexorable progress.

Sorrowful retreated into the tangle behind him. Then he climbed upward, forced higher and higher. The black goo oozed after him, things grabbing for his legs.

He climbed higher and threw stone after stone. He noticed that the stones were beginning to glow with a soft green interior illumination. After every explosion they grew just a little brighter.

Sorrowful scrambled higher and higher.

"OH MY!

He was at the top. To one side Smoke was crouching on top of a tangle of limbs and vines, staring intently down at the bright spot that was now next to the base of their perch, a base covered with the black. Tentacles of it scrabbled just below their feet.

"It fills the entire clearing. And I have almost run out of stones."

He shrugged his shoulders and sighed.

"It seems, dear Smoke, my most unusual companion of my most unusual trip ever, that we have reached the end. We are almost out of space and certainly are about to run out of weapons." He laughed.

"If we had the time I would tell you *The Tale of the Land That Shrunk.* However, I do feel that we would be overrun by those things of black ugly long before I could finish. I do not believe it would wait. So what good is an unfinished tale? Ah well, it appears that this segment of the quest is in that same state as well."

Sorrowful held up a bright green spot of light.

"This is my last one. The last of the stones of the Tree."

He held it high so Smoke could see it. The stone was a large one, egg-shaped, burning with its own cold fire.

"Is it not a beauty." He polished it on his sleeve, blew some small speck of dust from its surface. The stone flickered at him.

"This is it. One last throw and then, why then . . . it is all over. So, farewell, good friend. If we only could let those who are left to know of our adventure and know that we were true to it to the very end. One . . . last . . . throw. Then . . . THE END!"

His arm arched back.

Smoke's head whipped forward, jaws popping open. She grabbed the stone from his hand.

Farewell, Sorrowful.

She sprang, all the strength of her hind legs thrusting her out into space, well over the seething blackness below. Then she arched down, forelegs extended, and plunged into the white glowing eye. It burned brighter and brighter. Then flashed white . . . green . . . and roared upward.

The light blinded Sorrowful who just had the sense to grab a piece of the structure next to himself.

Leaves and debris were sucked into the implosion. Dust and particles of black swirled into the air. The tower shook and bent. The wind howled hurricane song around him. He could feel the tower collapsing. Then he couldn't hear a thing.

Silence.

Soft silence.

Cool silence.

Sorrowful opened one eye, just a narrow slit of a peek. The world was tilted, upside down. He was clasping a section of the tower, hanging upside down. He opened the other. Dust was settling everywhere. Down there all he could see was dirty brown.

No black.

No green.

The once green meadow was gone. The thing was gone. Nothing but churned earth, shattered stone. Barren.

Releasing his ankles he swung around and snatched wildly at a protruding piece of the tower. Then he clambered down to take a close look. At the bottom he carefully searched the clearing. On all sides, the trees were shattered and blackened, stripped of leaves, branches and bark. There was no sign of Smoke.

Through all this deadly silence, dust and leaves

fell softly. A slight breeze was dispersing the stench and haze. The air slowly cleared. Sunlight again poured down into the Blasted Spot.

Out in the brown shattered soil he saw something sparkle in the sunlight. Carefully picking his way through the scrambled earth he walked over to see what it might be.

It was a fist-sized gem of shining iridescence. Sorrowful picked it up. The colors shifted across the many facets, flowing from shade to shade. It felt faintly warm nestled in the palm of his hand.

"I am holding a piece of a rainbow. A very pretty piece. Hardly worth the price we had to pay to my way of thinking."

He dropped it into one of his pockets and spun around.

"SMOKE! Can you hear me, SMOKE? Where are you? . . . SMOKE!"

Suddenly he felt a presence behind his back.

Snatching his dagger free, he whirled around. The portal stood, waiting. The fire-snakes roiled and hissed at him. Flames danced across its surface. Through the heat distortion he could just make out a mountainous country.

"SO! The quest continues. Minus one."

Sobbing, he stumbled through.

The portal winked out.

His footprints ended in the middle of the clearing.

Mist on Cat's Feet Comes Creeping.

Tinker sat back, quietly sipping from his cup, relaxed, ready. He had made a decision. It wasn't all that much of an earth-shattering a decision, but, considering the circumstances and all, it was a fairly appropriate decision.

Take each day as it comes.

That was the decision.

It made some sort of good sense. This new reality he was stuck inside had become a kaleidoscope of change. So, if things were going to keep changing all the time, there was no sense in trying to plan ahead.

So there it was.

Take each day as it comes.

He smiled to himself and thought, such is life inside a fairy tale.

Goose smiled back, finished off the last few tidbits that remained of their breakfast, and turned his head to watch their host, who had just popped through their door. Unannounced.

"Greeting to you, Lord Tinker, and to all your fine company. I trust that the chambers were sufficient for your needs; the clothes cleaned right and proper; the food well cooked and savory, and sufficiently well supplied."

Goose patted daintily at his lips with his napkin. Their host beamed at them.

"Is there anything else that I may do, anything at all?"

Tinker glanced around the table, and waited.

"No sir, there certainly doesn't seem to be. Many thanks for everything you have done."

Tinker stood, shoving back his chair.

"Well gang, let's get outside and see what sort of a thing Dread is."

Their host gasped.

"Problem?" asked Tinker.

"Lord Tinker, Dread is the most terrible of creatures ever imagined. He has decimated Nature's Track from our gate to the Fern Fields."

The hosts face flushed, he struggled to reset it to a calm demeanor.

"I believe that it was only your sudden appearance that kept him from settling down outside our gates. We were, we are, unprepared for such a thing and did not know what to do. There is nowhere else to run. This killing and destruction will haunt our people for many generations. We will be in your debt for all of eternity."

"For what?"

"For riding us of this horror, for killing Dread."

"Yes. If we do."

Their host almost collapsed. But not quite although he did wobble from side to side.

Tinker clapped one hand on his shoulder.

"Let's go outside and see what we shall see. Huh?"

"Of course, of course, please follow me."

They were led back through the many twists and turns to the great hall. The Guard were already there, standing in two ranks, resplendent in bright and gleaming colors. As they entered, the Sergeant of The Guard took one step forward and saluted Goose.

"All present, SAH!"

"Very well, Sergeant." Goose looked at Tinker.

"Sire, we are ready."

"Then, we are ready. Let's go. Take us to the gate, if you would."

Their host hurried them across the hall. In what seemed like a very short period of time, they arrived at the gate.

Tinker grasped their host's hand.

"Look, when we get outside, just close the gates behind us. You stay inside, O.K.? There really is no need for any of you to be outside. You would just be in the way anyway. Understood?"

"Yes, Lord Tinker, all too well. If there was something we could do to aid you, we would."

"We know that." Tinker smiled at him.

"But, there really isn't. Not the way this quest is going. So, let us out. Once again, many thanks for all your hospitality."

Their host nodded at him. The inner gate swung slowly open.

They walked out into the inner courtyard and headed for the outer gate. It began to open. Behind them the inner gate thumped shut. Sunlight poured in.

Goose and The Guard cautiously stepped out and peered around. The vast stone yard was empty.

"We will take the center position, Sire. Tai and Two-Byte will roam at will."

"As you wish, Goose."

"Sergeant."

"Yes, SAH!"

"You heard. Clusters of two. Spread out."

"Yes, SAH!"

Tinker walked out into the middle of the plaza, that's what he thought it looked like, to him, a plaza, and looked around.

Chicken and Toucan remained close to him as he walked.

The Guard were neatly spaced, two-by-two. Tai and Two-Byte wandered around, seemingly aimless.

"Well, Toucan, what do you think?"

"Highness, I do think me that foul Dread do be a'playin some strange game a'us."

"You're probably right. Still, I wish he, or it, or whatever, would get here."

A soft hand lightly touched his elbow.

"My Lord, your wish do be filled in but a short moment."

"Where?"

"Yonder."

She pointed down the valley. At the narrow entrance some faint darkening was taking place. It swelled and flowed uphill toward them. As it drew closer they could see that it was a thick, black fog with a vertical leading face. A bright red speck floated on top, at the edge.

"Yep, here it comes."

"SIRE, we are ready. SERGEANT, stand ready!"

"Yes, SAH!"

The stuff surged into the great courtyard, or plaza, or whatever it was intended to be, lapping against the rock faces on either side. It stopped not far from them, a great fuliginous cliff pulsating with a slow, steady beat.

High above them, a figure glided back and forth, near the edge, staring down. It was a man, dressed in brilliant red, so brilliant that it seemed to blur his very outline. In his right hand he carried a great sword. Around his waist a wide belt hung, glittering with jewels. They sparkled with an internal fire of their own.

He stared down at Tinker who stared back up at him.

"I am Dread."

"Whoopee."

"I am the arm of The Evil One. Stand aside."

"Nice speech, fella."

"STAND ASIDE!"

"Buzz off."

Dread settled slowly down the face of the fog bank and stepped out onto the pavement and glared at Tinker.

"Neat trick." Tinker smiled at him.

"Stand aside. Or you are doomed."

"Same old song. All you guys sing the same old song." Tinker reached up over, snatched Slayer from his back and pointed it at Dread. Tinker could feel the faint vibration as his weaponkin waited for action.

"Take that black junk and get out of here. Go on, go away. And send a message to The Evil One. Tell him that we are looking for him. Go away, beat it, vamoose, skidaddle."

Dread lunged, a sword thrust with no warning. Slayer flickered up and sideways, deflecting the blow to one side, then down. Dread's blade bounced from the pavement.

Toucan and Chicken leaped to either side of Dread, attacking.

Dread leaped backward, pressing his back against the fog bank. They ringed him, swords making small movements.

He smiled at them.

"So, you would fight. Too bad, such a waste. Ebondeath will enjoy such a meal." He pointed with his left hand, eyes never leaving his enemies.

The fog had sent long feelers down either side and were even now almost touching, forming an enclosure.

Goose and The Guard charged through the narrow gap.

Dread lunged forward as Tinker leaped backward. Instantly Dread was surrounded. Goose, Toucan, Chicken and Tinker on four sides. Behind them stood The Guard, facing outward, ready to hack at anything that got too close.

They attacked. Dread was a flash of red as he twirled and parried and struck back. They couldn't penetrate his defense nor could he get past theirs. All stopped and watched each other.

Dread slowly shook his head.

"You cannot win, John Tinker. Soon, Ebondeath will overwhelm you all. Then I will step over your bones and finally take this city. Surrender and I will let you and your's live."

"Sorry, we are stuck. Do or die."

"Then die it will be."

"The belt," cried a loud, buzzing, crackling pair of voices. "You must have the belt, John Tinker."

Dread spun toward this new voice, Tinker lunged, his weaponkin slipping under a parry that was just an instant too late. A fragment of red cloth fluttered to the ground.

Dread slipped and weaved away from the flashing swords.

"Ebondeath! Come to me. To me, my pretty. FEED!"

The fog shuddered and began to slip inward, constricting the space around them.

Dread charged at them, trying to force them backward.

Blades flashed and clanged. Then stopped. They held the same positions as before.

Dread's right shoulder stained a darker red around a ragged hole torn in his shirt. He laughed at them.

"No matter, John Tinker, no matter. My beautiful pet will eat you all soon enough. AHHHHHH!"

Dread staggered as if hit by something heavy, and screamed, "Noooooooooo. . . "

Tinker whirled around to stare at whatever Dread was seeing.

Tai stood there. The great lizard was calmly munching on one of the tentacles. Slowly but surely she was eating Ebondeath.

Spinning back, Tinker lunged. Dread dodged and parried. Sharp buzzing/crackling sounds came from behind Tinker as the electronic twins ripped through the black barrier to stand just inside the opening. Suddenly a thick rope of blue hissing flame arched from them and fell over Tinker, sliding into his weaponkin.

New energy snapped up his arm. The jewel set in the hilt began to pulsate. The blade sang loudly as it slashed at Dread.

Toucan, Goose and Chicken pressed forward, trying to hamper this red-clad enemy.

A great ringing chant spilled from the cliff city, the song of a thousand bells.

"The Golden Eye, the Golden Eye," sang the multitudes inside the castle.

Dread swung away from his lessor antagonists, searching for this new enemy.

The trio, momentarily distracted looked over at Tinker.

Dread whirled, his weapon flickering brightly. Chicken staggered to one side, blood streaming from her left shoulder. Toucan's blade snapped sideways, deflecting Dread's followup thrust. Goose fell to his knees and slashed at Dread's ankles.

Leaping high, Dread hurtled his sword at Tinker's middle. Crouching, Tinker parried up and back, his blade flicking the missile high into the air. As the jeweled hilt of the weaponkin rose and aimed at Dread a golden flash of light shot forth and struck him in the face.

A startled cry.

A blinding flash.

Dread disappeared.

Tinker stared at the spot where Dread had stood, his eyes recovering from the sudden glare. Nothing but a dark splotch and a few tattered fragments of bright red cloth. Odors of ozone and something ugly drifted in the air. The jeweled belt lay in a heap.

"Well, I'll be." Tinker stood up and stared at the

mess, then at the jewel set in the hilt of his weaponkin.

Toucan shouted, "Look, Highness, look!"

Tinker did. Ebondeath was beginning to dissolve. A flood of dirty liquid began pouring down Nature's Track.

Soon, only a few oily puddles remained, rapidly drying into dark stains on the stone.

Tinker walked over and picked up the jeweled belt and hefted it in his left hand. Then he swung his blade up and over, resettling it on his back.

Turning, he looked at his companions.

Chicken sat, half-twisted away from him as Goose, knelling at her side, rapidly bound up her shoulder, resettled her blouse, fashioned a makeshift sling, and turned his attentions to The Guard.

"Princess, are you all right?"

As she stood, she turned and grinned at him.

"Tis naught but most shallow a'cut, My Lord, albiet inst fair anatomy best inspected in private as well as shoulder. All tis well as mine own Brother Goose be most able at this medico business."

Goose turned his head and smiled at Tinker.

"Mine sister shall be quite as good as new in mere few days." He smiled at Tinker and giggled, turning away again, "Sergeant!"

"Yes, SAH!"

"Report."

"All safe, Prince."

"Very well, Sergeant. Stand easy."

"Yes, SAH!"

Goose walked back to Tinker.

"It do appear, Sire, that we have escaped from most foul Dread most lightly. Brother, how fare thee?"

"Well enough. Although it do seem to be mine clothes do be in most dreadful a'state. No pun intended."

Toucan lifted the front of his blouse. The cut opened from side to side.

"It do pear I do jump back just far enough, what?" One eyebrow shot up.

Then his eyes popped wide as he stared past Tinker's shoulder, his sword hissing from its scabbard.

"What be that thing?"

Tinker whirled around reaching for his weaponkin.

The portal stood, shimmering and glowing. The surface flamed, the fire-snakes roiled and hissed at them.

Tinker laughed.

"That thing is our exit from this place. That is how I got here and that is how we will leave. GOOSE, round everyone up and follow me through. Everyone on their guard, we won't know what is over there until we get there. Ready? Toucan?"

"Believe so, Highness." He slowly nodded.

No-one moved forward. All their eyes were fastened upon his face.

"O.K., now what's the problem? Chicken, are those tears? Toucan, speak to me."

Chicken stepped up to him and lightly touched his cheek with her right hand.

"My Lord, tis only that we do be most sore afraid of losing you."

"You can't lose me, just step through."

She shook her head.

"We fear nought stepping through, it be only fear

of . . . " She looked at Toucan.

"Of changing, Highness," he explained. "We all do fear that if we step through that infernal machine we shall become as we were. We will become," his voice fell to the faintest of whispers, " . . . mere toys, unfeeling child play things. We," he waggled his arm at the rest, "would be naught but inert . . . things."

"OH."

Tinker stepped forward and threw an arm around Chicken's good shoulder and grabbed Toucan by the upper arm.

"I fear losing you-all as well." Then he dropped his arms, swung around and lightly brushed a stray hair from her forehead, his eyes fastened upon hers.

"We have no choice, you know. We must go that way. But if, ah, you should change, well, the only thing I could do is put you all in my pockets and keep you there forever. Ready? Princess? Hopefully I would eventually see Big Red again and he could change you all back."

She blinked away forming tears.

"Yes, My Lord."

He spun toward Toucan and the watching Goose, missing her final whispered words.

"Yes, my love."

"Toucan?"

"Where ever you shall lead, Highness."

"Goose?"

"TO THE DEATH, SIRE!"

Smiling broadly, Goose saluted with his sword. The Guard stomped their feet.

"Sergeant!"

"Yes, SAH!"

"Follow me!"

"Yes . . . SAH!"

Tinker had to smile at their enthusiasm and noded at them all.

"O.K., then, let's go."

He walked up to the portal and stepped through wondering what would happen next.

Chicken followed, holding onto Toucan's arm.

Goose, trailed by The Guard, marched after them.

Two-Byte and Tai followed.

The portal winked away.

The black and blasted splotch began to fade away under the intense glare of the sunlight.

Climb High, Climb Far.

Mountain woke with a start.

"DUMPF!"

He was rising, floating upward. The mists swirled away from his face. He could see. Nothing.

A leather-winged Floater drifted up and stared at him, fluttered its wings, and banked away.

He looked down. Far below, he could the rocky hills and the thin yellow ribbon of the Sand Bent with its string-thin blue-green line running down the center.

He craned his head back.

UP.

He was drifting up a cord of mist pluming down past him. Not far past one shoulder he could see the details of a rock cliff face.

Soft voices whispered to him, "Have no fear, friend. Not far above lies the Meadow of Origin. It is as far as we can take you on your journey. From there your path leads higher and higher, up into the realm of Darkness."

He bobbled up and over the lip of rock and was deposited into the middle of a large pool of bubbling haze.

"This is the Meadow of Origin. Standing here, you can see a green canyon. It leads into the heart of the mountains. In that canyon there is food and drink plentiful. From the far end, the path leads the way you must go. To Darkness."

Mountain felt his feet touch, something. He stood up. The voices faded over the edge and down the plume.

"Farewell friend, may your way be clear . . . "

"WAIT, BY DUMPF!"

He ran to the edge and squinted down through the mists.

The voices called up to him, "Rid us of Darkness, friend, rid us of Darkness."

Then silence.

The silence of being alone.

Mountain turned around and began to inspect his new surroundings.

The Meadow of Origin was a small flat spot. In the exact center, the mist boiled up, and flowed outward and down a slight incline, pouring through a sharp notch in the lip of rock. There were a series of steps carved in the stone. They led out of the depression into the wide, green canyon the voices had mentioned.

Shrugging his shoulders, he pushed toward them and started climbing, mumbling to himself, "Food and water is what they said. And it is about time."

His stomach rumbled and grumbled agreement to his thoughts and mumbles.

"Quiet down there, BY DUMPF! You will be taken care of soon enough."

He stomped heavily off the last riser of the stair and tromped out into the canyon vastness. A flat, wide floor rose slowly before him, twisting and turning into the distance, the far end hidden from sight.

The canyon was a crack splitting the mountain range. Somewhere, out of sight, he could hear a waterfall tinkling down a rocky face. Dense clumps of trees and shrubs littered the floor. Long stringers of tall vegetation ran along hidden water sources.

Mountain headed into and through the vegetation, found a waterfall and dropped to his knees, plunged his face into the cold water of the pool, and began to drink deeply.

Finally, he rose, shook the droplets from his face, and sighed, "AHHHHHHH, much better. That certainly recharges the old system."

He jumped to his feet, water sloshing in his gut, and looked around.

"Now, where is the food?"

His nostrils quivered as he turned his head, seeking, searching.

"There, BY DUMPF, food. I can smell it, just over there."

He walked rapidly over and into one the dense clusters of trees and shrubs.

Large, golden clusters of something hung from the trees. The soft breeze caused them to sway gently back and forth. Grabbing one, he took a tentative nibble.

"Delicious."

Mountain worked his way through the patch, stripping all the fruit away as he trundled on. When he exited, his belt creaked ominously. One large hand lightly patted his stomach.

"Well, you are nicely loaded and ready for a nap."

He found a soft place and sat down, smiled, lay back and fell asleep.

When he woke up, the shadows stretched black lines from one side of the canyon to the other. Yawning cavernously, he stood and ambled off toward the furthest reach of the canyon, veering from side to side to sample various of the fruits and vegetables he came across.

Then, in the dim light just before night, he wandered around one of the many bends and twists of the canyon and saw, not too far ahead, a vertical rock wall. It was a box canyon.

"URP! Best to stop right here and inspect this place in the full light of day. Wouldn't want to trip over something and break this or that. OOOOOOOPF!"

He stumbled over the exposed root of a gigantic tree.

"DUMPF!"

He sat where he was, leaned back against the tree trunk and watched the clouds casting a rosy glow on the tops of craggy peaks. Lightening flashed inside them, faint rumblings grumbled down, bouncing down unseen mountain walls.

He fell asleep.

Bright sun filled his eyes, jarring him awake. Mountain stood, blinked, and headed for the rock face. His huge frame was filled out again. All this clothes fit snugly, again.

Carefully he searched the cliff edge, searching for a way up. Some small crack, some tight crevice that would allow a climber access upward, for upward he had to go.

Mountain clambered around a tangle of fallen rock and saw it. There was a path cut into the rock face. It switched back and forth and disappeared from sight. He headed for it.

"BY DUMPF, I found it."

Then he heard it, scrambling noises. It was the sound of many chitinous legs crabbing over the rock above. A shadow fell and blocked his way, spiderlegs waggling, fangs snapping.

"GO BACK! NONE BUT DARKNESSSS MAY PASSSS THIS WAY!"

Mountain jolted to a halt and slipped his great club from his belt.

"By DOUBLE-DUMPF, what an ugly bug you are. Get off the way. Please."

The thing reared up and snarled, drool dripping from multifangs, hissing.

"Beware! I am The Fang of Darknesssss! None may passssss thisss way."

It sprang at him.

Mountain leaped sideways, one of its legs brushed him as it shot pass. Skittering and jerking, it halted and spun around. He was running for the rocky face. It hurtled at his back and sprang high in the air, reaching for him.

Mountain stepped sideways and spun. The sweeping blow from his great cudgel smashed the body of the thing and threw it back against the jagged rock face. The creature slid down the stone face to lie twitching and wiggling on the talus slope, greenish stuff puddling over the rock.

He walked over and kicked more of the loose rock over the mess he had made, carefully wiped the cudgel on the sparse grass and hung it back on his belt. Then he turned and began to climb the stairway.

"Go back, HUMPF!"

He moved upward, climbing at a steady pace. It

was a well-remembered pace that had taken him high into the rugged mountains on Stumpf, higher than many had gone. Among his folk he was well-renowned for scrambling to the highest of peaks. And for returning unharmed. On Stumpf that was something to be admired. Few managed to do so.

Mountain stopped and peered back down the face. Far below he could just see a dark stain on the rock.

"This place will certainly be a better place without things like that trying to frighten away poor but honest travelers. HUMPF MUMPF!"

The rock stairs wove ever higher.

Mountain trudged the serpentine course, admired the view, admired the rock itself, and longtime later, stepped out upon a ledge running across the face. He leaned back against the rock and looked out.

Far away and far down there, he could see the opening to the canyon he had walked through. Beyond that a small green dot that was the Meadow of Origin. And way, way out there, in the valley below, the Sand Bent with a thin green-blue string running down the center. The horizon disappeared in a haze of gray.

"Well, by all the rock and stone, great boulder, you have come aways, haven't you."

He looked up.

The cloud bank was much closer. Thunder rolled, thumped and echoed down at him.

Mountain started along the ledge, which pitched sharply upward. As he climbed, he admired the rockwork, the workmanship that had gone into its construction.

"Fine work, BY DUMPF, fine work."

At the end he found a steep stairway, clawing its way upward. Then another ledge. Then another stairway circling upward.

"BY DUMPF, this just goes on and on and on."

It did.

Over and over he climbed the repetition. Stairway to ledge, stairway to ledge. An upward rhythm: stairway . . . ledge . . . stairway . . . ledge . . . stairway . . . ledge.

Then the ledge ended at the edge of a wide, seemingly bottomless chasm. The path wound along the jagged edge. Fog billowed down there, obscuring the depths. It was flowing someplace, unseen.

"BY DUMPF!"

Just ahead a stone arch curved up and over the space, leaping into the air and landing on the far side.

Mountain smiled at the sight. It was just a slight twitch of the corner of his mouth, but a smile none the less. He hurried toward the bridge and approached the gatehouse.

Dark shadow shifted inside. Chitinous scrambling could be heard.

"GO BACK! NONE BUT DARKNESS MAY PASSSS THIS WAY!"

Multilegged horror jittered into the sunlight baring his way, waggling hungry fangs at him.

"Well, by DOUBLE-DUMPF, it is the twin of that bug-ugly from below."

Mountain ripped the cudgel from his belt and stalked toward it.

"I will BE DUMPFED if there is going to be any messing around this time."

The dancing, darting creature hissed at him,

fangs clattering.

"Beware! I am the Fang of Darknesssssssssss, none may passss thissss way!"

"HUMPF!"

It sprang at him.

A mighty two-handed, over the shoulder swing caught it in mid-flight. Spinning, he sent the thing twirling off the end of his club, crashing against an entrance post. A tangle of broken legs and torn body structure puddled green across the rock pavement.

"BY RUBBLE-RUMPF GRUMPF, it appears these Fangs of Darkness are not worth a good DOUBLE-DUMPF!"

Mountain clumped through the gateway and out onto the arch. He admired the view as he headed for the far side.

Suddenly, from somewhere behind him, came horrid screaming, the yowling of many angry voices.

He spun around and glared at the gateway as a mass of black jostled through the opening onto the arch and scrabbled toward him. Turning, he started for the opposite side.

And jolted to a halt.

Another mass was pouring toward him from that side. Screaming, yowling, fangs slavering.

"BY DUMPF, trapped."

Hefting the cudgel in his right hand, Mountain ducked his head, and charged at this new threat.

There was only one way to reach the side of the chasm he wanted, through the Fang.

The Fang surged along the arch, their numbers interfering with each other as they jostled for the front rank.

Mountain's feet beat a solid thumping counterpoint to the howling coming from both sides.

They collided.

Mountain's left arm swung up to cover his face.

"DUMMMMMMMMPF!"

The impact blasted black thrashing things up into a billowing shock wave. Black horrors tumbled over the low railing to disappear into the thick fog below. Broken bodies wriggled and twisted, fangs gnashing angrily. Mountain's passage created a crushed green path through the throng.

Just beyond the gateway, he stopped and slewed around, sweeping clear the space around him, this cudgel crushing all it met. The survivors ran screeching toward the mass still coming from the far side.

"UMPF-UGLY!"

He turned toward the narrow path and started up the steep slope that was this edge of the chasm. Looking back at the arch, he could see the Fang massed in the center, jostling and shoving. Their howls of rage clear and focused upon him. He began to trot.

Within minutes he had reached yet another stone bridge.

This one jumped a minor but apparently bottomless crevice that entered the main canyon. On the far side, Mountain stopped and peered at the structure, giving the anchor an experimental tap with the tip of his club.

"HUMPF!"

Rearing back, he gave it a heavy blow. Then another. The stone crackled. Another blow and there came a low rumble as dust puffed from opening fissures.

The anchor crumbled, the bridge, now unhinged, tumbled into the hole it once spanned.

Mountain turned and hurried ever onward, ever upward. Sometime later, he looked back. The Fang were crowded along the edge of the crevice, dancing in frustration, yowling imprecations at him. A few scrambled over the edge, searching for a way to cross, a way to get at him.

Shrugging his shoulder, he hung his club back on his belt and climbed higher, into a fog draped world

It was quiet.

The fog damped the sound and softened the light. And muted his senses as well.

As he wound up his way upward, he would pop from the fog layer into a clear air space and for a time be seemingly suspended between two blankets of gray cotton.

Then into the next level.

In and out, layer after layer, a new rhythm, a new cadence.

Up.

    Up.

        UP.

Suddenly he was facing clear space, blue clouded sky. And a long, open plateau. Behind him and just below, the soft gray cloud lake lapped silent waves against the gray stone. The clouds overhead, boiled in angry, disturbed patterns.

Squinting his eyes, Mountain could just see, perched upon a high neck of split and lightening scarred stone, a castellated structure, tall spires piercing the clouds.

"So, there you are, BY DUMPF! As UMPFING

ugly a place as one could ever wish to see."

He began to walk, long strides carrying him rapidly toward his goal, now finally reached, now finally in sight. On this sere rock, he could see no signs of life.

"Just my LUMPFING luck to find that Darkness has relocated. Make me waste my time and waste my energies going up and up and up, just to find the place vacant. Some little note on the door, telling the meatman to stop delivers, please."

Mountain stomped along, muttering to himself. A faint breeze rustled dank stunted grasses and twisted shrubs. Searching hard as he might, he could see no flying things hopping from bent limb to bent limb, no small creatures rustled in the shade.

It was a dead land, a quiet passage.

At the base of a wide stair, he stared up, his eyes following the tortured path that ended at the entryway to the castle. Four battlements marked stopping places on the way.

"BEDUMPF, four resting places. Good spots for admiring the view, such as it is."

He climbed.

Soon, all too soon, it seemed to him, he approached the first structure.

Mountain stopped and peered into the darkness within, some small movement had caught his eye. He saw it again, a small, furtive dodging, here to there.

"BY DUMPF, it seems we have a welcoming committee. One not likely to bring cakes and good drink with it. HUMPF!"

He stepped back a bit just to have more room.

A dark shape lurched forward and filled the

entry. It wore dark colored armor that glistened dully in the light, weapons were clenched in each of the hands.

"Four to one, BY DUMPF!"

Red orbs glared from deep set sockets. A deep bass voice snarled at him.

"HALT! None may pass the Gatekeeper of Darkness unless bidden to do so." It took a step toward him and blocked his way in.

Mountain stepped closer and scanned the stone structure. It seemed he had seen some small weakness in the stone. It was a recurring problem here. All the stone from the valley floor to here seemed to have stress fractures. Some force had treated the building materials poorly.

He jumped forward, jabbed the creature as hard as he could in the chest with the end of his cudgel, and paused.

The Gatekeeper stumbled clattering backward.

Mountain swivelled and struck the spot high on the supporting sidewall he had chosen.

The crack widened. The structure creaked, groaned and collapsed, burying the Gatekeeper as it tried to scrabble over the floor toward him.

A single sweep of his club snapped off the one arm that protruded from the rubble heap, wildly waving its weapon in a vain attempt to strike at him.

"HUMPF! Much too easy."

He clambered over the fragments of stone and stood on the platform on the backside, leaned on the parapet and looked down onto the plateau, tracing the line of the pathway he had followed. A faint howling drifted up to his ears.

He squinted and saw it. A dark squirming mass was pouring onto the plateau at the far end.

"DOUBLE-DUMPF it to here and there, the Fangs didn't give up."

He turned and started up toward the next structure along the stairway.

This time he slipped up as quiet as possible and carefully checked everything. Then he waited. Nothing moved. He stepped into the gateway.

One step.

Two steps.

Three steps.

He was inside, standing in the large open space that was the interior.

Two creatures stepped from the shadows on either side of the exit and bellowed at him, "HALT! We are the Gatekeepers of Darkness. None may pass unless bidden to do so."

They charged.

Mountain jumped forward into the space between them. His club struck one in the chest while he shoved the other sideways with his free hand. He ran for the exit and spun to meet their renewed charge.

Dropping to his knees, he swept the front one off its feet. The other jumped back to avoid the falling body. Mountain sprang into the air, landed on the chest of the fallen one and jabbed the other in the face with the end of his cudgel. A swinging backhand smashed it back against the wall. Crashing heavily it slipped downward and sagged limply to one side.

Mountain scuffed his boots down the side of the thing to clean them and stepped from the mess he made and out the exit to stand peering at the next way station.

"Two more stops. How many more of these Gatekeepers?"

Stalking upward, he watched the next battlement with very cautious eyes. There wasn't a sign of life, not one hint of anything. Of course, there hadn't been at the last place either. From down below the howling of the Fang came louder than before. He stopped and looked back and down.

The Fang were halfway along the plateau, scampering and scrabbling down the pathway. Even from this distance he could begin to make out individual forms and shapes. These things all seemed to be some variant based upon the theme of spider form. Masses of legs, snapping, drooling fangs, glowing red eyes. They clattered along, bent close to the ground, sniffing, following his scent.

Mountain turned and started up toward the third battlement mumbling to himself, "BY DUMPF, this could get most monotonous."

Then he was there, standing, watching, wondering what would be inside. He knew what he thought would be inside. And what it looked like was two shadow figures shaped most like Gatekeepers, trying to stay hidden, not doing a very good job of it.

Mountain leaned over the railing, the low stone wall that bordered the stairs to see whether there was any way around these places. A shear drop to jagged stones carefully set to catch and mangle the hapless visitor who fell. Or were pushed.

"HUMPF!"

He shrugged and stomped up into the battlement. This one had a roof. It was just a bit more ornate in design.

Two Gatekeepers grabbed him, clinging tightly to each of his arms. Their jaws clamped upon his upper forearms, rending and tearing. Another charged at him, multiple arms flailing a variety of cutting and crushing weapons at his chest. Two knives, a spear and a club battered his chest.

Reeling backward, Mountain pulled the arm grabbers with him. One foot thumped the front one in the gut and shoved it stumbling away. With a sweep of his left arm, Mountain lifted and smashed the Gatekeeper against the wall, twisting, dragging the other around, as he kneed the left one. One .. two .. three.

As it crumbled he used his weight to mash the other into the wall with his shoulder and warded off a three-pronged spear thrust at his eyes by Gatekeeper number three lurching back into the combat. Sparks flashed as the prongs struck stone. Mountain gasped the weapon just below the tines and wrenched it up and away, plunging it into the throat of the snarling Gatekeeper still attacking his right arm. Gurgling it pulled away, fingers grasping the weapon still firmly implanted and tugged.

Spinning to one side, Mountain's cudgel swung in an upward arc and caught number three under the chin, thrusting it back against the wall. The headless monster collapsed, arms and legs twitching, weapons falling from loosening grips to clatter on the floor.

The Gatekeeper against the far wall was struggling to regain his feet as Mountain leaped and kicked it in the forehead. He turned, searching for the third one.

Through the doorway he could see it lurching up

the stairs, headed for the fourth battlement. Mountain charged after it. Hearing the heavy footfalls, it spun, gurgled in terror and leaped over the railing.

Mountain ran to the spot and leaned over to peer down. Pieces of the Gatekeeper were scattered around the stone teeth below. Twisting his head, he could see the path running along the spine of the plateau.

The Fang were approaching the base of the staircase. They had seen the falling body and now saw him staring at them. Screams of rage and bloodlust roared at him as they hurtled toward the first stair.

He spun and ran up toward the last battlement, chanting in rhythm to his pulling feet.

"One to go . . . one to go . . . . one to go. . ."

Thundering up the staircase he tore into the fourth structure, noting as he slid to a halt that this one had high ceilings, was well lighted, and had massive doors at the entrance and the exit.

Whirling around he leaped at the great wooden entrance door and slammed it shut and quickly slid the blocking beam in place.

"There, BY DUMPF, that should slow down those things."

Turning back toward the other doorway, he ran.

Four Gatekeepers crashed into him, bowling him from his feet, throwing back toward the center of the gatehouse. In a tangle of arms and legs, punctuated by curses from Mountain and screams and snarls from the gatekeepers, they tumbled, scrambled and pummeled each other across the floor.

"UUUUUHHHHHHHHH . . . AHHHHHHHH."

Mountain heaved himself upward, staggering to his feet, spinning wildly, his attackers all trying to pull him back down.

One Gatekeeper tumbled away, then another. Mountain's forearm crushed a third against the wall as the fourth scampered away. Flashing elbows and knees battered one Gatekeeper slipping down the wall. Mountain gave the crumpled form a final kick and twisted around.

The three Gatekeepers scuttled back and forth in front of the exit, crouching and snapping at him, their many arms waggling a wide assortment of lethal appearing weapons at him.

Sunlight streaming through the doorway twinkled bright flashes across the room.

Whipping his cudgel around, he swung his arm up and back and around and with an underhanded sweep launched the heavy, wooden missile.

The loud smacking sound echoed in the closed space as the central Gatekeeper disappeared backward from the opening.

The two paused, then leaped toward him, fierce ululations hurting his ears, as they attacked.

Mountain sank downward, settled his feet, and threw his arms wide, and waited.

A knife banged off his chest. His hands clapped together, banging two heads, collapsing them, pushing the sagging bodies to one side.

Wiping his hands of his pants, Mountain walked out the doorway, bent down and retrieved his club, and sauntered upward, toward the castle perched not all that far above.

"UMPF, so far so good. But this is getting tiring. I wonder if there might be food in there."

His stomach rumbled softly.

Stepping carefully up onto the wide, stone platform that formed the courtyard in front of the main castle gate, he approached the front door.

He ignored the wild cries coming from the Fang as they coursed up through the second Gatehouse, stepped closer to the door, his eyes searching for some indication of how to enter.

The great gate in front of him swung silently back.

Mountain stopped at the threshold and peered inside. He couldn't see anything moving in there. Nothing made a sound.

"UMPF!"

He stepped through and past the open gate. It closed. The dull, resonating boom echoed and reechoed from the vast spaces before him.

He finally stood inside the Castle of Darkness.

Overhead, the ceiling disappeared in the dim light. Something flew by, soft twittering sounds drifted down from above. At the far end of this hall, he could just see a staircase that rose and then branched to the right and to the left.

Something lurked on the first landing. It was the vaguest of shadows.

"BY DUMPF, now what will it be?"

Hefting his cudgel, he stalked slowly toward the only way to go. Other than the main gate, he had yet to see any other opening to this hall.

He stopped, one foot one the first stair and squinted up at whatever it was that was waiting for him. The thing shifted from side to side. It was mostly shadow. Three glowing green eyes burned down at him.

Carefully, one step at a time, Mountain climbed toward it.

On the landing, he stopped.

The creature flowed to his right, guarding that flight of stairs.

"So, BY DUMPF!"

Mountain stepped toward it. It didn't move. Cautiously, he poked it with the tip of his club. It slipped right through it, no resistance.

"DOUBLE-DUMPF!"

Mountain stepped into and through the thing. He felt it as a cold, chilling cloud of frigid fog nothing. Three risers up, he turned around and looked down. It glared back at him but made no move to follow him. Shaking his head from side to side, Mountain turned around and started up.

"Mighty Boulder, as our twice-parent would say, that is a very strange thing, a very strange thing indeed."

He hiked higher and higher, finally reaching another landing. Something above was coming down the stairs toward him. It made a clattering, banging noise as it descended rapidly.

Out of the darkness hurtled an armor clad being. Mountain crouched and speared it in the middle with his cudgel. Pieces of armor showered around him, clanking and banging down the stairs, bouncing off the wall.

"This place is getting to be rather bothersome, BY DUMPF! If not just a bit boring. All I am getting is lots of HUMPFING exercise."

The second landing was not all that far up the staircase from the first. There was yet another staircase leading up.

Mountain started up, was just placing his foot on the first riser when another of the armor clad beings came crashing down the stairs at him. Battering this one out of the way he stepped up. Three steps and another came down toward him. Its parts were swiftly sent clanging down the stairs.

He twisted, placed his back against the wall and began to edge his way up as another, then another of the things, appeared. Striking, thrusting, battering his way higher, ever higher toward the upper reaches of the castle, Mountain sent, what he was beginning to think was a never-ending stream of the things, downward.

The din was beginning to hurt his ears.

Then it stopped.

He leaned against the wall, glad to take a rest, breathing deeply. Peering down the staircase, it seemed to him to be covered with bits and pieces of armor as far as he could see, Mountain booted a few pieces lying by his feet downward. Ricocheting from the wall, they started a small avalanche of parts cascading toward the last landing.

"HUMPF!"

He started upward, once again. He was beginning to feel the strain of endless combat. His arms were sore, his legs were sore, his back hurt. His stomach rumbled loudly, demanding large quantities of food, a reminder that he was burning up great quantities of energy. His clothes no longer fit as snug.

Mountain plodded up and up, suddenly recognizing an old feeling, one he had felt on the highest peaks of Stumpf. It was the bone weary trudge of the mountain climber driving himself to the top. It was the feel of an iron will forcing on a body that wished to quit and rest.

His foot reached for the next stair, he stumbled and lurched forward, into a room. After staggering a few steps, Mountain stopped, and stood swaying, checking his new surroundings.

This was more than a room, it was a throne room.

At the other end, a giant figure sat upon a throne and stared at him. A jeweled necklace glittered bright flame: red, yellow, amber, white, green. The jewels send rays of lights sparkling, flashing from their facets. As it watched him, the creature idly fingered the jewels with long fingers, silver talons reflecting multicolored light.

Mountain started toward whoever, or whatever, it was.

The creature rose to its feet.

"So. You are finally here. Place yourself in my service."

"No, BY DUMPF, not I."

"So sad, I could have used such a one as you."

A bolt of flame smashed into Mountain's chest, driving him to his knees. He lurched upward. Another bolt struck. He dropped. Then another bolt flashed out, another, another, another.

Mountain wobbled and sagged forward, shoulders slumping, head falling toward his chest. Slowly, painfully, his arms dragged his great club from his side and around past his knees. Squinting, he made his eyes focus, his fingers fumbling to maintain their hold. Using both hands, he stood the cudgel upright and using it as a crutch, hauled himself to his feet.

"Join me now?"

"NO!"

A bolt of flame threw him backward, crashing into a heap. As he struggled to sit up, then rise to his knees, he heard someone speaking to him. At first, he couldn't understand the words, then as he strained they became clear.

You, Mountain, with the gift of the Gett will correct this. Here. A small device. It fits your weaponkin . . .

He squinted at the hilt of his club. It was still there. Somehow the small lens-like thing had remained firmly attached, and in spite of all the violence it had been subjected to, undamaged as he had battered his way to this spot. Dragging the club toward him, he slowly raised it to an upright position, waiting for another blast from Darkness.

No enemy may harm you, no blow disturb you.

You are Gettish . . .

A golden eye, gleaming bright,
    Doth slay Darkness in his might . . .

Something was wrong with the jewel set in the end of his cudgel. It seemed to be pulsating, a soft golden light.

Placing one hand flat upon the floor, he readied himself for the thrust from weaken legs, ready to heave himself to his feet. He was so tired. The stone felt warm, comfortable. A mild tingle seeped from it into his fingers, up his arm. The energy eased its way from deep under the foundations of the castle. His fatigue began to fade. Suddenly he knew the answer.

"DUMPF!"

Mountain looked up.

Darkness was standing, watching him, even as it was molding a dense flaming orb in one hand. This would be the final thing to drain all the energy from Mountain's body.

"No, BY DUMPF, NO!"

Mountain shoved the hilt of the cudgel forward, pointing the lens at Darkness.

A flash of light flamed forth, ripped through the creature's chest, driving it backwards from the platform, stumbling, crashing into the back wall.

"Noooooooo . . ."

It was a final scream of rage and surprise commingling into a last gasp. Yellow flames flared and died. The monster slumped to one side and lay still.

Something tinkled and pattered to the stone floor. Mountain stared at the lens lying on the floor, broken into four pieces.

"One use, I only had one use."

He wobbled, struggled, and finally managed to stand, staggering from side to side. He headed for the form of Darkness, his eyes fastened upon the bright flames glittering around its neck. Reaching down he wrenched the necklace over the slack head and tugged it down over his own. The jewels felt warm, a light pleasant tickle that soothed.

Heaving himself around, he searched the hall for more enemies.

"AHHHHHHHHHHH!"

Fatigue left him with a rush that rocked him back upon his heels. The blood coursed wildly through his veins. He was alive, more alive than he had ever felt before. Energy seemed to be crackling from the necklace to his fingertips. The jewels flashed rays of color against the furthest wall.

Something behind him hissed. He whirled.

Darkness was dissolving, puddling across the floor. Wisps of acrid, yellow tinged smoke drifted from the disappearing thing.

The throne and platform erupted with a flash, flame blowing straight up through the ceiling and roof. Dense black clouds swirled above. Lightening crackled from them and struck down through the opening, splashing from the floor.

Mountain ran for the stair down.

A jagged crack shot in front of him as the front portion of the castle broke away, sweeping with it, the front wall, the highest battlement, and the yowling horde of the Fang just then charging toward the front gate.

"BY DUMPF, if this isn't a repeat of Doom's RAR-RUMPFING place, I will eat every stone in this place."

The side wall shuddered and fell outward. Pieces of the roof thumped around him. Ducking and weaving, he ran searching for some other way out of the throne room. There had to be a way out before the crumbling structure took him with it.

Something moved. His eyes caught the motion through the billowing dust. Leaping to one side he swept his cudgel between himself and whatever it might be.

It was the portal.

The fire-snakes roiled and hissed at him. Flames danced across its surface. Through the heat distortion, Mountain could just make out a large, open valley crowded with figures in motion.

Clutching his cudgel tightly, he charged through.

The floor fell from beneath his feet as the portal winked out.

I Was Yesterday, I Know Today, Who Is Tomorrow?

A small figure sat huddled on the ground. He was waiting, alone and miserable. He didn't know where he was, but he knew that he was alone and that he was lost.

Behind him a shape appeared, silent, unannounced. Someone stepped from it and stumbled over him.

"Watch it, watch it," announced this person, scooping him up and lunging to one side. "You almost got trampled upon, fella."

Others came jumping after, landing with light steps on the ground, stopping, peering around, and then running over to join the first one.

Princess Chicken threw her arms around Tinker's neck, kissed him hard, and beamed happily into his face.

"We did make it, My Lord, we do be most alive and well." She jumped back, startled at the lump he was cradling in his arms.

"But what strange thing be this you do be a'holding so dear?"

Tinker laughed at her.

"You're certainly alive all right. And here comes Goose and The Guard." He threw one arm around her waist, cradling his find in his other arm.

Toucan stood to one side and tried to be discrete.

They watched as Goose hurried over followed by The Guard.

Then Two-Byte and Tai appeared.

The portal winked out just as the dinosaur's long tail cleared the opening. Tai belched once, then again. Black smoke rings drifted away.

"Looks like her last meal didn't agree with her." Tinker set down the small person he was holding.

"But let's see what we have found. And almost stepped on."

The figure daintily brushed imaginary debris from its clothes, and tugged everything into just the correct shape.

"Why John Tinker, do you not recognize an old traveling companion when you pick them up?"

"SORROWFUL! Well, I'll be." Whipping his arm from around Chicken, Tinker grabbed him and lifted him up by the armpits, a smile splitting his face.

"It is you. Where have you been? Where are the others? What's been happening? Why such a dower expression?"

Sorrowful wiggled in his hands, and frowned at the wrinkles in his clothes that Tinker was causing.

"If you set me down, I would be glad to tell you. After you introduce me to your new companions, especially this demonstrative and lovely lady." He twisted his head and smiled at Chicken.

Tinker set him down. Sorrowful bowed gallantly to Chicken.

"Madame." She curtsied.

Tinker waved his arms, ushering the others over.

"Gather around gang, so everyone can be introduced to everyone."

They all crowded around, staring at this new person in their midst. Sorrowful stared back.

"This," explained Tinker, "is my boon traveling companion and raconteur, Sorrowful Mistiding, who I told you about before and whom one and all may address as Sorrowful." He turned and pointed.

"And these folk, are the dashing Princes Toucan and Goose, their sister, the Princess Chicken, that rowdy crowd over there are The Guard, commanded by Goose, the whirling buzzing pair are Two-Byte, and the huge animal is Tai. She is a stegosaurus."

Tinker clapped his hands together.

"Now that everyone knows everyone, how about we sit and visit before we head into whatever this place is." He dropped to the ground. Chicken sat next to him.

"So, Sorrowful, what happened to you? Where are the others, Smoke and Mountain?"

Sorrowful stood in front of Tinker and slowly shook his head.

"I do not know where Mountain is. Smoke and I assumed that he was with you."

Tinker shook his head by way of answer, then spoke, "Nope. Seems we were all separated from each other. But you said, Smoke and I. Where is she?"

He peered around them and called, "SMOKE, where are you? Smoke!"

Sorrowful gently touched his arm.

"She is not here, John Tinker, she is gone." Tears ran down his face as he struggled to maintain his composure.

"What do you mean, gone? Where is she,

Sorrowful?"

Sorrowful collapsed into a miserable heap, and stared up at Tinker's face.

"I do not know, John Tinker, I just do not know. She leaped out into the Light-In-The-Dark and it exploded and she was gone. I searched but there was no trace, she had just vanished."

"A 300-400 pound carnivore doesn't just vanish." Tinker craned his neck and looked at his surroundings. "Is this the elseplace where she vanished?"

"No, no, no, no no, no, NO! This is not Growing Deep. This is someplace else. What someplace else this is, I do not know. It is just where the portal put me. And now you and all these other folk. They had better all sit down while I tell of that place. It is a long tale and one that I thought, then, I would relish retelling. But now, I relish it not. Sit, please sit."

The company settled themselves around him as he began.

"SO! In a time and at a time and after we stepped through the portal taking us from the place where Big Red dwelled, we found ourselves in this strange place. We were alone, just Smoke and I. The portal had winked out and no-one else was around. We thought we had been forever separated from the rest of The Four. We saw a path and started to follow it. And after awhile . . . "

Sorrowful's voice, rising and falling with the rhythm and cadence of telling his tale, bringing the tale to life, captured his audience as his skills always did. In the retelling of the tale, he momentarily forgot his sorrows and anguish as well. All around them eyes widened in horror and fear as he described the final confrontation in the Blasted Spot and the arcing leap of Smoke.

". . . and so when I searched the rubble all I found was this strange jewel. The portal appeared and I stepped through and came into this place, where I found that I was, this time, totally alone. I sat where I landed, not caring what would happen next. Then, suddenly, there you all were, a great crowd of people and strange beings pouring from the portal just moments after I had arrived. That is the tale."

Sorrowful sat silently, surrounded by a silent audience. Tears streaked his face.

"Now, tell me your tale."

Tinker nodded.

"O.K. It's like this. As I stepped from the portal I tangled my feet in something, spun around and ran my head into a tree. And knocked myself out. When I came to, I found this bunch all standing around watching me and addressing me as Lord Tinker. As it turned out, they were . . . "

The audience nodded at places, agreeing with their parts in the story as Tinker talked on. Sorrowful sat immobilized, listening intently and registering every word, every detail, every piece of action in his remarkable memory. All of this he added to his great tale, the true saga of all that had occurred to one and all. And, as before, he forgot his sorrow and his loss.

His eyes gleamed as Tinker described the great city in the cliff and their final confrontation with Dread. Sorrowful noted the belt twinkling around Tinker's waist, and filed away all the details of that also.

". . . and so I picked it up and put it on, it seemed the thing to do. Then the portal appeared. And here we are. And no-one changed back into a toy. And it seems that this quest is winding its peculiar way along some rather strange paths." He looked from face to face and then back at Sorrowful.

"So Smoke is dead and Mountain is somewhere. Perhaps we will find him stomping around somewhere, just like we found you sitting here. What do you think, Sorrowful, is this the land where the Evil One lives? Can we finally finish and go home?"

"I do not know, John Tinker. I just arrived a few moments before you did." He stood and stretched.

Tinker rose to his feet.

"Well I guess we won some and lost some. Not much to say for all the trouble we have been through."

"But, John Tinker, we have gained some knowledge we did not have, have we not?"

"Like what?"

"For one, we now know that these weaponkin have strange attributes. They do things that The Thought did not mention, or, perhaps, did not have time to mention. I could talk with Smoke by touching the Golden Eye. Perhaps we might talk to each other in the same manner. I shall walk over here, you turn your back and speak to me. In your mind."

"O.K." Tinker turned around, his finger on the Golden Jewel.

"Ready?"

"Yes."

Do you hear me, Sorrowful?

I do, I do, I do, I do. "It works, John Tinker, it works!"

Sorrowful shot into the air and clicked his heels together. And thudded to the ground.

"Oh wonderful, wonderful!"

He pointed his dagger hilt at a nearby tree.

"I wonder if I can shoot a golden ray. Nothing. Nothing happens."

Chicken cleared her throat and spoke.

"Praps, Regent Sorrowful, it only do work pon evil things."

He turned and smiled at her, then frowned,

"Princess, I am not a regent, whatever a regent is, but you are probably correct. Blasting innocent trees is probably not what these things are for."

Toucan turned toward Chicken and nodded.

"Fair Sister, I do believe me most humbly that he do be correct ins't the latter but not in the former for me'thinks that he be most formally and properly a Count."

Sorrowful turned to Tinker for help.

"Regent? Count? What are these titles and what do they mean?"

Tinker stepped closer to him.

"They sorta like your title of Master Storyteller, or whatever, and it is how they see other people like you and me. You will just have to settle for a title." He bent over and whispered into Sorrowful's ear, "They will be uncomfortable if you refuse."

"Ahhhh, I see," whispered back Sorrowful. He spun around and bowed.

"Prince Toucan, the title of Count sounds like a good one to me. So I am, now and henceforth, Count Sorrowful." He made another bow, very low, very elegant.

Toucan, Goose, and Chicken returned his bow, their swords sweeping in elegant and fancy patterns as they did so.

Sorrowful jumped back and gasped, "My, oh my! They do that well." He looked at Tinker, a small frown forming.

"Is she dangerous?"

Tinker smiled and shook his head.

Chicken frowned at him.

He smiled back, and said to Sorrowful, "Not to us. I think." Laughing, he added, "Yes, she, and they, do that well. Fortunately her wound was not in her sword arm."

Sorrowful's interest shifted, he poked Tinker at the waist.

"Does that belt, those jewels, ah, do they glow from within?"

Tinker glanced down and touched the belt gently.

"Does seem that way. In some ways it has the same feel as the weaponkin. But I really don't know what it is supposed to do. But, somehow, wearing it seemed correct. So there it is."

The belt glowed with suppressed energy. If anyone had been listening closely they might have heard the small crackling sounds it made to itself.

"SAH!"

"Yes, Sergeant?"

"SAH, a path, over here." Goose turned and ran toward the call. In a moment he returned and pointed toward where The Sergeant was standing.

"Sire, The Guard have found path leadin' from here. Tis a wide'un paved with stone. Follow it?"

Tinker nodded.

"Might as well. It is as good a thing to do as any

other. For the moment."

"Righto, Sire. For the moment. We will utilize the same formation as before. Sergeant."

"SAH!"

"Two groups. Hustle, man, hustle!"

"Yes, SAH!" The Sergeant bustled off bellowing orders, The Guard running to obey.

Sorrowful tugged at Tinker's sleeve.

"John Tinker, I think that I shall walk with the first group." Tinker shrugged his shoulders.

"If you wish. But you will have to convince Goose, not me. The first group will run into whatever danger there might be first. And Goose takes his guardianship duties very, very seriously."

Sorrowful caressed the jewel in the hilt of his dagger softly with his left thumb.

"With the Golden Jewels we may converse between the groups. Thus I could tell you immediately what we faced and thus lessen the degree of danger to those who follow."

"I am convinced, but you still have to convince Goose."

"Of course." Sorrowful ran over to join the first group of The Guard as they made ready to start down the path. After much arm waving and animated conversation between Goose and Sorrowful, Sorrowful turned and waved a jaunty good-bye, and walked off with them.

The second group waited for the chosen interval and followed.

Tinker smiled at his companions.

"Well, Princess, here we go again. How's your arm?"

"As well as might do be expected, My Lord. In but some few days t'will be as good as gold. Shall we?"

They trailed after the second contingent of The Guard. Behind them came Tai and Two-Byte. Toucan walked on one side of Tinker, Chicken on the other.

The path was a wide, well constructed roadway made of think slabs of stone tightly fitted together. The surface was worn smooth indicating that heavy traffic came this way.

Tinker wondered what type of heavy traffic came this way.

"Certainly built this to last."

"Aye, My Lord, tis that. Lord?"

"Yes?"

"Tis truly a most strange gray sword you do wear in such most strange a'manner."

"How so?"

"Strange color and strange behavior, sticking bat-like to you." She smiled.

"The gem do be most beautiful though mounting do be fair odd in form and workmanship."

"Would you like to take a closer look?" Tinker reached up to sweep the weaponkin down and around.

She lightly danced away.

"Nay My Lord. Praps later, ah, when I might inspect it at greater leisure."

"O.K., just remind me when you want to do that." He swung it back to its resting place on his back.

"Oh aye, My Lord, that I will." She walked silently for awhile, then glanced sideways at him.

"Canst truly speak with Count Sorrowful, mind to mind, simply by touching fair gem set in monstrous hilt?"

"Sure can. Shall I ask him how things are going up front?"

"   "Aye. If you would, My Lord."

"O.K." Tinker reached up and rested his left hand over the Golden Eye.

Sorrowful?

Yes? John Tinker?

It's me all right. Anything happening up there?

No. We are just walking along. The Guard set a fair pace. There has been no sign of anyone, yet. Have you noticed the color of this land?

Noooooo. Why?

Everything here is in shades of gray: the trees, the shrubs, grasses, rocks, dirt. Everything. All blue and gray.

So it is. Talk to you later.

Tinker looked at Chicken.

"Sorrowful says that they haven't seen anything yet, no signs of anyone else going this way. He also called our attention to the color of the environment.'

She looked around and nodded.

"Indeed, this do most drab a'place be. All things colored by but the same hue. Passing strange a'place this."

"Sure is."

"My Lord?"

"Ummm?"

She cast a careful sideways glance around Tinker at Toucan who appeared to be lost in thought.

"Be this how you do be with the noble and fair Lady Smoke?"

"What way?"

"Speaking mind to mind."

"Seemed about the same only we didn't need to

use the jewel thing. There is one funny thing though."

"Some small jest?"

"No, not funny, strange. After a while the two of you sort of blend together yet remain separate. I think that is what happened to Sorrowful when they were separated. It was like a piece of yourself being torn away, like losing a piece of your mind, like losing a piece of yourself. A terrible lose."

"Didst feel this way, My Lord?" Her hand rested lightly on his arm.

He shook his head.

"No, I did not. Perhaps it was because you and the rest were there. Sorrowful thought he was alone and abandoned. But I had, have, company. Very pleasant company, I might add." He laughed.

"I think you are blushing." He smiled at her.

She frowned at him, yanked her hand away and stared fixedly at their surroundings.

Tinker looked over at Toucan. He was carefully looking elsewhere. So Tinker decided that he had better do the same.

The path meandered through a thin cover of the blue-gray trees and shrubs and debouched onto the top of a long and narrow gray ridgeline. They were high, very high: mountains and canyons stretched away into a hazy mist horizon. Far below, in the canyon bottoms, they could see thread-thin rivers coursing in the narrow and constricted flatlands. Faint white smudges indicated rapids where the valley floors suddenly broke and pitched downward. In front of them, flying creatures drifted and soared on the thermal air currents. Far ahead, toward the end of the ridgeline, Tinker could see the bright red dots, the bright white dot, that was

The Guard advance party.

Can you see us, Sorrowful?

Mostly assuredly, John Tinker. The brilliant yellow of Princess Chicken's garb stands out as a ray of sunshine in an otherwise drab countryside. Also when Two-Byte flashes. Tai is so large that she makes a noticeably shape. But down here we have yet to see a sign of life on the path.

O.K., just checking. Later.

He walked along musing on the view, the monochromatic landscape and his newest companions, now that he really had some time to do that. He decided that she was rather attractive. Rather forward though. And certainly surprising. He had never had the experience of waking up with an unknown woman in his bed before. Well, at least, not like that.

Far ahead he saw The Guard turning down and off the end of the ridgeline. This section of the path had small clumps of vegetation covered with spiny leaves growing along it. A small creature suddenly darted from one clump to the next. It was blue-gray.

"Toucan, what do you think of this place?"

"Passing strange place, Highness. Rather dull, but interesting. I find that, in spite of the color and overall simple tonal quality, that there do be a certain character to it. Yet, all in all, tis most strange. This pavement, well laid and heavily worn, suggests a people skilled in the engineer trade and with a well developed economy. Yet neither hide nor hair of fellow traveler do we see. Be that not strange, Highness?"

"Certainly is. But maybe this is the wrong time of year. Traffic this high up could be seasonal. I suppose."

Toucan nodded slowly.

"True, true. Still . . ." He pointed.

"What now do we approach?"

Just ahead of them, the pavement twisted and turned sharply downward, over the edge. A series of broad steps led them over the edge. At the bottom, the path widened into a square, open space. Part of that feature protruded out over the edge of the mountain flank, part was carved back into the solid rock. A low railing ran along the outer edge.

When they reached it, Tinker walked over and peered over the edge of the platform. He could see the massive stone pillars supporting the section he was standing upon.

"WOW, what a view." He waved and leaned further.

"Come take a look at this. If you fell from here you wouldn't touch a thing until you hit the bottom."

Chicken ran up, grabbed the back of his belt.

"MY LORD, nay lean so, thou mightst tumble down."

He laughed.

"Take a look, Princess." And straightened up.

"It is quite a view."

She stepped to his side, her arm still firmly clenching his belt, and stared out and down into the vast emptiness of this world.

Neither of them said a thing.

They watched the waterfalls, dim hazy, misty things, blurred by the intervening haze, as they drifted white plume down distance mountain sides. Small creatures soared and floated up to stare at these strangers, squeaking at them and to each other. One floated ghost quiet past them, rolling one eye at the silent pair.

"Ahem . . . AHEM, Highness, tis time for us to depart this place."

Tinker's head snapped around to stare at Toucan who was standing a proper distance removed from his other side.

"The Guard do be moving further and further ahead of us, Highness. It may not be safe to allow this."

Tinker stared at him before remembering where he was.

"HUH? Oh, yes, of course." He turned from the gray vista and started for the far side of the platform, Chicken loosening her grip as he did so.

"Then let's go."

Chicken shot a sharp look a Toucan and walked quickly after Tinker, regaining his side.

One eyebrow shot straight up, then Toucan composed his face and followed them.

From the platform the pavement slipped down the mountain side, a narrow ledge gouged from the parent rock. They were dropping lower and lower and deeper and deeper into one of the canyons.

As they traveled, the shadows lengthened and stretched and then they walked into twilight. And came to another of the open platforms.

The entire body of The Guard waited there, standing and talking. To one side Goose and Sorrowful stood in deep conversation. Both looked up as Tinker and his companions entered and walked over to join them.

Sorrowful bobbled up and down on his toes, and grinned at Tinker.

"Greetings, John Tinker, Princess and Prince, it

was a pleasant and fair walk was it not?"

Goose beamed at them.

"Hail, Sire. We do camp here for this night."

Tinker smiled at them both.

"Yes, it was a nice walk in rather pleasant country. Right, Goose, this is as good a place as any I've seen. But it is rather barren camping."

Goose nodded, and waved one arm at the platform.

"Most true, Sire, but defended easily. Two entrances, no more. This platform be perched most wrenlike on high ridgeline, bein' straight down on all sides. Easily defended, quite safe." He strode off to see to the depositions of The Guard.

Overhead the last rays of sunshine stabbed across the sky and then were cut off by the mountains.

Darkness dropped over them sudden and complete.

Tinker walked cautiously to the edge of the platform and peered downward and outward. The only lights he could see were unknown and strange constellations in the sky. If anyone lived down there, it seemed that they didn't use artificial light. Or they didn't show them. He wondered where the people of this land were.

A faint breeze blew across the stone platform. Tinker found that after sitting down, his back against the wall, that it passed overhead. The heat retained by the stone wall and floor seeped into stiff muscles and relaxed them. Through the darkness he heard soft footsteps approaching.

"My Lord, may I join thee?"

"Certainly may, Princess. Pull up some floor and

sit a spell. It is hard but warm and rather pleasant."

She sat next to him, leaned back against the wall, and stretched her legs out.

"Nice night out, isn't it?"

"Oh aye, My Lord, tis certainly that." She leaned gently against his side.

"Princess?"

"My Lord?"

"I am really glad that Big Red gave me that toy box. I, ah, don't really have any idea how all this quest that we are on will wind up, but, ummmm, well, I am very pleased that we will be sharing how ever many days there are left to it."

"Be there only a few more days?"

"That wasn't exactly what I meant. What I meant was that I am happy that we may be together however things work out."

"Thee do sound most be'vexed, My Lord."

"Vexed? Worried is more like it. I don't see any sense to what we are doing or to what is being done to us, however you want to look at it. All we are doing is being popped from pillar to post, so to speak. Each of these places has something ugly lying in wait for us. And while we are, while I am, surviving, we have lost Smoke for sure and probably Mountain as well. So, that is one-half of the original group, a fifty-percent mortality rate. And that is not a good number."

"But here do we be."

"Right. You guys are here. So, in terms of numbers, there are more than before. I guess I should be happy." He sighed.

"Why do thee worry so, then?"

"Because I do not want to lose any more people.

I do not want to see any more wounds. To tell you the truth, I just want to go home. I just want all of us to go home, alive and well."

"This do thee bother most deeply?"

"Oh, it does that, Princess, it does that. Losing Smoke was, is . . . painful. So, how's your arm, Princess?"

"Most surely on the mend, Fair Prince. If you should decide to slide most gentle a'arm around here t'would be no matter fretful."

"Like this?"

"Ummmmmm, most pleasant and friendly, My Lord. But, we must sit somewhat quietly, for a few more days."

"A few more days?"

"Oh aye. Brother Goose do say t'would be but a mere matter of two, three, days more for wounded arm do be good as new. Then we shall see, we shall."

Tinker didn't respond.

He had fallen asleep.

The first rays of sunshine poured over the mountain peaks and tickled the surface of the stone wall.

They woke Toucan, always the first riser, who stood, yawned, stretched, and walked over to stand and look at the slumbering pair. They had slumped together.

He turned and looked around the platform. All slept soundly except for two of The Guard standing and watching the entry ports. He looked down again, one eyebrow rising and falling.

"Ah, sister mine, what will come of this?" His

boot nudged Tinker's foot.

"Arise, Highness, fair dawn do smile pon us and bright day do be not far behind."

Tinker's eyes popped open.

"Huh? Oh, Toucan, morning already?" Lurching to his feet, he stretched and groaned.

"Ahhhhhh, I will be stiff for a week. Sleeping on hard rock is hard sleeping all right." He ruffled Chicken's hair.

"Wake up, sleepy head. Another day, another hike." He turned.

The first section of The Guard were already setting off, Goose and Sorrowful in the lead. Sorrowful waved at him.

Tinker bent down and shook her shoulder.

"Wake up, Princess, we are being left behind."

One blue eye opened and rolled and focused upon his face.

"Ummmmmm, My Lord. What?"

"It is time for us to go." He straightened up.

"OH." Her other eye flew open. She jumped to her feet, sleep rapidly draining from her face as she checked the platform, noting the disposition of the remaining Guard, who were just then starting out.

"Near time for us, My Lord. Morning, Brother Toucan."

Goose came charging back onto the platform and ran over to them.

"A thousand pardons, Sister, but I had seen not to thy wound. '

She turned her back on Toucan and Tinker as Goose opened her blouse to check the bandages and the progress of her healing. Then satisfied at what he saw, he rebuttoned her blouse, kissed her check, whispered in her ear, turned and ran swiftly out and away.

Toucan cast her a solemn glance.

"Sister?"

She smiled at him.

"Mine arm be well a'mending, Toucan. The Goose do state t'will be not but one day, two no more."

He beamed at the news.

"Indeed. Highness, it do be for us time for exit."

Tinker smiled at him and started toward the exit, "Lead on MacToucan."

"Mac Toucan, Highness?"

"Bad joke, Prince. One of these days remind me to try and explain it."

They started down the trail, followed by Tai and Two-Byte.

The stone shone brightly in the dawnlight, running straight and true down the slope. Suddenly the sun popped up from behind the near ridgeline.

Day had arrived.

Tinker strolled along, humming happily to himself, enjoying the early morning sunlight, feeling the air begin to warm. He really did feel pretty good, considering what he had to sleep upon last night.

Next to him, Chicken yanked off her sling, stuffed the material into a hip pocket, and began to swing her injured arm and rub the wounded shoulder.

"What's the matter, Princess?"

"Do itch itself most mightily, My Lord."

"Itches? You do heal fast."

"Indeed. I do suppose it do be naught but our blood blue."

Tinker gave her a wry smile.

"Well, I suppose royal blood is better than what we peasants have."

"Nay, My Lord, t'were nary analogy We do speak pon but most real blood color a'oozing out wound ugly. Hast thee see not?"

"Ah, no, I didn't. In the excitement of the moment I am afraid I was trying to watch too many other things. But I suppose that you are right, those of royal blood ought to heal faster." He thought that he might as well be agreeable.

"Blood blue, My Lord, tis color nay lineage pon that which we do be a'speaking." She glared at him and began to unbutton her blouse.

"Here! Cast eyes doubting pon lingering trace small yet a'staining fair bandage, do cast thee some sharp glance pon this."

"PRINCESS!"

"SISTER!"

She hesitated, about to yank her blouse from her shoulders.

"I will take your word for it, Princess. Button up."

Toucan frowned around Tinker at her.

"Sister Mine, this do be most unseemly behavior, even for you. Behave thyself. Or get thee hence and walk with Goose."

Chicken ducked her head and murmured softly but not well.

"Yes, Brother Mine. Yes, My Lord." She began to rebutton and retuck in her blouse, lengthening her stride, a new spring in her pace. She stalked along in front of them.

Tinker turned to Toucan and whispered, "That is

some sister you have there."

Toucan nodded slowly and spoke in low hushed tones, "Aye, Highness, tis most certainly true. One such as she be do take most heavy a'rein. Ahhhh, tis most fair a'warning me'thinks."

"Warning duly noted, Advisor."

Chicken twisted her head and yelled back at them, "Brother, tis most unkind of thee to so speak behind Our back. Wait till fair arm be really and truly healed, both of thee." She increased her stride.

Tinker leaned close to Toucan and asked, "What did she mean by that?"

Toucan carefully whispered back, very softly, "Truly, Highness, nary idea do I possess."

They walked on in silence for sometime.

Toucan admired the scenery as did Tinker.

They didn't know whether Chicken was admiring it or not as she stayed out in front of them.

Toucan thought that perhaps Lord Tinker's glance did admire that flash of yellow ahead of them far more than he did fair landscape. But he wisely kept those thoughts to himself.

The widely spaced groups walked on and through the day.

The path they followed sank lower and lower.

They met no-one, saw no signs of anyone. Periodically they passed through one of the wide stone platforms. The sameness of the colors and the countryside lulled them into a walking stupor. Little by little, the shadows lengthened. The afternoon breeze started drifting by.

Tinker reached up and caressed the golden jewel. *John Tinker?*

It is I.

We have found something at long last.

What?

A sign.

What does it say?

I do not know, I can not read it. We will wait for you here.

"Strange, very strange."

Chicken, who by this time had decided to walk by Tinker's side again, touched him gently on the arm.

"What do be strange, My Lord?"

"Sorrowful says that they have come upon a sign and that he cannot read it."

"What be so strange in that, for are we not in most different world?"

"What is so strange is that we were told that part of being on this quest was being given the ability to read and understand whatever language we should bump into. Now Sorrowful says he has found something that he can not read."

Chicken nodded.

"We do so see, most strange indeed. Hallo, there they be, just there."

They hurried up to the crowd clustered around the sign, Tinker calling, "That's it?"

Sorrowful pointed at the rock wall, and nodded by way of answer.

Tinker walked up and peered at it.

It certainly looked like a sign. There were three rows of marks carved into the smooth stone surface. They had no meaning to him either, they were just rows of strange marks on a wall.

He shook his head.

"Well, I can't read them either. Toucan, Goose, Chicken, anyone?"

A buzzing, crackling noise rolled up behind him and a mechanical voice, really two voices in unison, rattled forth.

"It says: Steep grade ahead. Pass during daylight only. That is the message carved there."

Tinker spun around.

"Thanks, Two-Byte. What language is this?"

"We do not know its name."

"Ummmmm, O.K." Tinker beckoned.

"Let's go, Goose, the light is fading rapidly. I want to see what lies just ahead around this bend."

"Righto, Sire." Goose ran ahead, waving a section of The Guard to follow. Sorrowful trotted at his side.

Toucan nodded at them.

"An interesting pair, Highness, the white Goose and his dark shadow."

Tinker laughed.

"They make quite a pair all right."

The Guard disappeared around the nearby bend.

Tinker and the rest strolled after them.

Well, Sorrowful, what do you see?

Absolutely amazing. Wait until you see it.

What is it?

Wait and see, John Tinker.

Tinker turned to his companions, and smiled.

"Well, gang, it seems that we have some sort of surprise waiting for us but Sorrowful wouldn't say what it was. Only that it is amazing."

They picked up their pace and hurried.

And turned the corner.

And stopped.

It was amazing all right.

Quite a sight.

They were standing slightly uphill and a short distance from another of the stone platforms. Passing down one side of it, stretching down the shear face of a seemingly endless cliff, was the path.

It pitched steeply downward, cut into the vertical face. It was disappearing into the gloom gathering in the deep valley before them and the shadows spreading up toward them.

They walked down onto the platform and rejoined the rest of The Company.

Tinker stepped over to the stone railing and stared out at the sight. The lengthening shadows were distorting the stairs and confusing the eyes. In the dimming light it would be easy to misjudge the stairs and take a tumble over the edge. There was no outside wall along this stretch.

Tinker pointed at the way down.

"Well, that sign was certainly correct." He spun round, and pointed at the platform.

"Looks like we get to spend another night sleeping on hard rock. Goose, make your preparations. We should start down that thing at first, and safe, light."

"Righto, Sire. Sergeant!"

"Yes, SAH!"

"Deploy the men, as before."

"Yes, SAH!"

The Guard scattered to their tasks.

Sorrowful strolled over to join Tinker and his group.

"Quite a sight, was it not, John Tinker? It will make an impressive section to the tale. Look!" He pointed toward the valley.

"It is already night down there. I can not see a thing. Wait, wait!" He bobbled up and down on his toes, stopped, and pointed.

"Does that look like a light out there, way out there, slightly to the left?"

"Toucan?"

Toucan stared in the direction that Sorrowful was pointing.

"He do have good eyes, Highness. There indeed do be lights yonder, some small cluster. It do seem that we do approach civilization. At last, some small cluster of dwellings."

Tinker smiled.

"Well, that is good. I was beginning to think that we had been landed into some vast blue and gray desert of stone and rock. Maybe tomorrow we will get to sleep in real beds and get something to eat. I am getting rather hungry. It has been two days."

Toucan nodded slowly.

"Indeed, Highness, two long days. I do think we shall, each and every one of us, enjoy more comfortable quarters. As you, I also do be most tired of rock sleeping. Some softer bed wouldst be rather enjoyable."

Chicken clapped him on the back, a hardy soldier's thump, driving him a step forward.

"Indeed, Brother, indeed." She strode away to peer over the edge at the faint lights in the distance, humming softly to herself.

Soon the company settled itself around the opening to wait out the night. Tonight the hard stone floor seemed, somehow, less hard now that they had an expectation of better lodging tomorrow. The evening passed quickly.

Sorrowful told the assembly *The Tale of The Rind'l-Rind'l.* Those of The Guard close enough to hear, and not on guard duty, roared with laughter at the comic ending. Finally, they all squirmed into positions as comfortable as was possible given their situation and fell asleep.

Tinker propped himself in a corner with Chicken nestled in his lap, a contented smile on her face.

Colors Speak in Many Hues

With the first glimmering of dawn, Toucan's eyes popped open.

He stood, stretched, yawned, and eased the kinks from his body. As he stretched and yawned, he thought about Lord Tinker's quest, then he walked toward where he slept.

The dawn was a faint red tinge on the horizon behind him. All around, he could hear the night creatures settling down as the day creatures began to prepare to emerge.

Tinker had slipped down the wall until he was lying flat on his back. It looked like a comfortable sprawl, but one wondered how comfortable anyone could be on hard rock. Chicken had rearranged herself as well. Now she lay partly across his chest, her good arm wrapped tightly across his chest.

He looked down at the sleeping pair. She did appear so protective of him although one would think her grip to be fearful in intent.

Toucan shook his head, and thought, Sister, Sister, what will become of you should he do be lost pon this quest? What will become of us all for we do be at his and only his service? Should he die, do we become naught but toys again? Truly, I do wonder me what the mighty magician be really scheming.

Toucan bent over and stared into Tinker's face. Mayhap that magician do be more subtle than Lord

Tinker does realize. Those deep lines of worry so etched pon his face when first we met do seem to be a'fading away. Do be that your fate, Sister? Be that the reason for our being summoned forth? Do we be but mere things for to lighten his burden for he do worry greatly about failing and death and injury to all? Ahhh, me'thinks the magician do play at purposes contorted that we shall nay understand till all be over and done with.

But, we warriors do be charged with his protection and that should be that. Yet there be much more. Enough, Toucan, keep thy pesky worries to thyself and give advice when asked and no more. Somewhere in all this lurks the pattern, if only it could be seen. Enough, enough of this.

He reached down and gently shook Tinker and Chicken.

"Awake, awake. Tis time, for first light do descend rapidly pon one and all. Rise up Highness, Fair Sister, rise up."

As they began to stir and rub sleep from their eyes, Toucan strode off to rouse up the rest of the company.

Finally satisfied at the hustle and bustle that signified that all were getting ready, he walked to the outside wall and stared down into the deep valley, mulling over everything that he had been told and seen of this strangest of strange quests.

Tinker stepped up to his side.

"Well, Toucan, what do you see?"

"Little, Highness, very little. Tis still inky night down yonder. Fair morn do greet us first. Look you there," he pointed, "the upper end of the stair do even now come into bright sunlight. Tis time for to be off."

"Right, let's go." Tinker spun on his heels.

"GOOSE, head'em out. We have a long way to go."

"Righto, Sire. Sergeant."

"Yes, SAH!"

"GO, man, GO!"

"Yes, SAH!"

The Guard started down, Goose and Sorrowful in the middle of the long line.

"Toucan? Princess? Ready to go?"

"Yes, My Lord."

"Whenever you wish, Highness."

Tinker stepped after the last guardsman.

"Princess, where's your sling?"

"Brother Goose did say t'was healed enough. He do say t'would best be for to exercise stiff muscles." She walked toward him swinging her arm.

Tinker stopped and turned toward Toucan.

"Well, she certainly wasn't kidding about healing fast. That was a major wound." He waited for her to join him.

"Do you really have blue blood, that is, blue colored blood? Or was that a joke?"

"Nay, My Lord, t'was most true. All of us, Goose, Toucan, myself."

"Time, Highness," called Toucan.

Tinker hurried onto the stair, Chicken staying at his side. Toucan followed them trailed by Two-Byte then Tai.

The staircase down was as steep as it had looked from the platform. For reasons only know to its designers there was no outer railing or wall, just a sharp edge and a long fall. The stairs however were quite wide, wide enough for four people to walk abreast with room to spare on the outside. This was fortunate as Tai, whose great bulk filled most of the space, would have had some problem getting down otherwise. She lumbered along, bringing up the rear, gazing out and back as if she were on flat land, nibbling now and then as she passed some small clump of growing things.

With the exception of Tinker and Chicken, the company was a long thin line walking single file, one shoulder brushing the inner cliff face. The stairs wound in and out following the undulations of the cliff face. Short stone bridges leaped over deep crevices down which small stones often clattered.

Eventually dawn penetrated to the valley floor. Now they saw a different color. The valley floor was yellow, multiple tones, multiple hues of yellow. The color washed up the cliff face until it merged and blended and became blue-gray. It seemed to Toucan, whose eyes were by far the sharpest, that he could detect at the far distant end of this valley the dull glow of red. The rising haze obscured his vision. Glancing backward toward the opposite end he could see the yellow blending into purple.

Good morning, Sorrowful.

Good morning, John Tinker.

How goes it so far?

Not too badly. Although I feel that this will be a long and hard day's walking. I would guess that we will hit bottom before dark. Have you noticed the colors?

Yes. Interesting place, isn't it.

It is that.

"Sorrowful thinks that we will be down by

evening."

Chicken beamed at him. "Good news that, My Lord, very good news."

The day dragged on as one of never ending monotony, long painful monotony. By mid-day, legs and backs were aching from the continual stress of stepping down. Now they could see the details upon the valley floor: fields and roads, here and there an isolated building. Once in a while they saw something moving along the central roadway. As they sank lower into the valley, the temperature went up.

Finally, as afternoon shadows were stretching out, lengthening into dark spears, the long line stumbled on quivering legs onto relatively flat ground. They were standing upon the valley floor at last. They were standing upon a well-paved road that ran straight away from the cliff face. Trees lined both sides. From what they had seen from above, they knew that this road connected with the main road out on the valley floor.

Tinker leaned against one of the trees. "Boy, am I glad we are down. My legs will ache for days. I can't imagine anyone going up and down that thing very often."

Toucan nodded in agreement. "Indeed, Highness. Praps that do be explanation as to why we do see none others along that rocky route. I would think only that business of a most pressing kind would hike such fearsome grade." "

"Right. Well, shall we proceed, or camp here? I thought that I saw a town not far from here. Shall we try for it?"

Then he laughed and gestured, hobbling down

the road. "Aw, let's do it. Come on, Goose, let's go to town."

Goose ran past him, trailed by a section of The Guard. "A right jolly good idea, Sire. Sergeant!"

"Yes, SAH!"

"Two skirmish lines, front and back. Hurry man."

"Yes, SAH!"

In moments The Guard were started down the road, one line on either side of the road. In the center of the road walked Goose and Sorrowful followed by Tinker, Chicken and Toucan. Tinker wondered at the ability of The Guard to show so little fatigue after such a day's exertions. Two-Byte and Tai brought up the rear as usual with Tai wandering from side to side as she sampled the native vegetation, munching happily upon yellow shrubs and trees.

Reaching the central road they turned and started in the direction of the nearest town. The road stayed empty. They had it to themselves.

"Toucan, I think we are expected."

"Indeed, Highness, I do believe you are most correct. We would have been most easily seen coming down. The inhabitants would have all the time in the world to prepare for our coming. For good or ill. See just there, yonder. It pears to be some sizable village."

They slowed up and walked cautiously into the village. The streets and buildings were all decorated with flags and banners. The place was a riot of color. The population lined both sides of the street, filling the sidewalks and the intersections. All stood in deadly silence and watched them as they walked past. Suddenly, as the company strode beneath the first of the banners stretching from side to side over the street, the crowd broke into loud noises.

Flowers began to rain down upon them from those standing upon the balconies. Then, as if at a signal, the population went wild. Dancing, cheering, screaming at the tops of their voices, they threw fountains of flowers, waved small banners frantically, and in general looked to be celebrating New Year's eve. At last, it looked that way to Tinker.

He called over to Toucan. "It seems that we are being welcomed."

Toucan yelled back. "Seems so, Highness, seems so."

Bending close, Tinker whispered in Chicken's ear, "What do you think, Princess?"

"We do Ourself think t'would be most wonderful if true, My Lord." She fondled the hilt of her sword.

Tinker frowned. "Yes, I suppose this could all be some sort of a trap. The Guard don't look particularly relaxed, do they?"

"Not until thee give the order."

"Um, yes. Well," he nodded toward the front, "it seems we have come to the town square, and that will be the town official, at least one of them, unless I miss my guess. We had better smile and look royal, it is politic time."

Tinker straightened up and stepped toward the central figure, walking through the now halted ranks of The Guard, a wide smile plastered across his face.

The figure ahead boomed out over the crowd noise, "Welcome, welcome. I am the Greeter. Welcome to Fulvidberg."

The Greeter threw both arms wide, then waved

happily to the crowd. "We have prepared feasts, merriments, songs and dances. Your quarters are ready." He beckoned at them, turning away.

"Follow me, follow me, honored guests. He passed through an open gateway, shouting, "Let the gala begin."

The surrounding crowd roared their pleasure, broke ranks and swept all before them into a vast courtyard. Along one side were arrayed long wooden tables, laden with food and drink. Along the other side another long table.

It was toward this place that Tinker, Toucan, Chicken and the rest were carried to be seated in the place of honor along with The Greeter. The Greeter rose and clapped his hands together. The feasting began.

Tinker leaned forward and stared up and down the table, then whispered to Chicken and Toucan who were seated on either side of him, "Looks like we have no choice. Might as well relax and enjoy what is to come."

He reached for a large earthen jug. "Some wine, Princess."

"Thank you, My Lord." She slid her cup forward. Tinker then passed the jug to Toucan who filled his cup and tentatively tasted it before allowing either of them to drink. "It do appear . . . ummmmm, tis quite good. Cheers, one and all."

Happy, laughing people brought large platters of food and began to serve all seated at the long table. Across the courtyard, Tinker could see others piling large mounds of leafy vegetation before Tai who huffed and wolfed it down as fast as they piled it up.

Throughout the courtyard, folk swirled and

laughed. Then Tinker noticed their skin tones. They were rainbow animated: yellow, blue, violet, orange, purple, white, brown, black, green. They reflected the hues of their land. He wondered if each of the colors he saw came from a different region of the same color. He made a mental note to try and remember to ask their host whenever a chance arose.

Musicians appeared from somewhere, playing and singing, while jugglers and actors bounded into the teeming masses. Music rang out, the food kept coming, the wine continued to pour. The crowd surged and grew denser, laughing and dancing.

In the midst of the cacophony of noise and color, Tinker thought that he saw a familiar white figure engaged in a most extreme, ungainly dance with a lovely wench whose blue skin contrasted pleasantly with his uniform.

Tinker leaned sideways and asked, "Princess, is that Goose out there doing that peculiar dance?"

"Oh aye, Me'Lord, tis The Goose. As We did say, the Goose do be rather silly be'times."

"Nothing silly here, it is a party, a rip-roaring blast." Tinker stood and tugged gently at her arm. "Come on, Chicken, let's cut a rug."

She rose, frowning at him. "But, Fair Me'Lord, why wouldst we desire to damage our host's property so?"

Tinker laughed. "It is just an old saying, it means, let's dance."

"Dance, do you say dance?"

"You betcha, Zorba."

"With mine greatest of pleasures. Do excuse us, Brother Toucan."

Toucan stood, making a slight bow. "Gladly. I shall stay and converse with The Greeter. Ta ta." He sat next to their host and leaned over to ask a few pointed questions as Chicken and Tinker swirled away into the confusion. He thought he hear her say, " . . . do tell Us what manner of thing this Zorba be."

The Greeter leaped to his feet and bustled into the crowd bellowing instructions about the dessert.

Then he returned only to bustle off in some other direction. This time he returned herding back to the main table various of the guests that had joined the merry crowds packed into the courtyard.

As soon as he managed to get them all reseated, dessert was served.

As the last dish was disappearing from the many plates, he rose to his feet and gestured for silence. The crowd rapidly settled down.

Into the sudden quiet, he spoke, "Honored Guests, I drink to your success." He lifted his goblet high then took a deep drink.

"To your success in the following days." He took another swallow.

"May your arms be strong." Another swallow. "May your lives be long." Yet another swallow.

From the far end of the table Goose's voice rang out, "I do drink to that."

Peals of laughter roared their appreciation for his jest. The Guard were the loudest of all. The Greeter beamed.

"And good health to all." The Greeter took a final swallow and banged his drinking vessel down on the table top with a sharp *crack*.

The village folk began to quickly file out of the

courtyard and back to their homes. Within a few short moments, the courtyard stood empty and silent.

"Honored Guests, if you would follow me, I shall now escort you to your quarters. In the morning, after the first meal, we shall talk of the thing most foul that despoils this our lands. This way, please."

The Greeter beckoned and led them into one of the buildings forming the edges of the courtyard and down a long hallway that dissected it. He stopped before a door and pushed it open. "The One and his companion have this place."

He pointed down the hall to the next door. "The rest of the multihues are there, just adjacent."

He pointed toward the outer door. "The great animal and metal beings have the courtyard."

Tinker and Sorrowful stepped into their room.

The rest of the company headed down the hall and into their quarters.

Tinker could see Chicken staring at him as she was hustled through the door.

As their doors were closing, The Greeter called to them, "May your sleep be deep and undisturbed." He turned and left the building.

Tinker stood just inside the room and inspected it. It looked comfortable enough, especially after having slept for two nights on hard stone platforms.

"Well, Sorrowful, shall we hit the sack? It has been a long, hard day, and after that party, such as it was, I am really ready for some sleep. Those beds look very comfortable."

He walked over, sat on one of the beds, reached out, removed his weaponkin and carefully leaned it against the wall in the space between bed and wall.

Then he fell backward, wiggled into a pre-sleep position and sighed. "See you in the morning, good buddy." And fell asleep.

Sorrowful carefully settled himself, making the bed covers just so, and replied, "Fair evening, John Tinker. I think that I shall keep my dagger under my pillow and a small light burning."

Then he fell asleep, a single tear trickling down his cheek as he thought about Smoke.

Screams of terror and panic ripped Tinker from deep untroubled sleep. He snapped upright, saw Sorrowful rolling from his bed, his dagger in hand. Tinker lunged for the wall grabbing for his weaponkin.

It was gone.

He hit the floor and scrabbled into a sitting position. Staring across the top of his bed, he stared at the strange group staggering back and forth across the middle of the room.

Five creatures were struggling with each other and trying to avoid a sixth who was flaying something wildly about. All were screaming and howling, terrified by something in their midst. They weren't paying attention to either Tinker or Sorrowful.

Tinker crawled over the bed and crept to where Sorrowful was standing in a crouch, the dagger gleaming in the faint light.

"What's going on?"

"I am not sure, John Tinker."

The group broke apart and reformed. In that moment, Tinker realized the central figure was clenching his sword by the hilt. It seemed as if it was trying to throw the weapon away. The other five were struggling with the sword arm and attempting to aid their companion in his struggles.

The weaponkin flicked to one side. A body fell, thrashing to stillness. The sword jumped, here and there, humming sound filled the room. Bodies and body parts fell outward. The survivor, still clenching the lethal thing, stood untouched, surrounded by carnage.

It ran for the door, fumbling for the hasp.

The sword flicked around and back. As the creature crumpled backward, the sword fell from its hand and struck the floor with a dull thump.

Tinker carefully walked around and over the remains littering the room and bent over to retrieve the blade. He could feel a slight tremor in the hilt as he lifted it up.

"Now what was all that about, do you suppose?"

Sorrowful sat on the edge of his bed, his legs swinging back and forth. "Those things were trying to steal your weaponkin, John Tinker."

Tinker sat next to him, the great sword resting next to his leg, its tip just touching the side of his boot. It still had a slight hum. His fingers could feel it.

"Think so?"

"Yes."

"Then why didn't they just take it and run instead of standing around and squabbling about it? Dumb. And ugly. Let's go down the hall and see if we can find a clean room. I don't want to sleep in here with all this."

Sorrowful cleared his throat, hesitated, then spoke, dropping one hand on Tinker's thigh. "Ah, before we go looking, perhaps I should tell you something that I have not had time to tell you about before?"

"O.K., so tell me."

"Remember my telling about Smoke and I utilizing the Golden Eyes to speak to each other in Growing Deep? Remember?"

"Sure. So what?"

"And you know how doing that also merges the minds into a kind of single entity? And how you also learn other kinds of things?"

"Yep, yep."

"Well, then, it seems that with the long usage of the Golden Eye, I learned of another being."

Tinker's head snapped around. "One of The Gryerd?"

"No, John Tinker, not one of The Gryerd."

"Then who, there was only you and Smoke?"

Sorrowful waggled his dagger in the air. "This thing, my weaponkin. It was something we really ought to have known from the first, but we did not pay attention. The facts that we were told was that they are weapon kin."

"Right, weaponkin. So what?"

"KIN, JOHN TINKER, KIN! Two words, not one."

Sorrowful sprung from the bed and whirled around to glare at him. "Kin implies a blood relationship. Remember the binding?"

Tinker nodded.

"These things are not just inert pieces of metal. These things are sentient beings that are permanently, PERMANENTLY, linked to that person whose blood they first drank. Sentient beings. Real alive sentient beings!"

He jumped up and sat next to Tinker again. "And who is linked to them? It is us. You. Me. Mountain. We each are bound to one of these creatures. They are weapons, and they are kin to the one to whom they are bound. We do not do the fighting. They do. They take control. When you are in combat, they do it. We are just the things that they use to do what they do. We become extensions of them, not the other way around. And they have only loyalty to their kin. If I tried to walk off with your weaponkin, it would probably kill me."

Sorrowful gestured toward the dead things in the room. "And that pile of carrion is an example."

Tinker stood and began to paced back and forth, his weaponkin still clenched in his right fist. "It doesn't stop does it? We being used by everything." He stopped and stared blankly at Sorrowful.

"I almost handed it to Princess Chicken just so she could look at it." The tingling he could feel running up his arm took on a new, more menacing meaning. He swung the blade up and around. It stuck to his back, contented to be there.

"Let's go find another room." He walked over and out into the hall.

The hall was empty and silent. They walked down and stood next to the door where the rest of the company had been put.

Tinker leaned his ear against it. Not a sound. Apparently the noise from their room hadn't penetrated the thick walls.

They turned back and started searching for a

place to sleep.

Tinker tried the first door, just opposite their room. It was locked.

"Next door, Sorrowful."

"RUN, JOHN TINKER, RUN!"

Dark shapes had begun to materialize at either end of the hall, pouring from the walls, from somewhere else. Silently they lurched toward their chosen victims.

"Huh? Right!"

They spun from the mass almost upon them and started to run toward the far end. And stopped. The hall was filling, surging past and through the other doorway, tearing it from its hinges.

The things began chanting.

Over the noise, Tinker heard a scream of rage.

He leaped toward this second horde, his weaponkin slashing a deep hole in the slithering ranks.

"PRINCESS!"

Then he had to jump backward, bumping into something, almost falling over.

"OOF."

"Just me, John Tinker. We cannot go this way either. We are trapped."

Something exploded, numbing their ears into silence. Orange flame enveloped them and surged along the hall in both directions, enveloping the howling demons. Orange glow shoved the hordes backward, rolling them into tangled heaps, leaving behind a liquid trail of bits and pieces, gore and slime. Then, pinned against the far ends of the hall, something began to take shape within the orange flame. Multiple arms, clawing and slashing, the creature pressed and pressed. Loud crackling, grinding, liquid sounds penetrated the screams. The walls cracked and bulged.

Thunder shook the structure in lightening flash. The orange disappeared. Dust trickled from ceiling cracks. Pieces of plaster fell on all sides. The belt on Tinker's waist flashed and flickered to a low ebb.

Nothing moved in the quiet after sudden death.

Chicken burst through the wreckage of her doorway, dirty and disheveled, sword in hand. Goose and Toucan followed.

Goose stared at Tinker. "Where do most foul beasties go? One moment we do be fighting for our very lives, the next, vile apparitions do vanish."

Tinker gestured toward the ends of the hall. "Down there."

Chicken stared and then turned back. "What manner of stuff do be this, Me'Lord?"

Tinker shrugged. "Don't ask me. But that is, was, them. That is all that is left." As she started to speak, he held up one hand.

"Lady, I will tell you in the morning, but right now all I wish to do is sleep."

Chicken wiped her sword on one pant leg and pushed it into its sheath. "But of course, Me'Lord."

"Do you guys have a couple of extra beds in your room. Our room is sort of a mess?"

Chicken stalked up to Tinker and peered into his face through a tangle of hair and purred at him. "Thee might share Our very own if thee do so wish, Fair Lord and Master."

Tinker brushed the hair from her face, spun her around, draping one arm over her shoulder. "Sounds like an offer I can't refuse. Shall we go?"

Toucan clear his throat. "Ahem, Highness, there do be one, um, small problem with our accommodations."

"What's that?"

"It do be Tai, Highness. The problem do be that she do be most mightily a'stuck."

Toucan led them into the room. The large head and long neck of the great lizard waved slowly back and forth watching them as they walked in.

Tinker smiled. "Oh, I see."

Toucan patted Tai on the nose. "She do thrust herself through small window when trouble do start. Now, I fear, she do be most stuck in place."

Tinker patted Toucan lightly on the shoulder as Chicken walked away toward one corner of the room.

"I think," he said, " that the solution is quite simple. TAI."

She cocked her head and looked at him.

"Back up."

Tinker whispered to Toucan. "Now we wait and watch."

Tai's head stopped swaying as she paused and thought about what she had been told. They waited as the idea slowly perculated down the extended neurological connections.

Suddenly she jerked backward. Dust billowed into the room from the space where her head had been. A few bricks clumped to the floor.

Goose walked over and leaned out the ragged opening and looked at the great lizard as she trundled back to her place on the other side of the courtyard, the window frame still around her neck.

"By George, Sire, t'was most neat a'trick, if I do

say so."

Tinker spun on his heels. "O.K., Princess, where's my bed?"

She came back, pulled him into the corner, stepped around him and gave him a sudden shove, buckling his legs. "Here, Me'Lord."

"WOOOOMP!"

He rolled over, eyes widening as she leaped on top of him.

"We do have thee enow."

"OOOOOOOOF!"

The bed timbers creaked, groaned, and collapsed.

Tinker thrashed his way free, laughing and cursing, sitting up. He grabbed his weaponkin from his back and slid it over against the wall, and announced to the room.

"Gentlemen, here I fell. And here I stay, hors de combat. Pray turn off the lights and hope that we can explain all this to our hosts in the morning."

He lay back, flapped a quilt over Chicken and himself, and sighed happily.

She nestled in his arms as the lights were snuffed out, one by one.

Hearts of Oak, Nerves of ?

"Highness, tis fair morn. Time for to arise."

Tinker looked up. "Eeeerrrrmmmmm?"

Toucan was bending over him, nudging him gently with one boot tip.

"Tis fair morn."

"All ready?"

Sunlight streamed through the ragged hole in the wall. Outside, low voices murmured.

"Act . . . ually, Highness, tis nearer mid-morn than dawn. All the company do be outside. There I do speak me'self with our new host, The Meeter, and he do explain all events that do pass in these lands. That ones job do be to tell us what manner of things we do face. T'other's job was but to arrange festivities and such. When you have prepared yourself, solid breakfast do await your noble pleasure in yon sunny courtyard. Hot water, towels, on the table, just there."

Toucan pointed across the room, bowed, and left.

Tinker rose to his feet, yawned, stretched and went about his usual morning rituals. Wiping his hands on the towel, he walked back to the mound of bed clothes and kicked it gently.

"Time to get up, Princess."

A head poked out, blue eyes blinking away sleep.

"A fair morn, Me'Lord?"

"Seems to be. We will all be in the courtyard. We are going to be told what is going on in this world.

Coming?"

"But mere few moments more, Me'Lord."

"O.K., see you outside."

He hurried through the hall. The stench was overpowering. He stopped and peered inside his first room. In there, it was worse.

As he stepped outside, he saw that the others were waiting for him, seated at the long table, finishing their breakfast. Across the courtyard, Tai was munching on a pile of yellow foliage. She wasn't wearing the window frame.

"Highness," called Toucan, gesturing at a large chair. "If you would but sit here."

Tinker did.

Toucan waggled one hand rather airily.

"This do be our host for the nonce, The Meeter. Meeter, this do be The Lord Tinker."

The Meeter smiled broadly and bobbled his head. "Ah yes, The One."

He hesitated, looked uncomfortable. "May I speak of our plight while you eat?"

Tinker reached for a fork. "Please do. And, um, many thanks for last night's festivities. We enjoyed it."

The Meeter gestured the compliment way. "It was only a small, pitiful token from us to you for all that you will face. I will tell The Greeter that he did well. To business?"

Tinker nodded, his mouth full of food.

The Meeter leaned sideways and spoke in a hushed tone. "Have you heard of Tremlor, Lord Vile?"

Tinker shook his head.

"NO? Oh. Ah well. Not long ago, Tremlor, Lord Vile as he calls himself, appeared far over the Vertical

Walls on the edge of the Crimson Lands. It has now taken most of these lands and is slowly destroying the colors of life. To do this is an abomination in the eye of the Heuden. We are basically a joyful people who have lived at peace with our neighbors, our surroundings, for far longer than can be remembered and our tales tell."

He paused.

Tinker reached for another helping of breakfast.

"At first, we did not believe what we were hearing. We sent Seekers. The one that returned filled our ears with terror and our hearts with anguish. This new thing was our doom for we had no way to resist. Those wise ones among us searched through all our legends and found a very strange tale. It said, to reduce it to its principles, that when we, as a people, would face the greatest test of our existence, then a strange company would appear at whose head would stand The One. This One would be an absence of color and so would be his companion. His company would be strange, multi-hued, multi-formed."

The Meeter gestured down the table and across the courtyard at Tai and Two-Byte.

"You were seen descending The Great Stair. All was as had been described. Your are the savior of our land, is this not so?"

Tinker sat, silently pondering the question. All the events and things he had seen and had been told flashing through his mind.

As the silence lasted longer than the normal conversational pause, The Meeter began to fidget and frown. This was not the sort of response he had been expecting.

Then Tinker turned, stood, and clasped The

Meeter's shoulder. "It does seem that way, doesn't it?"

Now The Meeter was worried. He hadn't been prepared for ambiguous statements or the strange behavior these strange folk exhibited.

Tinker laughed softly.

"Don't worry, Meeter, we are your saviors all right. As soon as we all have eaten enough breakfast and prepare to get under way, we will get out of your hair and see what this Tremlor thing is all about. You just tell Toucan everything you can think of that relates to that creature and anything else we might need to know. Toucan will ask as many questions as he can think of, so be prepared."

He smiled as Chicken brushed lightly against his side, sat, and began to heap large quantities of food on her plate.

"Fair Morn, Me'Lord."

"Looks that way, Princess. Sorrowful, let's take a little stroll."

"Coming, John Tinker."

"Toucan, Goose, will everything be ready pretty soon."

"Indeed, Highness. As you do wish and command."

"Into the fray with banners flying, Sire."

Tinker started walking toward the main entrance to the courtyard. "Let's go, Sorrowful." They strolled out into the street.

"Whither?"

"No where, I just wanted to stretch my legs a bit and ask your opinion about all this. We are still on that quest, aren't we?"

Sorrowful nodded. "I think we must be, specially

now that we have been told of this Tremlor creature. Why, do you doubt it?"

"No, not really." Tinker sighed heavily and stood looking down the street at nothing.

"It is just that it seems to go on and on and on and on, popping us from place to place, fighting whatever manner of madman or horror happens to be inhabiting that place. All we are is cosmic vagabonds, self-contained, set-apart, and controlled by someone or something else. We are following a path that appears predetermined and if we are not very careful, a lethal one as well. We are stellar ping-pong balls."

He twisted and leaned back against a sun-drenched wall and closed his eyes, arms folded over his chest, and sighed even more heavily.

"I am really tired of it. Nothing says that we are closing in on the end. I have the most frightful trapped feeling. And everyone has the mistaken idea that I am leading this in some rational way. I am beginning to think that I, we, will ever get home."

Sorrowful poked him lightly on the belly.

"And I fear that I will never see the Six Lands again, never get to tell The Tale of The Quest."

He poked Tinker again, this time much harder.

Tinker opened his eyes and looked down.

"But I have everything all recorded up here." Sorrowful thumped his forehead. "So, if I should survive, and return home, I will be able to tell and retell of our great adventure. On The Great Hike, I will tell it all, everyone's part. After all, John Tinker, this might be the last of the elseplaces. We have been learning more and more, so we must be approaching the end. It seems logical. To me."

"Logical? In a fairy tale?" Tinker shrugged. "Let's hope so."

He bumped his shoulders against the wall and thrust himself forward, looked up at the sky.

"Let's get back, it must be time to go."

They walked slowly back down the street.

"Tell me, does your dagger seem to hum softly?"

Sorrowful smiled up at him.

"Oh yes, that was one of those things I learned, the weaponkins sing to themselves. Had you not noticed that before?"

Tinker shook his head.

"Nope, not until last night. And so does this thing." He fingered the jeweled belt. The jewels flashed softly in the bright sunlight.

Turning into the courtyard, Tinker called, "Everybody ready? Princess? Goose? Toucan?"

"Aye, Me'Lord."

"I have the directions to follow, Highness."

"TO THE ROAD, SIRE!"

Tinker stood and searched their faces for traces of doubt or disbelief. Nothing. It made him feel all right, in spite of his apprehensions and doubts, it made him feel all right. He laughed, and though that it was *Tinker's Adventures in Wonderland* ready to start again.

"O.K., let's do it."

Tinker stepped smartly to one side as The Guard tromped pass. Goose saluted with his sword and gave him a broad, happy smile. As Toucan and Chicken came by Tinker turned, slipped his arm under her's, and followed.

Sorrowful trotted by, taking his position next to Goose.

Tai and Two-Byte formed the rear-guard as usual.

The little group walked toward the far side of town. As they strolled along, the sidewalks and intersections filled with villagers. They waved flags and banners, but made not a sound. It was a silent farewell. Here and there faces ran with tears.

"Looks like some don't think we're going to survive."

"Then they do be most wrong, Me'Lord."

"Where we going, Toucan?"

"Our directions do be to take ourselves to far end of this valley and into the Crimson Lands. Passing through those parts we travel up and in or over the Vertical Walls. Past there be where this creature named Tremlor abides."

"Very far?"

"If The Meeter t'was correct, two days, Highness, two days, walking with most steady but unhurried pace. It be planned for us to take our comforts this eventide in Carmineberg."

"Nice day for an outing, Toucan. Warm, not hot. Should unkink tight muscles from yesterdays descent."

"Aye, tis so, Highness."

Tinker looked at Chicken. "How's the arm today, Princess?"

"Well and truly healed, Me'Lord."

Chicken and Tinker walked along discussing the passing scene and this and that. It was a comfortable, wandering conversation. Toucan paid little attention to what they were saying, having recognized the duet being played. His mind searched for some clue, some hint that could be utilized to their advantage on this quest. Some way to end it, if possible.

Up at the front of the column, Sorrowful walked along beside Goose. The Guard walked on either side of the road in two lines eyes scanning their surroundings, alert to anything that might be out there.

It was a very relaxed group out for a stroll on a pleasant sunny day, more or less relaxed, that is.

"A very pleasant day, Prince Goose."

"Quite correct, Count, a very pleasant day. Pears my most Noble and Royal Sister do be enjoyin' this sunfilled day as well as you." Goose jerked one thumb over his shoulder.

Sorrowful grinned and bobbled his head. "Yes, I believe you are right. In my home, The Six Lands, we have saying for everything and the most appropriate one is 'She wears his face in her eyes'. I certainly think it is appropriate, do you not?"

Goose laughed happily. "Right on the old mark, old bean, right on the old mark. So you noticed, did you?"

"Oh yes. It was obvious from the first day I was with you."

"T''was?"

"Quite so, at least to me. Of course, we tellers of tales do tend to pay close attention to all the details in our surroundings."

"Count, it would take one most blind man to notice not enow. Course tis her fear, she be sore afraid."

"Afraid? Who, her?"

Oh aye."

"I thought you were all warriors?"

"Oh aye, that we be. Have you no fear regarding such matters as a'fightin' and a'brawlin'."

Goose clapped Sorrowful robustly on the back, staggering the small man. "She be no afeared of things that warriors get up to, nay, that one be more fearsome than most. Why she did pretty mangle and hack entire lot of ugly creatures come a'burstin' in pon us last eve. Course mine sister's own mood t'was most dark and stormy and exceedin' foul. Thus did she take great rage upon them things, she did. Good that she did."

"How is that?"

"Count, me'thinks you look like a fella couldst hold secrets well." Placing a finger against his nose, Goose took a quick glance backwards at the sauntering pair and then lowered his voice although there was no chance of his being overheard.

"T'was you, you see. Mine sister was bloody well pissed off, most ready to spit nails and do things unkind to this and that. She do say some rather unladylike things, she do. Do fair shock Brother Toucan."

Sorrowful's eyes popped round. "ME? What did I do? I can not think of anything that I could have done. Oh dear, oh dear!"

"Settle your self Count, t'were not you, t'were poorly managed, in her own fair mind, housin' arrangements. Whenst The Greeter placed you and him together and all the rest apart, she t'was bout for to cut smooth politico in some small pieces."

"I do not understand."

"Mine Sister Fair Princess did plan for to get Our Lord Tinker by himself, all to herself, so to speak. T'were first time when sweet opportunity do present itself since first she laid sweet blue eyes pon fair continence. She do be most rankled, even now."

"I see, I see." Sorrowful giggled.

Goose giggled with him. "Indeed. Luckily that lass understands protocol else things might have turned difficult. But, pon this sunny day, it do seem to mine own eyes that things do begin to work themselves out in this unendin' quest and all."

"Yes . . . yes." Sorrowful held up one palm. "But you said that she was afraid. Of what? Ahhhhh, that is, if you do not mind my asking?"

"Not at'all, Count, not at'all. Just as long as this be most carefully kept tween thee and me. Cany Toucan knows and worries, of all that ever has been, I fear. It be his nature. Not I. Mine Sister do be a most strong and sturdy person."

"Worry? Prince?"

"Ho, right, do tend to dither a'bit." Goose giggled to himself. "She be most a'feared of changin' back pon waltzin' through strange portal thing. It do cause us for to become. She do be most a'feared of not-bein'. As the Bard did say, 'To be or not to be, that be the question'. That be the essence, bein' or not-bein'. Not I. Enjoy what thee hast, a right jolly, excitin' life, short or long. Better than none at'all. For me, tis into bloody fray and devil take the hindmost."

"Afraid of changing back?" Sorrowful was hopelessly confused.

"Righto, Count. One step through magical thing and there we be, toys." Goose held up two fingers, measuring a small space. "Bits and pieces of stuff. No feelin', no emotions, nothin'. Not-bein' you see. Wonder what t'will be like? What think you, Count?"

Sorrowful slowly shook his head. "I really could not say, Prince, not even make a guess. It is quite beyond me. I certainly understand how the Princess must feel. That is a horrid future to have to face." He sighed, shoulders slumping and turned his face from Goose.

Goose waited just a bit, then patted Sorrowful on the shoulder. "And what of thee, Count?"

"Me? For me, it is quite simple. One life and that is that. But I would like to return home to tell The Tale of all this. One gains of kind of immortality that way. Of course, you never get to enjoy it. I do not think that matters, not at all. And you?"

Goose laughed. "I do think tis sufficient to live, to be, really and truly, alive. To sing, to dance, to eat and drink. And if it pleasures mine own self, to leap high."

Goose sprang straight up and clicked his heels together three times and landed lightly on his feet. "And click heels merrily. Me'thinks bein' alive do be most jolly good fun. Think you not, Count?"

Sorrowful grinned at him, and nodded. "Oh I quite agree, Prince."

"Princess, did you see what Goose just did?"

"Aye, My Lord, I do indeed. That do be our very own Goose."

"Certainly is. I would guess from all the arm waving that he and Sorrowful must be having quite a conversation."

"Indeed. They do get along most well, do they not?"

"Right." *Sorrowful, what's going on up there?*

OH. Hello, John Tinker. Nothing, nothing at all. Just having a little talk with Prince Goose. Why?

Just curious, that's all. You guys see anything to

worry about?

    No. It is just a very pleasant day for a very pleasant stroll.

    O.K. Later. "Seems that they are just having a talk. Toucan, Sorrowful says that they haven't seen anything to worry about."

    "Good news, Highness. Tis good and fair to relax."

    "Certainly is. I think we need to recharge our batteries. Oh well, another day, another dollar."

    Toucan furrowed his brow. "A dollar, Highness?"

    "That is a sum of money used in my land."

    Toucan snapped upright, squared his shoulders and glared. "Highness, I must protest. I DO protest. We be mercenaries not!"

    Tinker's head snapped around. "NO, NO, NO! That isn't what I meant, it meant, at all. That was just an aphorism of a sort, an old saying that means something like 'It's just another day of no real importance', just routine."

    Toucan tried to bow as they continued walking. "Your pardon, Highness, your pardon. I do react with nary a'thought."

    "Never mind, it is nothing to worry about."

    Chicken peered around Tinker. "Most unusual, Brother MINE, for thee to behave so. What do bother thy mind so?"

    "I ponder pon this quest, Sister. Tis most heavy a weight and murky a thing for to see. I trust not the progress we do make. Smoke do be gone as do be Mountain. Mighty Dread do almost succeed and thee came near mortal wound. The evil creatures become greater whilst we stay constant. Tis one race most uneven."

"Thee dost worry much too much, Mine Brother."

"Aye, tis so, Yet one's duty do lay most hard and heavy so Our Lord may lead, unfettered, to successful end of this strange quest."

Tinker began to violently wave his arms. "Enough, enough. Today is a nice day, let us enjoy it. Tomorrow is going to be ugly enough. Relax, relax, today we relax."

He tucked Chicken's arm under his own and gave Toucan a slight jab in the ribs with his free elbow.

"You too, Toucan."

Toucan tried to look meek. "Yes, Highness."

"Me'Lord?"

"Yes, Princess?"

"May I not ask thee some question of personal nature?" Toucan shot her a warning glance. She shrugged it away.

"Sure. What?"

"In thy land, wert thou a warrior?"

"Nope."

"You do walk and move most like one."

"Ummmm, long story. Ahhhh, it's like this. Many years ago I inherited a large sum of money."

"Thee do be wealthy then?"

"I wouldn't say that. However, I do not have to work for a living."

"Royalty do have of such need none."

Tinker suppressed a laugh. "Anyway, I was handed this large sum of money. And I was unprepared for that. So I partied and headed downhill in style.

Finally, I found myself in this little town, I still don't know how I got there, and was hauled literally from the gutter. Master Chen proceeded, for reasons that he has never been willingly to divulge, to teach me what he called *The Path of the Warrior.* I worked and studied with him for many years and at last began to see numbers of underlying principles. So I wrote about them. Now, in my home, I write, and study, and practice. You must be seeing the results of all that practice."

"Thee do handle most fearsome weapon in most astounding ways, My Lord. Was that part of thy training as well?"

"NO! That is the weaponkin's doing. My, ah, training was called empty hands."

"Empty hands?"

"How to defend yourself with empty hands."

A loud commotion suddenly interrupted their conversation. Chicken leaped away, hand flying to her sword hilt. Tinker spun, his hand flashing up across his chest. Then they relaxed.

It was Two-Byte whirling around Tai plucking packages from a number of pouches hung along her back. Clenching numbers of these packages in their hands, they buzzed forward handing one to each person as they passed.

Tinker looked at Toucan. "What's this?"

"Mid-day meal, Highness. Something to eat as we walk. Make better time if we do. All prepared by The Greeter under the direction of The Goose."

Toucan grabbed a bag from Two-Byte and rummaged around, removed an item and took a tentative bite, swallowed and beamed at Tinker. "Quite good, Highness."

They all strolled down the road eating. Tai joined them by ripping large pieces from the trees and shrubs as she passed. Whenever anyone was finished, Two-Byte rolled up and took the remains and stuffed them into small doors on their sides.

All afternoon the conversations waxed and waned, drifting from this subject to that, as the colors around them slowly shifted from yellow to red.

They trudged into Carmineberg as light faded from day to dusk. Crowds lined the streets, waving and calling. The Greeter of this town met them and led them into a courtyard similar to the one in Fulvidberg. This time there was no festival, just a long wooden table heaped with quantities of food and drink. It was a more somber occasion. Now they stood under the shadow of Tremlor, Lord Vile.

The meal was long and leisurely as the company finally felt the results of their long hike. The Greeter watched and waited, then jumped to his feet to lead them to their lodgings. Princess Chicken also leaped to her feet, grabbed him by one arm, and yanked the startled Greeter across the courtyard. He had to hop and skip to keep from falling. Then she bent forward and held an intent, whispered conversation with him. She perched on the balls of her feet, left hand clenching the hilt of her sword, her face intent and royally stern.

Toucan leaned toward Tinker and whispered, "Oh dear, Highness, I do fear mine most Noble and Fierce Sister do be giving him orders. It do be most clear from stance and expression that she wilt broach no disagreement."

"What is she doing with him?"

"I do fear me that we shall all too shortly be most

well apprised of that intent for here they do come."

Chicken walked back to the table by The Greeter's side, her face masked by a serene expression, a smile twitching at her lips. The Greeter walked up to the table. Chicken stood back a few paces.

The Greeter bowed. "Your lodgings are prepared. If you will follow me, I shall take you to them."

He turned and led them into one of the buildings. A long corridor bisected it. The building appeared to be identical to the one they had last stayed in. Leading them to the first door, he swung it open.

"The One and . . . and, ah, Princess Chicken. HERE." He cast a very worried glance at her. She nodded imperceptibly and stepped through the door into the room. Tinker looked at The Greeter who violently nodded his head up and down.

Toucan raised one eyebrow and covered his lower face with a hand. Goose giggled, waved on languid hand as he strolled down the hallway and threw open the door to the next room. Turning around, he winked at Tinker and called, "Sleep? . . . Well, Sire."

Then he waved and the rest of the company filed after him. The last Guardsman closed the door.

Tinker turned and entered the room. The door slammed behind him. Chicken stood with her back against it looking worried.

"Thee do be nay angry, Me'Lord?"

""Nope." He wasn't.

"Good." She began to tug her blouse loose from her waist.

"Who fixed your shirt?"

"T'was We, Sweet Prince. Most seamstress-like

do We tuck and sew great cut in mine garment fore that opening do fray downward and mine own soft anatomy do poke out for all and sundry to gaze pon with lustful delight. T'would be most unseemly, that."

She shook her head at the thought and shrugged her shirt from her shoulders.

Then she stared at him and frowned.

"Do We be so ugly, Me'Lord, that thee do so sadly for to gaze upon Our charms?"

"NO." He swallowed hard. "It is that scar."

"Oh," she said gaily. "Most a'glaring red line t'will soon fade itself away. Then one might gaze most close do one wish for to see." She stepped closer.

And began to undo the buttons on his shirt. As she yanked it off, giggled. "Tis only from shoulder corner down pon soft upper portion. Most shallow."

"Princess?"

"My Own Lord, if foul Dread had been hacker rather than slasher, Your Own Princess t'would be enow like great Amazonian Warrior with one chopped off. Now that t'would be most a'frowning matter, truly."

He found that her arm was well and truly healed. "Princess?"

She tugged him across the room. "We would Ourself have Us for to be thine in all ways, My Lord."

This time, when they fell into the bed, it didn't collapse.

The rest of the company slept deeply.

A soft, discrete rapping upon their door woke them. The door swung open and Toucan stepped in.

"Tis fair morn, Highness, time to rise. The company do assemble itself in warm courtyard at breakfast. The Meeter awaits."

"Huh? Oh, O.K., be right along. Thanks."

The door closed gently.

Tinker stretched, yawned, and reached deep into the pile of covers and quilts, and shook something.

"Hello, in there. Wake up, Princess, it's morning and your brother is anxious for us to get going. Time to rise and shine."

A muffled voice said, "Most noble idea, My Lord." An arm snaked out of the tangled pile, grasped him around the neck and yanked him under.

"OHHHHH, Me'Lord."

"It was your idea."

"T'were nary a complaint. Ummmmmm."

Toucan was in a deep, fairly animated conversation with The Meeter when Tinker and Chicken strolled out into the courtyard, ready for breakfast.

Tinker smiled. "Well Toucan, Meeter, the food looks good. I am famished."

From across the courtyard he heard Goose giggle. Tinker and Chicken hurried through their meal as Toucan received the last of the instructions from The Meeter on how to find Tremlor's domain. Goose finished packing what gear they would take with them and seeing that one and all were ready.

"At you wish, Sire."

"O.K., Goose, coming." Tinker wiped his mouth and stood up. "Many thanks for your hospitality, Meeter. Ready, Princess?"

"Yes, John . . . Me'Lord."

"Toucan?"

"Indeed, Highness."

Tinker headed for the exit calling, "Then, let's get this show on the road."

The company filed out of the courtyard, taking the direction indicated by The Meeter. They waved goodbye to the silent village folk. Chicken walked by Tinker's side and nudged him gently with one elbow. He smiled. And tucked her arm under his, their fingers intertwined.

The day was a repeat of the previous one.

Far ahead they could see their first obstacle, The Vertical Walls, a series of shear cliffs that ran across their line of travel. The stone faces seemed to stretch from horizon to horizon. Clouds scudded along their upper reaches.

In the late afternoon, the company reached the base of the cliffs and began to follow a twisting roadway that cut up and across the talus slopes.

Halfway up, the narrow road cut sharply around a jagged shaft of rock and entered a long, narrow, rapidly rising valley. This was the way in. It took them higher and higher, deeper and deeper into the foreboding mountain range.

They reached a sharp ridge as the last shafts of the setting sun stabbed into the gloom beyond. This was the dividing line. The road angled sharply down the backside of The Vertical Walls.

Up here they would camp for Toucan had been warned by The Meeter that they should not travel beyond this place in the dark. They must wait for daylight.

Goose quickly assigned The Guard their

positions, then everyone huddled in uncomfortable positions to wait for morning.

Mists swirled up and over them. Eddies of sulfurous fumes drifted from the backside.

Everyone dutifully ate the food that was passed out but few had much of an appetite.

It was a long night.

At first light, Toucan was up and moving rapidly, followed by the rest of the company. Peering around, he mumbled, "Gad, do be most unpleasant a'place this."

"Certainly is. However, I think down there looks far, far worse." Sorrowful pointed down into the darkness, into the unknown region they were soon to enter. In the twilight he could just make out a dark, murky, enclosed valley.

"Sire?"

"Sure, Goose, go."

Toucan laid one hand of Goose's shoulder as he started to walk away. "Brother, do take care. Find firm ground and be most wary, we know not what kind of thing foul Tremlor do be."

"Have no fear, Brother, tis time for most great a'caution." Goose turned and waved. "Let's go, lads. Sergeant!"

"Yes, SAH!"

The Guard trotted down the road, Goose and Sorrowful in their midst. Tinker, Toucan and Chicken stomped their feet and waited for the signal to proceed. Even Tai and Two-Byte were almost immobile.

They waited.

And waited.

And waited.

John Tinker?

Yes, Sorrowful, what is it?

There is no sign of life down here. Goose says for you to come ahead. One of The Guard will meet you partway.

O.K., we are on our way.

Tinker looked at Toucan and Chicken. "Well, here we go."

He strode down the road, swinging his weaponkin down and around and around. The dark blade hummed quietly to itself. He could feel the tingle traveling up his arm.

Behind him, Chicken and Toucan swished their blades back and forth as they warmed up.

At the base of the slope they were met by the assigned Guard, his sword resting on his shoulder, eyes carefully watching their surrounding.

He saluted. "This way, My Lords, Princess. It is but a short walk around this point."

The Guardsman led them through a narrow defile and then out onto a broad, sandy beach. Down the beach, they could see The Guard standing in a long line facing out. The body of water, once a clear lake, had been turned into a swamp.

It was a vast mire.

Bubbles rose slowly to the surface and burst, releasing yellow fumes reeking of sulfur. Periodically great ripples surged across the surface. Somewhere, deep beneath the matted surface, something large was moving.

Goose greeted them. "Here we do be, Sire. Rather ugly place, this. Nary a sign of life. Yet!" He waggled his sword at the swamp.

Tinker nodded at Toucan. "What do you think?"

One corner of Toucan's mouth puckered as he sucked it in. "Here may we do naught but stand and wait, Highness. The Meeter did specify this most surely. In yonder muck do dwell most foul monster called Tremlor. We do a'wait its pleasure."

Tinker nodded. "O.K." He turned and sat, leaning against his upraised knees, arms crossed and stared into the swamp. The weaponkin hummed softly in his hand. His arm tingled pleasantly from shoulder to wrist.

Chicken walked over and sat next to him.

Toucan wandered back and forth, deep in thought, flicking his blade this way and that. It reminded Tinker of the tip of a cat's tail when it is waiting patiently for the mouse to come out.

Goose had taken a position in the center, out front, of the long line of stolid Guardsmen, his arms crossed over his chest, waiting patiently. Behind this line wandered Sorrowful, Tai and Two-Byte.

It would only be a matter of time.

They all hoped.

They waited and watched.

Far out the surface of the swamp heaved upward and settled back. Low swells rolled toward the shoreline.

Tinker uncoiled, feeling the adrenaline beginning to flow. "Something is coming."

Out there a hump began to rise as a massive something pushed its way toward the surface and toward the shore, pushing the muck before it. The mire heaved and burst open as the huge misshaped body stepped onto the packed sand using four stumpy legs.

Clots of sulfurous ooze fell, spattering slug soft before them. The long tail swirled the muddy surface behind as a face, a parody of a face, peered down at them from the end of a long, sinuous neck. The face, ever changing, lowered itself to their level, dead white eyes staring at them, jaws agape, showing shark teeth.

Something liquid, something gurgled, as it spoke, "So you have survived my agents, have you. What do you want here? What do you have to do here?"

A wolf with red, glaring eyes, gore stained teeth snapped at them. "What do you have to do with TREMLOR, LORD VILE, new ruler of this land? WHAT?"

Tinker leaned forward and spit onto the sand. Behind him he heard the metallic slithering of great swords clearing their sheaths as The Guard moved as one man.

Just below the junction of head to neck, two short arms waggled at Tinker as Tremlor lifted his head. Jeweled fingers tinkled lightly as they rubbed together. Two long tentacles further down uncoiled, their three-taloned ends snapped.

Tinker turned his back on the creature and walked up the sloping beach to stand near Toucan.

Chicken trotted over to cover his other side.

Tinker turned, looked up at the slavering thing. "Lord Vile, we are your doom. We are here to end your foul reign. Permanently." He thought it sounded like the right kind of speech to make, given the circumstances.

"My doom?" Tremlor humped itself toward

them. "Say welcome to DEATH!"

The ends of the long line of Guardsmen swung inward attacking both sides of the creature simultaneously, great swords flashing in the morning light.

The thick hide of Tremlor absorbed the blows. One tentacle slashed across their ranks, sending two of the Guardsmen flying backward. Three more were thrown in the opposite direction.

Goose leaped forward shouting, "Up slope! Up slope!"

Dodging under a whirling tentacle he slashed it open as it whirled toward him. Ducking down, he slid under the creatures belly, exiting the other side, laughing, slashing the other tentacle as he did so.

The boar-snouted face of Tremlor thrust at Toucan forcing him backward to avoid the clenching arms beneath. He hacked at the snout, stumbled in the soft sand and fell backward. Eager fangs struck at him. Only to be intercepted by a small dark shadow that darted in, dagger ripping a furrow down the face as Sorrowful's free arm curled around the monster's neck.

Lord Vile's head and neck lifted carrying Sorrowful high into the air as he hung just above the creature's small appendages. He reached down, one foot at the junction of arm and neck and hacked the arm off, tumbling out and away. Sorrowful landed hard and off balance, rolling and sprawling in an ungainly heap.

Throwing sand in all directions, he sat up and grabbed one ankle. "OH, by all the tales to be told. OH, OH, OH!"

Chicken lunged toward the tentacle groping for Sorrowful as he violently thrashed away from it, his dagger whipping back and forth, holding it at bay. One muscular loop wrapped around Chicken's waist and lifted her from the ground even as she plunged her blade through it.

Tinker charged, snarling in rage, his weaponkin singing through the air, severing the rubbery thing from Vile's body, green gore splashing in all directions.

Howling with anger at the surrounding mob, Tremlor began to back into the swamp to reduce his opponents field of battle. And stopped.

Tai had moved behind the thing and was using her own great bulk, feet firmly implanted, blocking the way.

Goose spun around, waving the Guardsmen forward. "We have it! We have it now! CHARGE!"

Vile struck at his exposed back, fangs gleaming, spewing venom as it struck.

With an overhead, two-handed slash that had all of his body weight behind it, Tinker swung at the outstretched neck. Slayer snickered through the air and was buried in the sand as Tremlor's head was separated from its neck.

Tremlor's body heaved and thrashed. The Guard ran in all directions to escape the death throes. Tai lumbered off. The carcass backed partway into the swamp and collapsed, the long neck dragging a deep furrow in the sand.

Tinker straightened up from the crouch of his final blow, his fingers stiff and unwilling to release the sword hilt. He turned and stared around the scene of battle.

Goose lay crumbled on the sand, face down.

Guardsmen had been thrown far afield, those

standing had great rips in their clothes.

Tinker stared at Toucan who was swaying in exhaustion and attempting to stagger over to him. "My god, Toucan," gasped Tinker. "We've lost Goose and half The Guard."

As Toucan stepped past the gore leaking head, it snapped at him. The one attached hand and arm began to pull it toward the swamp.

"Watch it, that thing is still alive!"

Toucan lurched sideways, his blade slashing down, separating arm from neck.

Chicken ran over, plunged her sword down, and pinned the head in place. She whirled and stumbled toward the still, white form further up slope. Twisting in an agonized collapse she fell on her knees next to Goose.

"Oh Brother, sweet Brother, thy loss do be most sorely felt." Locking her arms across her chest she began to rock back and forth in silent mourning.

A sand-muffled voice rasped at her, "Do weep no more, My Lady, and do be so kind for to remove mine own face from bed so gritty. Me'thinks We have been most foully used and most heavily bruised, mayhap for life."

Wiping her tears from her cheeks, Chicken gently tugged Goose over onto his back and gently began to brush the sand from his face.

Carefully opening his eyes, Goose stared up at the sky. "Awwww ... ahhhhhhh, tis much the nicer this way. I may see fair sky." Pain contorting his features he jerked his head so he could see her face. A badly bent smile twitched at his features.

"Look not at Us so, for We do be not a'dyin' yet.

Praps thee might urge mine Brother and Our Lord Tinker to tug this battered body upright, We wouldst view this scene of such fearful work."

Toucan and Tinker stepped over to lift Goose to his feet.

"OHHHHHHH, owwww . . OUCH! Gently, damn it, gently!" Goose ducked his head."Your pardon, Sire."

He waved their support away and stood swaying from side to side carefully turning his head back and forth to survey the beach. He took a step, then another hesitating step and tottered further up the slope.

"We must do be well and truly alive for nothing dead wouldst feel so poorly. Sergeant!"

"Yes, SAH!"

"Assemble The Guard, We would inspect them."

"Yes, SAH!"

The Sergeant charged up and down the beach and finally reassembled the widely scattered group into a long line of battered figures, Jackets and pants hung in rags and tatters but all still clenched their swords. All were covered with patches and smears of green gore even now beginning to attract small flying things.

Goose swayed and weakly waggled one arm, calling, "My Lord Tinker, The Guard do await thy very own pleasure. Wouldst care to inspect their most battered but unbeaten ranks?" He stood crookedly to attention. "OH, ouch!"

Tinker smiled as he hurried to his side. "With pleasure, Goose. Would the Prince Toucan and the Princess Chicken accompany me, please."

"At your very command, Me'Lord."

"With pleasure, Highness."

Tinker stooped down and heaved his weaponkin from the sand. Carefully rubbing it clean, he swung it up and over, restoring it to its position upon his back. As he walked behind Goose, he stared at the battered ranks and wondered how any of them survived or why many were still alive. Deep wounds crossed a number of chests, great slashes bit deeply from face to shoulder, down arms and legs.

When they reached the end of the line, he asked, "Goose, I don't understand. How can some of these men still be alive, much less be standing there, smiling at us?"

Goose turned and stared proudly at The Guard.

"Oak, Sire, solid English oak."

"Oak?"

"Oh, aye, Sire." Goose stepped up in front of the end man and struck the torn and bare chest with one knuckle. It thunked.

"Oak?"

"Righto, Sire. It do take much for to do in one of The Guard. They do be," he announced proudly, "the stuff with which one builds empires great."

Tinker stared at the long row of battered Guardsmen. "How can they be solid oak? I've seen them eat and drink and carouse."

Goose giggled. "Don't really know, Sire. But tis true, none-the-less. Praps it t'were how all do come to be."

They walked toward the far end of the line, Toucan and Chicken had moved slightly away from them during their conversation. Tinker's eyes fastened upon them, he hesitated, then asked, "You are like The Guard, and Toucan, and yourself . . . Princess Chicken

. . . are plastic and fluff?"

The others had heard the gasped question.

Toucan stepped over, reached out and gently placed his hand on Tinker's shoulder. "Nay, Highness, for we do be as mortal as thee, mere flesh and blood. Although, as our Noble Sister do tell, our blood do be blue and do flow from wounds as readily as any. We all do be as open to final death as thee or The Count Sorrowful."

"Sorrowful? Where is he?"

"Coming, John Tinker, coming."

They swung around toward the call and watched as the small figure trundled up the beach toward them.

"Just gathering up a few trinkets, the spoils of war," he announced. "LOOK!"

Sorrowful pushed into their midst, holding out both hands. Cupped in his palms where five gold rings. Three of them had a pattern of intertwined vines carved into their surfaces. The other two were plain.

"Well, Sorrowful, just the right number. Where did you find them?"

"From Lord Vile's fingers, John Tinker."

Tinker handed the decorated rings to Toucan, Goose and Chicken. "Sorrowful and I can have the plain ones."

Tinker held out his left hand, turning it to show off the ring. "Pretty nice, huh?"

An ugly voice rasped at them, "Sssssssss, we will met again. Sssoon, John Tinker, ssssoon." Peels of demonic laughter echoed from the unmoving lips of Tremlor's head.

Chicken shuddered. "Ugh, My Lord, do let us be rid ourself and this elseplace of this thing."

"Good idea, Princess. Goose, have The Guard search this beach for all the pieces of burnable wood they can find. Then torch that thing."

"Righto, Sire, at once. Sergeant, on the double!"

"Yes, SAH!"

Soon a merry blaze marked the spot where Lord Vile's head had been. The body had vanished beneath the murky surface of the swamp. Finally, after the fire had died, Tinker walked over and kicked the ashes to the winds.

As the soft breeze blew them away, a gurgling surge of froth roiled the surface of the bog. In a great belch of yellow fumes Vile's body dissolved.

They all stood watching the final traces dissipate.

Something chimed a bell-like tone behind them.

It was the portal.

The fire-snakes roiled and hissed at them. Flames danced across its surface. Through the center they could just make out the features of a great, open valley.

Tinker looked puzzled. "That's the first time that thing has ever made a sound. Did it ever chime for you, Sorrowful?"

"Not until now, John Tinker, not until now."

"Well, it appears Big Red's toy has decided to start making noise. I guess we are done here. Shall we go?"

"Lead on, Sire."

Goose beamed broadly, The Guard forming into two ranks behind him.

"Ready Chicken?"

She nodded, her hand lightly touching his cheek. He took her hand in his and stepped through the portal.

Toucan, Goose and the rest followed them.

Sorrowful took one final look at the place, firmly fixing all the details in his mind, beckoned for Tai and Two-Byte to follow and stepped through.

As Tai's tail disappeared so did the portal.

The sandy slope was empty.

The soft breeze slowly smoothed away all signs of disturbance until no sign of their passage remained.

Darkness, Darkness, Foul and Deep

Tinker and Chicken stepped from the portal and quickly moved to one side.

He looked at her. Her eyes sparkled with happiness.

Throwing one arm around her shoulder, he stood and surveyed this new land while the company reassembled itself.

As Goose busied himself with The Guard, Tai and Two-Byte wandered about. The electronic twins buzzed and whirred to themselves. Tai gathered in large mouthfuls of vegetation and slowly chewed contentedly.

Sorrowful stood, taking in everything, then he walked over to join Tinker and Chicken.

"This is a rather beautiful spot, is it not? But it does have a strange shape."

The little group stood high on the upper reaches of a long slope thickly overgrown with deep grass. Below them, the valley formed a perfectly round bowl. Above them, tree covered ridges enclosed the depression.

Tinker scanned the valley before them, he estimated that it was about 18-20 miles across. Right in the center of the floor there was something from which all the roads radiated. From here, that area appeared to be totally devoid of vegetation.

BONG!

The portal winked into non-existence. Moments later an answering echo rebounded from the walls of the valley behind them.

Toucan, whose eyes picked out small details better than anyone's, reported that there had been some presence on the central spot that had waved at them.

Tinker frowned. "Fine time for that portal to start making noise. It certainly announced our arrival in no uncertain tones, no pun intended."

"Oh, aye, Highness, it most truly do that."

"Well Toucan, what do you think?"

"Highness, if we do stay here we may easily see anything that would fain come our way long err it would arrive. But I do me believe that our goal be there." He pointed at the central place. "Yonder, where all roads do meet. Pears to be the gathering place for this round land. And indeed, following subtle pattern of thy quest, yonder be whither we ought proceed. Of this, I have doubt not."

Tinker looked at his gathered group.

"O.K., Toucan, I agree. Let's go. This grass appears to be only knee deep, so nothing should surprise us while we walk down to there. We will just take it nice and slow. It's just the thing after leaving Lord Vile's beach behind. It is pleasantly warm. So let us enjoy it."

"Fair sun do look some strange, Me'Lord."

"Indeed, Highness, rather ruddy in color."

He stared up at it. The sun did have a distinct reddish tone and looked to be several times larger than the one that Tinker called familiar. Swinging one arm around Chicken's waist, he drew her close.

"We're not home yet, Princess. Just another time, another place, another something to do. How do you feel?"

"Some battered, some bruised, but most ready, Me'Lord. Thyself?"

He smiled. "About the same, battered and bruised. But nowhere as badly as Goose. I don't see how he does it?"

Chicken smiled back at him.

"Oh, Brother Goose wilt be right as rain by dusky eventide. We do ourself heal most rapidly, as thou shouldst remember, Sweet Lord."

"Right. I do indeed."

Tinker released her and swung around.

"Goose, head for that central area down there. But do take it easy, we have all day to get there. No rush. Sorrowful, stay with Goose, please."

"Aye, Sire, easy does it."

"Of course, John Tinker."

"Sergeant!"

"Yes, SAH!"

"You heard Our Lord, that way, slowly."

"Yes, SAH!"

The Guard formed themselves into a long, widely spaced line and began to stroll slowly down the slope, idly flicking their great swords. Bits of grass flew into the air before them. Goose and Sorrowful walked in the middle of the line holding another animated conversation.

Toucan, Chicken and Tinker followed while Tai and Two-Byte took a much more meandering course, Tai cropping a swath as she came.

Suddenly Tinker shuddered violently.

Chicken grasped his arm. "Me'Lord, what do ail thee?"

He grasped her hand.

"Don't look so frightened, Princess, it is just the aftershock from the last place. I am all right."

"Be thee sure?"

"Sure. Toucan was correct, you know. The monsters are getting worse. And look at this bunch. We are all staggering down through the grass like a bunch of old ladies. What is going to be down there? Oak or not, The Guard can only take so much beating until they are turned into a pile of kindling. What about us mere mortals? If any of us had been hit as hard as The Guard all we would be is a pile of blood and guts making ugly spots on the sand."

"Fret not thyself, My Lord."

"This is the fifth place we have been popped into. All we need is a sign."

"What manner of sign?"

"One that says, 'Welcome to the Rocky Horror Disneyland', that's what. See the Gypsies of the Universe, popping from place to place. All at the whim of an anthropomorphic Rhode Island Red chicken. To be a Shakespearean parody of to kill or be killed. So what kind of life is this?" He stared at the ground. Then he started walking.

"Tis life, Me'Lord."

Tinker's face had sagged into deep furrowed lines of fatigue. It was a fatigue more obvious to those who saw his face than it was to him.

Toucan reached out and lightly touched Tinker on the arm. "Highness, it is at least . . . existence."

Tinker raised his head and looked over. "Yes, Toucan, it is that." He straightened up, threw back his shoulders, and managed a wan smile. "O.K., no more grumbling. But you two will have to stop looking worried. What do you have to say about all this, Princess?" He waved his free hand wildly.

Chicken pulled him to a stop and stepped in front of him, brushing a hand across her eyes. "We do be most content to be, to be with thee, Our Own."

Tinker pulled her to him and held her. Then he turned her around and tugged her down the slope. She bumped him playfully with her shoulder.

Behind them, Toucan watched. And worried.

The company strolled toward their goal, the day wore on. Overhead, the sun crawled slowly across the sky, casting a baleful, reddish glow down upon one and all.

By mid-afternoon they straggled onto the central spot and stood and stared at it. Before them stood a large, round, flat-topped platform made of slate colored stone. It was about four feet higher than the surrounding pavement. Dead center sat a single, large throne-like chair draped with a soft, white cloth.

"Highness, just moment past I do see someone or some thing wave up toward us." Toucan pointed toward the platform.

"Wave? You sure?"

"Quite so. T'was most like the manner of some old friend in greeting."

"Well, I can't imagine any old friend of mine

being in such a place. Did you see where it went? Which way it headed?"

"Nay, Highness, I do not."

"Goose, have The Guard scour this place, see whether they can find any sign of life. Or whatever."

"Jolly good, Sire. Especially the latter, what?"

"The latter?"

"Whatever, Sire."

"Right. Especially the whatever."

"Righto, Sire. Sergeant!"

"Yes, SAH!"

"Search pattern, half a league out usin' yonder chair as marker."

"Yes, SAH!"

The Guard fanned out, probing and jabbing at the grass, examining the ground closely. Two-Byte whizzed around the open space crackling to themselves. Tai moved into the grass, making bald spots as she wandered, grazing here and there.

Tinker, Chicken and Toucan walked over and sat in one of the newly mown areas. Tinker slowly leaned back until he was sprawled flat on his back, his weaponkin along his side. The heat radiating from the ground felt good on tired back muscles.

"Now that does feels good. I think that I will just take a little nap. Princess, Toucan?"

"We do meself do sit a'spell, Me'Lord."

Toucan rose to his feet. "Highness, I would me inspect strange stone platform and chair. Your leave." He bowed.

Tinker waved weakly. "Bye, Toucan." His eyes closed.

Toucan walked down and over to inspect the

stone structure. Carefully he walked around it, inspecting its method of construction and the joinery of the stone block. After two slow circumnavigations, he hoisted himself up and lifted the cloth covering the chair to peer beneath it. Then, his curiosity satisfied, he jumped down and walked back toward the two still figures in the bare patch.

Tinker was sound asleep. Chicken sat next to him, her knees drawn up, resting upon them. Her left hand covered his right. Her right hand was tightly clenched around the hilt of her drawn word. She, too, was sound asleep.

He watched them for a moment, then wandered off to stand quietly, his eyes following the ever-widening search of The Guard.

Goose and Sorrowful were still in deep conversation. Tai continued to crop her way around the circle leaving a long trail of spots to mark her passage. Two-Byte had settled on one spot and were barely humming and crackling to each other. It was, all-in-all, a rather peaceful scene. Toucan walked over to join Goose and Sorrowful.

"What ho, Brother Toucan, come a'visitin'?"

"Quite so, Brother Goose, quite so." Toucan bowed to Sorrowful. "Count. Have The Guard found anything?"

Goose smiled broadly. "Neither hide nor hair. But, the hare jumps up where one do least expect it, as the wise folk do be want to say."

"Indeed. What think you of making camp roundabouts?"

"As safe as any. Tis most open and clear a space. Wither we from here on the morrow?"

"Six roads lead in as many directions. Who can say which of these Our Lord Tinker shall chose to walk. In this vast dish." Toucan waved one arm at their surroundings. "Yonder stone platform do be true center. All roads in, all roads out. Me'thinks strange dais tis nought but our final destination. Count, what say you? Be this grassy swale but merely another step on long journey? To me, this do feel most unnatural a'place."

Sorrowful frowned and paused before answering. He glanced over at his questioner. "Prince Toucan, it seems much the same way to me. There is an artificiality to this strangely shaped valley. I have not seen or heard anything here, or in the many places and times I have been, that yielded one clue as to where we are bound. I am afraid we can only wait and see." He shrugged one shoulder.

Toucan bent forward. "In that, Count, you do be most correct. We can do naught but wait and see. For the nonce, I shall stroll some small distance that way." He pointed back toward a bright yellow spot in the grass.

"Our Lord Tinker do sleep most deeply. As do our Noble and Fair Sister, Chicken. And yon Warrior Princess do sleep with mighty sword in hand."

Toucan turned and walked away, his hands clasped behind his back, head falling forward in thought.

Goose and Sorrowful returned to their previous conversation, telling one another of all that they had seen and done on this quest. They were adding little details, additional bits and pieces to Sorrowful's growing *Tale of The Quest*. The sun slowly approached the edge of the surrounding ridges.

By the time it was full dark, camp had been made, such as it was. Few of the supplies that had been hanging from Tai's back had survived the encounter with Lord Vile. But, all in all, there was sufficient food left that everyone had what Sorrowful called 'a very light meal'. All around them the great basin lay silent and still. No night creature rustled or sang. The Guard formed a defensive perimeter around the small group.

Everyone not on watch slept the night away.

Undisturbed.

Toucan roused the company at first light. They sat in small groups, talking, waiting for the sun to break up over the edge of the depression that was this valley. As the light brightened, Sorrowful pointed toward one point on a far ridge.

"Look just there, John Tinker, there is a notch cut into that hill. See. It appears that the sun will rise directly behind it."

It did.

As the tip of the sun slid up above the ridge, a beam of sunlight streamed from the notch and struck the cloth-draped chair.

It glowed dazzling white.

Brighter and brighter.

They squinted their eyes, shielding them from the sudden glare. A soft sound, a gliding, whispering sigh, spoke to them from that central spot.

A figure appeared, seated in the chair.

The light faded to normal daylight.

A medium sized individual faced them, comfortably slouched, feet crossed at the ankles, arms resting along the arms of the throne, his hands dangling from the ends.

The throne now glistened silver in the full light of the risen sun. His clothes were some shade of gray that matched the color of his hair and eyes. He spoke to them.

"Welcome, John Tinker, and exalted company. Welcome to my land. I am Dram. I am that which you have been seeking in your strange wandering."

Tinker thought Dram's face looked kindly with the deep creases in his face producing a world-weary look.

He nodded at Tinker.

"I am that individual that many have chosen to call The Evil One. A rather undignified title, heh? Really not very nice. But then, what can one expect, heh?"

Dram sighed. "I suppose that comes from having to use the sorts of things that I have been forced to use as my senior administrative staff. A rather unappetizing lot, heh? But what can you do when that is all the help you can find, heh?"

He stood, shrugged his shoulders. "But beggars can't be choosers, can they, as they say in your elseplace, heh?"

Dram strolled around the platform seemingly lost in thought. When he stood directly opposite them, he gave a start, eyes scanning every face.

"Let's see now. According to everything you have been told, you are supposed to rid all the multiplicities of all the universes of my, oh-so-terrible-and-evil, presence. IS THAT NOT CORRECT, HEH? John Tinker, I know of this quest.

And of The-Mountain-That-Walks, lost somewhere, heh? And of Smoke of the Velvetmist, gone in a frightful blast, heh? And about Goose, Toucan and the rest, heh? And, of course, of the beautiful and fierce, Princess Chicken, heh?"

Dram walked over and stared at her, raised his fingers to his lips and blew her a kiss. Then he stood deep in thought, eyes unfocused.

Suddenly his head snapped up, eyes popping wide.

"YES! All about everything, everything, heh? And I am here to tell you, Lady and Gentlemen, that you seem to have run out of luck, heh? This quest can not be finished, not at all, heh?" He spun around and flopped back into the throne, throwing one leg up and over an arm.

"You only have two choices. You've heard these before, John Tinker. From that dummy that I left behind in Murk Wildweald, heh? It has been a long time since then, relatively speaking, heh?"

Dram smiled and held up one finger.

"ONE! You may join forces with me and rule the elseplaces of your choice in any manner that you might wish. Ahhhhh, with me as your liege, of course."

A second finger rose to join the first.

"Or. TWO! You may chose to die."

He sat up, leaning forward to peer at Tinker warily, gray eyes staring. "It is quite a simple set of choices, isn't it, John? What do you say, heh?" His eyes scrolled slowly across the rest of the company while he waited for a response then returned to Tinker.

"Well, John, what do you say, heh?"

Dram's shoulders drooped, sagged, he sat back

in the throne.

"OH, me. I can see by your expression that you have taken the wrong choice, again. It is number two, heh? It figures after what that doddering old fool, The Thought, and that pesky chicken filled your minds with. Do not be too hasty, think about it. I am a good boss. Really."

Dram smiled winningly, flashing lots of teeth as he cocked his head to one side, and purred, "Awwwww come'on, Johnny, give ol'Dram a hand. I can use a man of your talents. I need people who can think, with lots of friends."

He waved one hand grandly. "You know how hard it is to find good people, top talent, capable administrators, heh? Come'on, join me."

Flopping back, he face fell. "No? Then that is that. Too bad, really, we would have made quite a team, you and I, heh? You would have been ever so much more palatable a staff that those things that I am forced to rely upon."

Dram whispered harshly at them, "They really have no taste, you know, not a trace."

Slowly he stood up. "Oh well, oh well, I do suppose we ought to end this as quickly as possible, heh?"

He made a short, stiff bow from the waist and snapped into a rigid stance. "I salute you gladiators before you die." Then he clapped his hands together, one sharp '*pop*'.

Wails and screams echoed from the corridors of nightmare horror as a mass of black, gibbering shapes and forms poured from all sides, down the slopes of the valley. Their eyes flashed red in the crimson sunlight, their teeth glittering glistening oozing slime venom.

Dram shouted, calling over the dim, "Ugly, aren't they, Johnny Boy. I will give you one more minute to reconsider."

The Guard quickly formed a defensive arc around the backs of the five as they still faced Dram, great swords snickering free. Goose, Sorrowful, Toucan and Chicken formed a loose box on three sides of Tinker, who still faced Dram. The other three faced out, watching the shifting changing mass charging toward them.

"THIRTY SECONDS, JOHN! TWENTY-NINE!"

Dram walked to the edge of the platform and looked down at them, his voice carrying easily. "You are almost out of time."

He turned around and strolled back to the throne, spun around and slouched into it, his legs sticking straight out as he slumped on his spine. He raised one arm and gave a limp-wrist good-bye wave.

"Bye, bye, Johnny."

The black wave poured into the stone clearing and converged, an ebony tidal wave eager to kill.

It flowed up and over Tai even as her tail tore gory swaths through their ranks while her feet mashed numbers into black pulp.

The Guards' wall held as great swords flashed high, hacking, slashing, driving back wave after wave crashing against their wooden breakwater.

Glancing to one side, Tinker could see flashes of blue lightening arcing and crackling as Two-Byte formed a defensive shield around themselves. Periodically they would disappear, swallowed up by demon hordes, only to reappear in the blinding flash of explosion decimating all that pressed so vainly upon them.

Slowly the front ranks were thinned only to be replaced by larger, even more deformed reinforcements.

The Guard's line swayed. And held.

Then, with a high-pitched screak that hurt human ears, the black surge coursed high and poured up and over The Guard.

Quickly, pushing Sorrowful into the middle, Tinker, Goose, Toucan and Chicken formed a hollow square. Their swords flashed and cleared a space around them as they tried to push toward the hidden rank of The Guard. The tangle of fallen bodies held them in place.

"Looks like we stand and fall in place, gang."

Goose laughed, slicing a three-headed monster from shoulder to stomach. "One, two, three. To the death Sire, to the death!"

Tinker nudged Chicken with his left shoulder as she yanked her sword free from the chest of something that was wolf-faced.

"A short but happy life, Princess?"

"Aye, Me'Lord, most so." She slashed another thing from crotch to sternum.

"And farewell to thee, Me'Lord . . . Love."

"GOOSE!" Tinker pointed. "I don't believe it!"

A Guardsman's arm rose above the black swirling mass and fell, hewing open a small space.

Goose giggled. "Solid oak, Sire, solid oak."

Dram watched as the battle swirled around them. He sat up, crossed one leg over the other and idly kicked his foot back and forth, musing to himself.

This was taking too long.

It was becoming a bore.

Yet, it was, after all, only a matter of time. And, he had all the time of the universe of universes. He smiled to himself. They would get tired soon. And then his never-ending multitudes would take care of this problem, permanently.

His smile broadened. Maybe he wouldn't let them kill them right away. He could let old John Boy watch as a few of those things played with Miss-Bright-and-Yellow-Chicken. Then he would see that it would be better to join up, that it would be the wise choice.

Dram almost laughed.

Then he stared.

A bent figure was hobbling rapidly through the black swirling demon throng swinging a monstrous two-handed sword, cutting a wide swath toward him.

It was muttering loudly as it came slashing, "A horse, a horse. My Kingdom for a horse!"

Tinker gasped as the figure strode past. "What was that, Goose?"

"Richard Crook-Back, Sire."

"Richard who?"

"The Third, Sire."

"I don't believe it."

"None-the-less, Sire. See yonder, at edge of stony platform."

Tinker looked in the direction indicated and saw the strange figure hoist itself up onto the platform and lurch toward Dram. A golden splash of light reflected from the crown attached to its helmet.

Dram slowly rose and stepped forward, transfixed by this new stranger.

"Who, or what, are you? And where did you come from?"

"I am The End of your reign, Foul Fiend!"

Piercing black eyes fastened upon Dram as the great sword was raised up and over one shoulder. "ON YOUR KNEES! It is your head that I wish, not your Kingdom."

Dram slowly sank. Then he jumped backward.

"NO!" He jabbed one index finger at this strange being. "BE GONE!"

A flash of crackling energy arched forth and struck the thing on the ornate breast plate blasting it backward and off the platform to crash into a demon which erupted into a gout of flame. Instantly the fire leaped from creature to creature. All around the conflagration roared, then died out. The arena was clear. Only wisps of smoke remained to drift gently where once demonic hordes struggled and fought.

"A TRICK! A TRICK!" Dram howled. "More meddling by that damnable Magician."

Dram continued to howled his frustration at the sky. Then he whirled to glare at Tinker and his small group.

"But you will die anyway."

He stalked to the edge of the platform and pointed one quavering finger at them.

"DIE, you will. It is merely a matter of minutes, if you'll pardon the alliteration."

Casting an oily smile at them, he turned and stomped back to the throne and resettled himself.

"Yes, only a matter of minutes, heh? Just recharging the batteries, as it were, heh?"

He gestured with the back of his hand.

"Oh, save your energies, termite bait, no-one can penetrate this space . . . now."

One of The Guard was hammering at an invisible barrier with the hilt of his sword, attempting to attack Dram.

"Sire," hissed Goose. "A respit, a respit."

"Won't be enough, Goose, you heard the man. It is really only a matter of minutes, then we will be attacked again, and again. We need hours of rest, not minutes. My arms ache, my legs ache, I ache. A couple of minutes rest really won't make much of a difference. It is a war of attrition and we are going to wear out first."

"Fraid you do be most correct, Sire."

Goose leaned forward, resting his crossed arms on the hilt of his sword, point on the ground, and sighed.

Chicken tugged at Tinker's sleeve.

"Lordlove, what do be strange case?"

"What case?"

"That one." She pointed.

Tinker looked behind himself.

Sitting on the ground, just behind Sorrowful, was a small wooden crate. Stenciled across its top were a series of red initials: C. A. R. E.

"Open it."

Sorrowful spun around and began to pry off the top with his dagger. He looked up.

"What does C.A.R.E. stand for?"

"I will explain later, if there is a later. What's inside?"

Pitching the top to the ground outside the small group, Sorrowful peered inside and thrust one hand into the packing materials and dug around. "Ummm, ummm, ummm, ummm, AHHHH." He yanked out five small, flat brownish colored objects and stared at them.

"They appear to be eatable, John Tinker." He handed one to each person.

Tinker took his and turned it back and forth, then read the small legend imprinted on the top: EAT ME.

He shrugged his shoulder and did, wondering whether he was going to grow bigger or smaller.

Neither one.

Nothing happened.

He looked at the others. They looked back.

Then he straightened up as something burst inside. His fatigue was gone, he bristled with new found energy. He could see the rosy glow of radiant health spreading across his companions features. They rolled and flexed their shoulders and muscles that were suddenly neither sore nor tired.

Tinker smiled. "A present from Big Red, I suspect. Looks like we are ready to withstand another onslaught."

"Just in time, Highness."

Blackness was pouring down the valleys walls as a screaming terror filled the air. Demon masses surged toward them.

Tinker glanced over at the platform.

Dram stood at the edge, a smile flickering on and off his face. He made an abbreviated bow.

"Sayonara, Mothers."

Now Is the Time to Put an End to This Quest

Turmoil, black ugly turmoil, swirled around them. They were an island in a sea of hate.

Dram danced and gestured at them, screaming curses into the tumult.

Chaos reigned supreme.

BONG

The bell-like sound echoed and reechoed from the surrounding hills. The sound cut through the roar of battle.

"What was that, John Tinker?"

"That, Sorrowful, I believe, was the sound of the portal telling one and all that it has arrived."

The little band struggled to move toward it, hacking, slashing, feet slipping in the gore, but to no avail.

"We will never get to it, not through this mob," grumbled Tinker.

BONG

"Damn, there it goes, back into never-never land."

They could see a great shape standing where the portal had been. It stood looking down at the swirling pandemonium. Then the figure gave a mighty bellow and charged down and into the demonic masses, the gigantic club tearing an open pathway in front of the headlong charge.

A shattered bow wave of crushed and mangled bodies flew upward as the immense figure plowed forward to the edge of the stone platform, swiping an open space around it, tramping wiggling creatures underfoot.

Dram, reseated in his throne, watched all this with a bemused expression on his face.

"Well, Mountain, so you have come at last. Did you bring me a present, heh? Some little, glittering something, heh? Something just for little ol' me?"

Dram blinked coy eyes at the giant standing unmolested and unbothered in an ebb tide of retching horror. Standing, Dram minced to the edge of the platform and draped one hand on an out-thrust hip. "Well?"

"Yes, I did." Mountain reached up and lifted a heavily bejeweled necklace from around his neck. He threw it. "Catch."

Dram caught it with one hand and swirling it around one finger, draped it over his head and around his neck. He patted it in place with one hand and smiled at Mountain.

"The Gett'tda'gaz, at long last. I thank you, Mountain, for this gift." His peels of laughter rang out over the surging battle, freezing the demonic hordes in their tracks.

"Oh, ha, ha. HA . . . HA! You fools, so misguided and misled. Now I have won. WON! You may as well lay your weapons down and face facts. I have won!"

Dram stared at Mountain and smiled broadly.

"For this gift, you may have anything, anything at all, even them. With this small trinket in my possession there is nothing that can prevail against me, nothing, NOTHING! They are all mine, each and every one. At long last, all mine. All the times, all the places, all mine!"

He held his hand next to his mouth and stage-whispered toward Tinker and his small group, "Oooooo, I just loooove to overact."

Then he straightened up and spoke to Mountain, "Mighty Giant, you may choose. Tell me your wish and it shall be so. Speak." Dram pointed dramatically at him.

"I choose . . . "

"Yes, yes?"

"To stand with my friends."

Dram's eyebrows shot straight up.

"WHAT? Oh dear, you also, heh? Well, so be it then. But it is so foolish, heh? I could have merely given them to you. However, do as you wish, it is your choice. GO!" He made shooing motions with his hands.

Mountain turned and walked over to Tinker and the rest, a pathway opening before him. He stopped, beamed at Tinker, bent over, reached down and carefully patted Sorrowful on top of the head, whispering in a low, rumbling bass that only they could hear, "He had to receive that gift willingly. The Gett said it must be so. Now we must fight." Straightening up, he announced in booming tones, "BY DUMPF, you can introduce me to your friends later."

Spinning around, he jumped forward and with one downstroke of his cudgel smashed one of the stones of the platform and mangled a number of the demons standing there. He managed another blow before the black ranks attacked.

Tinker stared at him as Mountain strode through the ripping, gouging masses in apparent total disregard for his own well-being. The giant stomped around and around the small group swinging his club in wide sweeps, mashing things under his feet while punching others with his free hand.

Demons leapt upon his front and back, tearing and rending, biting arms and legs. Mountain still paid them little attention, even as his clothes were being shredded.

Off to one side, a gout of blue flames blasted into the air. Two-Byte was still alive and functioning.

With Mountain circling around and around, Tinker and his party found that they had small moments of rest.

BONG

The sound echoed over the dim.

"John Tinker, the portal, the portal."

"I heard it, Sorrowful. But it sounded a long way off. MOUNTAIN! Let's push that way."

BONG

"BY DUMPF!"

"Certainly didn't stick around for long."

Chicken gasped, "ME'LORD! What manner of creature DO come at us enow?"

An explosion of black creatures flew into the air as slashing claws hacked a path toward the beleaguered group.

Well, mindmate, what have you been doing? Where have you been?

SMOKE?

Yes, mate of my mind, being of my being. Here I am. I bring you a gift and a secret. See.

The thoughts flashed forth and blazed through his mind. Tinker's voice roared out over the battle sounds.

"TAI! TWO-BYTE! TO ME, TO ME!"

"What is happening, John Tinker?"

"Me'Lord, what do be a'happening?"

"Sire?"

"Highness?"

"It's Smoke. She's alive and tearing down the slope to join us. Look."

A black shape flowed in sinuous curves, claws raking and tearing as she approached. Brilliant shafts of white light streamed from between her jaws.

Far to one side a wave of demons burst open as Tai surged toward them, shedding masses of things from her back as she plodded toward Tinker.

Far to the other side blue flames erupted, blowing clouds of ruptured flesh into the air. Black bits and pieces rained down upon friend and foe. Two-Byte was moving toward them.

Tai surged into view, clearing an open space with a sweep of her tail. Tinker pointed and quickly told Sorrowful and Goose what to do. They rushed from their group and climbed onto her back, sheltering between the thick plates running in a double row along her spine. Feeling them in place, Tai lumbered out into the clawing demon throng.

Blue flame erupted and Two-Byte blasted into view opening a space next to Tinker. As Mountain bent low, Tinker whispered his instructions into the proffered ear, then jumped aside as the giant stepped out and into the glowing blue field that surrounded the electronic Siamese-twins. One large hand grabbed Chicken and pulled her with him. They moved off in the direction opposite to that taken by Tai and her riders.

Toucan spun and guarded Tinker's back as they fought on, alone.

"Hurry, hurry, hurry," mumbled Tinker under his breath as his weaponkin flashed and danced before him, barely restraining the pressing hordes.

Finally Two-Byte and Tai reached their assigned positions, guided into position by Smoke who reared and danced over the surface of the surging black mass. The three groups now formed spots of turmoil equidistantly spaced in that sea of death.

NOW!

Smoke's command struck their minds, galvanizing their nerves and muscles into instantaneous action. Tinker, Sorrowful, and Mountain twisted their weaponkin's hilts towards Dram who stood watching this strange development in the battle, a puzzled expression upon his face.

Three Golden Eyes faced him. They opened wide. Three golden beams burned through all the intervening creatures and coalesced upon his chest.

"Oh no you don't. NO! You don't have me yet. Noooooooo."

Dram's screams of rage pierced the air as he struggled with the bonds that were rapidly forming around him. Fire flashed from his hands, hissing golden snakes coiled and twined, binding his legs and arms into immobility.

NOW!

Tinker bellowed, "GOOSE! TOUCAN! CHICKEN!"

Chicken raised her arm and pointed the gray jewel at Dram. A gray band snapped forth and merged with the golden coils tightening around Dram. Then another gray band flashed out, then the other. The gray inched upward and poured into the necklace around Dram's throat.

Dram jerked his head back and forth as he twisted to see what was happening. His fingers writhed in frustration as he fought to free himself.

The Gett'tda'gaz began to glow and pulsate. Scarlet color crackled from the jewels and seeped downward, drenching him in red.

CRACK!

The color snapped into a hollow column. Inside Dram struggled with the gray and gold bands that twisted, tightened, and curled around him. He screamed and mouthed words but no sound penetrated his prison.

Smoke leaped, landed on the platform and bounded high over the reddish tower, dropping a brilliant white object from her mouth as she sailed by.

It struck the top of the pillar.

And stuck.

The stone flashed white then a deep green fire that flickered a slow rhythm.

Landing lightly on her feet, she turned and looked out over the suddenly quiet, suddenly unmoving demonic hordes.

Green oozed downward, making marbled red and green patterns over the surface of Dram's entrapment. Now The Evil One could barely be seen, his mouth open in a long, silent scream. All around, the horrors called forth stared at the sight, the causal agent of their mephetic being totally encased.

Thunder rent the sky. Dense swirling clouds suddenly boiled into existence and boiled over this central point. A voice boomed down.

"DRAM!

    Turncoat.

DRAM!

    Traitor.

DRAM!

    Seeker of Power.

DRAM!

    Whose days are over, as was foretold.

DRAM!

    This web has been spun.

DRAM!

    The Quest is over.

DRAM!

    Once second to The Thought.

DRAM!

    Now second to none.

DRAM!

    Stealer of the portal.

DRAM!

    The portal has closed upon you.

DRAM!"

A monstrous fist flashed from the clouds, striking straight down upon the top of the multicolored column. Fire and lightening erupted in all directions as it was mashed deep into the platform and the rock below. In that last instant Tinker saw Dram's eyes glaring at him.

The clouds lifted, sunlight poured from a rapidly clearing sky. With whispering, gurgling voices the black masses surrounding them began to withdraw, fading, seeping into the valley walls.

Tinker turned and stared as the still standing forms of The Guards appeared, their red and blue uniforms hanging in tatters and rags.

Then he watched as the other two groups began to sort themselves out. He ran, ran toward the gigantic form of Mountain who stood with one large hand loosely settled upon Chicken's shoulder covering it.

Around them the blue crackling flame of Two-Byte hissed and disappeared.

He could see Goose and Sorrowful running in the same direction.

"Well, BY DUMPF," roared Mountain, "didn't that voice sound to you like a certain magician we once met in Paradise?"

"It certainly did, it certainly did. And do you know what else?" shouted Tinker as he bounded up to the huge figure, adrenaline wiping away all his fatigue.

"NO, BY DOUBLE-DUMPF, what else? What the HUMPF are you grinning about?"

"We did it. We did it. We did IT!" Tinker was fairly leaping as he punctuated each sentence. "We did it. The quest is over. At last, over. OVER!" The word roared out and returned moments later as the echo repeated and repeated.

"Over . . . over . . . "

Tinker grabbed as much of Mountain as he could and squeezed him, then jumped back. "It is over, by dumpf, it is over."

Mountain frowned down at him and mumbled, "HUMPF! You don't have to swear so much, John Tinker. I gather as much from what you have just said. There is just no need to swear, BY DUMPF! Now what? Who is this beautiful and fierce Lady who shared my company for such a short while?"

Tinker stared at him.

"Now? This is The Princess Chicken."

He threw his arms around her shoulders and mashed her against his side. "Mine, by god, all mine."

Then he wrapped her in his arms, their lips joined.

Mountain tapped Tinker on one shoulder nearly driving him to his knees as Tinker hastily released Chicken. "BY DUMPF, what else will you do?"

Tinker pulled back and looked over her shoulder at the green grass.

"Now? Come, let's take our weary souls over there and just sit and relax. We have a lot to talk about. I want to know where you have been and what you have been doing. And most especially, I want to know how come you didn't suffer a scratch through all this?"

Mountain stretched out one arm and pulling up his sleeve and peered at it.

"Well, BY DUMPF, I think there are a few scratches." He pointed. "There. You see, there is one, right there." He traced a faint line with his finger tip and smiled a crooked smile at Tinker. "That potion certainly worked, did it not?"

"What potion? How about we all sit down and you can tell us about it?"

Chicken swung around.

"Indeed, Sir Knight, pray do." Her arm wrapped around Tinker's waist and fastened upon his belt.

They walked out onto the grass and settled themselves into comfortable positions to relax and listen. The grass was lush, thick and cool, untouched by all that had occurred.

The rest of the company headed their way and soon all were gathered in a loose collection around Tinker. Smoke padded silently up and leaned against his free side, her long tail curled across their backs and around Chicken's waist.

Sorrowful raced up, tears streaming across his checks. "SMOKE! You are alive. By all the tales that were ever told, I had thought you to be dead and gone." He carefully keep his thumb on the golden jewel set in the hilt of his weaponkin

No, Sorrowful, I lived. As you can see and hear.

Sorrowful spun away and dropped down in front of Mountain who has just dropped to the grass.

"And what happened to you? Tell me, tell us. Then I will have the entire tale, the whole thing, the complete Tale of The Quest. All the pieces, the full Saga, from start to finish." He stopped the gush of words and spun around to stare at Tinker.

"It is finished, is it not, John Tinker?"

Tinker laughed at his expression and nodded violently.

"Yes, I think it is finished. Whatever it was that flattened Dram, it did say that the quest was over. So,

I suppose that means we are done here. No more worlds to go hippy-skipping through. No more monsters, demons and assorted bug-uglies to face. It is really and truly finished, over, alles ist kaput." He smiled at Chicken, then at Smoke.

"And thank goodness for small miracles."

Sorrowful jumped to his feet to throw an arm over Mountain's shoulder.

"SO! Tell us your tale, then."

Mountain shrugged, almost tumbling Sorrowful off his feet.

"HUMPF, Talking Mouse, you have no patience. But if you insist, this is what happened to me . . . "

In the midst of the tale telling, Goose burst in, "SIRE, see what I have found." Under each arm he clenched three loaves of bread. In each hand he grasped a bottle of wine.

"Truly amazin'. One moment empty space, the next, viola, a mound of bread and a cluster of bottles. It do seem that there do be at least one loaf and one bottle of wine for each of us. Here, Sire, have some. And you, and you, and you."

Goose walked amongst them handing out bread and wine. Several of The Guard followed him laden down with supplies. When he finished, Goose tipped an open bottle to his mouth and took a swallow. "By George, tis a most jolly red wine." He sat on the grass and waggled one hand at Mountain, urging him to continue with his story.

Mountain's deep bass voice rumbled out and onward.

Tinker's mind drifted away, lost in thought, barely paying attention to the tale being spun. Then he turned his head and whispered in Chicken's ear, "Can you sing?"

"Sing, My Lord?"

"Sing. All this," he waggled the bottle of wine, "reminds me of a poem that I heard not all that long ago."

"Speak to me, LordLove, this thy poem."

"Right:

> A loaf of bread, a jug of wine,
>> And thou, singing beside me in the wilderness.
> And wilderness would be paradise, enow."

But what song am I to sing, Fair My Prince?

"Huh?"

"I do say, Me'Lord, *What song am I to sing?*

Smoke?

Yes, Mindmate?

Did you hear that?

Yes.

So what is going on?

Only what ought to be. You are my Mindmate. In the Land of the Gryerd I set one of the quiet parts of my mind to think about things. By the time I reached this time and place, I had decided. It is my Right, as The Focus. I saw, also, that you and the Princess had become mindmates as well. Thus, we are the start of a new Dzent.

Dzent?

A new group among the Velvetmist. It is the way of my folk. We three are merging. Hold still, we must finish that which is started. Princess, hold his arm.

Chicken pressed against his side, one arm snaked around his waist, Smoke leaned heavily against the other side and reached out with her minds. Tinker twitched and looked out at the company sprawled around them on the grass. He watched with three pairs of eyes. He heard and understood through three separate minds. Then he was one, they were one. All memories, thoughts, desires, feelings, emotions, blurred together, merged, fused into a whole. One organism, yet three separate parts.

A Dzent, John Tinker, mindmate to Chicken and Smoke. Our consort, welcome to the group.

What group?

It is among the Velvetmist that more than one female shares one male. I spoke with her, Our Princess, and she said that she didn't mind. So, we decided.

Without consulting me?

But, of course, it is the ladies' prerogative. We love you deeply, each in their own way. And you know, do you not, that you do return that love, John Tinker, Chosen One?

Multiple images flashed through his mind: the throne room of Doom, Paradise, Dread and the Land of the Hueden.

Right, you are both right. This is certainly some fairy tale all right. I am in love with a Warrior-Princess and a Telepathic Carnivore. What would Sigmund Freud have to say about that?

Female laughter rattled through his mind.

Who cares, Mindmate, My LordLove?

Tinker laughed with them and suddenly realized something new. He was no longer worried about being trapped in this, or any other fairy tale. Or any other elseplace for that matter. Now he felt . . . complete, really complete.

Mountain finished his story.

Then Sorrowful launched into all his adventures, and Tinker's. Finally he told of Smoke's.

When he finished, Sorrowful stood up, his eyes darting from face to ace.

"SO! It is finished. Now what do we do now? Do you know, John Tinker?"

"Nope. I guess we just have to wait here and see what happens next."

"OOP, one last item." Sorrowful stabbed one hand deep into a pocket and fished out a fist-sized gem. Rays of varicolored light sparkled about them. The colors shifted from yellow to blue to green to red and on and on. He held it high over his head so all could see.

"There it is, the gem I picked up just before leaving Growing Deep." Then he lowered it and held it cupped in both hands. "I wonder what it was for?"

With a shrug of his shoulders he pitched it up and over one shoulder, high into the air. The jewel flew in a long arc and dropped into the wreckage of the stone platform. The explosion blew Sorrowful into Mountain's lap and the rest of the company tumbling in the grass.

They sat up and stared at the boiling cloud of dust belching up and over the central spot. As it slowly dissipated and drifted away, they could see a deep crater occupying the central spot. Haze rose lazily from the rubble filled bottom. Broken and cracked stone blocks edged the hole.

"Well, Count," called Goose, "now you do know." He giggled and patted the dust from his stained and torn clothes, then took another pull from his bottle.

BONG. BONG.

Tinker rose to his feet. "Well, Sorrowful, it seems that was the last event, the final touch for this place. It sounds like we are being beckoned onward."

BONG. BONG.

Chicken stood and took one of his arms. Smoke rose and stretched, her tail floated across his and Chicken's shoulders. The tip twitched slightly, back and forth.

Tinker glanced around.

"Ready to go? Sorrowful? Mountain?"

"Oh yes, John Tinker, let us go. Let's add another chapter to The Tale."

"HUMPF! More monsters, I suppose. Let us go."

Sorrowful and Mountain walked over to the portal and waited.

"Toucan? Goose? You ready?"

"Yes, Highness, quite ready."

"Lead on, Sire, lead on. Sergeant!"

"Yes, SAH!"

"Form 'em up."

"Yes, SAH!"

The Guard quickly formed into two columns and lined up behind Sorrowful and Mountain, Goose standing at their head. Toucan turned and walked over to Tinker and nodded. "The Company awaits thy pleasure, Highness."

Making a very stiff bow, Toucan announced formally, "If the Lord Tinker, His Lady Queen, the Noble Princess Chicken, and His Mighty Lady Smoke would step through yonder portal, the Counts Sorrowful and Mountain will follow. The Right Noble and Brave Prince Goose, with The Guard, will proceed next. Last will follow your most Humble and Obedient Servant, The Prince Toucan, accompanied by Two-Byte and Tai."

"Most nobly bespoke, Brother."

Toucan lifted her hand to his lips. "Your servant . . . Sister Queen."

"You know then, Brother."

"Thy face do speaks volumes, My Lady. As do My Lord's."

BONG. BONG.

"But let us away, for tis time to proceed."

Toucan turned and strolled to the end of the line. Turning back to face them, his expression changed. One eyebrow rose, then fell. He winked.

Tinker burst into laughter.

"Princess, your arm. Smoke, your whatever. Time to go."

They walked over to face the portal. It shimmered and glowed. Flames danced over the surface of the opening. The fire-snakes roiled and hissed at them.

Tinker paused and turned, looking over the assembled company, then spun back and gently kissed Chicken on the cheek and pulled her against his side.

Goose and The Guard cheered.

"Ready?"

"Indeed, Our LordLove, We do most be that."

They stepped through followed by Smoke.

The rest trundled after them.

Toucan motioned for Tai and Two-Byte to proceed him. He stopped and turned, taking one last, long look around the grassy basin and the smoking crater. Then he whirled around and stepped through.

BONG.

The portal winked out, leaving behind only the soft, sad echo rebounding from the surrounding hills.

Bong . . .

Bong . . .

Bong . . .

Home Sweet Home

Tinker woke with a start. "Huh?"

He was sitting in his favorite chair. He was sitting in the blue-gray twilight that always proceeded sunrise. He looked down. His favorite coffee cup sat on the floor next to the chair. The fire was crackling in the wood stove. The stove was muttering to itself as it always did whenever the wind blew hard.

The stove muttered.

The house creaked.

Those were comforting sounds for early in the morning.

Outside, through the window, Tinker could see the dawn creeping over and across the nearby, snow-dusted hills. The picture window was framing a Christmas card winter scene. He glanced up and over Frank's Flat. Nothing there. There was no bright star.

He shook his head. It had all been a dream after all. He hadn't been trapped in a fairy tale, only dreaming. So who would believe him if he ever tried to tell them about such a dream. It might make a fun book to write, but. He shrugged.

He stood and stretched, stiff from dozing in the chair. Then he heard it, a soft humming sound. It was a new sound, not a remembered sound. It was here, in his house, somewhere in the living room. He turned and slowly began to inspect the dimness of the room.

In a dark corner he saw it, a dark thing, standing there, humming softly to itself.

It was leaning, right there, behind the speaker box, hilt up, the golden jewel just visible from soft internal fire.

It was his weaponkin, Slayer.

He looked down. He was dressed all in black.

It hadn't been a dream.

"SMOKE! PRINCESS! Where are you?"

He ran over and pressed his palm down over the golden eye.

In his mind he could barely see her, the great cat-like face with its gleaming white, dagger sized canines.

Goodbye mindmate . . . goodbye . . . I, we . . . are . . . all . . . home, as promised. We . . . shall . . . miss . . . you, Mind . . . Mate.

As her image slowly faded, Tinker could see the bright points of light reflecting from the tears flowing glistening over the soft black fur.

"Toucan! Goose! CHICKEN!"

He spun around, rapidly scanning the room, searching for them, listening for them.

The first beam of morning sunshine stabbed through the window and picked them out. A small jumble of children's toys lay scattered across the living room rug.

Crashing to his knees, he gently picked up and cradled in his hands a small fuzzy bit of yellow fluff.

"NOOOOOooooooooo . . . !"

Faintly, through the distance of time and space, he heard the peals of demonic laughter.

About the Author

George R. Mead began to study anthropology in 1962 after being discharged (honorably) from the U. S. Army, Combat Engineers. He eventually received a B.A., M. A., and Ph. D. in his chosen field, before that an A.A. in Engineering. And many years later an M. S. W. in Clinical Social Work. He has worked in aerospace, taught at the college and university levels, worked in a community action agency, ran a restaurant, been unemployed, and worked for the U. S. Forest Service. He is now retired from the work-a-day world but does a certain amount of consulting, writing, and research. He lives seven miles outside of the small town of La Grande, Oregon, with his wife, two cats, and one dog from the animal shelter, Kona.